STACY M. JONES

Midnight Lilies

For Amy

Acknowledgments

Thank you to the detectives and forensics teams I've had the pleasure of working with through the years and the knowledge and expertise shared with me. Special thanks to 17 Studio Book Design for bringing my stories to life with amazing covers. Thank you to Dj Hendrickson for your insightful editing and Liza Wood for proofreading and revisions. Thanks to my family and friends who are always a source of support and encouragement and to my early readers whose feedback was invaluable.

A special thanks to my friend and former colleague, Jake, who spent countless hours on the phone with me talking through the anger and violence of young men that we have both witnessed firsthand. There are only complex solutions to complex problems, and we both hope that one day it can be addressed for the sake of all. His insight on this story has made it what it is. Any mistakes are my own.

CHAPTER 1

FBI Agent Kate Walsh wasn't sure she cared that Trevor Fontaine was dead.

She'd never dare say that aloud. She couldn't.

Trevor was the victim in her case.

He owned a four-story brownstone on the Upper West Side of Manhattan. It was sand in color, with a wrought iron railing guiding visitors up wide steps to double front doors. The nondescript brownstone blended with all the others on 74th Avenue between Central Park West and Columbus Avenue.

Trevor had lived a short walk from Central Park and countless high-end bars, restaurants, and everything else one could want with too much time and too much money. The whole world was at his fingertips, which is why Kate didn't understand why Trevor was such an insufferable fool.

Trevor was famous for his podcast, *Grit & Grind,* for telling every guest and every listener that nothing would ever silence him. Trevor feared and respected no one and cared for very few.

It was an ironic way to go out.

A little healthy fear might have saved his life.

Kate and her partner Declan James missed the body being removed by a few days. Their boss, Martin Spade, had been called in instead and showed up at the crime scene while they were busy handling another case. Kate couldn't recall the last time Spade was at a scene. She wasn't even sure she had seen him outside of his office in the basement of the FBI Headquarters in Washington, D.C. He directed all the work in their FBI special unit from there.

This time, it was the notoriety of the victim that dragged Spade out of the building and right into the middle of a media firestorm. He couldn't wait for Kate and Declan to get back.

The call in France had been direct enough. Spade told them Trevor Fontaine, the infamous podcast host, who was known for vile misogynistic rhetoric, even going so far as to say that men should take what they want from women with or without consent, was dead. He didn't think women should have the right to vote either. They should make him a sandwich, ensure he was satisfied in bed, and keep their mouths shut if they knew what was good for them. Trevor Fontaine wasn't the first podcast host of this nature, but he was certainly the loudest and most vile.

His housekeeper found his body and called 911. Once the detective got on the scene, saw the condition of the body and the home, he immediately called in the FBI.

It was exactly the kind of case Kate and Declan handled. She had been a long-time forensic profiler for the FBI and had worked in the special unit they called home for almost her entire career. Declan could see a scene in a way no one else could. In more ways than one, they were the perfect pairing.

Spade had told them to be prepared for the scene. Sharon Esposito, a crime scene supervisor with the FBI, who was a recent addition to their team, had been called in immediately. When Spade fled back to D.C., Sharon got down to work processing the evidence.

By the time Kate and Declan got to New York City, it had been three days since the murder. The media was camped out on the sidewalk, their vans taking up precious parking on the street. The neighbors were over the whole ordeal.

Kate and Declan were just getting started.

They stood in Trevor's bedroom. Its dark blue walls, heavy dark drapes, and thick wood furniture was too dark against the dark wood floors. The drapes had been closed during the crime and had remained that way. The room had the smell of blood, sweat, and fear combined with the solutions the crime scene team utilized.

Even days later, the room had a heaviness about it. Kate wasn't sure if it was the décor of the room or what had happened. A leather chaise sat against the far wall. Behind it, the remnants of dried blood and brain. It's where the housekeeper found Trevor's body.

The bed had been left unmade, according to the case notes. The sheets had been stripped from the bed and taken as evidence. Sharon had found a mix of semen and vaginal fluids, indicating that Trevor was probably in the middle of sex or just finished when the attack started.

Fresh.

That had been the word Sharon used. She also indicated that while the semen belonged to the victim, she found DNA belonging to several women. None in the system.

Scattered around the room remained the dyed black lilies. Kate glanced down at her phone to see the room as it had been found that morning. The lilies were on the floor, cascading over the body, the bed, nightstands, and almost every other surface in the room.

A note was left on a small index card, propped up against a bed pillow. It was simple enough, and the meaning was direct and to the point.

This is a reckoning.

The Midnight Lilies

Spade had indicated, probably rightly, that there was more than one killer. He also assumed that the killers were women. Kate wasn't sure if she agreed with that or not. It did seem the most likely. One woman to seduce Trevor and give her access to his home. The rest to torture and kill him.

Trevor was six-foot-two, muscular, and could have easily overpowered one or maybe even two women. The photos of the crime scene that had been provided certainly indicated there was more than one person. The thick throw rug that was under the bed had the shoe impressions of several people. The housekeeper explained that Trevor liked his bedroom vacuumed every day. When asked about the sheets, she indicated once every few days. The last time she changed them had been Wednesday before the Friday night murder. That meant the DNA from several women was in his bed over the course of those forty-eight hours.

Trevor's body had signs of torture. Someone had used a stun gun on him several times. Kate initially assumed the stun gun was used to incapacitate him, but then she was informed that there were several areas of his body with two red marks burned into his skin. It had been used to torture him, not incapacitate him.

There were several minor stab wounds, nothing that would have killed him, and bruising around his body. His wrists and ankles had been tied and he had a gag over his mouth. He'd been stunned, tied up, beaten, stabbed, and then the fatal shot to the head. Kate wondered if the killer was looking him in the eyes when she shot him.

Just when they thought the horror was over, Spade had received a call from the medical examiner. When Dr. Henry Woods got Trevor back to the morgue and pulled the tape off his mouth, he discovered that Trevor's tongue was missing – it had been cut out post-mortem.

The tongue was still missing.

Kate stood in the middle of Trevor's bedroom taking in the scene while Sharon pointed out locations where evidence had been found. Nothing else in the brownstone had been disturbed. They had walked through the entire six-thousand-square-foot structure already. The only place where evidence was found was the bedroom, and so far, nothing that pointed to the killer.

They had also searched the top floor, which was Trevor's recording studio, where he produced his podcast. Trevor had guests come to the brownstone, walk through the grand foyer, and up to the top floor. It was an impressive sight to behold. An initial intimidation factor for anyone who dared cross the threshold.

Kate had never heard a whole podcast episode, nothing more than short clips she'd had the misfortune of stumbling across on social media, before the man's death. After, on the flight back from France, Kate had started a deep dive. She'd need to know everything about Trevor, and what better way to do that than the podcast. She'd only made it through two full episodes before she had to stop for her mental health. Toxic didn't begin to describe what she had heard. But in those two episodes, it was clear what kind of women Trevor liked. He didn't like the kind of women who could pull off a crime like this, so Kate wondered how exactly he had been seduced.

On the flight, when they were listening to the podcast, Declan had asked her one poignant question that still needed to be answered.

How could they be sure that the persona on the podcast was the man in real life?

It was a fair enough question. Kate couldn't explain how she knew the persona and the man were one and the same. She just knew. No one could be that good of an actor.

Trevor believed the nonsense he spewed.

Kate's shoulders raised as Declan laid a hand on her back. It took her a few beats as she relaxed into his touch. "What do you think?" he asked as they stood at the scene.

He got what was coming to him.

"I'm not sure yet," was what she spoke aloud.

Declan responded, "Let's go over the evidence. Sharon has a working theory."

Sharon was several inches shorter than Kate, but a powerhouse of a woman. She ran through all the basic evidence that Kate knew from the file. No forced entry. No dishes or glassware in the kitchen. No evidence that the two had been having any interaction outside the bedroom at all. Sharon highlighted the DNA evidence and the footprints around the bed.

"You could see the barefoot marks. There was also a scuff of a heel near the bed where she probably took off her shoes," Sharon said, pointing to the left side of the bed. "No prints on the side tables or anywhere else in the room. She was careful not to touch much else. Then there are other shoe marks in the carpet we can't account for right now."

"Why wasn't she worried about her DNA during sex?" Declan asked.

Sharon didn't have an answer for that. "I wonder if she was a professional."

"Hitman?" Declan asked, then said *hit woman*, correcting himself but still not sure that worked.

Sharon shook her head. "Prostitute. I wondered that because she seems to have come into his bedroom, not touched anything else in the house, then left after sex. Whoever this mystery woman was, she didn't eat or drink anything with him here. He let her in, and then she was gone without a trace."

"We can't be sure she participated in the murder," Kate reminded them.

Sharon agreed. "Spade said the same. As you know, he thinks it was multiple women. Sexist if you ask me. I don't need a posse to kill a man."

Kate glanced down at her. She was sure Sharon wouldn't need a posse to kill a man. "I probably wouldn't either. But we are trained. I think the average woman would need some help."

"Unless this isn't her first kill," Declan said, getting to the heart of what Kate had been wondering. "The torture, cutting out his tongue, the lilies. If we thought the killer was a man, then you'd assume this wasn't his first."

That much was true. Kate was still on the fence about whether it was a man or a woman. It was easy enough to leave those kinds of clues behind to make it look like a woman, which the flowers and card certainly did. They were assuming it was a woman based on the recent sex and no forced entry.

Kate remembered something Spade told her before she arrived in New York. "What about the threats Trevor had received before the murder? Spade mentioned them in passing."

Sharon glanced around the room one last time. "We can get to that. Is there anything else in here right now you need to know?"

There were too many questions to count. Kate gestured toward the chaise. "I assume he was sitting when he was shot?"

"Upright. You can see the mess on the wall." Sharon took a few steps toward the chaise. "There wasn't enough blood on the front of him to indicate his tongue had been cut out while he was still alive. As the medical examiner said, it was done post-mortem. What they did with the tongue is anyone's guess."

Kate locked her gaze on her. "You said *they*. I assume you also think this was more than one person?"

"I do," conceding her earlier point about being able to handle the murder alone. "You can't see it now because there's been more than a few detectives and techs in here. The early photos clearly show several different-sized shoe patterns on the carpet. At least three plus Trevor's and the barefoot woman."

"You don't know that they were caused on that night," Kate argued.

"The housekeeper said she vacuumed the carpet around two that afternoon," Sharon reminded her. "He was a neat-freak, remember? Look at the rest of this place. Not a thing out of place. Go look at his closet. He even color-organized his clothing." She pursed her lips. "I'm sure there were several people in this room. What I can't say for sure is that several people participated in the murder. That's where the threats come in."

"Let's go talk about the threats then," Kate said, turning and heading out of the room.

CHAPTER 2

"Manosphere," Kate said, repeating the word Sharon had just used. They were on the first floor in the back of the brownstone in the kitchen. It was a mix of high-end appliances in stainless steel and dark features. Much like the bedroom and the rest of the house, the kitchen had a masculine feel. The walls were a chocolate brown with a butcher block for an island. Dark leather chairs perched high at the counter.

LED strips of light cast a warm glow, providing sufficient lighting while serving as a captivating decorative accent. The lights above focused down on a luxurious black, heavily veined marble backsplash, creating a play of light and shadow. It wasn't Kate's taste, but she couldn't argue that it wasn't well designed. The whole brownstone screamed wealth and power.

Kate repeated the word *manosphere* as she eased herself down on a chair at the center island. She wrinkled up her nose. "What is it exactly?"

Sharon's features were tight. "It's a collective of websites, blogs, and online forums. In the last few years, podcasts have sprung up. They are popular among a certain crowd, getting millions of views. The clips from those are what trends on social media."

Kate had seen those. "What's the overall focus?"

"Misogyny. It's all anti-feminism. There are a few groups involved including men's rights activists, incels, pick-up artists, and father's rights groups. Their views and focus are different for each of those. The common thread is the belief that society is biased against men due to feminism, and that feminists promote misandry, a hatred of men."

Declan, who had been quiet until now, said, "They call accepting these ideas as 'taking the red pill' from the movie *The Matrix*. They are red-pilled. There is also the term black-pilled. That means accepting that feminism isn't something that can be fought against. Those men accept it and should either kill themselves or commit violence to be heroes."

Kate cursed softly. She was glad she had stayed off the internet and social media for the most part. She had heard the term incel. That was as far as she had gone down that rabbit hole – involuntarily celibate men. She knew their rhetoric.

This was… She shuddered… *something else.*

Sharon shared the same disgusted look on her face. "The manosphere has also been associated with online harassment and has been implicated in radicalizing men into misogynist beliefs and the glorification of violence against women. Did you know there was recently a forum found of more than seventy thousand men discussing how to sexually assault women?"

Kate wished she could say she was surprised. She wasn't. "I hadn't heard, no."

"It's horrifying," Declan echoed.

She turned to him as he sat next to her. "You heard about it?"

"My mom was telling me about it last week. She's on social media a lot these days, connecting with her friends and her knitting circle. She called to ask me if I had heard."

Kate waved with her hand as if struggling to find the words. "All of *this* is mainstream?"

"It is," Sharon confirmed. "You're a bit out of the loop because you aren't on social media all that much. You have enough on your plate with the real-life killers you take down. It's out there and radicalizing younger and younger men. I hear from my nieces in their twenties how hard it is to date these days. Some men want outright submission and ask for it on a first date. They demand information like how many people the women have slept with. They are parroting content they hear on these podcasts. A woman who has had a lot of partners can't pair bond with a new man."

Kate shook her head. "Pair bonding isn't impacted like that."

Sharon agreed with her. "It's just another way to slut-shame women. No matter what happens out there in the world, it's a woman's fault. She's told not to sleep around. Then she's on a date with a man who wants intimacy and she's a prude if she doesn't. He wants sex for the price of a cheeseburger at dinner. It's a lose-lose situation. They tell us to raise our standards so we don't end up single mothers. Then when we raise our standards, our standards are too high. Some of them use the bible as a means of reinforcing the message that women need to submit to their men."

Declan cleared his throat. "If women naturally submitted, we wouldn't have to keep reminding them to submit."

Kate's head turned sharply to him. "Is that what you want?"

Sharon steadied her gaze on him as if to tell him he better get the answer right.

"No, of course not," Declan said through nervous laughter. "Even if I did, I wouldn't dare say it to the both of you alone in a house where there was just a murder. There might be one more." Declan bumped Kate's shoulder affectionately. "It's not what I want. I like the challenge of a strong woman. I'm just stating the obvious. If it was a woman's natural disposition to submit, there wouldn't need to be podcasts and forums discussing how to make women submit. That's all I'm saying."

Kate had heard about incels. She had studied that for a previous case. Sharon was right that she wasn't online enough to see these kinds of things. The handful of clips she had stumbled across and two episodes of Trevor's podcast were vile enough that she didn't spend much time viewing the content. Kate assumed the algorithm probably decided it wasn't for her.

Kate raised her eyes to Sharon. "You said you spoke to Spade about the threats. Were they specific to Trevor Fontaine?"

"No," Sharon responded with a shake of her head. "There is a forum online started by women about how to combat the manosphere. There have been threats that if men continue down this path there is going to be more than a loneliness epidemic."

Kate had heard that research too. Men are lonelier. They have fewer friends, fewer male-only spaces in which to connect with peers. On the flip side, women are delaying marriage longer and having fewer children. Women are outpacing men in academics and in general the United States has moved away from trades education to college degrees. Many men are struggling to find work, friendships, and relationships.

Kate explained some of the findings in the research to Sharon and Declan. "I fail to see, however, how content by the manosphere is going to help them. Social media is also driving isolationism and discontentment. Hating women isn't going to help their cause. I'd suggest that it's only going to make it worse."

Declan agreed with that. "A lot of this is driven by insecurity. I've never met a man who felt good about himself who had a problem being in partnership with a woman."

Kate knew that when there was a group like this, there was also a common vernacular. "Is there a common language they all use?"

Sharon tsked in disgust. "You'll hear words like masculine and feminine energy. A woman who is an adult taking care of herself is too masculine. Men who have feelings or are kind to women will be called a simp or soy boy. They toss around words like high-value and low-value. Their favorite term is alpha. You hear a lot of them claiming to be alpha males. They love to tell other men they are betas. It's all made-up nonsense. I think the most ridiculous is that all women want a man over six feet, with six-pack abs, a six-figure salary, and six inches." She glanced down at Declan's lap.

"Hey," he snarled, looking up at her. "I fit the bill perfectly. Above average in all areas."

Kate rolled her eyes. "I'm not sure how to respond to this. I've never been involved with a man for any of those reasons. I can assure you that list doesn't even make my top twenty for romantic partner selection."

"Me either," Sharon said. "Most men I've dated are five-foot-seven on a good day."

"The threats," Kate reminded her. They were getting off track. It seemed like there was a lot to cover, though. If she could understand the victim better, she might better understand the person who wanted him dead.

"Nothing specific that the FBI has been told about," Sharon reiterated. "Certainly nothing connected to a group called the Midnight Lilies. That wasn't a reference to any threat. A few women online suggested that if men didn't stop their behavior, then violence against them might be the only answer. There is a rise in women giving up on dating. They don't want to get married or have children. They are feeling like it's not worth the effort. Many don't want to deal with emotionally unhealed men who they have to cook and clean for while also working a full-time job. I don't think anyone wants to do all of that work, and at the end of the day, be told they have to submit to that man. Times have changed, and in my opinion, men didn't keep up with the change."

"Homicide is a bit extreme," Declan said.

Sharon raised an eyebrow. "The number one cause of death for pregnant women is homicide. The rates of domestic violence and sexual assault are staggering. Few crimes are prosecuted, and even when they do go through the criminal justice system, women are usually ripped apart, and the sentences are light. I'm not condoning this kind of violence. I don't think violence, unless it's self-defense, is ever the answer. They brutalized that man. That said, I can understand it. I can understand the rage. I can understand wanting to take back their power, particularly at a living, breathing symbol of the kind of hateful, horrible rhetoric he spewed."

Kate could understand it too. "Are we in agreement that this is probably a woman who committed this crime?"

"Women," Declan said. He could see the look of doubt on Kate's face. "I still think, given the evidence, that we are looking at more than one offender. The medical examiner reported that even some of the knife wounds seemed to be at different angles and suggested both right-handed and left-handed offenders. The consensus is that we are looking at more than one offender. I tend to agree with that. Based on that scene up there, they know what they are doing. This was well-planned."

Kate couldn't disagree with that. What was causing her the most tightness in her chest was considering a group of homicidal women. "The killers are organized, methodical, and came in with a plan. They were able to get in and out without being seen, as far as we know. Do we believe the woman who had sex with him is also involved in the murder?"

Sharon wasn't sure. "There's no way to know. The medical examiner indicated that there had been sex before the murder, but couldn't pinpoint the time. He put the time of death at two in the morning.

He doesn't seem like the kind of man who'd want a woman to spend the night. I think you're going to need to figure out his last hours to determine that."

Kate assumed as much. It was still worth asking the question. "Is there anything else about the scene or the evidence we need to know?"

"I'm still going through the evidence and testing. What I have been able to sample hasn't been in the system."

"What about witness statements?" Declan asked. "Spade gave us some files, but there weren't any witness statements from neighbors. Didn't anyone speak to them that night?"

"I know the NYPD canvassed the neighborhood during the initial hours of the investigation. It was turned over to the FBI quickly. Spade wanted both of you to have the first shot at any potential witnesses. The people who were home when the NYPD went by didn't have much to say. No one heard or knew anything. Trevor wasn't an involved neighbor. He worked from home and had people in and out of the brownstone for both work and personal reasons. He bought the place five years ago."

That explained why the file Spade had provided them didn't contain much at all in the way of statements. They were starting from ground zero.

Declan shifted in the chair. "Has the whole house been searched? We are missing his tongue."

"Never found," Sharon said. "The whole house was searched by the NYPD. They had three detectives in here along with a few officers who went all over this brownstone top to bottom. By the time I arrived, they had already searched it and were able to point out some evidence, mostly in the bedroom."

Kate hadn't thought there was evidence anywhere else. "Are you saying now that evidence was found outside the bedroom?"

"We aren't sure it's connected to the murder." Sharon pointed to the

French doors at the back of the kitchen. "Out on the small patio in the back were three glasses. One of the glasses had Scotch in it. Two others were empty. I tested the glasses and found male DNA on all three. We assumed it was from the last time Trevor had people over or maybe the men who worked with him."

"We can't rule out that it wasn't someone responsible for the murder?" Kate asked again.

"We don't know," Sharon admitted. "We also don't know how long those glasses had been sitting out there."

"Yes, we do," Kate countered with a little more force than she intended. "The housekeeper had been here in the morning before the murder. She would have cleaned up the back patio." She gestured around with her hand. "This place is spotless. I'd venture to say the place doesn't even look lived-in. The glasses were definitely from Friday. I'm not saying that it has anything to do with the murder, but people were here."

"Maybe it was the men who worked with him on the podcast," Declan suggested. "We are going to need to speak to them. We can find out if Trevor believed all the things he said on the podcast. For all we know, it was just a persona he was putting on for show."

Kate knew she'd have to come face to face with them at some point. She wasn't looking forward to it. Unlike Declan, she believed that Trevor believed every word. The one clip of him she saw reverberated in her mind. Either he believed it or he was the best actor she'd ever seen.

"Let's start with the neighbors."

CHAPTER 3

After Sharon departed for her hotel and Kate started her ascent of the stairs at the neighbor's house, Declan reached for her and pulled her back down to the sidewalk. "I want to talk before we knock on that door."

"Sure," she said, not sure what was on his mind. Since they'd received the news about the case while in France, they had both been unusually quiet. "What's on your mind?"

"You don't seem yourself," Declan said. "I want to make sure you're okay."

"You don't seem yourself either," Kate countered, looking up at him. The sincerity on his face broke the little bit of defensiveness she felt in her chest. She wasn't even sure that's why she was feeling that way. "I'm a little jetlagged. I'm also having trouble imagining a group of women getting together to torture and murder a podcast host, even one as vile as I believe Trevor to be. Since Spade told me his theory, I've been in my head about it. I don't even have a working profile for something like that."

Declan rubbed his hands up and down her arms. "You've never failed on a case yet."

Kate didn't want to jinx herself. This might be the case that they couldn't solve. "You've been quiet too."

"Yeah," he admitted. "I don't want to say the wrong thing. I've listened to a few of those podcasts. Other guys I know have listened to those podcasts. I don't buy into what they are saying. I can see how it's radicalizing men, especially younger men. I can also see that it's giving an outlet to the frustration men are feeling right now. I think we probably just need healthier male-focused podcasts to take their place. I still don't think killing these guys is the answer."

As much as Kate didn't care that Trevor was dead, she couldn't disagree with Declan there. "Can you make me a list of the men who run the most egregious podcasts? I think they will probably be the initial targets."

"You don't think this is a one-and-done?" Worry creased Declan's forehead.

"I don't. If they have organized enough to call themselves a name like Midnight Lilies and leave their symbol over his body and around the bedroom, there is more to come. They called it a reckoning in the note. There is more, probably many more."

Declan locked his gaze on her. "Are you coming around to the idea that it's women doing this?"

Kate shook her head. "I'm not running with any theory right now other than there will be more murders if we don't stop them. That's all I know for sure."

The front door to the brownstone they were standing in front of opened. A tall woman in her early forties in yoga pants and a tee-shirt stepped outside. She had her dark hair twisted in a topknot and wore understated makeup, giving her a natural glow. The creases around her eyes pinched as she narrowed her focus on them. "I saw the two of you standing on my bottom step. Can I help you with something?"

Kate turned her body to fully face her and lifted the badge from the chain around her neck. "I'm FBI Agent Kate Walsh and this is my partner Agent Declan James. We are here investigating the murder next door. As you might know, Trevor Fontaine was killed on Friday night."

The woman's hand went to her chest. "I heard about that. I saw all the police officers over there on Saturday. I didn't realize the FBI was involved."

"Nature of the crime. The NYPD called us in," Declan explained. "Could we come inside and speak to you for a few minutes?"

The woman glanced over her shoulder. "The nanny is here with my two kids." She eased the door closed and walked halfway down the steps. "I'd be happy to speak with you out here. What do you need to know?" She took a seat on the fourth step up from the bottom and folded her hands in her lap. "I didn't know Trevor well."

"Can we start with your name?" Kate asked.

"Oh, I'm sorry," she said with a light laugh. "It's Evaline Marks. Most people call me Evie. My husband is Daniel Marks."

If the name was supposed to mean something to Kate, it was lost on her. "How long have you lived here?"

She glanced back up at her brownstone. Then she turned back to Kate. "Longer than Trevor Fontaine if that's what you're asking. My husband bought this soon after he started his practice."

"He's a doctor?" Declan asked.

Evie's face registered surprise. "Dr. Daniel Marks?" she said with a raised eyebrow. When neither of them ventured to respond or guess, she relented. "He runs the most famous plastic surgery practice in Manhattan. People come from all over the globe to see him. If those doctors in Los Angeles think they are swimming in business, they haven't met my husband."

"We're both from Boston," Kate said.

"We travel a lot," Declan echoed as a way of explanation.

Evie took it all in stride. "Well, my husband is as famous as you get. A lot of people know where we live. When Trevor moved in next door and ran his podcast from there, you can imagine that Daniel wasn't happy to be associated with such a thing. He spoke to Trevor a few times and asked him to tone down his rhetoric."

Declan perked up with this information. "You mean they had a few arguments? I don't understand why your husband would care what a neighbor was doing. It's not like he endorsed the podcast."

"Trevor asked Daniel for sponsorship for the podcast. Asked him if he wanted to run a commercial. Can you believe that? That's what sparked the whole thing."

Kate didn't understand that. "I'd think most of your husband's practice is women, and most of the podcast audience are men. It doesn't seem like an ad would work."

Evie laughed. "I guess you don't know much about plastic surgery these days. More and more men are going under the knife. They want a certain aesthetic that comes with a glamorous lifestyle, like the podcast promotes. Peak masculinity. Men are turning to surgery more to achieve the look they can't get otherwise." She got up and took a few steps toward them. She leaned down, appraising Declan's face. He pulled back from her. "He could take that line right out of your forehead, and those little lines starting around your eyes, they'd be gone too. You're a classically handsome man, rugged even. But my husband could make you look like a model."

Declan stared at her. "I don't want to look like a model."

Kate resisted the urge to get between them. They were getting off track. "You were saying your husband had a few words with Trevor. Did it ever turn physical?"

Evie didn't step back from Declan as she leveled an icy glare at Kate. "And have my husband hurt his hands? God, no." She pulled back with a laugh. "It was never physical. Daniel tried a few times to talk to Trevor, explaining that he wasn't going to advertise on a podcast where the host said it was okay to sexually assault your wife. He's not insane. As for why they had words, it's because Trevor brought all kinds of unwanted attention to our doorstep. His fans would lurk around the block, and these are some shady characters. The kind of men who listen to those podcasts and soak in those toxic messages aren't the kind of men I want creeping around my house. My husband was worried about our safety. When Trevor wouldn't be reasonable, Daniel dropped it. He wasn't going to keep wasting his time arguing with him."

Kate could understand the man's concern. "What about your interaction with Trevor? What was that like?"

"There wasn't any. We might see each other in passing and wave hello. That was it. I never had a conversation with him. Nor did I want to."

"Do you think he believed the things he said on the podcast or was that just a persona?"

"By the number of women in and out of here and the way he spoke to them, I'd say he lived what he preached."

"You heard him?" Declan asked.

"It was impossible not to if our windows were open. One woman showed up here a few nights ago while I was in the living room. The window was open a crack letting the cool breeze in. I heard him meet his date on the steps and tell her that he wasn't letting her in because he didn't have sex with fatties. A vulgar thing to say to anyone. This young lady couldn't have been more than a size six. I don't understand women who flock to men like that. She apologized to him and promised she'd lose ten pounds. I wanted to rush out front and shake her." Evie shook her head and sighed. "I minded my own business and went back to playing with my daughter."

Kate swallowed her disgust. "Did he routinely treat women like that?"

"All the time. I don't think I saw one interaction I would consider kind or respectful." Evie went back to sitting on the step. "Is it wrong that I don't much care that he's dead?"

Kate held back her response. "Were you here Friday night?"

"We got back home late. There was a charity dinner earlier in the evening. My husband received an award for some volunteer surgeries he had performed last year. We were gone from about six until a little before eleven. I'm not exactly sure what time we arrived back home. I know it was in time to see the eleven o'clock news. As far as hearing anything that took place, no. These walls between us are pretty thick. We have a bit of soundproofing too on our windows to keep out the city noise. It's only if they are open and he's outside that we can hear him."

"Back to your husband," Declan said. "You came home from the event a little before eleven. What did you do then? Did Daniel stay home?"

Annoyance graced her features. "Agent James, at no point did my husband leave this house to murder Trevor Fontaine. The guy was a horrible person, sure. He was an annoying neighbor to have. He put out hateful rhetoric, but Daniel wasn't going to throw his whole life away for him. Neither one of us left the house after we returned on Friday night. Daniel watched the news while I got changed and checked on the children. We were both asleep by midnight. Daniel left for a run around seven that morning. By the time he came back, the block was swarming with police. All they would say is that someone was deceased inside the home. No details or anything. We didn't learn until that afternoon that it was Trevor who had been murdered. We don't even know the details surrounding the murder. Most of the people on the block are wondering if they are safe. People have hired security. It's been a real nightmare."

Kate wasn't going to offer up any information about the murder. "We don't believe anyone else is at risk. This was targeted at Trevor."

"How can you know that?"

"The nature of the murder," was all Kate would say. "We will be giving the media a statement probably late today or tomorrow. We only arrived in the city this morning."

Evie locked her gaze on Kate. "There are rumors that he was tortured. Then he was shot. I didn't hear any gunshots that night. I didn't hear him yell or call out for help. I didn't hear anything."

"Did you see anyone coming or going from the brownstone when you arrived home that night?"

Evie paused to consider it. "The porch light was on. I do remember that. I also remember that a downstairs window was open. I thought it was odd. We might still have a few nicer days, but the nights are cold. I've had heat on already. I didn't understand why he'd leave a window open like that."

Kate wondered if the woman who had been with him had left it open so the others could get in. "Anything else unusual? We know that there was a woman with him at some point that night. Do you know if he was seeing anyone regularly?"

Evie shook her head. "They all looked alike. Carbon copies of club girls around here. Short dresses, spike heels, thin, pretty, and living on Daddy's money. Those kinds of girls are a dime a dozen. A little interchangeable if you ask me. Dress the same, talk the same. I can't tell one from the other."

"All Caucasian?" Declan asked.

Evie scoffed. "That man didn't discriminate his abuse against women."

Kate could feel the anger radiating off her. Evie had played it close to the vest at first. Now, her true feelings toward Trevor were seeping out. She couldn't blame the woman. Kate had felt it too. She certainly wouldn't have wanted to live next door to him. "Is there anyone you can think of that might have threatened him?"

"No," Evie said, shaking her head. She took a few deep breaths, centering herself again. "Honestly, as you said, he was a neighbor. If he hadn't asked my husband to advertise with him, and we didn't know the hateful things he said on the podcast, we wouldn't have had much interaction with him at all. This is a family block. Most have children. They all go to the same school a few blocks away. Trevor was the odd one out. I can see why he moved here. It's a lovely block with nice access to Central Park. I tried not to pay any attention to him." She stood. "Sorry I couldn't be of more help."

Kate pulled out a business card and handed it to her. "If you think of anything, feel free to call me directly. I'll be honest that we don't have a lot of leads. Anything you think of might be of help. Do you know if any of your neighbors knew Trevor well?"

"None more than us," she said, taking the card. "No one spoke to Trevor here. Most of the men stayed away, and the women were disgusted. He didn't have a lot of support in the neighborhood. No one I know wanted to kill him. We were hoping he'd move."

Before they left, Declan had one last question. "What about the men who worked with Trevor on the podcast? We know he had a partner. There must have been a studio manager or sound engineer who worked with them. I listened to the podcast and there were three of them. Two on camera and one off. Do you know their names?"

"No," Evie said, her voice stiff. "I never listened to the podcast, so I don't know anything about it. I saw a handful of men around here. I wouldn't know if they were friends or co-workers. I don't believe Daniel knew them either. Trevor was the only one we had minimal contact with over there."

Kate thanked Evie for her time and waited as she went back into the house.

CHAPTER 4

"We know Trevor's partners' names. Why did you ask her that?" Kate asked as they headed down the block. They were walking distance to the hotel where they were staying. It was far beyond the FBI stipend, but after France, Kate wasn't in the mood for a cheap government room.

Walking in step with her, Declan responded, "I wanted to see her reaction. There was something a little bit off about her. You saw the way she was calm, jovial even, then she flared in anger. I wanted to see her reaction when I brought up Trevor's partners."

Kate wasn't sure she understood.

Declan shrugged it off. "There was something about her I didn't like. I believed her when she said she didn't know Trevor's partners. She'd have no way of knowing unless she listened to the podcast or met them. If she had met them, then she was lying about the interaction."

"Okay," Kate said, conceding the point. She checked her watch. "We have enough time to speak with Reggie Miller." He was Trevor's co-host. The one who provided a counter-balance to some of Trevor's worst rhetoric. Not that Reggie was much better.

"He lives in the heart of Times Square."

Kate wrinkled up her nose. She couldn't think of a worse place to live in New York City.

Times Square was alive with its usual chaos as Kate and Declan approached the block where Reggie lived. The towering buildings loomed over them, their neon lights blinking like the pulse of the city. It was the kind of place that never slept, never stopped buzzing, and Kate found herself a little worn by its energy. It started as soon as they were off the subway and only grew as they got deeper into the chaos.

Reggie lived in a high-rise that looked as though it belonged in the future, all glass and steel, with a blackened chrome façade reflecting the constant stream of yellow cabs and people rushing by. The buzz of the intercom echoed through the entrance as Kate pressed the button for Reggie's apartment.

A second later, a voice came over the intercom – strained, but unmistakable. "Yeah?"

"That's him," Declan said. He had promised he knew the man's voice from the podcast. He had listened to far more than Kate.

"It's the FBI. We're here to talk about Trevor Fontaine," Kate replied, trying to keep her tone neutral.

There was a hesitation before Reggie buzzed them in, the door unlocking with a soft click.

Declan glanced at Kate before following her into the building, his eyes scanning the lobby. A clean, modern space with polished marble floors and a bright, sterile atmosphere. No warmth. No character.

"Up to the penthouse," Declan said after double-checking the address in his phone. He swiped the elevator button as they stepped inside.

The elevator doors slid closed. The tension in Kate's shoulders rose as they went higher. On the flight to New York, Kate had read a few newspaper articles about the relationship between Reggie and Trevor. Undeniable chemistry, one reporter stated. Another said the relationship bordered on toxic, much like the podcast. There was sometimes tension between the two on air. Both played up their "alpha" roles. The irony was that there was only one alpha, and even the research that had developed the concept had been flawed about wolves. It was never about humans, and the researcher had walked it back.

The elevator came to a soft stop. The doors opened to reveal a long, narrow hallway, dimly lit by recessed lights. Kate took the lead, her hand brushing the cool wall as she moved toward the door at the far end.

She rang the doorbell and seconds later, the door opened, revealing Reggie Miller. He was dressed in a black hoodie and jeans, his unshaven face drawn tight with strain. His eyes were bloodshot, like he hadn't slept in days.

"Come in," Reggie said, his voice shaky. He stepped aside to let them pass, then quickly closed the door behind them. His movements were quick, almost jerky. Kate didn't miss the way his eyes darted around the room as if expecting someone to show up at any moment.

She glanced around the space. Reggie's apartment was nice, but it was far from welcoming. The sleek furniture, minimalist décor, and floor-to-ceiling windows that overlooked Times Square made the place feel cold and impersonal. A glass coffee table sat in the middle of the room, stacked high with magazines and an empty mug. The faint sound of traffic filtered in through the windows, the city's relentless hum adding to the tension in the air.

Kate flashed her badge and introduced them both. She had wanted to take the lead and see how Reggie would respond to her. "I understand you refused to speak to the detective from the NYPD."

Reggie pulled at the strings of his hoodie. "No. That's not right. He showed up here and told me Trevor was dead – murdered. I needed a moment to process it and he kept hammering me with questions. I asked if we could slow down. I mean, give me a minute to process what he told me. He wouldn't stop. I asked him if I was under arrest and he said no. I asked him to leave. I said I'd follow up with him and

I tried. When I called to set up an interview a day later, he told me the case was going to be handled by the FBI. He said you'd be in touch. If I was going to refuse, I wouldn't have let you in." He gestured toward the couch for them to sit. Reggie perched himself on the edge of a leather chair.

Reggie's eyes darted around the room, his jaw tightening. "What do you want to know?" He looked almost desperate, far from the alpha he portrayed himself to be.

"We need information," Kate said, keeping her tone even but firm. "We have listened to snippets of the podcast. Agent James more so than I. I won't lie that I find the subject and the things you both say reprehensible. That said, Trevor didn't deserve to die. I need to know about what happened."

His face stiffened. "I don't know anything about the murder. I wasn't there when… when it happened." His voice cracked slightly at the end of his sentence. "I found out later, as I said."

"When were you last there at his brownstone?" Declan asked, folding his arms across his chest. When Reggie didn't respond to the simple question, Declan pressed him. "This isn't a hard question, Reggie. We know you all recorded the podcast from the top floor. We know you were there on Friday or someone was. There were glasses of Scotch on the table on the back patio. Three of them. I'm going to ask again, and I expect an answer this time. What time were you there and who was there with you?"

Reggie swallowed hard, his eyes shifting uneasily. "We recorded around noon. We are about two weeks ahead in recording compared to when something airs. Devon Rainey is our editor and producer. He also acts as our sound guy. He does a bit of everything. We recorded the podcast, then went out back and had a glass of Scotch. It's a bit of a ritual at this point. We didn't have a guest for this particular episode, so it was just the three of us. Devon left around four and I left shortly after. I didn't speak to Trevor again."

"That's good," Declan said, encouraging him. "What did you do on Friday night?"

"I was with a friend at a local bar that night. I have an alibi all night. I didn't find out about the murder until the next day."

Kate would get the alibi information later. Now she pressed on, unfazed. "What about Trevor? Was he expecting someone that night? A woman, maybe?"

Reggie's expression faltered. For the first time, he looked truly uncomfortable. "Trevor—yeah, he was talking about a woman when we were over there. He didn't give me any details. Just that she was coming over around ten. Trevor had a lot of women come over to his place. There was nothing new about that. I stopped asking him for details a long time ago."

"You didn't ask who she was?" she asked, raising an eyebrow.

Reggie avoided her gaze. "Look, I didn't think it was any of my business, okay? He was an adult. He had his own life, his own choices. Besides, he was a one-and-done kind of guy. I knew I'd never meet her, so there was no point learning her name or even having a conversation about it. Trevor might talk about her on the podcast later. I knew not to ask for details. I didn't care, and I knew he wouldn't have told me anyway. We were friends and colleagues but didn't share everything."

Kate could see the way he was shifting, the tension in his posture. He was hiding something. "I can tell there's something you're not telling me. Was there something about this woman that concerned you? Something about what Trevor was doing?"

Reggie's eyes flickered toward the door again, a near-panic beginning to seep into his expression. "I don't know what you want from me," he muttered, his voice rising in agitation. "I told him that he needed to be careful. I told him we needed to tone it down on the podcast. I warned him. They warned him. Trevor was reckless, okay?

I don't know what more I can tell you."

"Reckless, how?" Kate asked, not taking her foot off the gas. He knew more than he was saying. "You said *they* warned him. Who are they? Advertisers?"

Reggie clamped his mouth shut and cast his eyes to the side, not looking at either of them or responding.

Declan wasn't having it. He uncrossed his arms and leaned forward on the couch. "We need to know what you know." He pointed toward the door. "The scene in Trevor's bedroom was among the worst I've ever seen. Did the detective tell you what the killer did to your friend?"

Reggie nodded slightly, his eyes wincing closed. "It's sick. Torturing him like that. Shooting him in the head." Reggie turned his head, a gag rising in his throat. "I can't imagine it. I didn't have anything to do with this. I wasn't there. I can give you the name of the woman I was with all night. We met at the bar around eight, stayed to hear a band, and came back to my place. She spent the night with me here, and we went for brunch in the morning."

"When did you hear of Trevor's murder?" Kate asked, trying to keep the timing straight.

"After brunch. I was just getting back here when a detective with the NYPD showed up and told me. I swear I don't know anything about who killed him or the woman he was meeting that night. Devon doesn't either. We've already spoken. I called him as soon as the cops told me." He cast his eyes off to the side again lost in a memory.

Declan tapped his foot on the floor to get Reggie's attention. Once they were eye to eye, Declan said, "I don't believe you. I suggest you start talking before it's too late. Trevor was the first, but we know he won't be the last."

Reggie got up and paced the floor. He ran a hand through his messy hair. "I don't know anything. I don't know the girl he was seeing other than that he met her at a bar a few nights ago. It was just sex. They weren't hanging out or dating or anything like that. Trevor didn't do that. It was always sex, nothing more. He didn't even let the women spend the night."

"What do you mean he never let them spend the night?" Kate hated to interrupt his ranting in case he shared something good.

"What I said, they did the deed and he kicked her out. He didn't want to deal with the morning after or go to brunch. He wouldn't even call her a cab, just send her on her way." Reggie stared at Kate. "I assume it was good he did that because she wasn't murdered with him, right? They only found one body."

"We don't know her role in this," Kate admitted, finally settling into the fact that it might be women involved. "The woman could have either been among the killers or she might have left well before he was murdered."

Reggie pinched the bridge of his nose. "What do you mean killers? Like more than one?"

Declan asked, "What do you know about the scene that was left in his brownstone? You said he'd been tortured and shot. Do you know about his tongue and the flowers?"

Reggie's head snapped up. "Flowers? What flowers?"

Declan explained, "The lilies. They were dyed black. The killer called themselves the Midnight Lilies. That's what the note said."

It was curious to Kate that out of tongue and flowers, he had focused on the flowers. "Does that mean something to you? They left a note saying the murder was a reckoning."

For a moment, Reggie just stood there, breathing heavily. Then he dropped his head, his shoulders slumping. He didn't answer Kate's question. Instead, he asked, "What did they do with his tongue?"

Declan stood then and took a few steps toward him. "They cut it out of his mouth after he was dead and took it with them. It's not anywhere on his body and it's nowhere in that brownstone."

Reggie's hand flew to cover his mouth as his eyes bugged. He shook his head furiously back and forth as if he were having trouble understanding the news. He uncovered his hand inches from his mouth and spoke in barely a whisper, "We were warned."

The admission hung in the air, thick and heavy.

"Warned?" Declan asked. "What do you mean you were warned?"

Reggie's eyes shifted around the room, not settling on anything. "About six months ago, we got a letter that was addressed to the podcast – Trevor and me – that said we had to change our focus. We had to tone it down and stop promoting violence against women or there would be a reckoning and they'd silence us. It was signed by the Midnight Lilies. We joked about it on the podcast."

Bile rose in the back of Kate's throat. "They warned you six months ago?"

Reggie nodded. "They warned us, but I swear to you we thought it was a joke or the normal hate mail we get all the time. Women hate us. Some men hate us, too. We use it on social media to showcase how fragile people are. Words can't hurt people. There's free speech."

"That's not what free speech means," Declan started to say, his tone tinged with anger.

Kate got up and touched his arm, pulling him back. It wasn't time for a Constitution lesson. "Do you still have the letter?"

"No, we threw it out like we do most of our stupid mail." Reggie stumbled back, his breathing becoming uneven. "Do you think they are coming for me too?"

"Yes, Reggie," Declan said, gripping him by the arm so he didn't fall any farther back. "I think they are coming for you too."

Declan tried to ease him down gently as the man dropped to his knees and started to cry harder than Kate had seen anyone cry in a long time.

CHAPTER 5

An hour later they were standing in Devon's apartment on the second floor of a Greenwich Village brownstone. He had scuffed hard-wood floors and the living room looked more like a workspace with sound equipment, laptops, and other wired contraptions that Kate couldn't name.

After they made sure Reggie was headed off to relatives in New Jersey where hopefully he'd be safe, Kate and Declan rushed to Devon's to warn him. They found him wearing ripped jeans, a Metallica tee-shirt, and his hair looked like it hadn't been combed in a week. There was a stark difference in appearance between Trevor and Reggie and Devon. He was Kate's height at five-foot-eight and didn't have the muscular build of the other two.

"I'm sort of the runt of the litter," he joked as he let them in. "Sorry, the place is a mess. I'm a producer for several podcasts, and I edit from here most days." He moved things out of the way so they could sit on the couch. He stood near the edge of the living room that flowed into a small dining room. The table was filled with stacks of books and magazines. "The detective with the NYPD told me that the FBI would be coming to speak to me. What do you need to know?"

Kate asked him the same initial questions they had asked Reggie. Devon was at his girlfriend's house after leaving Trevor's brownstone on Friday. They had spent the latter afternoon together, went out for dinner and then back to her place for the remainder of the night. He was there all the next day too when Reggie called him to tell him about Trevor. Devon offered up the name of his girlfriend and her phone number without being asked. He even offered to call her on the spot so Kate could speak to her. What he didn't do was indicate how he felt about the murder. There were no words of sympathy for Trevor.

"I'm a contractor for the business," Devon explained, putting distance there. "Trevor and Reggie own it. I'm not involved with much of anything other than the production side." He kept his focus on Kate. "I don't decide the content," he said almost as an afterthought.

Kate appraised him, noting the puppy dog look about him. His hair flopped down over his forehead and he brushed it back. His eyes were a deep shade of blue, almost navy, and he had the scruff of a man who couldn't decide whether to shave or grow a beard. "Does that mean you don't approve of their message?"

"If you're asking me if I share their viewpoint on women and relationships? No, I don't. I think if I ever said some of the things they did, my parents would disown me. My sisters would probably kill me. My girlfriend is doing her medical residency. She's going to be a pediatrician. I have no problem with strong, independent women."

Declan agreed with him. "Why work for them then? Doesn't it bother you to listen to all of that? I listened to a few podcasts and it enraged me."

"It's a job for me. Pay's excellent and it's easy work." Devon crossed his legs and eased himself down to the floor in one fluid motion. It left him in a position of looking up at them. Kate wondered if he did yoga. "You can judge me for taking the work. I understand that. It's just work for me though. I'm not even sure how much of it Reggie believes. Trevor was a true believer. He knew better than to talk one-on-one with me like that. He learned early on that we didn't share the same beliefs. He was convinced he'd convert me one day."

Kate moved into a more comfortable position on the lumpy couch. She would get to the specifics of the murder later. Right now, she wanted to know more about Trevor from someone who knew him but hadn't bought into his mindset. "What was Trevor like to work with?"

"He was controlling at first. He'd come back to me and question why I edited the podcast in the way that I did. I had the expertise, he didn't. Trevor learned quickly to trust me. Once he gave me the trust, we were fine." Devon stared off as if looking for the right words. When he refocused back on them, he said, "I believe Trevor was deeply insecure. He grew up with rich but absent parents. His father was always working. His mother didn't have much time or use for him. He said she was a drinker. Always at some charity event or lunching with friends. He's an only child. He was radicalized on the internet. I had a good male role model at home and played sports in school. Trevor didn't have that. I think he was trying to figure out masculinity and got all the wrong messages along the way."

Declan glanced over at Kate. She gestured for him to go ahead. "What about his relationship with women? Was it as dysfunctional as he portrayed?"

"That's the irony. He didn't have relationships with women. I don't think he's ever had a girlfriend," Devon admitted. "Trevor would go on and on giving all kinds of stupid relationship advice. He never had anything more than a series of one-night stands with women. He could get them into bed. He said he cast them aside when he was done with them. I'll be honest, I didn't see a lot of them coming back to him for more."

"Do you have any examples of that?"

"A few," Devon said, brushing the hair off his forehead. "One night, Reggie, Trevor, and I were at a bar after work on a Friday. My girlfriend was going to be at the hospital all night and they convinced me to go out with them. At least three women told Trevor off to his face. Two of them he was trying to take home that night. He had slept with them prior and they weren't interested in a repeat. He couldn't take the rejection. After one of them rejected him, he told her he wasn't interested in her anyway, that she was fat and ugly. She was neither, but even so, he had already slept with her. He liked her enough at some point. It was only once she rejected him that she wasn't good enough for him. Trevor was doing that a lot that night. He'd pick out a woman and size her up. If she appeared intelligent or beautiful, anyone out of his league, he'd say something disparaging about her."

Declan asked a few more questions that drove home Trevor's character or really lack thereof. He sounded like a nightmare to be friends with and to any woman who had the misfortune of encountering him.

Kate almost felt bad for Devon. "How do you feel about Trevor's death?"

Devon's eyebrows shot up, a gesture of surprise as if he hadn't been anticipating the question. "I'm not sure if I'm going to be honest with you. Look, I don't think anyone should be murdered. I'm not condoning what was done to him. Will I personally miss him? No. I'm not sure anyone will and that's sad to me. He was a terrible person. With him gone, maybe there will be one less person spreading such hate." He looked down at his hands. "But I'm sure someone will try to replace him. Unfortunately, that's what happens these days. One loser like that is gone and there is a space to be filled. Instead of filling it with someone who has something positive to say, it will be filled with more hate."

Kate wanted to remind him that he had participated in that hate. She knew that even if Devon wasn't there to produce the podcast that someone else would fill that gap. "Can you tell me about that Friday? How did Trevor seem to you?"

Devon took a breath and sighed it out. "He was hyped up as usual. That's always how he got during the podcast. He was always *on*. It was an episode with him and Reggie talking about the politics of the day, giving their opinion and such. We didn't have a guest scheduled for this episode. After they were done, we had a celebratory drink on the back patio. Trevor was talking about a date later that night. She was coming over around ten. He was meeting another woman for drinks around eight. He was going to decide who was going to be the better lay, as he put it. If he connected with the woman over drinks, he might ditch the woman coming over at ten."

"Classy," Declan said, his tone dry. "Was that common for him?"

"Yeah," Devon said with a nod. "I'm not even sure Trevor saw women as people. They were interchangeable to him. There was no respect. He didn't want to get to know any of them. It was just what women could do for him. The irony is that the more women said yes to him, gave in to being with him, the less he respected them. If they rejected him, they were worthless losers. Something was wrong with them for not seeing his high value. His brain was warped."

That was one way to think about it. Kate had other, choicer words for it that she didn't express. "Do you know anything about the women he was meeting? Did he mention any names?"

Devon pinched the bridge of his nose. "The woman at the bar was Madison McBride. I don't know why I remember that. Maybe it's because he never mentioned women's names. But this time he did."

"Did Reggie know her name?" Declan asked.

Devon shrugged. "I don't know. When Trevor mentioned her name, it was just him and me on the back patio."

Kate made a note in her phone. "What about the woman coming over around ten?"

"That I don't remember."

"Do you remember the name of the bar?"

"Crescent & Oak. It was his favorite bar. He had a booth in the back where he always sat. Trevor knew the owners and they treated him like a king. He didn't specifically say he was going there that night, but he said the bar, and I took that to mean Crescent & Oak. Trevor once called it his hunting ground to pick up women."

Declan cursed under his breath. "Did the man have any redeeming qualities?"

"I'm afraid not," Devon said evenly. "That's why I'm hoping you'll overlook my inability to feel too bad that the guy is gone. Are there any leads?"

Kate had no problem being honest with him. Even though she didn't understand his choice of job, there was something warm about Devon. "We are just getting started. We've reviewed the initial files, been by the house, spoken with Trevor's neighbor, and met with Reggie. We only have a little to go on. Reggie said that they had been threatened. Do you know anything about that?"

Devon leaned back on his hands. "I seem to recall a few months back them having a heated discussion about a threat that came in the mail. While Trevor was the lead on the podcast, Reggie did most of the work. He researched guests and invited them. He handled all the financials, marketing, and all of the administrative tasks. He was the one reading the threats that came in via the email address listed on the website and in the mail."

"There was that much hate mail?" Kate asked.

"There was a lot. Reggie told me once that he was surprised given their popularity. You can take a look at the comments left on their social media profiles. Not only are there hate comments, but there are comments from the men who listen who then bash the others, mostly women, who comment. It's vile," Devon added with a shudder. "I've only looked a handful of times, and it's straight up disgusting what people will say to each other."

Kate refocused him. "The specific threat you heard them arguing about. Tell me about that."

"A few months back, while I was working on setting up a few things for the upcoming podcast, Reggie and Trevor were arguing on the floor below me. Reggie was saying that there was something different about this threat – that it was cryptic and specific. He said it felt different than the usual stuff they got. He wanted Trevor to tone it down, at least for a few months. Let some of the heat blow over. It only enraged Trevor, both the threat and Reggie asking him to tone it down. Trevor said there was no way they were going to give in to it. Then he did something stupid and mentioned the threat on the podcast. He laughed at the sender. Told them to bring it on."

Kate turned her head to glance over at Declan. They shared a surprised look. "Do you know the episode number this would have been?"

"I can get it for you." Devon offered a few guesses but promised to confirm it for them.

Declan asked, "What do you remember about the threat?"

"The writer said there would be a reckoning. It was signed by the Midnight Lilies. That's what creeped Reggie out the most. He argued to take a break, get out of the city for a while. I had never seen Reggie so freaked out."

Kate was curious why Reggie had underplayed the fear. He didn't express anything remotely this emotional to her. "What did they do with the mail?"

"Trevor took it from him and ripped it up. When I went back downstairs later, I remember seeing pieces of it still on the floor."

Kate wondered if his taunting the killer was the reason they had been so brutal with him. "Did they speculate at all about who the killer could be?"

"No," Devon said dismissively. "They never spoke to me directly about it. I could see when they came upstairs that Reggie was worried. I don't think I've ever seen him that stressed out. Whatever that letter said, it caused him to worry. Trevor didn't seem bothered by it at all – except he was angry about being told what he could and couldn't do."

Kate and Declan took turns asking a few more questions, not yielding much more. At the end, Kate issued a stark warning. "We believe Trevor was killed by whoever sent that threat. There was a note on Trevor's body from the Midnight Lilies, as well as black lilies tossed on his body and scattered around his room. It hasn't been in the media yet, and we expect you to keep this quiet. Trevor was tortured and shot. His tongue was cut out after death."

Devon's face twisted in disgust and horror.

"We believe Reggie might also be in danger. He has left Manhattan for now. We can't say for certain if you'd be a target or not, given you weren't a public face of the podcast."

Before Devon could respond, the door to his loft creaked open.

His head turned and Kate and Declan sat at attention, assessing the threat. A woman with a blond ponytail and messenger bag pulled up short when she saw the three of them.

Kate noted the lilies embroidered on the bag and her eyes went wide.

CHAPTER 6

Devon got to his feet in the same fluid motion as he had sat. "Ava," he said, immediately embracing her. "I didn't know you were coming by so early. These are FBI Agents Kate Walsh and Declan James. They are here to talk to me about Trevor."

Ava allowed herself to be enveloped in Devon's embrace. She was only a few inches shorter than him, and as her chin rested on his shoulder, she peered over at Kate. She ducked her head back and let go of him. "I'm sorry, I can come back. I finished classes early today and thought we could grab some dinner."

Kate stood and Declan followed. She didn't know if he had spotted the flowers on her green messenger bag. She didn't even know if he could recognize a lily when he saw one. Kate held back from rushing the young woman. "I heard you're in medical school," she said, as a way of engaging.

Ava stepped around Devon, tossing her bag on the floor near the door. "I'd like to be a pediatrician. It's a lot of work but worth it." She glanced back at the door. "I can give you all some privacy if you want. I didn't mean to interrupt."

"It's fine," Kate assured her. "We were just wrapping up. We were telling Devon that we can't be sure that the threat leveled against Trevor and Reggie doesn't extend to him."

Ava reached for him. "Why would he be at risk? He edits and

produces a lot of podcasts, even a few that have a feminist focus. Wouldn't that cancel out any risk against him?"

Kate hadn't been aware of all the programs that he produced. Devon described several of the podcasts that he worked on. It was a range of subjects. "Devon's risk might be lower, but there's still a risk. Is this the only podcast you produce that's of this nature?"

Devon assured her it was the only one. "I have a no-competition clause in my contract. I can work with other podcasts but none that are in direct competition."

Kate reiterated that it might be a lower risk but still a risk. Devon told her he'd remain at home for now. She turned her attention back to Ava. "Did you know Trevor?"

"I only met him twice," she explained. "Devon and I were out to dinner once and he was at the same restaurant. Then the second time, I was out with a group of friends and he saw me. He came over to the table and tried to flirt with one of my friends. She knew what he was all about and wasn't interested. Trevor got angry and called us a bunch of old hags, said we were past our prime and left."

"Past your prime?" Declan asked with confusion in his voice.

"Because I'm over twenty-five. According to Trevor, I should have already had a few kids. He had this whole theory that once a woman reaches twenty-five, if she's not married and doesn't have kids, she's basically a dried-up old hag." A smile hinted at Ava's lips. "If being a dried-up old hag means men like Trevor stay away from me, I take it as a compliment. He wasn't someone I had to interact with much, and I was glad for it. I'm even happier now that Devon won't be producing the podcast. It was the one thing that caused a bit of tension between us."

The young woman's openness surprised Kate. "Do you know of any women he slept with?"

Ava shook her head. "No one from my friend group is that

desperate."

Kate stifled the laugh that rose in the back of her throat. "Is there anything you can tell us about Trevor?"

"I don't know anything." Ava glanced over at Devon. "We've been together three years. He started working with Trevor about two years ago. In that time, as I said, I only met Trevor twice."

Kate pointed over at her bag. "Are those lilies embroidered on your bag?"

Ava's face brightened. "They are. There's a shop near the NYU campus that sells bags with all kinds of things embroidered on them. I thought it was pretty and the kids like them."

Declan side-eyed her, a sure sign that he had missed the flowers.

"Lilies have a particular meaning in this case," Kate said, not sure where she was going with this. "Did you realize that?"

Ava looked over at her. "No. I don't know anything at all about Trevor's death. Devon and I spent that night together and he got a call the next morning from Reggie telling him Trevor was murdered. I was surprised that it wasn't on the news much. I figured it would have gotten a little more airtime. Maybe Trevor thought he was more important than he was."

Declan was assessing her now in the way Kate had. "We are keeping details quiet for now. There were lilies thrown over Trevor's body and around his bedroom. Do you know of anyone who dyes their lilies black?"

"Black?" Ava asked.

"Black," Declan confirmed. "The lilies were dyed black. Is that familiar to you?"

"You mean midnight lilies?" Ava asked, not registering the look on Kate's and Declan's faces. "Were they dyed or were they midnight lilies, which are purplish black?"

"I'm honestly unsure," Kate admitted, realizing they should probably have examined them more. Other than seeing them scattered on the floor and over the body in photos, she hadn't had time to explore their meaning. "We'd have to examine them more. Our crime scene tech has a sample of them."

"If there were a lot of them, maybe they were dyed black. Midnight lilies are expensive." Ava paused, considering. When she spoke again, her voice was clear and confident, haughty almost. "When I was an undergrad, I took a symbolism course related to great works of art. Lilies are often associated with purity, renewal, and transience. Midnight lilies are about mystery, transformation, and rebirth. I even recall something about the hidden depths of the human psyche. Do you think they were used symbolically?"

Kate studied this young woman. She wasn't sure if she was testing Kate or if she was trying to be helpful. "I'm sure the lilies had meaning to the killer or killers. The one thing we haven't told the media yet is that we are considering that it might be more than one person. Possibly a female killer, too."

"That wouldn't surprise me," Ava said. "I don't know one woman who liked Trevor."

Devon could see the looks on their faces. He pulled on her arm. "Ava gets worked up about Trevor sometimes. She and I were together the whole night when Trevor was murdered. She's had that bag long before I started working for Trevor."

It was only then that Ava understood what he was trying to do. She gasped. "I had nothing to do with this murder," she said in a rush. "I was only trying to be helpful, Agent Walsh. You mentioned the lilies and I know a bit about them. I'm getting my medical degree. I want to help people, not harm them."

"You're fine," Kate assured her, still a bit unsure of the young woman standing in front of her. She certainly didn't look like she was strong enough to take down a man of Trevor's size. Ava and Devon alibied each other and she had no question about him. "We'll be in touch if we need anything else." She turned to Declan to see if he had any other questions. When he didn't, they headed for the door.

As he opened the door for Kate, she turned back. "Madison McBride. Do you know anything about her? Where we could find her?"

It wasn't Devon who answered though, it was Ava who stepped forward. "Madison McBride, who goes to NYU?"

"I don't know," Declan said. "Do you know someone by that name? Trevor was supposed to meet her on Friday night."

Ava stammered out, "I know her roommate. I don't know her well."

"Do you know where we can find her?"

Ava gave her the address in NYU's graduate student housing. "I don't know her schedule. I've only met her a few times when I go over to see my friend. I'm not even sure this is the same person. Might be a common name."

Declan thanked her for the information and closed the door behind them. He waited until they got to the street and down a little from the building. "Was that as weird for you as it was for me?"

Kate glanced back up at Devon's windows. "He seemed normal. I don't have any questions about him. I'm not sure how to read her."

"Something about her struck you as odd. I could see it on your face."

Kate didn't want to be reactive. "It was an odd interaction," she said to confirm. "I saw the lilies on the bag when she came in. I didn't realize midnight lilies were an actual type of flower. The fact that she used the term threw me off. We should have done more research."

Declan pulled out his phone and typed off a quick text. He shoved the phone back in his pocket and raised his head to Kate. "I texted Sharon and asked her to test the lilies to see what we are dealing with. If they are dyed, that's one thing. If someone is buying actual midnight lilies, we might be able to use them to find who is buying them in bulk."

"It's one murder, Declan. I don't know how many flowers they used, but it didn't look like more than a dozen."

Declan put his hand on her back and guided her to the side of oncoming walkers she didn't notice approaching. "You said there'd be more, Kate. I believe you."

She had said that. It would mean more flowers would be needed. "Let's find Madison. I want to know who was with Trevor that night."

The student housing complex loomed ahead, a brick pre-war building that fit right in with the neighborhood. They walked through the front courtyard past students who were lounging on benches, books scattered around them, headphones on, typing on their laptops. They paid no attention to Kate or Declan.

They walked up to the building's main entrance. Kate's fingers brushed the cool metal handle as she pulled the door open, and they entered. The lobby was minimalist. A row of mailboxes off to the left and straight ahead a receptionist sat at the front desk, a young woman with thick-rimmed glasses and her nose buried in a textbook.

"Can I help you?" she asked as they approached, her voice distracted but polite.

Kate flashed her badge. "FBI. We're here to speak with Madison McBride."

The receptionist didn't hesitate. "Room 204B. Go up those stairs and down the hall on the left. She might be in class."

"It's fine. We must speak to her, so we'll wait if we need to," Kate said, nearly interrupting her.

With a quick nod, the receptionist returned to her textbook, the conversation over. Kate motioned for Declan to follow as she led the way toward the stairs.

The second-floor hallway was narrow with walls lined with doors. There was a distinct smell of microwave popcorn and freshly brewed coffee that lingered in the air, reminding Kate of student life at

Harvard. She hadn't lived in the dorms but had spent considerable time in them with friends. They were some of her happiest memories of college.

Kate's eyes flicked to the numbers on the doors as they passed. Each one had its own character – some were covered in posters for obscure bands, others with half-finished assignments taped to the wood. They stopped in front of a door marked 204B.

Kate knocked once, her knuckles tapping sharply against the wood. There was no answer. She knocked again, this time louder. Moments later, the door creaked open just a few inches, revealing a pair of bright eyes staring through the gap.

"Madison McBride?" Kate asked, peering down at the young woman.

She had chestnut hair that curled in delicate waves around her face. Her eyes were wide but guarded, her lips slightly parted as if she were preparing to speak but wasn't sure what to say. She wore a loose sweater, comfortable jeans, and sneakers. "Can I help you?" she asked, tentatively. Her voice was soft but clear, her gaze flicking between the two agents.

"We need to talk to you about Trevor Fontaine," Declan said, his tone casual but with an edge that made the air between them feel heavy.

Madison's face didn't betray any immediate reaction, but Kate could see the faintest tension in her posture. Her hand gripped the door handle tightly.

"I don't know that I can help you."

"You do know him?" Kate asked, hoping they had the right young woman. Although, Kate was having a hard time seeing Madison with the likes of Trevor. When Madison nodded ever so slightly, Kate went on. "We're just trying to understand what happened the night Trevor was killed. We've been told you were supposed to meet him."

"We were supposed to meet, yes," Madison said slowly, opening the door a little wider. "I didn't stay at the bar long that night. He was rude to me shortly after meeting and I was uncomfortable. I left and even took a cab back here because I didn't want to walk."

Kate studied her carefully. "What did he do?" Before Madison could respond, Kate asked if there was somewhere else that she'd rather speak than in the hallway.

"This is fine," Madison said to Kate's surprise. "I don't have much to say. I met Trevor one night at a bar. He was insistent that we meet for drinks. I wasn't sure about him, given his reputation on the podcast. I didn't even know who he was at first. He had to tell me, which I don't think he liked. I got the sense he saw me as a challenge. Trevor was persistent that night. I agreed mostly so he'd go away and I could go back to enjoying time with my friends. I should have cancelled the date, but I went."

Declan leaned his shoulder into the wall, looking down at her. She couldn't have been more than five feet three. "You said Trevor did something to make you uncomfortable."

"He negged me." When she saw the question on Kate's face, she smiled. "It's that thing people do where they gently insult you to get you to prove yourself. It's supposed to knock down your self-confidence to make you more open to their sexual advances. It's stupid and we know when guys are doing it. When I shrugged it off, Trevor didn't seem to know what to do. He got increasingly angry."

Three doors down from Madison a door creaked open and a young woman with heels and a short dress exited. She looked like she was heading to a club rather than an evening class.

Madison shrank back into her room and started to close her door.

Declan's hand shot out to stop her. "We need to finish this conversation."

Madison looked up at him with worried eyes. "There's a coffee shop a block away, meet me there in ten minutes." Before closing the door, she gave them the address.

Kate eyed the woman who had come out of the other room as she walked down the hallway past them, not acknowledging them in the slightest. She brushed past them like they weren't even there.

"Weird," Kate said under her breath.

CHAPTER 7

Kate and Declan sat in a back booth away from other customers. It was easy to see why Madison had picked this place. It had a dark, gloomy vibe of a coffee house visited by struggling writers. The thick scent of brewing coffee hung in the air, the lights were dim, and the overhead music moody. Kate felt like she should be hunched over a laptop struggling to write a badly crafted poem.

Madison arrived moments after them, tugging her blue cardigan around her tighter. She slid into the booth next to Declan and across from Kate. "Sorry about that. I didn't realize she was home."

"Who is she?" Kate asked, hoping they would get an explanation but not planning to push it.

"Kristen Carney. Her father is some media mogul or so she tells us. I don't know why she's in student housing if that's the case. She said once she wanted to live like common people." Madison scrunched up her nose. "Who says common people?"

Declan agreed with her that it was weird. "Do you have some kind of thing with her that you didn't want her seeing you speak to the FBI?"

Madison shifted in the seat. "I umm…" She paused as if she wasn't sure what to say. She looked between them, maybe seeing if there was a way out of the question. Kate and Declan remained silent waiting for her response. Finally, she relented. "She dated Trevor. That's technically how I met him. I didn't want her to know I was speaking to the FBI. I didn't want her to hassle me about it. I'm sure she doesn't want the FBI to know she was involved with him, so if she asks, I'm going to lie."

"Trevor Fontaine?" Kate asked, fairly certain that's what Madison said. It was so shocking that she had to double-check. "The victim in our case."

"Is he really a victim?" Madison asked dismissively.

Declan rested his folded hands on the table. "Yes, he's the victim. He might have been a despicable human being. That doesn't mean he deserved to die as he did. We can hate what the man stood for and what he had to say. No one is entitled to end his life."

"Fine. But you should know a lot of women don't feel like he's a victim. In fact, many of us feel like he's getting far more attention than most women who go missing and are murdered."

Kate couldn't argue with her there. Women were assaulted and murdered every day, more often than not by someone they loved, and it rarely made more than a couple of sentences in a newspaper, if even that. "The nature of the case brought us in. Less to do with who Trevor was and more with how he died. I can understand your feelings. Sometimes there isn't much fairness in what cases we investigate." Kate wasn't going to let her skirt the question. "You said Kristen was dating Trevor? Is that correct?"

Madison nodded. "Trevor and Kristen had an ongoing relationship of sorts. I don't know how much dating there actually was. It was more like she was using him to annoy her father and Trevor was using her for sex and possibly for her connections to her father. It was a use-use situation all around. I think Trevor asked me out that night to annoy her."

The situation was more complex than Madison had initially said.

Kate was beginning to think Madison was more complex, too. "If you are friends with Kristen, why did you say yes?"

"Because she encouraged it," Madison said. "I said no to Trevor initially. He sat down with us and wouldn't go away. It was like some game they were playing. Kristen was trying to get me to say yes to prove she wasn't interested in him. They had a terrible relationship, nothing that I would have kept going long-term. They couldn't seem to quit each other. She was as bad as him."

"We were told there wasn't anyone Trevor was seeing regularly," Declan said, questioning her. "The men he works with told us Trevor was the one-and-done type. He slept around extensively, but there was no one he saw more than once. They didn't seem to know about Kristen."

Madison shrugged. "I've never met the guys he works with. All I know is Trevor and Kristen have been a thing for months, possibly longer than that. I don't know when they first met. I know it's not serious and it's not committed. Kristen said he still sleeps with other girls and she doesn't care. She was dating some other guys too."

"Doesn't sound like something I'd get in the middle of," Declan offered, saying exactly what Kate had been thinking.

"I didn't want to get involved," Madison responded, affronted as her cheeks flared red. "The last thing I wanted to do was get in the middle of it. But that night Trevor wouldn't go away and Kristen was egging me on to agree to a date. I did so they would stop. I had every intention of cancelling. Then Kristen showed up at my room and asked me what I was wearing. I told her I didn't want to go and she told me I had to. I figured I'd go, meet him, and leave early. I barely made it a few minutes with him that night. I knew I shouldn't have gone."

"The negging?" Declan asked.

"Yeah, it started as soon as I walked in. He asked why I wasn't wearing anything designer. Then he said that I should consider different makeup and hitting the gym."

Kate would have dumped his drink on his head. "That sounds more like straight insults than negging."

Madison shifted her attention to Kate. "He wanted me to respond. He wanted me to tell him that I was on scholarship and couldn't afford designer clothes or bags, so he could impress me with his money. He wanted me to compete for him, knowing that Kristen was the kind of woman he dated normally. I believe he thought I had low self-esteem or something. Trevor wanted to believe I wanted to be there with him. That I would be in competition for him. Like it was some kind of treat for me and I'd be jumping through hoops like a trained monkey to get his attention."

"How did you respond?"

"I called him a few choice names, called out his obvious insecurities, and bailed. I called a cab, chatted with a few guys outside as I waited until the cab came. I was worried Trevor was going to follow me out and keep harassing me. He did not, which I was glad about. The cab came and I went back to my room."

Kate had several questions. "When was the last time you spoke to Trevor?"

"We met at eight and I was gone by eight twenty." She pulled her phone from her pocket and scrolled back through her recent calls. She showed the phone screen to Kate. "I called the cab at eight twelve that night. I was standing outside the bar by then. I thought I'd hail a cab, but that's a quiet street, so I called one. There was one around the corner. I barely had to wait. I wasn't with Trevor in the bar for more than a few minutes, as I said."

"Was he talking to anyone else at the bar?"

"No. He was sitting at a back booth. He said it was his table. I didn't even order a drink before he started with me. Trevor did say that if I wasn't going to sleep with him that night, he had another date lined up. That was the point at which I left. We were already arguing, and I figured he wanted me to fight for his validation and attention. It wasn't going to happen."

Kate raised her eyes to Declan. "Did he mention the other woman's name?"

Madison shook her head. The look on her face indicated she might know more.

Declan pushed. "If you suspect something, please tell us. We are working to solve this before someone else is murdered."

Madison turned her head sharply to look at him. "You suspect there might be more murders?"

"We do. Based on the crime scene and what happened to Trevor, we suspect that there might be more murders. That's why they called us in. Otherwise, the case would be handled by the NYPD."

"I kind of wondered why the FBI was involved." Madison sat back and stared at Kate across the table. "I'm not saying this is true and I'm not saying I have any evidence to back this up."

"I understand," Kate said. "You were with Trevor that night. If you have a feeling about what he was doing, that's good enough for me. We can confirm it or dismiss it."

Madison nervously licked her lips. "I was so angry by the time I got back that I wanted to scream at Kristen for making me go. She wasn't home. I didn't see her until Sunday. By that time, the news had broken that Trevor had been murdered and my anger seemed pointless. When I found out Kristen wasn't home, I thought she might have gone to see Trevor. I assumed she was the one who might meet him later if I didn't have sex with him. I got the feeling it was a game to them. That I was just a pawn in whatever sick sex game they were playing."

"What do you mean?" Declan asked, not hiding his confusion.

She turned to look at him. "I figured it was a game. Kristen encourages me to go out with him. Trevor tries to get me into bed. One making the other jealous – all so they can get angry then go at it. Kristen had said they often had angry hate sex, whatever that means. I assumed I was part of some sick foreplay between the two of them."

It made a twisted kind of sense to Kate. "You don't know for sure?"

Madison shook her head. "No one seemed to know where Kristen went that night. She never came home. When I didn't see her on Saturday, I thought maybe I was wrong. She never spent the night with Trevor. He didn't allow her to sleep over. He also never came to the dorm to see her. As I said, I don't have proof of anything."

Kate started to wonder then if Kristen might have been involved in the murder. That kind of passion could spill over into violent rage. "What has Kristen told you about Trevor?"

"Little things here and there. Mostly, she was using him to make her father angry. She said the sex was hot, even hotter when they were angry with each other. She said she had Trevor wrapped around her little finger. He was begging for it. And she liked that a man who considered himself an alpha was begging. As I said, it was a dysfunctional relationship."

"Do you think Kristen had something to do with his murder?"

Madison leaned back against the booth. She pursed her lips as if thinking. "I can't say for sure. As I said, it was a crazy relationship. Kristen said they were always arguing and fighting then having sex. I asked her once if it ever got physical and she said it had. She had shown me bruises around her neck that happened during sex."

Declan stopped her. "What kind of bruises? From being choked or from kissing?"

"I have no idea. That isn't my idea of a good time. They were around her neck. If it was from kissing, I'd be surprised."

Declan glanced over at Kate and she could see his mind spinning. He was thinking the same thing. She asked, "Have you ever seen Kristen get violent with anyone?"

"No. I'm not accusing her. You asked me if I thought it was possible and anything is possible with the two of them." Madison turned her head to look at Declan. "You said you suspect there might be other victims. I can't see Kristen doing that. She might have hurt Trevor, but she's not insane."

Kate wasn't going to rule it out. "You said after you left the bar you went straight back to your dorm. Can anyone confirm what time you got back?"

Madison hesitated, turning back to her. "I saw a few girls down the hall when I went looking for Kristen. But otherwise, no. As I said, I barely saw him for ten minutes. I should never have agreed to meet him. I regretted it as soon as I got there."

"Is there anything else you think we should know?" Kate asked.

"I can state the obvious – I had nothing to do with Trevor's murder. I've never even been to where he lives. Met him in one bar and left him in another."

"What was the name of the bar you met him at that night?"

"Crescent & Oak. It's like his bar. He's there all the time."

"Thank you," Kate said, her tone softening just a fraction. "We'll be in touch if we need anything else." As Madison got up to leave, Kate called her back and asked for her phone number and carrier information.

"Why?" Madison asked.

"We need the phone records," Kate said without hesitation. She didn't know if they'd pull them but easier than requiring a warrant later. "If you could call the company too and give us permission."

"Oh. Sure." Madison provided the information. "Will you be able to tell that I was in my room all night if you look at my phone records?"

Kate cocked her head to the side. It was a curious question. "We'd have to get a warrant for that, but yes, we'd be able to see what cell tower your phone was connecting to. Although you could have left your phone at home and gone back out without it." She paused to see if Madison would react. When she didn't, Kate added, "If you haven't done anything wrong, we wouldn't have a reason to get that information."

"Okay," she said evenly. She pursed her lips as they watched her. "I figured it might be a way to prove I was in my room all night."

"We have other methods for that," Kate explained. "We'll be in touch if we need anything else."

With that, Madison left the coffee shop, their gazes following her as she walked out the door.

Kate wasn't sure how she felt about Madison. There was something about the young woman that piqued her curiosity. She felt she was being truthful but also holding back.

"Think she's hiding something?" Declan asked, reading Kate's expression.

Kate exhaled sharply. "I'm not sure. There's something about her I can't quite put my finger on. She doesn't seem like the kind of young woman who'd get in the middle of relationship drama like that."

Declan ran a hand through his messy dark hair. "I don't think anything is going to surprise me about this case. To the bar or hunt down Kristen?"

"Bar first," Kate said. "I have a feeling she's going to deny the relationship, and I want to get ready for that fight."

CHAPTER 8

Crescent & Oak sat on a quiet corner in the Upper West Side, almost like a secret tucked away in plain sight. Its exterior, aged but refined, had a dignified air about it that Kate liked. She could see herself heading to the spot after a long day of work. The brick façade was weathered but sturdy. The windows were framed by dark mahogany, and above the door, a faded, gold-leaf sign with the name in a curving script. Right under the date 1888.

The door, heavy wood with brass handles, creaked slightly as Declan opened it. Once inside, the air was thick with the scent of aged whiskey and wood. The dim lighting cast long shadows across the room, flickering softly from vintage sconces that lined the walls. The space was long and narrow, with rich oak paneling that hugged the walls, giving the room a warm, intimate feel. The bar itself was the centerpiece, a gleaming stretch of polished wood that seemed to have soaked up the history of countless conversations, deals, and whispered secrets. The bartender tended to the patrons with practiced ease.

The floor was dark hardwood, worn in places where people stood talking, laughing, and probably even sometimes arguing. Booths lined the back wall, deep and plush, with crimson velvet cushions that still managed to hold a certain elegance despite their age. They offered a sense of privacy, of concealment, making it the perfect spot for both business and pleasure – or something a little more dangerous. Kate could see why Trevor might have chosen it as his spot.

A few tables were scattered between the booths, their surfaces gleaming under the low, amber light. The bar itself was a rich expanse of oak, its surface smooth and shining, polished by decades of use. Behind it, shelves stocked with liquor bottles gleamed in the soft light, each bottle arranged with the care of a collector's prize. A mirror ran along the back wall, slightly cloudy with age, reflecting the entire room with a quiet elegance.

Kate felt the weight of history as she stood near the end of the bar. The place was a time capsule and probably a booming hotspot during the Prohibition era. While it had since shed its more illicit reputation, today it was more the place where upscale singles met and business deals were sealed.

Declan pulled out a short-backed high stool for her to sit on while he gestured to the bartender to come their way. The man finished with a customer then headed down to the end of the bar. Declan flashed his badge and the man glanced back at other patrons.

"What can I help you with?" he asked with hesitation in his voice.

"Trevor Fontaine," Declan responded, keeping his voice low. "We know that he was here the night he was murdered. We believe it was his last stop before heading home that night. We were hoping you might be able to tell us about the time he spent here."

The man finished wiping his hands on his apron. "Let me finish helping these customers and call for help at the bar. You can take a seat in one of the booths and I'll be right over." He started to walk away then turned back. "Would you like to see the surveillance video first?"

"Of course," Declan said before Kate could respond. The bartender walked down the length of the bar and returned with an iPad. He handed it over to Declan. "You'll see our security app. You can search in the app for history and pull up anything within the last thirty days.

I was surprised the cops hadn't shown up sooner for this. Trevor was a regular customer."

"That's what we were told," Kate confirmed. "The NYPD only had the case briefly before it was given to the FBI. We only found out today that he had been here that night."

The bartender took a credit card from a customer and ran it, giving him back the slip and a pen. He angled himself to look at Kate. "Trevor was here every night. That back booth, the last one in the row. That was his. He sat there all the time. If customers were sitting there when he came in, he'd make a stink about it until they moved. I didn't like the guy, but I'm not the owner. The owner liked having Trevor here, so we were supposed to accommodate him."

It didn't surprise Kate in the least that Trevor was not liked. She was getting that from everyone they spoke to about the man. She followed Declan to the back booth, Trevor's booth, and they sat opposite each other.

Kate surveyed the bar, understanding why Trevor might have liked the seat. It gave him some privacy away from other patrons while also offering him the clearest line of sight for the whole establishment. Kate could see each patron at the bar, the front door, and catch the bartender's eyes from here. It also allowed her to scan the floor. The only thing she couldn't see was who was sitting in each booth. She assumed that as the place got more crowded he'd be able to see less and less. But she assumed he would have been a few drinks in and holding court by then and the view wouldn't have mattered as much.

"Here," Declan said, his eyes rising from the iPad. "I found the right night. Trevor comes in about seven and sits here in the booth where you are sitting. He gets two glasses of whiskey before Madison even comes in. He talks to a few guys at the bar but is mostly on his phone. He's typing then waiting and typing again. I assume he's texting someone."

Kate leaned into the table to see what Declan was pointing at. The footage was black and white and a little grainy. She could make out Trevor. This was the first time she'd seen him like this, outside the podcast, out in the wild, so to speak. "He sits with the confidence of a man who commands a room. His eyes rise and fall from the screen, always moving. He's not one for sitting still. He's waiting, talking, and back to looking and typing on his phone."

The timer counted down to a little before eight. As she said, Madison walks in, looks around, and finds him in the booth. She stands at the side of it, looking uncertain if she should sit or not. Trevor looks as if he's about to get up when she slides in. Trevor puts his phone down on the table, finally leaving the device alone for several minutes. He's gesturing wildly with his hands as he speaks. The video surveillance doesn't capture the conversation. Trevor seems engaged while Madison looks tense, her features tight and no smile on her face.

"They don't look like a couple on a date. They appear more like enemies meeting. Her posture is rigid, and she visibly shrinks back against the booth at least three times." Kate assumed it was when he threw the insults at her. Moments later, just as she said, she points at him sharply, her mouth moving quickly as she strikes back. Then she's out of the booth in a flash, retreating toward the door. She doesn't look back as she leaves Trevor sitting there watching her go.

There's a sick, satisfied smile on his face.

Declan hit the pause button and leaned toward the screen. "He almost looks happy that she left."

Kate didn't need to lean in. "He looks pleased with himself. Whether he's happy she left or he enjoyed how he insulted her. He might have even relished how rude she was in response. Men like him get off on the reactive abuse."

"Reactive abuse?" Declan asked, laying the iPad flat on the table to focus on Kate. "What does that mean?"

Kate explained the term was often used with victims of narcissistic abuse. "It's once a victim finally blows their top and responds to the narcissist. It's their reaction. Often it takes a victim a long time to build up the courage to react in anger. Once they do, it's seen as an extreme reaction. The narcissist likes that they can get the victim to respond like that. Manipulate their emotions in such a way. It also allows the narcissist to feel like the victim, which they feel like all along anyway. It's reinforcing their behavior. Madison reacted this way and Trevor enjoyed that he got a reaction out of her. He probably also enjoyed the confirmation that women were emotional. Men forget that anger is an emotion, too. Women get a bad rap for being emotional. I've never seen anyone more emotional than an insecure man who has been rejected."

Declan's eyebrows went up, but he didn't respond. He hit play on the video and the screen jumped to life. The minutes ticked by as Trevor got another whiskey and went back to texting on his phone. Declan hit the fast-forward button and the screen sped up. No one else came over to the table during this time. Trevor barely even raised his head from his phone.

Shortly after Madison had left, a woman who looked a lot like Kristen glided into the bar, stopped briefly to order a drink, turned her back to the bartender, and glanced in Trevor's direction. She offered him a coy smile then turned her back on him. She did not walk over to the table. Kristen waited there until Trevor got up and walked over to her.

He moved slowly across the floor, never taking his gaze off her. Trevor moved the chair next to her out of his way as he pressed his body against hers and let his fingertips trail down her back. It was the physical move of two people who had been intimate before. This wasn't a casual acquaintance but an intimate gesture from someone who knew the other well.

Trevor leaned down and whispered something in her ear, causing Kristen's mouth to turn up in a satisfied smile. She never turned her body fully into his, keeping herself just slightly off from him.

"She's teasing him," Declan said, expressing Kate's thought. "She's allowing herself to flirt with him but not fully engage with him. Do you see the way she keeps a focus on the bartender and the other people around her but never fully looks Trevor in the eyes?"

Kate did see it. "It's foreplay." It made her think that Madison might not have been off in her assessment that she had been used as a pawn in their twisted sex game. Kate kept her eyes focused on the screen as Kristen finished her drink, placed the glass on the table and moved toward the front entrance of the bar without saying another word. She stopped only when she got to the door. She turned back to Trevor with an eyebrow cocked and she licked her lips suggestively.

Trevor hurried back to his table, knocked back the last bit of his drink, tossed a few twenties on the table, and followed her out. Once Kristen saw he was on the move, she didn't even wait for him. She pulled open the door, letting it close behind her only seconds before Trevor reached it.

"She constantly remains just out of his grasp," Declan said, hitting stop on the video. He rested the iPad on the table before sitting back. "Kristen knew exactly how to play him. I wonder if that's who he was texting before Madison came in."

"Why drag Madison into it at all?" Kate didn't pretend to know all the kinks out there. Her romantic life would be considered boring to most.

Declan didn't seem to know either. "Is it possible they were trying to goad her into a threesome?"

Kate shook her head. It didn't feel like that to her. "Maybe Trevor gets off on the rejection and chasing after Kristen, knowing in the end, he will have her."

"They play that game often," the bartender said suddenly at the end of their table. He slid into the booth next to Declan and introduced himself. "Brian Torella."

Kate gestured toward the iPad. "You said it's a game they play often. What do you mean?"

"Trevor and that woman. I think her name is Kristen. They are involved with each other, clearly. But they often come in separately and pretend they are strangers. She tries to steal him away from other women and he tries to steal her away from other men. It's something they do before leaving together. Well…" he paused. "Not quite together. They leave like you saw them on the video. She always goes out first and he follows. I get the sense she's the one in control in that relationship."

It was an astute observation. Kate applauded him for it.

Brian brushed off the compliment. "I've been running this bar for the last ten years. When you're here all the time, you spot these things about people. I can usually tell someone's drink before they order." He paused to see if they'd respond to that. When they didn't, he gestured toward Kate. "You're not much of a drinker, but when you do, it's strong Irish whiskey. You do a variety of things with it – a good Irish coffee, a mule, and occasionally just a glass neat."

Kate couldn't help but smile. He wasn't wrong.

Brian turned his head to Declan. "You'd drink what's served. You've got a blue-collar vibe about you even though you might have gone to a fancy college. A dark beer, whiskey…you're not picky."

Declan gestured for him to go on without confirming that he was right. "Tell me what you think about Trevor?"

"Insecure, desperately seeking male approval in all the wrong ways."

"You think it's male approval and not female approval?" Kate asked, wondering about his reasoning.

Brian nodded. "Most of these guys want to out masculine the other. Prove they are the alpha, but there's no such thing. The only thing they are proving is that they aren't good people and they aren't good men. Trevor didn't do that podcast to win over women. He did it to win over men in his culture of hate. Do you know he actually said on a podcast once that it was gay to be friends with your wife?" He held up his hand to show his wedding band. "My wife is one of my favorite people. That's why I married her."

He shook his head in disgust. "If it wasn't for the owner, I would have made his stay here so uncomfortable that he left. He disrespects women, doesn't tip the staff, and is an all-around creep."

Kate had heard the same from so many people. If it wasn't for the flowers and notes, anyone could be the suspect. "Do you know of anyone who might have wanted to kill him? He have issues with anyone in the bar?"

"Other than women, he mostly kept to himself. He'd jut his chin out and talk to a few guys here and there, but nothing I'd consider friendship. He didn't start fights because he wasn't the kind of guy who could finish them. He talked a big game on the podcast. In real life, he kept to himself."

"What about the women?" Kate asked. "He must have angered a lot of them. Can you recall anyone that he had a particular public altercation with recently?"

"Ali Brewer. She's that hard-core feminist. She has a rival podcast and she stages protests. She showed up here one night and started a fight with him in the bar. She threw a drink at him. The glass shattered and cut his hand. She went after him." There was a faint smile on Brian's face. "I get it. She did what a lot of us wish we could do. I couldn't have it in the bar."

"Was she arrested?" Declan asked, jotting down her name in his phone.

"No. I wasn't going to call the cops. Even though Trevor whined about it, he knew it was going to be good clout for his podcast. He would have looked like a wimp if he had needed to call the cops over a woman."

They asked Brian a few more questions about the altercation and what he knew about Ali. Kate left the bar feeling like they were making a little ground.

Ali Brewer sounded exactly like the kind of woman who'd orchestrate the Midnight Lilies.

CHAPTER 9

Kate didn't want to find Ali Brewer right away after the meeting at the bar. She wanted time to do a little research first. It had been a long first day of investigating and she wanted to take a break from the field. They headed back to the boutique hotel on the Upper West Side.

After having dinner at a nearby place and taking a long, hot shower, she felt ready to sit down in front of her laptop and learn more about Ali. Declan had earbuds in and was deep into more episodes of Trevor's podcast.

Kate noted the way his face contorted with anger at certain points. She was glad that he had been raised by a strong mother and stable father who instilled good values in him. She thought that, then stopped herself, because Kate wondered if it was true. Declan's brothers were all criminals in South Boston. Declan had had a bit of a drinking problem in the past and had slept around more than she liked. She had never taken the time to explore Declan's background beyond what he told her. Tonight wasn't the night for that, though.

For now, Kate would be happy he turned out exactly as he had because she had fallen completely in love with him over the last year. While she snuggled into one end of the couch, Declan was across the coffee table from her in a chair with his feet kicked up on the ottoman.

Kate pulled the headphones up to her ears and started the first episode of *Her Voice, Her Fury.* She learned how aptly named it was within the first ten minutes. Ali had a feminist rage tee-shirt on, ice blue eyes, and parts of her long blonde hair had been dyed purple. She wore it loose around her shoulders. To match the rest of the look, she had a sleeve of brightly colored tattoos up one arm, several rings on her fingers, an array of earrings up and down each ear, and one through her nose.

Kate couldn't quite place the woman's age. The way she spoke portrayed the intelligence of someone much older with considerable life experience. Ali's youthful, glowing skin and appearance hinted at someone younger. It was a toss-up.

Kate sank back into the couch and listened to Ali discuss dating violence and protecting women and the history of the feminist movement. She highlighted upcoming guests and why the podcast was so important. She said she had an army of women who were rallying behind her. That the podcast was a counterpoint to all the bro podcasts out there.

Ali stated in the podcast that she was a women's studies adjunct professor at Barnard College while also working on her doctorate in the same subject. She was highly qualified to run a podcast such as this. Kate wondered what the college thought of Ali's appearance and the podcast name. She assumed that having a professor and student so heavily invested in their subject area of study might be beneficial.

Kate lay back on the couch, taking quick glances at Declan, who was as absorbed in his podcast as she was in Ali's. As Kate progressed from the first episode to the third, Ali honed her style and voice. The rocky bits in the first were smoothed out into a coherent dialogue and presentation. The style was relaxed yet educational and conversational. It was easy for Kate to lose herself in the information. When discussing the statistics about violence against women, Ali presented accurate information. She didn't inflate the numbers, and she didn't sensationalize the content – not that she needed to. The factual statistics were horrifying.

The questions Ali and her guests debated were the answers – how to solve the issue of sexual assault and violence against women in American society. There was no easy answer and many things were thrown into the discussion. Kate liked that they didn't settle on any one way because it was a complex topic that required complex solutions. Kate thought the discussion was fair and balanced. But then again, she agreed with almost everything that was being said. She had expected more rage from Ali and her guests, given the name of the podcast.

She had assumed there'd be calls for violence. But she found none.

Kate listened for a while longer then shut off the podcast in the middle of an episode and switched to the FBI database to learn what she could about Ali. There wasn't much of a file. She had been arrested a handful of times in her early twenties for protesting. There had been one incident of throwing paint on the car of a convicted rapist who was given a light sentence of only six months in jail by the judge. Kate didn't know anything about the case to say whether the sentence was justified or not. There was a lot that went into sentencing. She didn't know if the man had pleaded out and saved the victim from having to testify, or if the case possibly wasn't all that strong.

It was enough that Ali committed the act of vandalism and that's what Kate honed in on. Ali had received probation and community service. Kate noted her birthdate on the police report. She was thirty-four.

She scrolled through the file but found nothing else of value. There was no assault. Nothing to indicate violence. Kate went to the internet and did a broad search on Ali's name. Several academic research sites came up with papers that were authored and co-authored. They were all on the topics of gender violence, sexual assault, women in the workplace, and similar topics. One of the more recent papers caught Kate's attention.

It was focused on the rise of radicalization of young men in the incel culture.

Kate clicked on the paper and started to read. Ali and her co-authors had done a deep dive into the rise of the movement, the key players, the symbols used with emojis, and social media slang. They interviewed several young men about what the culture means to them and why they consider themselves a part of it. The subjects that were interviewed were taken from a pool of those who had been initially surveyed and were willing to leave their names. The survey was otherwise anonymous. They had even spoken to law enforcement in several major cities and a handful of rural towns, as well as the FBI counter-terrorism agents who focused on domestic terrorism. Kate knew that the threat of domestic terrorism far outweighed any other kind of terrorism, but that's not where the money was funneled.

One agent who Kate didn't know was quoted in the paper as stating that many of these young men are being radicalized online at younger and younger ages, some as young as twelve, through gaming forums initially and social media. It was giving them an outlet for their insecurities and a place to put the blame for their feeling of inadequacy – women. The paper cited several of the podcasts as potentially helping to radicalize these young men. Much of the content they were viewing on social media was coming from these podcasts.

Kate scrolled through to the next page and saw a list of the podcasts that were problematic. Trevor Fontaine's name and his podcast *Grit & Grind* were front and center. She grabbed the notepad sitting next to her on the couch and jotted down the names of the others, highlighting both the podcast name and the hosts. While Trevor's name was mentioned Reggie and Devon were not. Kate wondered about Ali's reasoning for this.

Kate clicked out of the research and searched for the name of the paper elsewhere on the internet. She wondered if Ali and her co-authors had spoken at any conferences. After a few minutes of searching and coming back with nothing, Kate gave up. She felt Declan's gaze on her. She slipped the headphones off and turned to him.

He was staring right at her. "I love it when you talk to yourself," he teased, a smile on his face.

Kate hadn't realized she was talking to herself. "What did I say?"

"Nothing of any importance. While you were searching, you were just chattering away about what you were looking for. I take it you found some good information."

Kate explained what she learned about Ali, some highlights about the podcast, and the paper she co-authored. "I didn't realize she was an adjunct professor. I'm having trouble squaring this woman on the podcast and who co-authored the paper with the woman at the bar. I know we were told she went in and started a fight with Trevor and ended up throwing a glass at him. I need more context because I'm struggling to see it. The only real arrest she had other than peacefully protesting was vandalism against a convicted rapist's car. She isn't accused of doing anything to him. The paper does mention Trevor and the podcast by name." Kate hitched her chin toward Declan's laptop. "What more have you learned?"

Declan sighed, pushing his laptop off his lap and setting it down on the coffee table. "It only gets worse the more you get in. There's a lot of inaccurate information being used to justify their misogyny. Things taken out of context. As Brian at the bar said, it's a lot of insecurity being masked as bravado. Early on, before the podcast was well-known, Trevor would bring reputable guests on for debate and he acted like a clown. He'd shout and yell at them, call them names, and wouldn't listen to counter-arguments. There was no intelligent exchange of information."

"Have you known men like Trevor?"

Declan shrugged it off. "There are always men like that here and there. I knew a few in college, but they were creeps. They got a reputation early on as using women and women stayed away. They got angry and started to blame women for not choosing them and their anger and creepiness grew, turning off more women. It was a vicious cycle."

Kate could see how that would work. "What about you when you were younger? I knew you at the academy, but I don't know much about you in high school and college. Same? A lot of girlfriends?"

Declan shook his head. "Not in high school. I was too focused on hockey. I had a big group of friends. Some might even say I was popular, but I wasn't paying much attention to anything other than my core groups of friends, hockey, and getting good enough grades to get into Boston College for hockey. College was hockey, parties, and studying. It's never anything I gave much thought to."

"Because it came naturally to you," Kate said evenly. "For these men, it doesn't come naturally. You had parents as role models and brothers who were keeping you in line."

"They are criminals, Kate," Declan reminded her. "My brothers were out of the house getting in trouble while I was studying."

"Criminals, maybe. But two of them have successful marriages and have never once been accused of violence against women."

Declan nodded. "My brother went to prison for assault for hitting a man who he saw hit a woman. I guess you're right in that regard. I don't know how they ended up as criminals. My parents didn't raise us like that."

"They didn't have your sports or academic talent." Kate didn't know if that was true, but it was the only thing she'd ever been able to reason. She had met Declan's parents, and he was right that they were not raised that way.

Declan's phone rang and he reached for it on the arm of the chair. "Sharon," he said as he answered. He spoke to Sharon on speaker, alerting her that Kate was there too. "What have you found?"

"The lilies are dyed black. They aren't the flowers known as midnight lilies. They were white and dyed the black shade that you're seeing at the crime scene."

Kate had assumed that might be the case. "Do you know what they used to dye them?"

"It's not food coloring, I can tell you that much," Sharon explained. "I'm still running some tests on that. I'm leaning toward a professional floral dye. I'm going to a florist in the morning to speak to someone directly about how they'd do it most cost-effectively. I'm assuming you don't have professional horticulturists on your hands. I will say they did a good job dying the flowers. They are well-coated and no white was left. I assume this would be a messy job."

That meant they'd need some space to do it. Somewhere to either buy flowers in bulk or grow them. Kate was out of her depth. She knew nothing about flowers. "Can you ask about either purchasing large quantities of lilies or how someone might grow them? There isn't a lot of room for gardens in New York City in your average apartment, and someone is going to notice large quantities of lilies being bought."

Sharon promised to gather all of that information for them. "Any leads yet?"

Declan leaned forward toward the phone. "Nothing worth sharing. We pieced together Trevor's last few hours."

"Did you figure out where the DNA came from?"

"We might have. Still leads to run down." Declan assured Sharon that he'd update her once they knew more. He ended the call and stretched his arms overhead. "We need some sleep. I don't know about you, but I'm still jetlagged."

Kate agreed that sleep was something they both needed if they were going to be fresh for the case in the morning. They'd go see Kristen first, followed by Ali at Barnard. It would be easier to find her on campus.

They went through their nightly routines and as Declan was pulling back the covers to crawl into bed beside Kate, his cellphone rang again. "It better not be Sharon again," he said as he reached for it. He looked at the screen and groaned. "Spade."

Declan sat on the edge of the bed as he engaged the call. There were no pleasantries as Spade delivered the news they knew could eventually come. Kate had been hoping for more time.

Another podcaster – Corey Weber from *The Alpha Narrative* was dead.

CHAPTER 10

Corey Weber did not live in Manhattan. He didn't even live in New York in the tri-state metro around the city. He lived in San Francisco and his body was found in Central Park off a trail in The Ramble section of the park.

It was located mid-park between 73rd and 79th Streets and encompassed thirty-six acres that were designed to look like upstate New York's forests. The paths and trails were winding and featured rustic bridges, streams, dramatic rock outcroppings, and dense plantings.

His body was found by a man walking his dog, who first noticed the man's feet several yards off the trail. He went to inspect and found the body. He immediately called the NYPD, who brought out a team that decided it was connected to the Trevor Fontaine murder, and Spade was called.

It was a short walk from the hotel to the entrance of the park where the body was found. It was in the most accessible part of the park where Kate and Declan were staying.

The NYPD did a good job of closing down that section. At that hour, the park was officially closed, which had been Kate's first question.

Why was someone walking their dog in the park that late?

Kate got the answer to her question moments after arriving. NYPD had held the witness a few yards from where the body was found. He had on sweatpants and a Colombia sweatshirt. The dog, a black

Labrador, was lying calmly at his side.

While Declan met with the few NYPD officers who had been first on the scene, Kate went to the witness – Steve Winslow. Kate walked up to him, resisted the urge to bend down and pet the dog, and introduced herself. The man looked up at her through shellshocked eyes.

"I know this must have been difficult for you. What were you doing in the park so late?"

He pointed back toward the entrance of the park. "I worked late and Ollie wanted to go for a walk. He was running around the place full of energy. I figured a nice long walk might calm him down. As you can see, the paths are well lit. You won't find too many people in here after hours, except neighbors walking their dogs. It's not late enough yet that the criminal element shows up, or so I thought."

Steve went on to explain that there were drug deals and other things that happened in the park late at night that made it unsafe to wander around. He noted that he wouldn't be caught dead in the park after midnight then quickly backtracked on his choice of phrasing.

Kate said she understood. "Can you tell me about finding him?"

Steve pointed down the narrow path right in front of him. "That path loops back around down there." He pointed to the left, deeper into the park. "I figured we'd walk down there, loop around to this main trail, and head back. We got maybe thirty feet down and I saw what I thought was a sneaker among the leaves. I didn't think too much of it at first. Then Ollie started pulling me toward it. I tried tugging him away. I was looking over there. That's when I noticed all the black. There are a lot of leaves, as you can see. None of them are black. I thought that it was just because it was dark. The closer I got, I started to realize they were flowers of some kind. I don't know anything about flowers."

Steve took a deep breath as he struggled with what he witnessed. Kate told him to go slow. She didn't want him to hyperventilate. She knew finding a body was traumatic for nearly everyone.

"You're doing great," she told him, encouraging him to go on.

Steve glanced down at the dog. "You can thank Ollie. Even seeing those flowers, I was going to let it go and keep moving. I didn't see the body under it. Ollie kept tugging and lunging toward him. He had his nose to the ground and kept sniffing, pulling me. He didn't give me much of a choice. He pulled me right off the trail to the man's body. It was only after I was standing right over him and shined the flashlight app on my phone down to the ground that I saw there was a person under all those flowers." He winched his eyes shut and shook his head. "It was so creepy. I couldn't see his face too well, but I knew he was dead. He wasn't moving, and it looked like there was tape over his mouth. I got out of there as quickly as I could and called the police. It took some effort. Ollie is about ninety pounds and he didn't want to go. I pulled him back out to the main path here and called the police. I considered leaving. I didn't know if the killer was still around."

Kate understood that. She might have gone all the way back home to call it in. "What made you stay?"

"I don't know," he said with a shudder. He tugged on Ollie's leash and the dog raised his head. "He's a good protector if I need it. With the flowers all over the body, I assumed he was dumped here. Not like it was a robbery or something."

Kate couldn't rule out that he'd been killed close by. "Do you know the victim?"

"I don't think so. As I said, I didn't get a good look at his face." Steve paused to take a deep breath then squinted up at Kate. "You said you were with the FBI?" Kate confirmed again. "Why is the FBI out here and not just the NYPD? I don't understand why the FBI would be involved in a homicide in Central Park."

Kate didn't mind telling Steve the truth. It was going to hit the news anyway. "We believe this homicide is connected to another. Trevor

Fontaine was murdered in his brownstone. We believe that this case is connected to that one. That's why the FBI was brought in. Certain markers about the crime needed FBI expertise."

Steve grimaced. "Like a serial killer or something?"

Kate nodded. "You're correct that your run-of-the-mill killer isn't leaving black lilies all over bodies. Did you happen to see a note or anything on the ground when you went to look at the body?"

"There are too many leaves, and it was too dark to see much of anything. Once I realized it was a body, I got out of there and pulled Ollie back. I hope we didn't destroy any evidence." Steve peered down the path at the cops milling around. He angled his head to look back up at Kate. "I'm sorry if we disturbed anything. I didn't know until I knew. Then it was too late."

"You're fine," Kate assured him. "If you hadn't found him, it would have taken us much longer to get out here. Who knows who might have found him in the morning or what creatures overnight. You didn't see anyone else out there in the park tonight?"

"No one. I'm not usually out here at this time, but I worked late." Steve reached down to pat Ollie on the head. "When I first entered the park, there was a group of women standing on the sidewalk near the entrance. They were all in jogging gear like they were going for a late run or coming back from one. They weren't in the park. I did notice one had dirt on her knees as if she had fallen. I didn't see anyone other than my doorman when I left."

A group of women.

"How many women were there?"

"Umm…five, I think. Yeah, five of them, standing in a circle talking. I didn't think much of it. You don't think they could have done this, do you? They looked like they were exercising."

Kate didn't answer one way or the other. "Did you recognize any of them?"

"No," he said with a shake of his head. "I couldn't even pick them out of a lineup for you. They weren't looking at me as I passed. It's not like I stopped and spoke to them. Ollie wasn't even paying attention. He saw the entrance to the park and pulled me along."

"How old would you say they were?"

"I have no idea. Honestly, I was staring more at the dog than I was at them. That's how I saw the dirt patches on the one woman's knees. I was looking down. I couldn't even tell you what her face looked like."

Kate told him she understood. She asked him a few more questions, double checked that he had given a formal statement to one of the NYPD cops then gave him her card. "If you think of anything, call me. Even if you don't think it's important, you never know. Anything at all." Now that she was done, she leaned down and ruffled Ollie's head and told him he was a good boy.

Kate watched Steve and Ollie head back toward the gate where she and Declan had entered. Then she surveyed the area. The metal lampposts gave enough illumination that she understood why someone would walk the path at night.

Kate stood there for a moment, soaking up the scenery, trying to get a sense of the women who might have killed a man here. She tried to envision him being killed elsewhere but couldn't figure out how they'd carry a body unseen and dump him here. That didn't make sense to her.

The Ramble, even at night, held an eerie, enchanting beauty. The air, sharp with the scent of damp earth and fallen leaves, carried a chill that prickled Kate's skin. She started the walk down the smaller, narrow path, said hello to the few cops standing around, and got deeper into the wooded area. She wouldn't have come down this path alone at night even with a dog.

This was a part of the park that felt wild, untamed, even in the heart of New York City. The trees, tall and twisted, loomed like shadowy sentinels, their boughs creaking softly in the breeze that whispered through the underbrush. The faint light from distant streetlamps barely penetrated the thick canopy overhead, casting long, distorted shadows across the uneven terrain. It felt as though the park itself was alive, the rustling of branches and scuttling of small creatures creating a low, constant murmur against the silence.

Kate's boots crunched over the carpet of dry, brittle leaves that now covered much of the ground, their crisp edges skittering away with each step she took. A few gusts of wind stirred them, sending them spiraling in small, chaotic dances. The earth smelled of decay. And tonight, there was something about it that made the hairs on the back of her neck stand on end.

Ahead, beyond the thick line of trees and tangled underbrush, the glow of flashlights bounced in the distance. The NYPD had cordoned off the area with yellow tape marking the boundary. As Kate stepped under the tape, it was only a few steps to where Declan stood over the body, his flashlight illuminating the scene. Sharon hunched on the other side. Their voices were low and rushed.

The body of the man was draped in a blanket of dyed black lilies. The flowers, vibrant and out of place, glistened in the low light, a stark contrast to the muted browns and oranges of the fallen leaves that surrounded her.

The flowers had been arranged with care, as though the killer had crafted some sort of macabre offering. There was a sense of ritual in it, a deliberate coldness that Kate couldn't shake. Her breath caught, the chill of the air biting deeper now, or maybe it was just the unease creeping into her chest.

She stood still for a moment, taking in the scene – the dark pool of shadows, the thick trunks of the trees looming overhead, and the stillness that was somehow unsettling in its perfection.

Kate knew one thing for sure right then. These killers had only gotten started.

"Kate," Sharon said, her voice cutting through the low murmur of voices. "He has tape over his mouth. Declan and I were just discussing whether we should pull it off to see if his tongue is missing like Fontaine's or we wait for the medical examiner."

Kate knew she'd be the one to make the call. "What other evidence have you found? Is there an obvious cause of death?"

Declan pointed to the man's head. "One of the officers first on the scene recognized him. There's a gunshot to his head, like Trevor Fontaine. We have not done much with the body, so I have no idea if there are signs of torture."

Sharon handed Kate a pair of gloves and she snapped them on. She moved past Sharon, who stood back so Kate could get a closer look. Her breath caught in her throat as she saw the burn marks and wound on the man's forehead. He'd been shot at close range, close enough that it had left the mark from the barrel. "We have photos?" she confirmed again. The last thing Kate wanted to do was disturb the scene more than it already was.

When Sharon confirmed, Kate moved more of the flowers off his body and pulled up the man's blue Henley. The first signs of trauma to the man's rock-hard torso came into view. He'd been sliced and stabbed several times. She glanced over at Declan. "Help me roll him. I want to see his back."

Declan helped Kate roll the dead man to his side. Sharon bent down to help them. Corey was a big guy. The medical examiner would have to measure and weigh him, but it was evident he had lifted weights and probably stood at least six feet three. In the middle of his back were two round red marks – the marks Kate had been looking for when she rolled him.

Taser marks.

This is how they were bringing these men down.

Kate explained what she found then they rolled him to his back again. "I don't think even a group of women would have been able to carry him here. I assume he was killed on the spot or up a little on the trail. If they moved him, it wasn't far."

Declan tugged up the man's sleeves. "He has ligature marks on his wrists but no ligature."

"They must have taken it with them." Kate cursed softly. This wasn't a crime of happenstance. They had lured Corey out here to the middle of The Ramble to kill him.

While Kate was still kneeling in the wet patch of ground, she gestured toward his mouth. "Let's get the tape off and confirm."

Declan started at one corner and tugged the tape back, going carefully enough that he didn't rip the man's skin or the tape. Once he had the tape completely off, Kate put her hands to his lower jaw and pulled it down. She knew by the stains of blood around his mouth that his tongue was gone. What she hadn't been expecting was the piece of folded paper in its place.

She held his jaw down with one hand and tugged out the paper. She unfolded the small note that had been folded in on itself twice to fit in his mouth.

The message was direct and clear and exactly what Kate feared.

We won't stop until they are all dead.
Midnight Lilies

CHAPTER 11

At nine the next morning, Kate and Declan stood outside the student housing building waiting for Kristen Carney. They had stayed late in Central Park well after the medical examiner came, retrieved the body and left. The post-mortem was scheduled for this morning, a rush on the case given the circumstances.

Kate and Declan needed to investigate to understand Corey's last moves and what led him to Central Park that night. They didn't even know why he was in the city for the evening. Spade was taking care of the death notification to Corey's family. A press conference was scheduled for eleven that morning. Kate wanted to talk to Kristen and possibly even Ali if they could track her down before that press conference.

"Do you think she's going to talk to us?" Declan asked, stifling a yawn. They hadn't gotten much sleep the night before. They didn't get back to the hotel until close to three in the morning. Both collapsed into bed and woke up around seven. Some sleep was better than none.

Kate wasn't even sure that Kristen was anything more than a witness. More than anything, she needed to know if the young woman had been at Trevor's house the night of his death and if she had heard or seen anything. "I'm not planning to approach this like she's a suspect. We know she's connected to Trevor, but we have no idea if she's connected to Corey." The only person so far that Kate knew connected, at least loosely, to both men was Ali because she had drawn up a list with their names on it. Not that it was much of a connection.

Fifteen minutes later, Kristen exited the building.

Declan pushed himself off the bench where they had been seated. He stepped in front of her and flashed his badge. "Kristen Carney, I'm FBI Agent Declan James and this is my partner Agent Kate Walsh. We need to speak to you about Trevor Fontaine."

The young woman lowered her round sunglasses long enough to sneer at him before pushing them back up her nose. "I don't speak to cops. My father said if I were ever approached, I should tell you to speak to my lawyer." She started to brush past him, but Kate pulled up at her side and walked with her.

The young woman didn't even acknowledge her. "We know you were with Trevor Fontaine the night he was murdered. It's up to you if we consider you a suspect or a witness. We have several witnesses who have confirmed a relationship between you."

Kristen said nothing but her steps faltered slightly.

"That's right. We know you left a bar with him the evening he was murdered. You were the last one to see him alive. We also believe it was a woman who killed him." Kate turned back to Declan, who was a few steps behind. "I wonder what her father is going to think today when we name her publicly as a person of interest in the investigation."

Declan played along. "I think at that point her father is going to get his lawyer involved and she'll have to explain why she was sleeping with a creep like Trevor Fontaine. Maybe that was why she was involved with a guy like that. What do you think, Kate? Maybe Kristen here was just trying to get her father's attention."

"Is that it?" Kate asked her. "You didn't have enough of your father's attention, so you slept with a creeper like Fontaine? I didn't think anyone was desperate enough. Low self-esteem, maybe?"

Kristen stopped dead in her tracks. She whipped around to Kate.

"You're not allowed to speak to me like that."

Kate shrugged it off. "I can speak to you however I like. You should give me your attorney's name so I can set up a meeting. But either you speak to me now or we are going to have to make this public. You were the last one to see Trevor alive and there's DNA all over his bed. We know that he had sex with you before he was murdered. It only stands to reason you are a suspect."

Kristen clicked her tongue and held firm.

"Okay," Kate said, retreating. "Let's play it your way. Your father's business is going to suffer, having a daughter connected to a major homicide like this. Not to mention, once your name gets out, the threats you might get from Trevor's supporters. My understanding is they aren't the nicest group of men. You might even need to leave school to keep yourself safe." Kate knew she was playing dirty. She turned on her heels and walked to Declan. They retreated toward the student housing building.

It only took about thirty seconds before Kristen scurried after them. "Wait! I'll speak to you but not out here on the street." She marched past them to the door and pulled it open, gesturing for them to follow her.

Once they were inside her room, Kristen turned to them. "How did you get my name?"

Kate shook her head. "We can't tell you that. All we can say is that we heard from several people that you were involved with Trevor. Is it fair to say that you were his girlfriend?"

"I wasn't his girlfriend. It was casual and flirtatious and not serious at all." Kristen folded her arms across her body as if she were hugging herself. "Trevor wasn't the kind of guy I could get serious with. It would make my father angry, but that's not why I was seeing him. Trevor wasn't a serious guy."

"He seemed serious enough on his podcast," Declan said, zeroing in on her.

"I mean with women. Relationships. He didn't want to get serious." Kristen stared past Declan to Kate. "He also wasn't as horrible as he came across in the podcast. I'm not saying he didn't believe all those things he said, he did. It just didn't impact what was going on between us."

Kate didn't understand how any woman could spend time with a man like Trevor. "What did you get out of the relationship?"

"Fun. No strings. A little danger." Kristen let her arms drop at her sides. She pulled up her desk chair and sat. "Trevor was dangerous in a way. He said things no one around me was saying. He had crazy ideas and bizarre beliefs. We argued about them. Debated. Had sex. It was hot. He also let me express a side of myself that I'd never express with someone that I'd be serious about in a relationship."

"What do you mean?"

Kristen cocked her head to the side, offering a sly smile. "Come on. There's relationship sex, then hot sex you'd have with someone you didn't care about. There's a difference."

While Declan's expression hinted that he agreed, Kate wasn't so sure she saw a difference in her own life. "The night that Trevor was murdered, you saw him. Tell us about that."

Kristen lowered her eyes to the floor. "We met at a bar around eight-thirty and went back to his place. We had sex twice, then I went home. I was planning to go see my parents that weekend, and I had an early flight to catch. I didn't normally spend the night. That wasn't unusual."

"Do you have your flight information?" Declan asked.

Kristen raised her eyes to him. She turned around to her desk and grabbed her phone from her bag. She pulled up the airline app and showed him her most recent trip information. Kate leaned over to see it as well. The flight left on Saturday morning at seven from

LaGuardia to Atlanta. The return was for Tuesday. The problem is that they had no way of knowing right then if she was actually on the flight.

"Do you still have your luggage tags?" Kate asked.

Kristen stood, her frustration evident. "I only had a carry-on. I didn't check a bag." She scrolled through something else on her phone and showed Kate a rideshare app. "I was surprising my parents for my father's birthday, so I took a rideshare from the airport. Here's the receipt for that."

Kate leaned in and confirmed the information.

"Look," Kristen said, her tone tinged with annoyance. "I'm sorry Trevor was murdered. I didn't even know about it until I saw it on the news over the weekend. It was hard to believe. I keep waiting for him to text me. You say that I was the last one to see him alive. I left around eleven and came back to my room here. I was up at the crack of dawn to catch a cab by four-thirty. I left Trevor in his bed and never saw or heard from him again."

Declan cocked an eyebrow. "He didn't walk you out? Text you to make sure you made it home okay?"

Kristen rolled her eyes. "He wasn't my boyfriend. It wasn't like that between us. I left his place, found a cab about a block away and came home. That was it. I left him satisfied and half-asleep. What happened after I left is anyone's guess."

"We don't need to guess," Kate reminded her with some heaviness to her tone. "We know exactly what happened to him that night. Did you lock the front door when you left?"

Kristen considered the question for a moment. Her response was a drawn-out *no*. "I never locked anything when I left his house. I guess I assumed he got up at some point and locked it himself." Kristen took a few steps back to the chair and sat. "Are you suggesting I might have let the killer in?"

"I'm not suggesting anything." It was exactly what Kate was suggesting but didn't want Kristen to feel any undo guilt. The facts of the situation mattered, especially because there was no forced entry. "Do you know if he locked the door when you came over to his place that night?"

"I don't know," Kristen said, the worry creeping into her voice. "We were already in the middle of things when we entered. We kicked off our shoes, undressed by the time we made it to the stairs and barely made it to his bedroom. I couldn't tell you what he did with the door."

Declan sighed. "Was he normally safety conscious?"

"No. Trevor thought he was untouchable. There were always threats being made against him and he didn't care. First off, he didn't think anyone knew where he lived. Secondly, he was armed and third of all, he didn't think anyone had the balls to go after him. His words, not mine."

"He was wrong on all counts." Declan looked over at Kate. She encouraged him to go on. "Did you know about the threats against him?"

"We didn't talk much about that. I knew there were threats. I didn't know the specifics." Kristen glanced between them, settling on Declan. "What happened to him that night? The news didn't give much detail. I don't know any of his friends to ask."

Kate was hesitant to get into the details. She shifted her eyes to Declan, who was looking at her with the same expression. "Trevor was tased to incapacitate him, stabbed a few times, both deeper and more shallow cuts, and then shot in the head. After death, his tongue was cut out."

Kristen recoiled in horror. She didn't cry and she didn't look away. There was confusion on her face. "Why would someone do something like that? All of that seems personal."

"We believe it was in response to the rhetoric on the podcast. It was personal, very personal, to the people who did this."

"People?" Kristen asked without missing a beat. "You think there was more than one person involved in this?"

Kate answered the question with a question. "Have you heard of a group known as the Midnight Lilies?"

Kristen shook her head. She cast her eyes to the floor for a moment. Kate wondered if she was trying to process what had happened to Trevor, or if the information overwhelmed her. When she raised her head, Kristen said, "I knew Trevor got threats, but he never told me the details."

Declan leaned forward. "What can you tell us about Madison McBride? Our understanding is she was also with Trevor that night."

Kristen guffawed loudly as if the mere suggestion that Madison was connected to Trevor was outrageous. "Have you met that mousy thing?" Declan confirmed they had. "Trevor wasn't interested in her. He was just trying to make me jealous. I encouraged it because it was never going to happen. I knew he was trying to test me, so I didn't bother playing into it. Madison was with him for maybe half an hour at most at a bar. She isn't smart enough or strong enough to kill him. She didn't have anything to do with this." Kristen narrowed her eyes. "Is that how you got my name?"

"No," Declan responded sharply. "Madison didn't mention you at all. We got your name from another source close to Trevor. Do you have any connection to Corey Weber?"

"Who is that? Never heard that name before." Before Declan could answer, Kristen stood, pushing down her skirt. "I have to go to class. There's nothing else I can help you with. If you keep bothering me, I will call the school and then my lawyer."

Kate stood without saying anything else. She had gotten what she needed, for now anyway.

CHAPTER 12

Once they hit the street, Declan reached for Kate's arm to stop her. "What did you think?"

Kate stared back up at the building. "I don't think Kristen's involved. It sounds to me like they had a toxic relationship and Madison got in the middle of it."

Declan agreed with that assessment. "Did you believe her when she said she didn't know Corey Weber? She didn't even mention anything about the murder from last night. She didn't ask if it was connected or anything."

"She might not have heard the news," Kate reasoned, not recalling seeing a television in her room. Not that she couldn't have seen the news on her phone. "Kristen might be telling us the truth. If she hadn't heard about the murder, she wouldn't know to ask about it. I'm not sure too many women know these podcasters. I didn't know much about them at all before this case. I still don't. Those names on the list that I found from Ali's research, I only knew two of them and that's only because they were interviewed on another podcast that I happened to see a clip of on social media."

"Fair point," Declan said, moving closer to her. He tucked errant strands behind her ears and kissed her lightly on the lips.

Kate smiled. "What was that about?"

"I want to remind you I'm on your side here."

"What do you mean? Of course, you're on my side."

Declan could see that she had taken it the wrong way. He reached for her, trying to pull her into a hug, but Kate resisted. "Katie," he said slowly, drawing out her name. "This case feels like it's going to be a landmine. I'm eventually going to put my foot in my mouth."

"I appreciate it," was all Kate said. The last thing she wanted was for this case to impact their relationship. "Have you talked to Sharon this morning?"

"Yeah, nothing found on Corey's body as far as evidence. The killers are doing a good job of covering their tracks. No errant hairs, fibers, or fingerprints."

The one question Kate had still lingered – why was he in New York? "Did we ever figure out what he was doing here?"

Declan shook his head. "Corey was registered at the hotel for a week. Last night was the third night here. The hotel didn't have much information, and we have yet to find his cellphone. Sharon was searching the room for that."

Kate knew he would have had it on him. No one left home without their cellphone. "I wonder if they took it. Trevor's phone was wiped clean. I think we need to call in Ditch to help us go through the tech."

Ditch – Kevin Detrick – was a member of their team. Ditch had been plucked from a life of crime, hacking everyone and everything, including the Russian government, and was brought onto the team by Spade. He was needed more and more on cases as technology advanced. While he and Declan had a contentious relationship, Ditch had grown on Kate over time. He was high maintenance but worth the effort.

Declan sighed. "Do we need him here?"

"Yes, we need him here. I'll deal with him if you don't want to," Kate offered.

"No. I'll call him." Declan looked at his watch. They had a video call scheduled with one of Corey's colleagues from the podcast. Declan made her an offer. "Do we want to split up today? You go talk to Ali Brewer. I'll speak to Corey's colleague and handle everything for Ditch?"

Kate chuckled, sensing he wanted to avoid Ali so much he was willing to deal with Ditch. "She's not going to bite you."

Declan shrugged it off. "You can talk woman to woman."

"You heard the words feminist and gender studies and got scared," she teased.

Declan was trying to hold back a smile. "I'm not scared. She looks perfectly sane to me in the photos we saw. I'm just thinking if she's targeting men…"

Kate wasn't going to remind him of all the serial killers she had sat across from that not only targeted women who looked like her but had threatened her directly. "You're such a chicken. I'm going to tell Spade you need to go back to the academy."

Declan knew she was teasing him. He leaned over and planted a quick kiss on her cheek. "You'll be fine with all those gender studies professors and students. I'm not walking into the lion's den unless I have to." He was backing away slowly as he was trying not to laugh.

"You're pathetic," Kate shouted after him. It was just as well. With two murders, there were so many people to interview and still so much to understand about why Corey was in New York City and what, if any, threats he might have faced.

Kate stood on the sidewalk adjacent to Lehman Lawn facing the imposing brick buildings of Barnard College in the Morningside Heights neighborhood. Her sharp eyes scanned the campus as students milled about, heads buried in their phones, the bustle humming in the background.

Ali might be more talkative alone with Kate. She might let her guard down in a way she wouldn't with Declan around. That's what Kate had convinced herself of anyway.

Kate had done a deep dive on Ali's social media earlier that morning in preparation for the interview. She had been outspoken on social media for years, railing against the rise of the manosphere, decrying its toxic rhetoric. Her followers idolized her for her unapologetic feminist views. But Kate had uncovered something chilling – Ali had also claimed the world would be a better place without those kinds of men in it. She even cited that it was only going to be a matter of time before women rose up and dispensed with them. She didn't clarify how that would be or who would lead the charge. It was enough that it riled her supporters. It wasn't a direct death threat but still chilling.

Kate entered Ali's department building. The walls were lined with dated academic posters and flyers advertising lectures that no one seemed to care about. The air smelled faintly of old paper and cheap coffee. She made her way down the corridor, checking her phone for Ali's schedule.

Kate passed the lecture halls – most of them empty or holding the tail end of some quiet seminar, hearing a louder voice off in the distance. It was distinctly feminine. It was met with the sound of raised voices from the last lecture room at the end of the hall.

Kate slowed her pace as she got closer to the room. The door was slightly ajar, and as she stepped closer, Kate could make out the unmistakable tone of Ali Brewer's voice. She recognized it from the podcast. It was loud – passionate – almost as though she were holding court to an audience far larger than the one in front of her.

"They deserved it!" Brewer's voice rang out with a venomous clarity. "These men, these – what did they call themselves? Intellectuals of the manosphere. All they did was spread hate, and now look what's happened. Their deaths are a reminder of what happens when you propagate poison in the world. A reminder that not all of us will sit back and let you tear down women without consequence."

Kate stepped closer to the door. The words felt like a punch to the gut. Ali was speaking freely, loudly, without any hint of hesitation. The professor's voice was brimming with righteousness, a twisted sense of vindication that only intensified the knot in Kate's stomach. She certainly hadn't expected her to be discussing the case this openly and with such vitriol.

Kate's eyes narrowed as she peered into the lecture hall. There she was – Ali Brewer, standing in front of a small group of students who were listening, rapt. She wasn't just lecturing. If Kate had to label it, she'd call it inciting. Ali's demeanor was far too comfortable with the topics for someone who had just heard about the murders. The students sat in their seats, some looking uncomfortable, others nodding along. Kate wondered if she had upended her regular lecture to cover the topic.

"These murders," Ali continued, "are proof that there are consequences to the kind of hate these men spread. Let's not pretend their deaths are anything but a result of their own making. It's a harsh world for men like them, isn't it? Would we go as far as to say they deserved what they got?"

A few of the students shouted yes while others glanced around at their classmates with uncertainty.

Kate had seen enough. Taking a deep breath, she stepped into the room, pushing the door open just enough to enter. The faint scent of dry-erase markers filled the air.

Kate stood at the back of the room, unwavering, her eyes fixed on Ali. She'd interrupt the firebrand lecture if she needed to. As she was about to speak, Ali noticed her in the back. A slow smile spread across the professor's face.

"We have a visitor, class. Come on down here and introduce yourself." If Kate wasn't reading into it, it was almost like Ali knew her, expected her.

As all eyes in the classroom turned to her, Kate introduced herself. "I need to speak with you, Professor Brewer." Kate's voice was calm, but the authority in her tone was unmistakable.

Ali hopped up on the corner of her desk, letting her legs dangle freely. "Class, let's welcome Agent Walsh into our discussion. We are discussing the murders of Trevor Fontaine and Corey Weber. What's your take on these recent murders?"

Kate didn't respond to her. She was purposefully putting her on the spot, trying to access information the FBI might have, and Kate wasn't going to take the bait. "How long before your class is over? We need to speak privately."

Ali laughed. "Ahh, Agent Walsh doesn't like it when people question her. She likes to be on the other side of the table." She turned back to her students. "Agent Walsh has had several public serial murderer cases in the news where she has brought justice to many victims, mostly women, because we all know how much men like to kill women. It's almost like it's their favorite hobby. Agent Walsh works primarily with men. Don't you, Agent Walsh."

Kate took a deep breath, sighing loudly. "Is there a point to this? Yes, the FBI is primarily men."

"Women aren't given a fair shake in law enforcement. Wouldn't you say that? But they often make better investigators because they are more empathetic and intuitive?"

Kate wasn't going to allow herself to be baited into the discussion. "I lecture at Harvard sometimes about the criminal justice system and criminology. It's a much more in-depth discussion than can be had in a few minutes." If this woman wanted to bait her into an academic discussion, then Ali had to know Kate could play hardball too. She wasn't going to do it. She didn't have the time or the patience for it today. "As I said, I need to speak to you... *alone*."

Kate took a seat on the aisle and crossed her legs.

Ali held her arms open wide. "Anything you need to say to me, you can say in front of my class." She beamed a smile up at Kate.

Kate relaxed back into the chair. If Ali wanted to play it this way, Kate would oblige her. "Great, we can do it this way if you'd like. I'm investigating the murders of Trevor Fontaine and Corey Weber. You've come up in the investigation as having had a confrontation with Trevor Fontaine not too long before he was murdered. Given your recent comments on the case, you're quickly rising to become a person of interest."

The class let out an audible gasp.

Ali stumbled back, finally shaken out of her bravado. "There's been some mistake." She turned to her class. "Read the next chapter and we'll discuss it next class. You're dismissed."

Kate remained seated while the students filed out. They glanced her way, but Kate remained focused on Ali, who no longer seemed as sure of herself. She stood at the front of the room, her rosy glow having faded to white. She remained leaning on the edge of her desk until the last student was gone.

Only then did Kate get up and take her time walking down the few steps to the front of the classroom. "That wasn't for shock value," she explained when she reached Ali. "You were an interest to me before I came into your class, but hearing you praise the men's deaths put you a little higher up on my list of suspects."

Ali licked her lips as she slowly nodded. "Then you need to come to my office so I can show you something I got in the mail. I think it's a recruiting flyer for the killers."

"Excuse me?" Kate asked, not sure she heard correctly.

"Let me show you."

CHAPTER 13

Kate held the small, heavy card stock, black and white invitation in her hand. The size and weight of it reminded her of a wedding invitation. The message was clear enough – it was an invitation to join a secret women's collective to discuss feminist issues and plan for how to dismantle the patriarchy. There was nothing on it that hinted of violence. Nothing mentioned the Midnight Lilies. It was not the smoking gun that Kate had hoped for.

She handed the card back to Ali. "Why do you think this is from the killers?"

"When these murders first started, this is what I thought of."

"Why?" Kate asked. "There's been nothing on the news to indicate the killer in any way."

"There was some chatter in my class that the victims' bodies were covered with black lilies, and there was a note from a group claiming responsibility. Now I can't connect that to this group, but it's suspicious to me all the same."

"How did your students hear that information? None of it's been made public yet."

"People talk." Ali leaned against her desk and gestured for Kate to sit. "There's been rumblings all over campus since Trevor Fontaine was murdered. We were discussing it in class this morning because one of the girls heard about Corey Weber on the way to class. She said he had been murdered in Central Park last night and that the crime scene was similar to Trevor's. I don't know where she heard it, but I assume cops told someone who told someone else. Things have a way of getting around."

Kate knew that with the sensational murders that things would inevitably slip out. She wanted the shock value of telling Ali directly and seeing her reaction. "Did you hear that the men were tortured before their deaths?"

Ali closed her eyes and nodded. "There was mention of it."

"How about that their tongues were cut out?"

Ali's eyes flew open wide. "No. No. Is that really what happened?"

"It is. We haven't found their tongues." Kate sat down in the chair and told Ali to sit as well. She chose to take the seat next to Kate rather than going behind her desk. The shock on Ali's face seemed real. She could have been faking it, but Kate wasn't sure anyone could pull that off.

"Did you attend the meeting?" Kate asked.

"No. I have enough work here at the college. Between teaching classes and working to finish up my doctorate, it's a lot." Ali reached for the invitation. "As you can see, there also isn't a name of the group. There is no date and time for a meeting. If I wanted to attend, I had to go to a special website and drop in my email. Then later, I'd be given a special code. With the code, I could access another part of the website where I'd be given the time, date, and place of the meeting. It all seemed a little…" Ali's voice trailed off.

"Strange?"

"To say the least. I barely have time to get to the gym. I don't have time for anything cloak and dagger. If I'm going to focus on feminist issues, I'm going to do it out in public. I want my voice to be heard. Education needs to be prominent. I don't know what they are trying to accomplish."

"What made you think they were tied to the murders?"

"I'm not sure exactly," Ali said, pausing to stare down at the card. "When I heard from some of my students the details of the murders, I assumed it was a group of women."

"Why?" Kate asked.

"It seems ritualistic in nature, which I know isn't far off from what serial killers do. But some of the details don't feel like a normal serial killer." Ali tossed the card on the desk. "I don't know for sure that the details I heard were correct."

Kate watched Ali with a little bit more admiration. "How do you know so much about serial killers?"

"I read a lot as a kid," Ali explained. "Part of the reason I have such a focus on women's issues is because of the sheer number of women killed by men each year. Even with those murders, we hear more about the men who kill them than the victims or anything about their lives. Look at all the documentaries. None are ever made about the victims and their background. It's all about the killers. They don't deserve the notoriety."

Kate agreed with her there. "Did you ever take any criminal justice or psychology classes?"

"Some psychology and sociology. I wanted to understand why people do what they do." Ali backed up her chair a little and crossed her legs. "This case, if the details I heard are correct, feels different than the kinds of murders I read about. Is that fair to say?"

"It is," Kate agreed with her. "Tell me about your interactions with Trevor?"

"He attacked my reputation first." Ali folded her hands in her lap. "I believe it started because he met a handful of my students on campus. He was here looking for women to bring on his podcast to humiliate. Two of my students stood up to him. My name got tossed around, and then Trevor went on his podcast and started ripping into liberal professors warping the minds of young women to turn them against men. That's not what I do here. I want to empower women to make the best decisions for themselves. I also caution them about losing their identity and power in relationships. I tell them to make sure they have their own money and a way out if abuse becomes a factor. I caution women about predatory men. We talk about it all in a relevant social construct. Trevor didn't like that. He called me names I can't bother to repeat."

"How does all of that end with you threatening him in a bar?"

Ali took a breath and sighed it out. "He got one of my students drunk and had sex with her without her consent. Then he tossed her out of his house like she was garbage. You have to understand, Agent Walsh, he can attack me. I can take it, but when you assault a young woman, I can't sit idly by and do nothing about it."

"Did you make a police report?"

Ali snickered. "You think anyone is going to take it seriously? She got drunk with him and willingly went back to his house. He said the sex was consensual, but the young woman did not. Trevor is famous and has the ear of many young men, many of whom are cops. No, she didn't want to be any more traumatized by the system than she already was."

Unfortunately, Kate couldn't argue the point with her. "Going to the bar that night to confront him was about your student?"

"My student and any other young woman he thought about doing the same with. I wanted him to know the cops might not be aware that he was a predator, but people were watching." Ali looked away from Kate. "I lost my temper in the process. I have a record of being arrested for protesting. I sometimes go too far. I'm passionate about what I believe and what I do."

"Where were you last night?"

Ali looked at her again. "I was here teaching a class from six to nine.

Then I ate a late dinner in the dining hall next to this building, and I went back to my apartment to grade papers."

"Did anyone see you?"

"They saw me teaching my class. You can see a record of my card being scanned at the dining hall. After that, I'm not sure who saw me."

Kate knew then she didn't have an alibi for the time of the murder. She mentioned the date of Trevor's murder. "Where were you that night between eleven and four in the morning?"

"Asleep," Ali said with a shrug. "I don't do much else other than work, study, and sleep. I'm certainly not out there killing a podcast host. I may have confronted Trevor that one night, but that was my only face-to-face interaction with him. I wouldn't know Corey if I tripped over him. I don't listen to the podcasts religiously."

"You do listen?"

Ali nodded. "It facilitates discussion in the classroom. It's important to know what they are discussing. It's part of the zeitgeist. It's quickly becoming a culture that's spilling down into how men behave with women. It has a real impact on our society. It's not just impacting women, but men too. There are other victims of this kind of content we don't talk about enough. That's young men. They are not connecting with women and it's leading to loneliness. That, in turn, is making them angry and violent. That's an oversimplification, I know. I can't remember a time when the divide between young men and women was this severe."

Kate was quickly becoming aware that it was true. "I'm afraid I'm a little out of the loop on that," she admitted. "This case took us all by surprise. I hadn't even heard of half of these podcasters until this case."

"It's been a growing trend. As the rise of podcasting took over, so did the rise of a bunch of losers with microphones making their insecurities their whole personalities."

Kate had felt the same. "You started a podcast, too."

"I was asked to start one," Ali clarified. "Like I'm not already overworked. The thing is, when you're an assistant professor, you're not making much money. Barely even enough to live and certainly not enough to live in New York City. The podcast was a way to engage in insightful conversation on relevant topics related to women's issues, interview experts in the field, and earn a decent living. If it wasn't for the podcast, I don't know how I'd be making it. It's educational. I try to leave the firebrand side of my personality off the podcast."

"Really?" Kate asked, thinking back to what she had viewed. If Ali's personality was stronger than what she had seen, Kate wasn't sure what to think.

Ali laughed, rightly sensing Kate's disbelief. "I said I try. I don't always accomplish it. I told you I'm passionate about this work, not just for women but men too."

"Explain that to me."

Ali crossed her legs under her and got comfortable. Her tone of voice even changed to one similar to her *teaching* voice. "There was a period in our recent history when women started advancing faster than men, and we didn't help men keep up. Home life and dating changed. Suddenly, women didn't need men for financial resources anymore. Women wanted men to have more to offer than just money. Women were traveling alone, buying their own homes, living amazing lives while decentering men. The culture shifted, and we were supporting women through that. At the same time, we were losing male-dominated fields – manufacturing, the trades, and so forth. Men were suffering economically and socially. That led to the rise in these male voices, blaming women for the state of things and saying that we needed to be dragged back under men's thumbs. That's not the answer. We cannot go backwards. I feel bad for men, and I feel terrible for young men who think this is the way. The work that I do hopefully impacts young men as much as it does young women. We need to continue to move forward and bring the collective with us."

Kate agreed with her there. She asked a few more questions and even learned a thing or two. Kate had walked into that classroom earlier, convinced that Ali might be among the people killing these men, but now she wasn't so sure. Kate mentioned Ali's research paper, which mentioned the podcasters. "I can't help but notice that the killer is going in order from that list. How widely known is that research paper?"

Ali winced. "There have been two. I think that's probably nothing more than a coincidence. The paper is known. It's been the basis for lectures, conference workshops, and guests on the podcast. The news from *The New York Times* to *The San Francisco Chronicle* covered it. The podcast bros trashed the research. It's been talked about wildly."

As Kate was listening to Ali, her eyes kept drifting over to the invitation. "Weren't you even curious who sent that to you?"

"Not really. I'm a public person on these topics. I get invited to conferences and to be on panels all the time." Ali reached over and pulled the invitation from her desk. "This sat in my mail for about two weeks before I even opened it. I thought it was weird that there was no return address or information on who to contact other than the generic email address to start the initial process."

"You don't know anyone connected to this? Not a student or another professor?"

Ali raised her head. "No. I swear to you, I don't know anything about this. It's weird though, right? A secret group like this and they don't even really spell out what they are doing. That's why when the murders started and there was all the imagery involved with the lilies that I thought of this group. I can't say exactly what made me go to them, an instinct, I guess."

"It is weird," Kate agreed, putting her hand out to take the invitation. "No one else contacted you about this invitation? No calls or emails?"

"Nothing. It came in the mail. I never responded. I didn't hear another thing about it."

"Can I take that with me?"

"Sure," Ali said, handing it over to Kate. "I threw out the envelope that it came in. I didn't think it would be important. I'm not even sure why I held on to that. I threw it in a pile of other mail I need to sort through."

Kate held the weighted invitation in her hand, gesturing with it. "Did you tell anyone else about this?"

"No. I didn't think much about it, honestly."

"No other students asked or hinted around about it?"

"No." Ali uncrossed her legs. "I'll work on keeping down the talk about being glad they are dead. I was merely suggesting that if someone cultivates hate and violence that it's bound to come back on them. I didn't suggest that someone *should* have killed them." Ali looked up at the clock on the wall above her desk. "I have another class starting soon. Is there anything else you need?"

Kate stood, not sure if pressing the matter more would be worth it. "Nothing for now. But I might be in touch. I appreciate your time and for telling me about this invitation." As Kate was headed for the door, Ali called to her.

"What's it like working for the FBI? I was serious with what I said in the classroom. I'm sure it's difficult being among only a few women."

No one had ever asked Kate that question. "I was lucky because I showed an aptitude early on and was asked to be in a special unit where my skills are appreciated."

"How many women do you work with?"

Ali had her there. "Until recently, I was the only woman in my specialized unit. We recently brought on a woman who is in charge of crime scene analysis."

"Well," Ali said and smiled, "if you ever want to chat about work, I'm here."

"I'll be in touch," Kate said, knowing this wasn't the last time she'd be talking to Ali and it wasn't going to be discussing her career at the FBI.

CHAPTER 14

Kate met Declan and Sharon at the bar in the hotel where Corey Weber had been staying. She had walked a few blocks after her meeting with Ali, then ended up taking a cab the rest of the way. She had thought that the walk would clear her head. With the hustle and bustle of the city, getting lost in her thoughts wasn't possible. She dodged business people, mothers with strollers, and the occasional woman clad in leggings and long athletic tees who decided a run on the sidewalk was the best choice of exercise.

Kate walked into the hotel bar to find Sharon and Declan sharing a plate of wings, their heads bent toward each other. She assumed talking about the case. They had developed a good working rapport while Kate had been sent to Morocco on a terrorism case a couple of years ago. Declan had been needed at the field office in Boston. They were rarely split, and it had been the longest they had worked apart in the history of their partnership.

Kate waved when Sharon lifted her head long enough to see her standing across the bar.

"We were waiting for you to order. Then Declan got hungry, and you know you can't deal with him long when he's hungry," Sharon said, pointing to the plate of half-eaten wings.

"I'll still be hungry for real lunch." Declan wiped his hands on a napkin and pulled out the chair next to him. He waited until Kate sat down before he asked how the meeting went.

Kate gave them the overview of the meeting and said that she found Ali credible. She pulled the invitation from her bag and put it on the table. "There might be something here. We can get Ditch to explore it. It's an invitation to join some secret feminist group. It's all a bit cloak and dagger. Ali said she couldn't be bothered with it. She held onto it. Ali even said she had wondered if they could be the killers."

"She said that?" Declan asked.

Kate nodded. "Information has leaked out about the murder scenes. Too much information, so we need to get in front of the news as soon as possible. The information is out there, probably from the NYPD first on the scene."

Declan cursed softly. "I knew it was too sensational to keep quiet for long. We can go public today to confirm. Are we saying it's a serial killer?"

"No," Kate said a little too loudly. "I think we can say we know the cases are connected and we suspect there might be others. I want to stay away from that term and anything that might indicate it could be a group of women killing these men. We don't have anything substantial to go on yet, and I don't want to speculate that broadly yet."

While they were talking, Sharon was inspecting the invitation. She gestured for Declan to look at it too. When she was done, she raised her head. "This looks a lot like something we found in Corey's room. It was an invitation to speak on a panel at Columbia University. The only problem is that it didn't come from official channels. Declan called and found out that no such meeting or conference existed. When we called the number, it went to a generic automated voicemail, and the website address indicated doesn't exist."

Kate cocked her head to the side. "Are you suggesting that Corey was lured to Manhattan under a pretense? His people didn't check this out?"

Declan finished looking over the invitation. "That's exactly what we are suggesting. It's the same color scheme, embossing, and weight as the other invitation. The card size is the same. Other than what's written on it, they could be identical." He put the invitation down. "I spoke to Corey's colleague. They checked out the information from Columbia and it appeared legit. The website and phone had been working at one time."

Kate didn't want to jump to conclusions. "That card size is a standard five-by-seven invitation. Any stationery store is going to sell it. I assume black and white is a common color scheme. The embossing looks fairly basic as well. I don't think we can assume that it's the same. Is there a serial number or anything on the back of it?"

Declan flipped it over to look at the back. "No. It's clean. The same with the one we found."

Sharon gestured toward the card. "As I told Declan, with the rise of online stationery retailers, it's unlikely we are going to be able to find the specific store that sold the invitation."

It sounded to Kate like a long hassle to find something that might not even be connected. "If you feel like there might be something there, go for it. If you find some invisible marking or serial number on the backs and they are the same, by all means, we can run that to ground. Until then, I don't feel comfortable saying the two are connected. We don't know anything about the invitation sent to Ali. I'm more concerned that someone lured Corey here to kill him."

Kate turned to look at Declan. "Did you speak to anyone in Corey's family?"

"I spoke to Ronald, his father," Declan started. "He's getting a flight out of San Francisco later today. All he knew was that Corey was coming to Manhattan for work. He gave me the phone number to his best friend, Matt. He confirmed everything Corey's colleague said about the conference. He suggested we check Corey's laptop. Matt said Corey didn't delete much."

Kate knew the emails could be tracked. "Do we have access to the emails? Did he save them?"

Declan nodded. "We found Corey's laptop in the hotel room along with his cellphone. Ditch will take possession of both when he arrives." Declan checked his watch. "He should be here in a couple of hours."

Kate sighed in relief. Once Ditch was involved, things would move along. If there was a digital footprint to be found, he'd find it. "Is he coming in by train?"

Declan nodded. "I got him a room in a nice hotel near Penn Station. He doesn't even have to take a cab."

"Upgraded room?" Kate asked with her eyebrow arched. She knew Spade would cover Ditch's eccentricities, and she wouldn't have to pay out of pocket. Ditch was a diva. It was the price of doing business with him.

Declan laughed. "Upgraded room. His favorite snacks and drinks are in the fridge, and a steak and baked potato are on the menu for tonight to be delivered to his room."

Sharon pulled back in surprise. "I feel like I should be more demanding."

Declan shot her a look. "One diva on our team is one too many. It's Kate and Spade who humor this nonsense. If it were up to me, Ditch would be sitting in some nice Russian prison in Siberia for the rest of his life."

Kate held her arms open wide. "He's the only one who does what he does. I don't love it, but I do what I have to so we get him to focus."

"Sounds like he needs a good slap upside the head." Sharon and Ditch had only met on one other occasion. It had been a brief interaction. Their work didn't cross much. "I want a nice steak dinner out of the deal."

Declan laughed. "If you buy for me, I'll buy for you and we can pretend."

"What else did Matt say about Corey? Have there been any threats like what Trevor received?"

Declan apologized for getting them off track. "Yes, he received the same threats. The letter came a little more than a month ago. Corey had the same reaction as Trevor – he dismissed it. He told his colleagues at the podcast and a few friends but reassured them he got angry emails all the time. No one had done anything to him."

"Yet," Kate added. "Does Matt have the letter, or did he see a copy of it?"

"He said Corey threw it out. I called the local police in San Francisco, who will go through Corey's house looking for it and any other potential evidence. They are aware of the particulars of the case and what kind of evidence we might be seeking."

"What about anyone else connected to the podcast?"

"There are a handful of regular guests, but Corey didn't have a co-host like Trevor had. Just a producer I spoke to. There are a couple of guys who frequently show up on the podcast with him to banter back and forth. All the interviews he does are one-on-one. Matt was going to notify the others. I gave him my cell number in case any of them had pertinent information to share. I assume we might need to interview them at some point. I'd rather they call me if they are willing to speak and have something to offer. We can get into one-on-one questioning later if need be."

Kate assumed that would be a good way to start. Otherwise, they were going to be like dogs chasing their tails. She hitched her chin toward Sharon. "What can we present related to crime scene evidence at the news conference?"

"Not much evidence. We confirmed the lilies are dyed. My team back in Boston is calling some of the bigger florist shops here in the city to see if there have been any bulk purchases. They will also be calling some of the online shops. We can see if anyone ordered in bulk. My guess is someone is growing them inside in a space big enough for the right lighting and watering system. It's not ideal, but it can be done."

"What about fingerprints or other DNA?"

"The few fingerprints found don't come back to anyone in the system and the same for the DNA. We can assume some of the DNA will come to Kristen. We can ask her for a sample, but based on what Declan told me, she might not be willing."

Kate shook her head. "I don't want to go that route unless we have to. I don't think she will be compliant and she already admitted she was there that night for sex. Right now, Kristen is the only one we can put at the scene. She also doesn't have a solid alibi. If she did this, she didn't do it alone. We need to explore any connection she might have to Corey."

"What about the rest on the list, Kate?" Declan asked. "We probably should warn them."

"We don't know they will be targets, not yet anyway. I think the news conference can address that. We can mention the threats and encourage them to call us if they received the same threat."

Sharon noted, "I've been looking at that list, Kate. Some of those men are diabolical. A few have called for the total removal of women in the workforce and called for stripping away their rights to housing, banking, and, of course, the right to vote."

Kate released a breath she didn't realize she had been holding. "That's the most insane thing I've ever heard."

"There is some fringe backing in Congress," Sharon said evenly, mentioning two House Representatives who mentioned similar rhetoric. "One of them tried to introduce legislation to force banks to enforce co-signers for every mortgage and loan a woman applies for. It would eliminate her ability to get the funding on her own. The other guy co-signed the bill. It didn't get any traction even within their party. Just the fact that there are legislators who think this way terrifies me."

Kate couldn't think about that now. "Let's give the blanket warning and see if anyone reaches out to us. It's still going to be more efficient than trying to track down everyone that might have been threatened."

Kate had no idea how high the number of deaths could go. It was staggering to consider.

CHAPTER 15

Kate stood off to the side of the podium while Declan spoke directly to the media. All eyes and cameras were trained on him as he went over the Trevor Fontaine and Corey Weber murders. He detailed how the men had been tortured, shot, and their tongues cut out after death. There was a gasp among the reporters in the crowd. Declan mentioned the black lilies that had been found but left out mention of the name of the group taking responsibility. So far, the notes left with the bodies signed by the Midnight Lilies had not been made public and Kate hoped to keep it that way.

The name Midnight Lilies hadn't reached the public either.

Halfway through the press conference, Kate's phone rang. She glanced down at the screen and wanted to take the call. She stepped off the back of the podium.

"Leo," Kate said, glad to hear from him. Leo Lamiere, once known as the Phantom – the most infamous and impossible to catch international art thief – had made a deal with Spade. The FBI would stop hunting him and shield him from any international justice if he came onto the team and worked with Kate and Declan. It had been Declan's idea, much like they had done with Ditch.

Kate had been reticent at first, even though Leo had saved her life. After a couple of cases working together, she was glad he had chosen to join them. After the last case ended in France, Leo returned to his chateau in Cassis to work with the FBI's art theft team to catalogue and return art that Leo's stepfather, Lucien, had bought and kept hidden in vaults beneath the property.

It turned out Leo was an art thief with a heart. What he had been stealing all those years was Nazi-looted art. He had been stealing it back and returning it to its rightful owners.

"Still in France?" Kate asked as she answered.

"No, I'm here in Manhattan. Just checked into a hotel. Spade asked me to join you. He just called me and asked me to deliver a message." Leo paused for a moment before delivering the blow. "There's been another murder connected to the case."

With the noise of the press conference, Kate wasn't sure she had heard him correctly. "What do you mean another murder? We haven't been called about anything."

"It's been kept quiet until they could notify the family. It's…" Leo paused and seemed to trip over his words.

"Spit it out."

"It's a politician, Kate. House Representative Marty Nubeck. He was here for some kind of meeting. The man had security with him. He went into his hotel room around nine last night, told his team to stand down because he wasn't going anywhere. When they went to get him this morning, he was dead. The scene is bad, Kate."

Kate had no idea who this politician was, but Sharon's earlier words came back to her. "Do you know anything about him?"

"I don't. I haven't followed much in the way of United States politics. What do you need me to do? I have all the details here."

Kate turned back to the podium as Declan was still answering questions for the press. "When was the body found?"

"This morning."

Kate didn't understand. "Why are we being notified now, hours later?"

"His security team found him and immediately sealed off the room. They haven't allowed anyone to enter. They haven't informed the hotel either. They told housekeeping that Rep. Nubeck wasn't feeling well and service for the room wasn't needed. They called the Speaker of the House but asked him to keep it quiet. Then they notified the man's family and asked them to keep it quiet. The head of the security team, Jay Sterling, called in the FBI. Spade wasn't happy with the delays."

"When was the last time someone had eyes on him?"

"Sterling remained at the door until nine. He was worried that Nubeck might hire a prostitute as he'd done in the past. Sterling waited a bit to see if one showed up. When none did, he called off for the night."

"What did Sterling do after?"

"The security team met in the hotel bar and had a few drinks before retiring to their rooms a little after midnight. Sterling went to wake him at seven this morning after Nubeck didn't answer his phone. Security had his room key, and when they entered, they found him."

Kate was trying not to jump to conclusions. "How does Spade know the cases are connected?"

"The lilies, Kate," Leo said with emphasis. "They were all over the room. Security already went to look at the security footage and it's been erased or didn't record. They aren't sure."

"Erased?" Kate's voice boomed. "How did it get erased?"

"We don't know. The hotel doesn't know. But as I said, they aren't telling the hotel what happened. They just said for security reasons that they needed to see who entered Nubeck's room overnight and the footage was gone. All the footage from the entire hotel is gone for most of the night."

Kate cursed more loudly than she intended. "We had another murder in Central Park last night. That means that they killed two people in one night."

"That's Spade's worry. There were at least a few days between the first and second murder."

Kate tucked strands of hair behind her ear. "Was security staying on the same floor as Nubeck?"

"Just down the hall and none of them heard anything. The one thing the security detail did do today was start asking people close to Nubeck's room if they heard anything. If their goal was to not drum up attention, they aren't doing a good job of it. They didn't even call the FBI until about ninety minutes ago. That's when they were put through to Spade and he spoke to one of them."

Not that Kate didn't appreciate Leo calling her. She didn't understand why Spade hadn't been the one to deliver the message. "Where is he?"

"Congress, Kate. Spade has been called to Congress to brief them about what's going on. They aren't happy that the FBI hasn't issued a warning before this."

Kate rolled her eyes. They expected the FBI to be superhuman sometimes. "We didn't even know what we were dealing with. In some ways, we still don't. We certainly never expected them to move beyond podcasters." Kate wasn't sure if that was true or not. She had considered it but hadn't wanted to speculate that far. "Give me the details of the hotel and Sterling."

Leo provided her with all the information as she requested. "Do you want me to meet you at the hotel?"

"Get over there if you can and let them know we are on our way. I need to wait for Declan to finish and call Sharon to get over there." Kate hung up with Leo and immediately called Sharon. "You're not going to believe this, but there's been another murder. Representative Marty Nubeck. I don't know anything about him," Kate admitted. "I don't even know what state he's from."

Sharon was looking up information for her in real time. "He's from Missouri. There's an article here that he was in his late fifties and had been accused of sexually harassing a few female staffers, and there's a rumor going around that he sexually assaulted two women. Nothing was ever done about any of it. He's been in Congress for more than a decade and keeps getting reelected."

Kate knew that it fit the pattern of the victims. But if these killers were going to take down every powerful man who had accusations made against them, the bodies would pile up quickly. "I need you to get over there and meet with Leo. He arrived not long ago. Spade asked him to come back from France to help us. I think we are going to have a full team."

Sharon had three staffers from the FBI lab in Boston helping. "How did they kill two people in one night?"

"I honestly don't know." Kate knew for sure now that it wasn't one killer. "This got complicated fast. I need to get Declan off that podium and over to the hotel." Kate gave Sharon the address and told her they'd meet her there as soon as possible.

After they hung up, Kate went right back to the small staging area that had been erected for the press conference. She passed by the few NYPD officers who were there as a show of force and passed the New York City's mayor and put her hand on Declan's back. He asked the crowd of reporters to wait as he stepped back to Kate. She wasn't going to say aloud that there had been another murder. She let her facial expression tell him what he needed to know.

They had worked together for so long that while he might not have known there was another murder, he knew something was wrong and the press conference needed to end. Declan stepped back to the podium. "I can take one last question," he said, so as not to stir up the crowd too much. Hands shot up across the sea of reporters, both local to New York City and national.

A young woman in the front row was called on. "Do you believe these murders will continue?" she asked.

"Yes, this killer has a mission," Declan said as calmly as he could. "That's why all those with similar podcasts need to remain vigilant with their safety. We know that the killer sent warnings to the two who were murdered. If you received any kind of warning or threat, you need to take it seriously and call the FBI." Declan provided the number to the hotline that had been set up. "If you believe you've been threatened, ask to speak to Agent Kate Walsh or me. They will get in touch with us."

Declan thanked the reporters and stepped back as they continued to shout questions. He pulled off the mic attached to his shirt and left the staging area, following after Kate. Once they were out of earshot of everyone, Kate gave him the rundown of everything that had happened.

Declan's eyes got wide as he ran a hand down his stubbled face. "What does this mean, Kate?"

"It means this killer is luring their victims to New York City and murdering them. Who knows how many invitations were sent." Kate's heart rate had not returned to normal. They needed to get to the hotel as soon as possible without being followed by any of the media. "This hasn't been made public yet. I think we should keep it that way until we get over to the scene and see for ourselves."

Kate and Declan went across town as fast as they could. Nubeck was staying at the Marlowe, one of the city's most exclusive hotels. It's where the pulse of wealth and influence thrummed just beneath its polished exterior.

The hotel's façade was an imposing blend of old-world charm and modern luxury. Ornate limestone columns framed the entrance, gilded lettering spelling out the hotel's name in gold above the glass doors. Inside, the lobby was a cavern of opulence, with marble floors that gleamed under the soft, ambient light. Crystal chandeliers hung like frozen waterfalls from the ceiling, casting delicate glimmers over the hushed chatter of guests who sipped cocktails at a bar crafted from black granite.

Kate walked past the quiet buzz of the concierge desk, her gaze scanning the room, noting the way the hotel's staff seemed oblivious to the tension hanging in the air. They hadn't been briefed on the murder yet, and that was just as well.

A tall man with a swath of blond hair standing near the bank of elevators raised a hand in their direction. He had a stern all business look on his face. Kate noticed the slight tremor in his hand as he waved to them. She also noted the twitch in his left eye.

The man was scared, even if outwardly he was keeping a professional demeanor.

Kate approached with her hand extended. "Jay Sterling?" The man confirmed. Kate introduced them.

"Your other team members are upstairs already. I haven't let them access the crime scene yet. There's a sitting room at the end of the hall for everyone on the penthouse level. That's where I have them waiting. I thought we should talk first before heading up."

"You could have given them access," Declan said. "You delayed getting us here and we are losing time."

Sterling shook his head. "I'm not letting anyone in there but you. I've never witnessed anything like this. It's why I called the FBI instead of the NYPD." Sterling swallowed hard. "He told us to turn in for the night. If I had any idea something like this was going to happen…" He trailed off.

Declan let his brief annoyance about Sharon being blocked from the crime scene fade. He put his hand on Sterling's shoulder. It was clear he was shaken up. "We've been to two of these scenes so far. I understand what you saw up there and how it can impact you."

Sterling offered a curt nod. "I've known Marty Nubeck since college. We played football together. When he told me that he had started to get threats, he turned to my security firm. We've never had a failure like this." He ran a hand down his face. "We rarely have security breaches at all. I can't think of the last one we had."

"This isn't a normal killer," Kate said, trying to offer him a little solace. She was sure that no matter what the security team did or didn't do, this killer was going to find a way to strike. "You said there were things about the scene that had you call the FBI. Do you want to tell us what they are now?"

"No," Sterling said, stepping toward the elevator. "I couldn't explain it if I tried. It's best if you see it for yourself."

CHAPTER 16

Kate stepped into the elevator with a slow, deliberate motion. The cool, polished metal of the doors slid shut behind her, leaving her with her reflection in the brass, the faint hum of the cables pulling the car upwards, and the tension that seemed to vibrate through the air. Her heartbeat was steady, controlled. They had to get in front of these cases.

Kate couldn't help but think of the way the public would react once the press caught wind of this one. A high-profile congressman, the kind who had a hand in the lives of millions, his murder would send shockwaves through the political elite. The message would be clear because the targets were all one brand of men. Kate wondered for a brief moment if they might think twice about their misogynistic rhetoric. Men like that never did – they'd double down.

The elevator slowed to a smooth stop, and the doors opened. She stepped out into the plush hallway of the hotel. The carpet beneath her feet was soft, and the overhead lights, dimmed to an intimate glow, seemed to halo the space in muted golds. Declan was by her side and Sterling was a few feet ahead, guiding them to the room.

"I should've been watching him more closely," Sterling said as they reached the door, his hands clenched into fists. "It's my fault he's dead. I should've known."

"What kind of threats?" Kate asked. "Let's stop here now that we are out of the lobby. There's going to be enough work once we get inside. Can you tell me first what brought Nubeck here to Manhattan?"

Sterling chewed on his lower lip. "He received an invitation to speak at a men's conference, but he wanted to get into the city early and get settled. He also had some donor meetings set up."

"You got here just yesterday?" Declan asked. When Sterling confirmed, he went on, "What did you do after you arrived?"

"We came straight to the hotel after landing at three. Nubeck spent some time alone in his room, then had a meeting with a donor at a restaurant. After that, we came back here. Nubeck said he was going to turn in early. He wanted to do some prep for the meeting anyway. He gave us the night off. I was here in the hall outside his door until eleven."

"I was told you were gone at nine?" Kate recalled what Leo had said.

"We were called off at nine. I didn't leave until eleven."

"Why was that?"

Sterling stared past Declan as if he didn't want to say.

Declan said it for him. "Nubeck was known to hire prostitutes. We know this. Can I safely assume you were making sure that didn't happen?"

Sterling nodded.

"Is there a reason why you didn't want that to happen?" Declan pressed.

"There were some issues the last time. He got rough with her. I had to step in."

Kate's blood pressure went up. "Is it safe to assume that you talked her out of calling the police and pressing charges?"

"I did. We paid her off not to talk."

"You were enabling his behavior." Kate stepped toward him, tilting her head back to look directly at him. "Should I assume that you have the same views about women as your boss?"

"No. My wife doesn't like that I work for him. My daughter feels the same." He paused as if trying to find the right explanation. "We just go back so far, and when he asked, I had trouble telling him no. I didn't know about the prostitutes then or…" It was as if he couldn't say it.

"The violence against women," Kate said what he wouldn't. She let it go because Sterling wasn't on trial here. "We all have a job to do. So, you were waiting here at the door to make sure that he didn't hire a prostitute. Does he usually do that before eleven?"

"He does. If one were coming, she'd have been here by ten-thirty. Nubeck likes his sleep. I figured when eleven o'clock rolled around, it was a safe bet to call off for the night."

"What about the lock? Did he keep the room secured?"

"Normally," Sterling said, explaining how the bolt locks and whatever other locks that were offered on the door remained in place. "He's been security conscious."

Declan pressed, "You said there were threats."

"Right." Sterling ran a hand threw his hair. "Nubeck has a lot of extreme ideas. He's not as vocal about them on the floor with initiating bills as some. He has quietly supported them behind the scenes. As subjects get a little less taboo and he doesn't worry so much about his reelection, he's been more vocal. He's gone on a few podcasts and spoken publicly about what he believes. He's been a big advocate in pushing the idea that women shouldn't be able to initiate divorce."

Kate stopped him. "Are you talking about getting rid of no-fault divorce or just no divorce at all?"

"Neither," Sterling clarified. "He believes only men should be able to initiate divorce. As you know, divorce is mainly initiated by women. He wants to take that power away from them. If they commit to a marriage, then the only way out for her is when a man decides he wants out. Otherwise, no divorce."

"There are other ways out," Kate said evenly. When confusion fell over Sterling's face, she explained, "When divorce wasn't allowed and husbands were cheating and abusing their wives, husbands would routinely die of poisoning. If we go the direction Nubeck wants, we are going to end up with a lot more dead husbands." Kate gestured toward the door. "I think they have already gotten started."

"What does that mean?"

Kate answered his question with a command. "Tell us about the threats first."

"Run of the mill. Threats to find someone to primary him. Threats to target his donors with boycotts and acts of physical violence against him personally. There were threats to shoot him and blow up his offices in D.C. and Missouri. None of those threats have materialized or got more specific than that. They were enough that he wanted security. More of the same has come during my time with him."

"Nothing more specific than that? Any group taking credit?" Kate asked, knowing that none of those threats sounded like the Midnight Lilies.

"No. Nothing more specific than that. A few fake names but nothing that checked out." Sterling turned toward the door to let them in, but Kate stopped him.

"Did someone on his staff vet the conference he was attending here? Was there a point of contact?"

"Thoroughly checked out," Sterling said. He pulled out his phone and gave Kate the contact name and phone number. "I spoke to the woman already this morning and told her that Nubeck wouldn't be able to attend. I didn't explain why."

"What was the name of the conference?" Declan asked as he pulled out his phone.

"Masters of the Pack. I was a little surprised that a woman was running the conference. I looked at some of the other attendees and it's a who's who of men in that alpha male space."

Kate's heart started to race. It meant there were many potential victims right there in the city. She turned to Declan. "Make sure this is real."

"What do you mean?" Sterling asked, raising his voice. "Do you think it's not real?"

Kate explained how Corey Weber was lured into the city under the guise of a fake conference. "He was murdered last night in Central Park."

"They killed two in one night?" Sterling paled.

"I'll need to get in there to confirm," Kate started but stopped, seeing the look on his face. "What were some of the podcasts he was on?"

"Well, Corey Weber's for one. It aired a few weeks ago. He never saw Trevor Fontaine as serious. He said all the right things for Nubeck, but there was a certain frat bro vibe about the podcast that didn't sit well with Nubeck. He said it was not serious." Sterling listed off a few more that were all on Ali Brewer's research list.

They walked down the hall to the private suite where Sharon and Leo were waiting. They got gloves and booties for them all.

"Where's Declan?" Sharon asked as they got themselves ready.

Kate snapped on a pair of gloves. "He's in the hall researching something for me." She turned to Leo. "Are you sure you want to go in? Once you see it, you can't unsee it."

"I'm fine, Kate," he assured her as he pulled on his gloves, snapping them at his wrist. He might have said he was fine, but Kate knew Leo well enough by now to know that he was unsteady about the decision. It was written all over his face.

She wasn't going to fight him on the decision. He'd need to harden himself to the realities of what they faced in their cases sooner or later. Leo had seen a few things already. Kate had a feeling this was going to be much worse.

They reached the door to the suite. Declan joined them and nodded at Jay, and the man hesitated only a second before unlocking the door. It opened with a soft click. Kate stepped through first, her eyes immediately taking in the sitting room.

And there it was.

A trail of black lilies lay scattered across the floor in an almost careful pattern. Petals glistened under the muted lighting, their contrast stark against the ivory carpet. It was the same signature, the same calling card the killer had left at every other crime scene.

Kate's breath caught. She could feel the hairs on the back of her neck rise. There was something distinctly creepy about the flowers this time – almost as if they were breadcrumbs leading right to… her thoughts trailed off because that's exactly what the flowers were intended to do. As she walked along the path, Jay explained to her that he hadn't touched the flowers, but they led right into the bedroom.

"There's a cluster of them across the door's threshold."

Kate could see that for herself. It was clear the security agent was nervous. He chattered on, narrating what they were now seeing firsthand. Sharon called out from behind her that she was photographing and marking everything as they went.

Declan moved in from behind her, his gaze flicking over the petals, a low curse escaping his lips. "I don't think we've ever seen anything like it. It's like stepping inside of a horror movie."

Kate moved forward slowly, her shoes making soft impressions in the plush carpet. Each step took her closer to the bedroom. The killer had taken time with this. It wasn't the dumping of flowers over the body as it had been with Corey. And it wasn't the scatter of flowers across Trevor and his bedroom that the first case had shown them.

Each flower was placed just so to make a path.

Kate walked the path laid before her, the faint scent of the dyed flowers filling the air, overpowering, almost sickly sweet. As she approached the threshold of the bedroom, the sense of dread hit her like a physical blow. Her hand hovered over the doorframe, ready to push it open. She hesitated for only a second before swinging the door inward with a creak.

Careful to step over the row of lilies on the floor, she entered the bedroom. The stale metallic smell of decay filled her nose, making her recoil. It burned her eyes and she took shallow breaths to fight the nausea that grew in her gut.

"We need some lights," Sharon said from behind Kate.

Kate wanted to tell her to wait so she could prepare herself, but the lights flipped on before she could say a word. Congressman Nubeck's body was in the center of the bed on his back with arms and legs splayed out. His palms were face up with a lily in each palm. His once-vibrant features were drained of life. His eyes were wide open, staring up at the ceiling with a vacant, frozen expression. He wore navy sleep shorts, a gray tee-shirt, and his feet were bare. The clothing seemed to have been straightened over his body after death. Not a hem out of place.

What caught Kate's eye – what made her stomach tighten – was the positioning of his body. Nubeck wasn't just lying on the bed. He looked posed. The killer had gone to great lengths to make it look this way. The way the flowers were arranged, not only around the bed but around the body, had been deliberate and carefully placed. They framed his head and outlined the body.

Kate knew what she'd find if she tore off the tape over the man's mouth – his tongue missing.

What Kate didn't see was the cause of death.

She turned back to look at Jay. "Do you have any idea how he was murdered?"

Jay moved toward the body, but Sharon asked him to wait while she snapped a few photos. "I was just going to show Agent Walsh the strangulation marks. I didn't see them at first either."

Kate assured him it was fine. They would get to that. "Let Sharon do what she needs to do. Preserving this scene for the record is critical if this ever goes to trial." As Kate said the words, she wondered if that day would ever come and what that might look like. It would be chaos.

Leo stood back from them still near the doorway. He kept taking quick glances at the body before looking away. While Sharon worked, Kate stepped back. "What do you think?" she asked, not wanting to ask him if he was okay.

"It's ritualistic, almost," Leo said softly.

"Not almost. It is ritualistic," Kate corrected. "With everything they do, they are sending a message. The lilies, torture, posing of the body, and the tongue."

"Tongue?" Jay asked, looking back at her. "What do you mean?"

Kate hitched her chin toward the body. "The thick gray electrical tape over his mouth might have been used to keep him quiet. We can't be sure about that. What we do know is that with the two other victims, once that tape was removed, we came to learn that their tongues had been cut out."

Jay gasped as his hand went to his stomach.

"If you're going to throw up, don't do it in here," Declan cautioned him.

Jay closed his eyes and took a few breaths. "I'm fine. It's just horrific. I thought the message on him was bad. That's—"

"Message on him?" Kate interrupted, concern in her tone. "What do you mean?"

Jay opened his eyes and looked over at Kate. "When I first came in, I found him exactly like he is now. I had to touch the body to figure out if he was still alive, but I didn't want to touch too much and mess up the scene. I noticed the marks around his neck and a little of his shirt got pulled up when I was moving him. There is a word carved on his stomach."

Rapist.

CHAPTER 17

After finishing with the crime scene, Kate stepped out of the suite, nodding her head so Declan would follow her. She made her way down the hall to the small meeting room. Kate wanted a chance to speak to Declan alone, out of earshot of Jay and his team.

"You okay?" Declan asked, sensing rightly that she wasn't okay at all. He pulled his gloves off, dropped them in the bin, and went to her. "I know that scene in there is bad."

"I don't even know what to say." Kate pulled her gloves and tossed them in the bin. She wretched the ponytail holder from her hair, then redid her ponytail. "I feel sick. Not only did Nubeck have more trauma on his body, but that scene was staged so dramatically. How did they get all of that done without anyone knowing they were in there? How did they kill Corey Weber at the same time across the city in Central Park?"

Nubeck's body had more trauma than the last two – burns on his back and a mix of shallow and deep stab wounds, mostly on his back, pooling the blood under him. It saturated the fine dark comforter and the fine linens under him. This victim, unlike the others, had been strangled to death with a cord-like weapon.

Kate pointed back toward the room. "You know he wasn't strangled once. There are so many marks on his neck. It looks like they kept strangling him, letting off, then going back to try again. It's like they never strangled anyone before or were purposefully stopping, allowing him to breathe and starting again."

"It takes a lot of force, pressure, and time to strangle someone like that. Maybe they hadn't before and didn't know." Declan cast his eyes toward the door. "The other possibility is that there was more than one person who wanted in on the action."

Kate had thought that but hadn't said the words aloud. "I believe there had to have been more than one person on the scene here." After carefully looking over the body, they came to learn that his hands and ankles had been bound and then released after death. There were significant marks around both to indicate that he had been restrained.

Then there was the word carved into his body. They believed, given the lack of blood, that it was most likely post-mortem. As with the others, once Sharon got the tape off, they discovered his tongue was gone too.

Kate said again that there had to have been more than one person. "What do you think? At least three?"

"We have no way to know, Kate." He ran a hand through his hair. "It's like a whole murder club."

"Instead of pickleball, the ladies of Manhattan have turned to torture and murder," Kate said sarcastically, only there was some truth to what she was saying. "I'm not even sure how to create a profile on this. I know the media is going to be asking. They are all going to want answers we simply don't have. They also aren't leaving any evidence behind. Someone among them knows what they are doing."

"You think there's a ringleader then?" Declan asked.

"There has to be. Someone came up with this idea and knows how to coordinate and facilitate these murders without getting caught. What did you find out about the conference?"

"Oddly, it's being held in an event space above a gallery in Greenwich

Village. The list of guest speakers is people this killer would target." Declan read off a list of names from podcasters to media personalities. "Any one of them could be a target."

Kate's mind swirled with the possibilities. "Do we think the person who set up this conference is connected to the Midnight Lilies? Were the presenters targeted to come here under the guise of this conference only to be lured to their deaths?"

"I have no idea," Declan pulled his phone from his back pocket. He scrolled through a website while Kate looked on. "There is no information about who set up this conference. All there is is the phone number that Jay has. I haven't called it yet."

Kate sighed. "We have no leads. Nothing." She couldn't recall being this far into a case and having nothing to go on. "We need to get you in front of the media again to address this. Word of Nubeck's death is going to leak. I'm glad Jay didn't call the NYPD but called the FBI instead. It bought us a little time. The hotel is getting suspicious. I'm sure the guy down the hall who was questioned by Jay is wondering what is happening. They should have notified the hotel immediately and had him removed from this floor."

"Let me go handle things with the hotel before the medical examiner arrives." Declan leaned over and kissed her on the forehead. "All we can do is take this one step at a time. You go talk to Jay about his conference contact. We can tackle that next."

Declan left the room, leaving Kate alone with her thoughts. He was right, all they could do was take things one step at a time. Moments later, Leo stood in the doorway. "You don't look too great," he said with a half-smile.

Kate raised her eyes to him. "You look less green than you did in there. I know it's rough, but I'm glad you're willing. I'd like to tell you that you'll get used to it."

"I won't ever get used to that. The evil that people do to one another."

Leo swallowed hard. "Who do you think is doing this?"

Kate took a breath. "We believe it's potentially a group of women murdering these men as revenge for the misogyny they have been spewing. The group taking credit is a group called the Midnight Lilies. They are leaving dyed black lilies, and they are cutting the tongues out to silence them. I believe they are working from a list and luring these men to Manhattan. Trevor Fontaine lived here and was the first. Corey Weber was here for a meeting. Marty Nubeck was going to speak at a conference. We know the conference exists, but we need more information. Many of the people who are listed to speak could be potential targets. We need to find out if someone connected to the conference might be involved."

"You're sure the conference is real?" Leo asked.

Kate wasn't sure of anything. "There's a website that's still up. Jay said he spoke with someone about Nubeck not being able to attend. It seems as if it's real."

"Let me help you with that," Leo said. "You and Declan have had so much in such a short time, let me do something."

Kate appreciated that he wanted to help. "I need to interview them. If this is connected, I need to know. I don't know who you'll meet there. It could be the killer."

Leo said he understood. "Let me come with you. Do you think this is a murder group?"

"I do," Kate said, finally feeling firm in that assessment. "I also believe they are working together and not independently. This was a planned, coordinated attack against Marty Nubeck and Corey Weber."

"To confuse you?"

Kate shook her head. "They would know the crimes are too similar. Staged in the same way. They had to know we'd connect them. If I'm not mistaken, they want us to know who is doing this. Their goal is to send a message. They even warned Trevor and Corey ahead of time.

They came here to do exactly what they had practiced and planned."

"Practiced?"

The word had slipped out of Kate's mouth without too much consideration. The more she thought about it, the more she realized she was right. "They were able to get into this hotel, up here to this room, torture and murder him, and stage the scene all without being caught. All without anyone suspecting a thing. Yes, I think they had to have practiced this." Kate didn't want to throw Leo's past crimes in his face, but she wanted to know. "Before a big heist, I assume you'd practice, right?"

Leo nodded. "Down to the minute. There were even times we created replicas. I had bought many different kinds of safes to practice breaking into them. I got away with it for so long because I was practiced." A hint of a smile graced his face. "I would have gotten away with it for much longer, but I chose to come out of the shadows."

"I would have caught you eventually."

"That's debatable," Leo teased. "Honestly, Kate, you're the reason I came out of the shadows. So, you did catch me in a sense."

"We will call it a tie."

Kate was sure that the Midnight Lilies were planning this – strategy meetings, going over what was going to happen the night of a murder, who was going to do what, how they were going to leave the scene. There were probably contingency plans too for when something went wrong.

The killers were motivated, strategic, and determined. Their motive was far different from most serial killers, who were killing for the thrill or some sick twisted sexual gratification. This wasn't about any of that. These killers weren't driven to kill for the sake of killing – the murder was a means to an end. It was revenge and retribution. It was a political statement.

Kate stopped herself at that last thought.

This was political.

She had been thinking about this all wrong. It wasn't a serial killing in the traditional sense – this was terrorism. She expressed as much to Leo. "It doesn't necessarily change anything we are doing in the case to recognize this. But the media needs to know. This is by all definitions a terrorist group. They aren't going to stop until they feel like their point has been heard. Until they have exacted the last bit of revenge. It's why they have been able to bring a group of people together who, on their own, wouldn't have resorted to murder."

"Is it cult-like?" Leo asked.

Kate couldn't dismiss the possibility. "It probably has a leader with cult-like attraction. Someone came up with the plan and put it into place, recruited others to help. The leader would have to be someone dynamic and powerfully convincing in their message to get others to follow. She'd have to recognize others who were willing to join in. You can't just walk up to someone and say, 'I'm thinking about murdering a bunch of popular misogynistic men, want to help?'"

Leo stifled a laugh. "I think today you might find a lot of women willing to help."

"You're probably right. Women are fed up."

"As they should be." There was a level of conviction in Leo's tone that made Kate take notice.

She raised her chin to look at him, remembering that his mother had been a victim of emotional and physical abuse in her marriage to his stepfather. It had been one of the driving forces for Leo to leave home at a young age and seek revenge on the man who hurt her. She admitted something to Leo that she might not to Declan. "This is a hard case for me. I'm conflicted. I don't agree with what they are doing, but there's a certain satisfaction in knowing these men can't keep spewing the vile nonsense they have been. If we find that Marty Nubeck was a rapist, I'm not going to care that he's dead at all. I have to get justice. That's my job. I'm going to need you to remind me of that."

"Me?" Leo asked. "I'm right there with you, Kate."

"That's why we have to keep each other in check."

Leo stuck his hand out and Kate slipped her hand into his. "You have a deal."

"Let's start with how they got him to Manhattan." Kate started toward the door, calling Leo to follow her. She found Jay leaning against the wall in the hallway. He had his head down as he scrolled through his phone. He glanced up as Kate approached. "Tell me about this conference Nubeck was going to speak at. Was your only contact the name you gave me? Patrice White?"

"Yes," he confirmed, providing her the few details he knew about the conference itself "Do you think the conference is connected to what happened?"

"I think the conference might be bait. We need to confirm that it's real. Corey Weber was also lured to New York City, and the reason turned out to be fraudulent. I'm surprised by everyone else on the list to speak at the conference that Corey Weber and Trevor Fontaine weren't on the list. I'm wondering now if they weren't asked because the conference organizer knew they'd be dead by then."

"When I called Nubeck's assistant and told her about his death, I also asked about the conference and she said she didn't handle any of the arrangements. That Nubeck must have handled it himself, which is unusual. She had seen the invitation come in the mail and asked him if he wanted to attend. He told her at the time he wasn't sure, but that he'd look into it and check his schedule. He never got back to her, and the next thing she knew, it was on his calendar. He called me directly to ask for security support. I think Nubeck made all the arrangements for travel himself."

"Would that be strange?"

"Rather. I've never known him to handle his travel. I don't know why he would, but it appears he did. Is that important?"

"It could be. There might have been something he was hiding and didn't want anyone else to know about the travel or planning," Kate explained, not sure of Nubeck's reasoning. "You said he met with a handful of donors? Were these people he knew as long-time donors, or were they new donors?"

"A mix of both."

"I need you to get me the list of their names."

"I can do that."

"Was he slated to meet with anyone else while he was here?"

Jay shook his head. "Not that he told me, and he normally would have told me."

"What about the rape allegation? Someone thinks he was a rapist. You said he frequented prostitutes. We know there were sexual harassment allegations. Did it ever get physical besides the one you paid off?" Kate didn't think this murder was about the rape of a prostitute. She had a feeling it was more.

Resigned, Jay said, "There have been rumors swirling for years. But I don't know the details. I wasn't working with him then."

Kate believed him. She explained she was headed to speak to Patrice. "If you think of anything, call me."

CHAPTER 18

The narrow streets of the West Village were as charming as they were cramped, their cobblestone paths winding beneath the drizzle that had started to fall, casting a sheen over the old bricks of brownstone buildings. Kate had spent enough time in New York to know that even a light rain could make the city seem somehow more alive, more magnetic. She adjusted the collar of her coat against the chill and kept her pace steady, her shoes clicking against the slick pavement as she neared the art gallery.

Leo remained by her side. She had let Declan know where she was headed as he worked with the hotel and medical examiner. He was all too happy to concede the task to Leo if it allowed him to remain at the scene doing what he did best.

The gallery stood tucked between two older brick buildings, its storefront a striking contrast to the drab brick on either side. A minimalist black sign with sharp, white lettering spelled out White Art Gallery, with her last name in a larger, more stylized font. The window display was an eclectic mix of modern and classical, curated in a way that called for pedestrians to stop. A tall, thin sculpture – a half-human, half-geometric figure, distorted but alluring – loomed in the window's corner. Its sharp angles seemed to bend and shift with the changing light, creating an eerie sense of movement.

Inside, the faint hum of ambient jazz music floated just beyond the door. It wasn't loud enough to dominate, but it created a quiet, seductive pulse to the space. Kate reached for the door, her fingers brushing the cold steel of the handle, and pushed it open. The warm air inside was a contrast to the damp chill of the street, and the musty scent of old wood mixed with the sharp scent of fresh paint.

The gallery was sleek, with high ceilings that seemed to stretch endlessly upward. Its open-plan layout felt almost like a loft, with polished concrete floors beneath her feet and clean, white walls that begged to be filled with art. The walls were lined with large canvases – some abstract, others detailed – but all with one thing in common: they evoked a sense of darkness, even if the color palette was subdued. Deep blues, grays, and blacks predominated. In one corner, a large, disorienting painting of a city street blurred into something unrecognizable, as though it had been drowned in rain and shadow. The kind of work that invited questions, yet offered no answers.

A few well-placed sculptures and sleek modern furniture dotted the space, but nothing seemed to compete with the artwork on the walls. In the center of the room, a long, narrow table was strewn with open books, papers, and a bottle of fine wine, as though the gallery's owner had just stepped away for a moment. The soft light of antique pendant lamps hung low, casting a warm golden glow on the room, but the play of shadow over the pieces made them feel almost alive. It was an atmosphere that put Kate on edge, yet kept her entranced. She had trouble focusing on one image. The gallery's minimalist elegance was the perfect backdrop for someone who wanted to remain hidden while still presenting an image of openness.

Kate stepped further in, scanning the space. The room was empty other than the art. "It's open, right?" she asked Leo, who looked back at the sign.

"Been open all day since nine this morning," he said, his voice echoing in the space.

While on the cab ride over, Kate had read a recent article about Patrice White. The journalist noted that Patrice had a reputation for being elusive, for running a gallery that attracted the city's elite while remaining just out of reach, like a secret only a select few knew.

"Can I help you?" a voice said off to Kate's right behind a row of sculptures that she couldn't even begin to guess what they were supposed to represent.

"I'm here to speak with Patrice White," Kate said as the woman came into view.

"I'm Patrice," she said with no hesitation in her tone.

She stood at just over five feet ten with a presence that seemed to fill the room as she entered. Her features were sharp, almost sculptural, with high cheekbones and a narrow jawline that gave her face an otherworldly quality, like one of the statues that dotted around her gallery. Her skin was pale, almost porcelain, and framed by shoulder-length, jet-black hair that was impeccably styled – neat but not overly fussy, much like her wardrobe. She wore tailored minimalist clothing, her blouse and wide-leg trousers in muted earth tones. A silver cuff bracelet adorned her wrist and a delicate black silk scarf was tied loosely around her neck. Everything about her suggested precision, control, and an understanding of the power of subtlety.

She watched Kate and Leo carefully. "How can I help you?"

Kate flashed a badge and introduced them both. She took a few steps toward the woman and stopped. Her eyes were dark – almost unnervingly so – set beneath arched brows that gave her an air of both intensity and calculation. "I'm here about the conference you're having tomorrow night."

"Conference?" Patrice asked, her tone soft. "I'm not sure what you mean." She exuded an air of detachment that could easily be mistaken for coldness, yet beneath that, there was an undercurrent of something else that Kate couldn't quite discern.

Kate pulled out her phone and showed Patrice the screen. "You're having a conference here focused on men's issues. The speakers are a mix of podcasters, media figures, and Congressman Marty Nubeck. I believe you recently spoke to Jay Sterling, Nubeck's head of security, who told you that he wasn't going to be able to make it."

Patrice looked down her nose at Kate. "I wouldn't call it something as pedestrian as a conference. It's a salon I'm hosting. A time for intellectual exchange with like-minded people."

Kate pointed to the ceiling. "The space above the gallery. How many people are you expecting?"

Patrice leaned to the side so she was looking around Kate to Leo. "Do you speak or does she run the show here?"

"Agent Walsh is in charge. I'm only a consultant with the FBI, not an agent. Regardless, with her experience and knowledge, I'd defer to her."

Patrice offered him an icy smirk. "You might do well to come to the salon. You might learn a thing or two about being a man." She noted the lack of a ring on his finger. "You're not married either. That's strange for a man of your age and stature. I detect an accent – French?"

Leo didn't answer the question. "It seems strange to me that as a woman," he gestured around the gallery, "and as a business owner, that you'd take this stance and support the kinds of men that you're bringing here. You're also a terrible judge of character." He didn't wait for any kind of response from Patrice. Leo left the conversation and focused on the art on the walls.

Kate was impressed with the way Leo handled her. "Back to what I was saying."

"I don't understand why the FBI is here about an event I'm holding, no matter what you want to call it or the topics we are discussing. There's still free speech, after all."

Kate held up a hand to stop her. "I don't care about the topics you're covering. The reason I'm here is three murders that have happened in the city recently. Were you aware that podcasters Trevor Fontaine and Corey Weber were murdered?"

Patrice's eyes got wide. "I saw the news conference a few hours ago. There was a man who gave that news conference. It wasn't you."

"That was my partner, Agent Declan James. He's busy on another homicide right now."

"There's been another?"

The news would come out eventually. Kate made the call to disclose it now, even though it wasn't public yet. "Before coming here, I was at the hotel where Congressman Marty Nubeck was murdered."

For the first time, Patrice's cold exterior cracked. She stepped back as if to stumble but caught herself. "I don't understand. Someone murdered him in his hotel?"

Kate didn't call attention to the fact that Patrice's demeanor hinted that she knew Nubeck and not as a presenter at her upcoming salon. Kate suspected there might have been a personal relationship there.

"Yes," Kate said evenly, no trace of emotion in her voice. "Marty Nubeck was killed in his hotel room last night. His body was staged like the others and there were hallmarks of the scene that were similar to Trevor Fontaine and Corey Weber. The FBI believes all three cases are connected. The reason I'm here is that I need to check to see if the meeting you set up was legitimate."

"Of course it was," Patrice stated, confusion evident. "Why wouldn't it be?"

"We believe Corey Weber was lured here to Manhattan under a pretense, and we needed to see if the same thing happened to Congressman Nubeck."

"Oh," Patrice said softly, nearly a whisper. "The salon is real and happening tomorrow night. Some speakers have come from out of town. I thought Marty had changed his mind. We are going to have media here. I figured he decided he didn't want to speak so publicly."

The use of his first name didn't escape Kate. "When was the last time you spoke with him?"

"Yesterday."

"What time?"

Patrice licked her lips and glanced away.

"Look, it's clear to me you had some kind of personal relationship with him." Patrice started to deny it and Kate asked her to stop. "I'm not here to judge you or get personal details about that relationship. It certainly answers some questions we had about why he set up his own travel."

"He didn't," Patrice corrected her. "I set up his travel and the hotel. He requested that specific hotel and I set it up. He's been needing to travel with security lately and he wanted to stay at a hotel. I'd have preferred him to stay with me, but he said it wasn't possible on this trip. Now I wish he had. He might have been safe." Patrice stepped back from Kate, excusing herself. She walked out of the main gallery area, back around the corner from where she had entered the space. She didn't explain what she was doing, only that she'd be back in a moment.

Kate turned back to Leo, who had been watching them. "I liked your answer."

Leo dismissed her with a hand wave. "I am secure in my masculinity and will not debate it. I don't need to prove I'm man enough by putting down women or other men, for that matter. These men, who fall into this kind of rhetoric, are insecure, Kate. I won't play that game. I stand by my question about why a woman would be setting up a salon like that."

"Women have been carrying water for the patriarchy for a long time. Patrice must be getting something out of it, more than seeing Nubeck."

Kate wondered if Patrice knew about his sexual assault history or his predilection for prostitutes.

Kate grew impatient waiting for the woman to return. She checked the time on her phone and started to walk toward the back of the gallery to the side where Patrice had disappeared. She stopped in her tracks when Patrice showed herself again. The woman's mascara had run and been cleaned up. It left a smudge on the side of her eye, a spot she had missed.

"I needed to compose myself," Patrice said as a way of explanation.

Kate didn't know if she should offer the woman some comfort. She chose not to as Patrice straightened her back and held her head high, looking down her nose again at Kate. "Can you help me to understand your reasoning for holding a salon with these men?"

Patrice scoffed. "These men, as you call them, have a right to express their views."

Kate held her hand up to stop her. "I'm not questioning that. I was asking why now, why here? Did someone encourage you to do this? Are you the only backer of this plan? My goal is to understand because we don't want any more deaths. I'm trying to figure out if the killer is behind bringing all these men here or if they heard about the salon and are using it as an opportunity."

Patrice smoothed down her blouse. "I understand. This was Marty's idea. He wanted a forum for all of them to come together and discuss the issues. It wasn't something he could pull together himself. He suggested it to me and asked if I was open to the idea." She paused and took a breath deep enough that her chest rose. "I can't say that I agree with everything these men say, but I support their right to say it. Marty asked, and I was willing to help."

Kate pointed to the ceiling. "You have an event space upstairs."

"I do," she confirmed. "We are expecting eleven speakers." Patrice paused and shook her head. "Ten now and about twenty people coming to hear them speak. I don't think I can cancel because the speakers traveled here. Arrangements have been made."

"Is there anyone else involved in the planning? Anyone who knew the speakers who were coming and the arrangements that had been made?"

"I haven't told anyone besides staff here at the gallery. They haven't been involved in the planning, but we did expect some blowback. There hasn't been any. The website has been up for a while. I did a short interview on the local news a few months back when all the speakers' names were released. The information has been public."

Kate asked for the names of her staff. As Patrice told her, the handful of people who worked for her there didn't have a common name among them. It wasn't anyone she knew connected to the other cases. "Do you know Ali Brewer? She's an associate professor at Barnard."

"I know the name, but I'm not sure why I know it. Should I know it?"

Kate shook her head. "Not particularly. She has been involved in protests before against groups like you're bringing together. I wondered if you heard any rumblings about protests."

Patrice gestured with her hand. "That's how I know her. I've read a few articles and Marty mentioned her."

"He knew her?" Kate interrupted.

"No. He just said that he had read how she protests and wondered if she'd put up a stink this time. I think he was preparing for the worst."

Kate asked a few more questions, saving the two most important for last. "Where were you last night?"

"Here. I had a gallery showing until midnight. I stuck around until two with my staff. We were cleaning up and talking. I was trying to distract myself since I knew Marty was in town and didn't want to see me." Even at that admission, Patrice's voice didn't crack the way some women's might. "I can give you their information. I assume you'd want to verify my alibi."

Kate confirmed she did. "Lastly, what can you tell me about the rape allegations against Marty Nubeck? We believe it might play a role in his death."

Patrice let out a tired sigh. "Let's go back to my office to speak. There's a lot I can share."

CHAPTER 19

Kate left the meeting with Patrice with far more information than she thought she'd obtain. Leo had waited in the gallery and hadn't rejoined them during the discussion. By the time she was done, Leo was sitting outside on a park bench waiting for her.

"You could have joined us," Kate told him as he stood when she exited.

"I thought she might be more forthcoming if it was just you." They walked away from the gallery together, neither quite sure where they were going next. "How did it go?"

"There's been two significant rape allegations against Marty Nubeck. Patrice only knew one of their names. The other she didn't know, said it was from a long time ago when he was in college."

Leo didn't ask for the name. He seemed to have something else on his mind. "I don't understand women like Patrice. She knows he had been accused of rape twice. She must have known about the sexual harassment. What about the prostitutes?"

"She knew that, too." The truth was Kate didn't understand women like Patrice either, so she didn't have much to offer Leo. Patrice was intelligent and highly successful, and she probably could have had her pick of men. Yet, she chose someone like Nubeck. It defied any logic. "She didn't defend the rape allegations in the way I thought she might. Nubeck always denied it. Patrice chose to believe him. I think in the back of her mind, there were doubts."

"She seemed to be more focused on the free speech aspect of it."

Kate understood that about the woman. "She owns a gallery. She helps to nurture artists. Of course, she's going to be an advocate of freedom of expression. I feel the same way about that. I don't like what these men have to say at all. But I understand why it's important that they are allowed to express themselves."

Leo fell into silence and walked side by side with her for a few blocks. "What about Declan?" he finally asked. "How does he feel about the case?"

"About the case or what these men say?"

Leo shrugged. "What they say. I am hoping he doesn't agree with them. I'd hate for you to be in a relationship like that."

Kate chuckled. "Do I appear to be in a relationship like that?" Leo shook his head. "When Declan and I met in the academy, he was having his fun. He dated, slept around a bit too much, and drank far too much. I was attracted to him but knew he wasn't for me. We became friends quickly and then he became my partner. Spade knew Declan needed someone like me to settle him down and make him focus on work. I suppose I needed someone like Declan to get me out of my comfort zone. I'm far different now from how I first started. Rules were meant to be followed and never broken. That doesn't always work during an investigation."

"That certainly wasn't the woman I met," Leo said, his eyes never leaving her. "If you had been that way when we met, we wouldn't be here now."

"No, you're right about that." Kate knew if she had been as rules-driven as she was at the beginning of her career, nothing would have stopped her from arresting Leo. "You can thank Declan for softening my stance some over the years. But my point is, Declan met me as an FBI agent. I led our team and he was my partner. Our relationship is much the same way. He knows I have family money, which sometimes bothers him. Only because he's living in my house. He moved in before we got together, as he was going through a divorce. We haven't done things conventionally, but it works for us. He appreciates that I'm smart and driven."

"That's good. You need that, Kate," Leo said, stopping on the sidewalk and looking around them. "Do you know where we are walking?"

"I need a little air and to process what Patrice just told me." She turned her head to look at him. "You didn't ask me the name of the rape victim."

"You're right, I didn't. Does it have meaning for the case?"

"Kristen Carney," Kate said, realizing only then that Leo hadn't been brought up to date on the Trevor Fontaine details. "She was involved with the first victim. She also doesn't have an alibi for the night of the murder. She was the last person with him that night. Kristen said she left his house and went back to her room to pack. She caught an early flight home and didn't even know about the murder until it was on the news."

The implications of that caught up with him. "She's connected to two murder victims."

"Correct."

"Did Patrice know the details of the rape?"

"It happened years ago. Kristen did a summer internship with the Congressman. She was living in D.C., and he got friendly with her. Started taking her to dinner after work, paying special attention to her. Kristen assumed he was doing it because her father runs a media empire. She figured he was going to hit her up for a connection to her dad. That's what she told friends in D.C. anyway. One night when he brought her back to her apartment, Nubeck went in. The allegation was that he sexually assaulted her. Nubeck said it was consensual and she cried rape afterwards. She went to the cops, who discouraged her from formally pressing charges. She left her internship early and that seemed to be the end of it."

Leo couldn't seem to wrap his mind around how the police wouldn't take it seriously. "How does Patrice know all of this?"

This was the nexus of the situation that Kate was having a hard time understanding. "Patrice is the one who recommended her for the internship. That's how she knew everything. Between what Nubeck told her and what Kristen told her after she was back in the city after that summer, Patrice put the story together. She's not sure what to believe after Nubeck went into Kristen's apartment."

"Wait," Leo said, trying to make sense of it. "Patrice is connected to Kristen, who is connected to two of the victims?"

"Exactly," Kate said, wondering if this was all a coincidence or if there was more there. "Kristen had been working at the gallery during her undergrad years. It was important to her father that she have a job. She took the job at the gallery, then found out Patrice knew a congressman and mentioned she had been hoping to get into politics one day. It took a few years before Kristen had the experience for that kind of internship, so it happened at the end of her senior year before she started graduate school."

Kate understood the look of concern on Leo's face. She was feeling the same. "After Kristen got back from the internship, she immediately went to Patrice and confided in her about what had happened. That's why Patrice knew all the details."

"Did she influence her not to call the police?"

The jury was still out on that. "Patrice said she didn't encourage Kristen to do anything other than take care of herself. She told me she had asked Kristen if she had called the police, and she was told no. Kristen didn't know what to do. Nubeck told her that no one would believe her. After all, she had been going to dinner with him and allowed him to go up to her apartment."

"That's not consent," Leo said sternly.

She was glad he understood what some men didn't. "We both know that. Nubeck knew that, too, but he was using it to dissuade her from calling the police. Sadly, some cops don't understand that either. Some victims find going through the criminal justice process a compounded trauma and they stay away. I guess that going up against someone well-connected like Nubeck, the bar for proof would be even higher. If Kristen walked in there with nothing but her word and no real evidence to offer, cops might not have done much."

"What about her father? You said he's a media mogul. If so, he must be rich. No one could accuse her of going after Nubeck for the money."

Kate agreed with him there. "Her father's business might have Kristen second-guessing if she wanted to be public with it at all. I assume it was complicated all the way around. I'd like to find out about the other victim, but Patrice said she didn't have that information."

"Is there a way to get it?"

"I don't know." That was as honest an answer as she could give. It might take time and considerable resources that they just didn't have right now.

They caught a cab and made their way back to the hotel as quickly as the afternoon traffic would allow. As Kate entered the hotel, her phone chimed with a text from Declan. While standing at the elevator, she glanced down at it, a surge of relief filling her. She glanced up at Leo.

"Declan said he found something. One of the cameras in the bar didn't cut out when the rest of the security footage was cut. He said the bar manager had a small camera that he rigged to watch the bar area from his office. It wasn't connected to the main security line."

The security room was dark except for the flickering glow of multiple screens, each one offering a different angle in the hotel's bar. The upscale setting was dark enough to seem intimate, with a plush feel that was welcoming. The bar was open to the public, not just hotel guests. The menu offered signature cocktails and appetizers to keep them there, chatting and eating, but more importantly, handing over cards for twenty-dollar drinks. It was the kind of place that would make a young twenty-something with too much ambition feel like they'd somehow stumbled into the inner sanctum of New York's elite.

Kate leaned forward, elbows resting on the cool surface of the desk, eyes narrowing as she watched the bar from a new angle.

Declan sat across from her. He didn't say anything at first but allowed her to review what he already saw with his usual razor-sharp focus. His intensity for minute details made him one of the best in the field.

"Pause it," Kate murmured, her voice low but firm.

Declan clicked a few keys and the scene froze. He asked her what she wanted to see more closely and he zeroed in on the screen on the same three women he had mentioned to her.

Kate's eyes flicked over them immediately, not just because they were stunning, but because they moved in a way that set off a quiet alarm in her head. "Do you see how they are looking around? Trying to appear casual but looking for someone?"

"That's what caught my eye from the start," Declan said, agreeing with her. "Keep watching them. Nubeck's security is coming in soon."

The three women, Kate noted, had that effortless grace that was so common among the wealthy. Their clothes weren't ostentatious – no diamonds or fur coats – but they exuded a kind of polished ease that screamed money. One wore a chic leather jacket over a high-neck sweater and tailored pants, another a silk blouse and slim-cut jeans, while the third wore a sleek, form-fitting dress that wasn't too revealing, but drew the eye nonetheless. They looked like they belonged, without trying.

But there was something about them. It wasn't just their clothes, or the way they glided past the bartenders with a subtle but unmistakable air of authority. It was the way they lingered.

"They don't order drinks," Kate murmured, still focused on the screen. "And they don't talk to anyone. Not even to each other. It's like they're waiting for something."

Declan nodded, tapping a pen against his notepad, eyes flicking between the footage and his scribbled notes.

The women made their way toward the far side of the bar, near a set of tall, art-deco windows that overlooked the city. They hovered there, not engaging with anyone. One of them pulled out her phone, swiping through it with one hand while her other hand rested casually on the back of her chair. She didn't seem to be in any kind of hurry, but there was something about the way her eyes darted occasionally toward the entrance that made Kate pause.

They both watched as the security detail finally entered – two men in khakis and Polo shirts, dressed differently from most of the other guests in designer suits – and cut through the crowd with military precision. They weren't subtle, and the whole bar seemed to take notice. The women didn't flinch when the men arrived. They didn't react at all, just continued to linger, their expressions unreadable.

Kate couldn't shake the feeling that they were watching the security team as the two men ordered craft beer and relaxed at the table after a long day of work. Declan sped up the footage, past the hour mark, when Jay Sterling entered the bar, sought out the men and joined them.

The women continued to do nothing more than they had been doing the whole time – watching and waiting. They had eventually ordered drinks when a server came over to them, but the drinks remained untouched on their table.

"Something is going on there with them," Kate said, pointing at the screen.

Declan agreed. "They are waiting for something. Did you notice the woman in the dress? Look what's under it?"

"Under it?" Kate asked, not having seen anything that caught her eye sooner. But as Declan zoomed in, sure enough, it looked like she had black Lycra leggings on under her dress. He zeroed in on the other two women, and sure enough, peeking out from the bottom of their pants was the same black Lycra.

"Let's keep watching," Declan said, pointing to the screen.

The atmosphere in the bar changed when the women made a subtle move. The one in the leather jacket leaned in and said something to the other two. Their heads came together for a brief conversation, their lips barely moving. In the stillness of the hotel bar, even the smallest movement stood out.

As soon as Jay Sterling loosened his tie and put his drink to his lips, two of the women stood and began walking toward the center of the bar, where the access to the main lobby of the hotel was located. Their steps weren't hurried, but their pace was calculated, deliberate. One of them glanced over her shoulder just before she was out of shot of the video. The other remained where she was, watching the men carefully, too carefully.

Kate leaned in, her breath catching. "They waited until they were sure he wasn't going to leave and until they believed Nubeck was alone. They knew to wait until his whole security detail was there. That tells me they knew his security team ahead of time. Then they left the other one as a lookout."

Declan nodded. "That's exactly what I thought."

CHAPTER 20

After Kate and Declan watched the video feed and had a copy made, they brought it upstairs to the suite and showed Leo, Sharon, and Jay. Kate pointed to the three women in the corner. "Do you recognize these women?" she asked Jay.

He leaned in and kept his gaze on the women briefly before looking back over at himself and his men. "I don't remember seeing them at all. It's dark in there, and as you can see, we were done for the day. I don't remember what we were talking about, but it was nonconsequential."

They focused their eyes back on the screen.

"Keep a watch on the one they left behind," Declan said, gesturing to the lone woman who appeared younger than the rest. They hadn't noticed it at first, but once she was alone, her short, dark hair brushed back from her face revealed someone much younger than the other two. Kate would venture to guess she might even be college-aged.

Declan hit play as all of them huddled around the laptop and watched as the men had two rounds of drinks, shared two appetizers, then paid the bill. Each of them, appearing tired and worn from the day, got up from the table and headed for the door. As they did, the woman reached for her phone and typed something. Kate assumed a text. She got up from her seat and followed the men off-screen.

"You didn't see her in the lobby or near the elevators?" Kate asked, assuming the woman followed them out.

Jay ran a hand down his face. "I hate to say it, but no. I didn't notice her in the bar and didn't notice her following us out. We didn't linger in the lobby. We went upstairs to our rooms. I figured Nubeck was asleep by then. He didn't like it when I bothered him after he turned in for the night. I didn't check on him again until morning."

Kate assured him that he was fine. "I'm not sure I would have noticed her either. The women weren't noticeable to most. It's only by zeroing in on them with the footage that they appear suspicious. We don't even know for sure that they are connected."

"They could have been tailing a cheating husband," Sharon offered from behind them. When none of them bit, she conceded. "I know it doesn't appear that way. To Kate's point, though, we don't know what they were doing or why the two women left the other waiting there. They could have gone back to their room, or she was waiting for someone who didn't show up."

Declan cocked an eyebrow. "I appreciate you offering to play devil's advocate here, but it's fairly obvious what's going on. They were watching the security team, two of them left to kill Nubeck and left a lookout. When the team left, she texted the others, then followed." Declan turned to Jay. "Do you remember if she followed you up in the elevator?"

Jay stared down at the laptop. "There was a woman who entered after we did. A couple was waiting for the elevator. To be honest, I was exhausted and wasn't paying any attention to anything other than getting to my room and going to sleep. We had a long day planned for today. I'm sure she didn't follow us off at our floor. That I would remember."

Declan noted that in the pad where he was keeping notes. "Did any of the people in the elevator with you look familiar?"

Jay shook his head. "No one in the hotel looked familiar. Nubeck is on a floor you can't access unless you have a specific key access.

That's why I met you downstairs."

Declan pulled a hotel card from his pocket and flashed it to Kate. "They gave us one to use as we have been coming and going."

Kate stopped him there. She hadn't noticed Jay put a card into the elevator slot earlier. Then again, she hadn't paid that much attention to him. Her mind had been on other things. This was the first time Declan had mentioned the card. "Then how did they access the penthouse floor?"

"We don't know," Declan said. "That's something we haven't figured out yet."

"Jay, you said that you were standing guard because Nubeck sometimes hires prostitutes. How would they have accessed the floor then?"

Jay realized then he hadn't explained himself well. He apologized. "Nubeck would tell the front desk that he was waiting for a guest to arrive and that they could give her a key to use in the elevator. Hotels are discreet. They aren't going to question the congressmen. They would do as he asked. He only hires high-end call girls. I'm sure they know at the desk what they are, but again, they are discreet."

"That still doesn't answer how these women got in," Kate said, wondering if Nubeck had maybe called for a prostitute that night and instead gave his killers access.

Reading her mind, Declan shook his head. "We checked his phone and he didn't call anyone last night. After security left him, there were no calls on his cellphone."

"There is the room phone," Kate argued.

"True enough," Declan conceded. "We still don't believe that's what he did. We think they probably got a key from the hotel. There are four rooms up on the penthouse floor. Other than Nubeck, two were rented."

"By whom?"

Declan said. "One of the rooms was rented by a tech consultant. Angela Kramer. Jay hasn't met her. She wasn't in her room last night when he knocked, and no one has come back today."

"The other room?"

Jay explained, "Some medical consultant. A guy in his forties. Seemed harmless enough. I spoke to him briefly last night and introduced myself. He said he was here for work and that he wasn't around much. I don't know how those women accessed the floor."

Leo cleared his throat. "Hotel keys are easily cloned," he said quietly. "They could have targeted someone else on the floor. When did the guy arrive?"

"Three days ago," Jay said. "It's certainly possible they could have stolen his key. He didn't seem to be the brightest of men."

"Is there anything else?" Kate asked.

Declan gestured toward the screen. "I wanted you to see this first before we approached the front desk. I can screen grab these images and show the staff to see if anyone recognizes them. I can also give them to Ditch to see if he can run some facial recognition. I wanted your thoughts before we proceed."

Kate appreciated that. "It sounds like a plan to me. We don't know why these women were here, so we need to be cautious about this video and any photos taken from it. We don't want it circulating to the media with the message that these three women were involved in the murder. We simply don't have enough to go on right now. The announcement of Nubeck's murder is going to draw international attention to the case, especially when we tie it to the murders of Trevor Fontaine and Corey Weber. I need you to make a statement as soon as possible, so we can be in front of this with the media. We need the appearance at least that we are on top of things."

Declan raised his head to Jay. "Has everyone who needs to be notified about his death been notified? I don't want a shocked family member seeing this on the news for the first time."

"I made all notifications this morning."

"We are ready to go to the media then," Declan said but was interrupted by Sharon, who stuck her phone in his face.

"It's too late," Sharon groaned.

"What do you mean?" Kate asked, as she kept her focus on Declan, who was reading something on Sharon's phone.

"It seems the killers leaked the story themselves," Declan said slowly as he read them a few sentences. "The Midnight Lilies are taking credit for the murders. They have linked all three together and said there will be many more."

Kate's heart raced as she reached for the phone, trying not to rip it from his hands. "Where is this published?"

"The *New York Times*," Sharon said. "There is what I can only call a manifesto that they published."

"The paper published it without speaking to the FBI?" Kate couldn't believe what she was hearing.

Declan's head was still buried as she reached into her pocket for her phone. Before she could grab it, Leo handed her his. "Right here," he said, pointing down at the article. "The reporter said they received this manifesto and were told that if they didn't publish it online one of their reporters was next. They decided that publishing it was the right thing to do for the reporter's safety and the newsworthiness of the story. They were told not to speak to the FBI before the story was published. It's long, Kate. They said they will keep killing and that no one, not even the great FBI Agent Kate Walsh, can stop them."

"They named me?" Kate asked, practically yelling.

Declan glanced over at her. "They named both of us. I'm a target if we don't back off."

Kate held the phone in one hand and rubbed at her forehead with the other. "Let me read."

She lowered her eyes to the screen and read through the article, starting with the editor's note at the top. The *New York Times* was conflicted about publishing the manifesto, their word, because of the sensitive nature of the information provided. Kate understood that it would have been terrifying to have one of their own threatened, but it was no reason to publish this without at least speaking to the FBI.

The manifesto railed against offenders of sexual harassment and assault. It highlighted the lack of investigation and how few cases go to trial. The author of the manifesto shared statistics and relevant research, as well as highlighting recent cases where even a convicted offender of horrendous violence against his wife got less time in prison than a robbery case where the offender didn't hurt anyone but had stolen more than ten grand in goods.

As they noted, most crimes against women and children go unchecked, even when the victims come forward and do everything right, according to the system. They were here to level the playing field. Women had been afraid long enough, and it was time the tables were turned on those they considered the biggest offenders – the ones who were speaking loudly and proudly and facilitating the ongoing misogyny in the country.

The author said it was time for them to live in the fear that their victims had been living in. Again, they called it a reckoning. Kate knew by the use of that word and the style of the writing that this was authentic. There were also details about the murders that the FBI hadn't released to the public yet – cutting out their tongues and the lilies dyed black.

They praised Kate for solving previous cases and bringing down offenders for killing women, but they were clear that she'd be useless in this case. They implored Kate, for the good of the feminist cause, to let them continue. When they were done praising Kate, they questioned Declan's involvement with her and the cases they solved.

They speculated about his good looks and that he probably wasn't as good a man as he presented. They highlighted rumors that he might have been a bit of a drunk and a playboy earlier in his career. Even if that wasn't true, they said he was guilty by association of his gender alone. Then they threatened that taking him down might be beneficial to stop Kate from coming for them. Collateral damage is what they called him. It sickened her to read the words.

The way the manifesto closed is what stopped Kate cold.

There are more of us than you realize.

We are your mothers, sisters, friends, and co-workers. We have joined together for a common good.

You cannot stop us until the mission is complete.

We will rid this world of this scourge.

The Midnight Lilies

CHAPTER 21

The words from the manifesto echoed in Kate's mind as she and Leo made their way to the *New York Times* office. She had called ahead to schedule a meeting with the editor and the reporter whose names were attached to the story.

Kate hadn't wanted to leave Declan. She truly believed that the Midnight Lilies would go after him to stop the FBI. Declan had brushed off the threat. Leo had offered to stay. Declan had encouraged him to go.

"Is he always so stubborn?" Leo asked as they walked from the subway. Kate had left the car service for Declan in case he needed it. The last thing she wanted was him on the streets of Manhattan alone, or worse, riding the subway or getting into a cab alone.

"I don't think any agent takes well to being threatened," Kate explained. "He needs to process it. That's going to take a couple of hours. By the time we get back, he'll be okay."

Leo smiled. "You two really know each other."

"Long time working with each other." Kate tipped her head back to take in the imposing *New York Times* building on Eighth Avenue, occupying the eastern side of the avenue between 40th Street and 41st Street, one block west of Times Square. The building loomed like a modern monolith – sleek and imposing, its glass façade reflecting the surrounding chaos of Manhattan. The crisp, reflective surface of the building was punctuated by the bright red, illuminated sign of the *New York Times* logo, glowing like a beacon, announcing its presence to the city.

As Kate approached the entrance, the air felt colder, the towering shadow of the building blocking out the sun. She could hear the low hum of traffic as she went through the massive revolving doors. The security guard at the front was watching her as she approached, his uniform sharp and formal, but his gaze was neutral, accustomed to the comings and goings of high-profile visitors. Kate showed her credentials as she stepped forward.

Inside, the lobby was vast, open, and starkly modern, with tall, clean columns stretching toward a high ceiling. The walls were decorated with framed front pages, iconic moments in journalism captured in glossy print – stories that had shaped history, or at least captured the world's attention. The air smelled faintly of freshly printed paper and polished marble, a mixture of old-world gravitas and cutting-edge design. To her left, a row of elevators stood, their chrome doors gleaming under the soft lighting. A marble desk sat in the center, where an attendant spoke in hushed tones into a phone, her voice barely audible over the soft murmur of footsteps echoing across the space.

They rode the elevator to the fifth floor and stepped out into the hum of noisy chatter of an office in full swing – journalists talking and typing away and phones ringing.

As Kate made her way down the narrow hall toward the editor-in-chief's office, she couldn't help but feel the weight of the building's history pressing down on her – this was the nerve center of one of the most influential media organizations in the world. Whatever was about to happen in that office would be important. For better or for worse, they had made their choice to publish the manifesto.

Kate and Leo entered the bright corner office, announced themselves to the administrative assistant behind the desk and were ushered into a large conference room off to the right. A woman about forty stood with her back to the door as she stared out the window to the street below.

"I'm looking for James Braeden," Kate said as she entered. She introduced them before the woman even turned around. "We're here to discuss the manifesto you published."

The woman turned to face her, her arms curling around her body. "I'm Elise Hoffman, the journalist who handled the reporting." Her eyes scanned over Kate. "I thought you would have been older. I've seen you on television. You're younger looking in person."

Kate wasn't sure if that was supposed to be a compliment or not. "We can wait for your boss because I have several questions. First, where is the manifesto now?"

"James has it. He put it in a sealed bag. We limited how many people handled it." Elise turned her attention to Leo. She asked his name even though Kate had just introduced him. Leo told her again. "You're part of the FBI?"

"A special consultant," Leo said as he had been trained to do.

Elise seemed satisfied with that answer. She pulled out a chair and sat at the table, gesturing for Kate and Leo to do the same. "These murders are horrific. Was Congressman Nubeck really killed in the same way as the two podcasters?"

Kate pulled out a chair and sat. She'd remain tightlipped about the details until the right time. They fell into an awkward silence until Braeden arrived. Even in the doorway of the conference room, he was a commanding presence. He stood over six-three, his broad shoulders and muscular build making him an undeniable presence in any room. Kate had been warned of his sharp, calculating eyes that seemed to cut through the noise of conversation, always focused, always assessing. A man of few words, Braeden was known to value honesty and directness, cutting to the chase without hesitation. His reputation for being a no-nonsense, straight-shooter had earned him respect – and fear – in equal measure. His gruff exterior was matched only by his unwavering commitment to uncovering the truth, no matter how much it might cost.

The staff at the *New York Times* bowed to his authority. Kate wondered if he expected her to do the same. He practically charged her with his hand extended, introducing himself. "We were going to call you," he said instead of hello. "We were trying to get everything squared away here first." He introduced himself to Leo before sitting next to Elise across the table from them.

Kate didn't waste any time. "You shouldn't have published the manifesto. At the very least, you should have called the FBI and consulted with us first."

"That's not the FBI's call," Braeden said, matter-of-factly. "No matter what you would have said to us, we were still going to publish. It was sent to us and for us to decide."

"It's evidence in three horrific murders," Kate countered. "You knew the FBI was involved, given one of your staff was covering the press conference."

"I'm that journalist." Elise raised her hand and gave a little wave. "The fact is, we were sent the manifesto, one of our reporters was threatened, and we did what we had to do. Besides, the FBI hasn't been sharing much information. I can only assume you don't have much to go on. As I said, your reputation precedes you, so much so that this serial killer called you out by name."

"I noticed in the writing that bookended the manifesto that you referred to this killer as a serial killer. Had you spoken to me, you might have learned that this killer is not considered a serial killer."

Elise raised a perfectly arched brown eyebrow. "Then what are they considered?"

"Terrorists," Kate said evenly, making even Leo turn his head to look at her. When Braeden said he didn't understand, she explained, "It's much like the Unabomber case. Ted Kaczynski killed enough people that some might have considered him a serial killer, but that wasn't his motivation. He used a mail bombing campaign against people he believed to be advancing modern technology and the destruction of the natural environment. That was the focus of his manifesto. He wasn't killing for the thrill of it or sexual gratification. He was killing to terrorize and carry out a political agenda, much like this killer. Normally, traditional serial killers don't have a manifesto. This killer is focused on men they believe are promoting extreme misogynistic views and violence against women. They believe, wrongly, that by killing them and terrorizing those remaining that they will force them to reconsider the kind of content they are pushing out to the world. I don't believe for one second that it will have any impact – it might embolden them more."

The information made Braeden and Elise sit back, silent for a moment. He collected his thoughts. "Are you willing to go on the record with this?"

"I would have been willing to go on the record with you if you had done us the courtesy of allowing us to review the manifesto before it was released to the public. Now, I can't be bothered with you." Kate sat back and folded her hands on the table, staring them down. "We don't take kindly to interference in the middle of our investigation. You allowed threats against an FBI agent to be made public. That information could at the very least have been redacted."

Braeden took a breath through his nose loud enough that Kate heard it across the table. "Agent Walsh, the instructions said to release it in its entirety. As we said, there was a journalist here who was threatened."

"I see that name didn't make the paper."

He shook his head in dismay. "They didn't give us a name."

Kate wasn't sure she understood him. "Are you saying you got a blanket threat against some unnamed male journalist and you took that seriously?"

"That's correct," Braeden confirmed. "We have a handful of male journalists who are young, some of them listen to podcasts like Corey Weber and Trevor Fontaine. What they do on their own time is their business. That said, we don't tolerate sexual harassment of any kind, and there have been no allegations against any of our staff that I'm aware of. I wasn't going to chance it. Lives are at risk. As we can see, this killer is highly motivated and has killed three times already. Not to mention our integrity. We can't get communication like that and not go public with it."

Kate held her tongue on the matter of ethics in journalism. "How was the manifesto received? Was it mailed or hand-delivered?"

Elise answered, "Mailed from the Bronx. We checked the postmark. It was mailed two days ago and arrived early this morning."

Kate stopped her there. "If this was mailed two days ago, that was before Corey Weber and Marty Nubeck were even murdered. I need to see the manifesto myself, the original." Kate knew that it had been written in the past tense, as if the murders had already occurred. She knew that the murders were well planned, but it meant they were so confident in pulling it off that they were willing to go public with the information before it even happened. It also meant they knew how to get onto the penthouse floor of the hotel days ago.

Braeden instructed Elise to get it from his office safe. She got up from her chair and left the conference room. When she was gone, he said, "We tried to limit the number of people who touched the envelope and the letter." He offered Kate a smile. "I am sorry we didn't call you right away. In retrospect, maybe we should have."

"You should have. We probably would have let you publish it. But we were blindsided by it while in the middle of a case." Kate wanted to drive home the point. "To be frank with you, we hadn't even released to the public that Marty Nubeck's murder was related. His next of kin had only just been notified. Can you imagine if we hadn't been able to reach them yet? This is a distraction for us. I should be out in the field interviewing potential suspects and running down leads. Instead, I'm here."

Braeden's features tightened. He seemed almost lost for words. "I didn't even consider the timing of notifying his family. I thought that would have been the first thing the FBI did."

Kate explained how they weren't even notified right away about the murder and that his security team was at the hotel. "When it comes to a murder investigation, there are a lot of moving pieces. We had two homicides last night."

Braeden took a moment to digest the meaning of that. "Are you saying there are two killers? I know the manifesto references *we* and calls themselves the Midnight Lilies. Can there really be more than one person?"

"We believe there are several involved with the Midnight Lilies. We aren't looking for one terrorist, we are looking for a terrorist cell."

A loud gasp in the doorway turned all of their heads. Elise stood at the threshold of the door holding a clear bag with a few loose pages inside. "A terrorist cell? You can't be serious."

"Don't print that until the press conference," Kate warned her. "We are dealing with what I would consider a terrorist cell. Two murders in one night. A manifesto. I can't even tell you how many people are involved. We have three potential persons of interest from last night at Nubeck's hotel alone. That doesn't account for how many were involved with the Corey Weber murder in Central Park."

Elise slid the bag toward Kate as she sat. "Do you have any viable suspects?"

Kate noticed the woman's hands for the first time and averted her eyes to the bag. "I hate to say it, but no, we don't. We have leads, but that's about it. The men in this city are in danger."

"Just men?" Elise asked with a shudder.

Kate had assumed so, but it was the first time that she considered that not only men might be the target. "I honestly can't answer that. I think we are safe to say that anyone spouting misogynistic views or carrying water for the patriarchy might be in danger."

CHAPTER 22

It wasn't until they got to the street and far away from the *New York Times* that her phone rang. She handed Leo the clear bag with the manifesto while she answered. "Ditch, please tell me you have something."

"I think I have something," he said, not sounding too confident. "Two of the women from the bar last night aren't showing up in any facial recognition. They aren't in any database I can find. The younger woman, the one who looked college-aged, she's showing up in a college database. Can you come to the hotel where I'm staying so I can show you what I found?"

Kate told him she'd be there as soon as she could. "Did you find anything in any of the cellphone or email data Declan provided to you? What about the invitation?"

"Invitation link is dead. It probably only lasted for a few days then was out of commission. They don't want anyone tracing them. It was intended for quick use. As per email and cellphone data, I still have a lot of it to go through."

"Okay," she said, trying to hide her frustration. "Leo and I will be there soon."

Kate stepped into the hotel lobby, greeted by the cool rush of air conditioning and the faint hum of distant conversation. She barely registered the polished marble floors beneath her feet or the faint scent of floral perfume hanging in the air.

She and Leo moved quickly to the elevator bank and pressed the button for the second floor. The ding echoed in the quiet space, and she stepped into the small, unremarkable elevator. The doors slid shut with a soft chime. As it ascended, her mind raced, ticking through the details of the case.

The elevator doors opened with a soft whoosh, and Kate and Leo stepped out. They found room 212. Kate rapped her knuckles against the door. "Don't be too bothered by him. Ditch has a distinct personality that can sometimes be overbearing."

Leo chuckled. "I met him on a previous case, Kate. I think I like him more than Declan does. We'll be fine."

Kate was sure everyone liked Ditch more than Declan did. The door opened and Kate came face to face with Ditch, who looked markedly different than the last time she saw him, which wasn't all that long ago. His longish hair had been cut short and his perpetual five o'clock shadow was replaced by a clean-shaven face. The mischievous glint in his eyes remained.

"You're late," he said with a smirk, stepping aside to let them in.

Kate wasn't bothered. His appearance might have changed, but this was the Ditch she knew. He always had something to say. She'd learned not to take his words too seriously. She stepped past him into the room, taking a quick mental inventory of the chaos. A half-open suitcase lay discarded on the floor, its contents spilling out haphazardly. The bed was covered in layers of clothes – some wrinkled, some still in their plastic bags from the dry cleaners. A fast-food cup sat perched precariously on the edge of a cluttered desk, surrounded by empty pizza boxes, crumpled paper, and a tangle of computer cords. The air smelled faintly of stale coffee and the acrid tang of electronics.

"What happened in here?" Kate asked dryly, her gaze flicking from the mess to Ditch, who was already back at the desk.

He grinned, clearly unfazed. "I like it messy. Reminds me of home." He gestured to the chair in front of the desk, where a tangle of papers and old snack wrappers had been hastily swept to one side.

Kate bit back a sigh but chose not to argue. She settled into the chair, her eyes narrowing as she surveyed the monitors in front of Ditch. He had three running, each displaying something different – one with a deep dive into the girl's university records, one with a feed from a live facial recognition program, and one showing a map with pins scattered all over the city.

Amanda Larson's face had come up in a college database. Political science major. Barnard College. It didn't escape Kate that's where Ali Brewer taught. She wondered then if there was a connection to the college.

Ditch's fingers were flying across the keyboard, the clatter of keys filling the room. He didn't glance up. "Leo, take a seat, man. This is going to take a little time. I have a lot to show Kate."

Leo backed away to the bed. "You really should take care of your things better."

"No need," Ditch said absently. "I take care of my tech and that's all that matters."

Kate's eyes flicked to the second monitor, where a still image of Amanda Larson appeared. It was her, no doubt. The facial recognition software had done its job. The image of Amanda in the bar had been clear, but this shot from the college's facial database was clearer. Amanda had dark hair, a sharp jawline, and pale skin. A girl next door, if Kate had to describe her, but there was something about the set of her eyes, the almost imperceptible tilt of her chin, that unsettled Kate.

"This is her, right?" Ditch asked, his voice low. When Kate confirmed, he read off a list of things about her. "She's originally from Seattle. She is a junior in college. She's been involved in some political causes on campus, but no criminal history. At least none that shows up here."

Kate studied the image again, tapping her fingers on the armrest. "She doesn't look like the type to get involved in something like this."

"I would agree with you there." Ditch scanned the next screen. "Her grades are impeccable. No issues on campus that are recorded in her file."

"You're able to pull those up?" Leo asked from behind them.

"Haven't you told him how good I am?" Ditch asked Kate, a grumble about his genius not being recognized. He clicked a few more times, and a document appeared on the screen. A file labeled Amanda Larson - Political Involvement. Kate read the summary quickly. Amanda had been part of several student-run organizations, most notably one that had protested against a proposed city council development project. She had spoken out at a protest against sexual harassment – one of those referenced in the protest was Congressman Marty Nubeck.

Kate's eyes flicked back to Ditch, who was watching her carefully. "Not a coincidence," she said, her voice firm. Kate felt her pulse quicken. She'd found the first real thread. They didn't have much on her, but Amanda's involvement was a start. "Can you see her class schedule from the semester back or just her grades?"

"I can see all of it. What do you want?"

Kate named the classes that Ali Brewer taught. "I want to see if there's a connection between the two."

Ditch leaned forward and read off Amanda's class schedule. "Right here," he said, pointing. "The first semester of her freshman year, she took a class about women in politics with Ali Brewer. It looks like she is in a class with her now, too – a more advanced women's studies course."

"Anything else in her background I should know?"

"There's a police report with her name attached." Ditch pointed to the other screen with an NYPD incident report, clear as day. "Amanda showed up with a friend who had been sexually assaulted after a night out at a bar. She was there to provide a witness statement to what occurred at the bar before her friend left with the guy. She didn't witness the assault, but she was angry the police weren't doing more."

Kate absorbed that information, knowing that kind of anger could spill over. "Is there anything else? What about the other two?"

"Not so far. As I said, the two other women don't show up in the database. They don't show up anywhere. I even cross-referenced all of Amanda's social media and can't find those women anywhere."

"We know she's not working alone," Kate said, still staring at the screen. "At least two teams are working independently. Probably coming together to meet. They'd have to, the scenes are too similar for there not to be specific planning. Declan and I are going to have to bring Amanda in."

Ditch looked over at her with a broad smirk. "You don't even have enough for a warrant. How are you going to bring her in? If she refuses to talk to you, you are toast. It isn't a crime to be in a hotel bar."

Kate knew all that. She knew there wasn't a smoking gun. What they had on Amanda and the other women was circumstantial at best, flimsy speculation at worst. "Declan and I will figure it out."

Ditch whistled loudly. "This case is bugging you. I can tell by that twitch under your eye and that snarky tone you got going."

Leo started to defend Kate, but she shot him a look. She could defend herself. "Do you listen to any of the podcasts that fall under this..." Kate struggled for the word. The genre wasn't exactly right. "Sharon called it the manosphere." The word still felt off rolling off her tongue.

"No. I can't be bothered with all that. A bunch of insecure men who can't get women, bragging about all the women they get while also acting straight up like they don't like women at all. I think I'm what they call a beta. But frankly, I can steal all their money, shut the power off in their homes, infect their cellphones and laptops with spyware, infiltrate their smart homes, and cause general havoc in their lives. Plus, I get women. I'm not too worried about what a bunch of numpty men think of my masculinity."

Ditch turned around in his chair to face Leo. "I bet you don't care about all that either. You look like the kind of man who'd eat those losers for breakfast. Like you're a legit tough guy. I haven't figured you out yet, Leo. You're like a puzzle with a bunch of missing pieces."

Leo tried to hide his smile. "I respect women and strong women at that. The problem is that these men are creating an issue for society as a whole and for younger generations of men who listen to them. The violence they perpetrate against women is real. While I'd like to pretend that they don't exist, it's a real issue."

Ditch gestured toward him. "See. A real puzzle." He turned his head to look up at Kate. "What's your boyfriend's take? He seems like he might have been one of them at one point in his life. He only gave me the specifics of the case. He didn't elaborate much, but he said he'd been listening to some of the podcasts."

Kate shook her head. "Declan isn't like that at all and you know that. We were listening to the podcasts to understand the victims better."

"Sure," Ditch said with a snarky tone. "You can do better than him, Kate."

"We aren't going down this path again."

Ditch tipped his head back and laughed. "I had a date with a Victoria's Secret model the other night." He gestured to Kate, looking her up and down. "This tomboyish thing you got going on doesn't do it for me anymore."

Kate rolled her eyes. "I'm so glad." She had better things to do than stand around and yammer on with Ditch. She pointed to his computer setup. "Keep digging. We don't need any slipups. This case is going to end up in court with at least a few defendants. I don't need any mistakes."

Ditch grinned. "Don't forget to send the thank-you card. I don't do this for free, you know."

Kate ignored the jab. "Just get it done, Ditch."

CHAPTER 23

It had been one of the longest days of Kate's life. After leaving Ditch, she sent Leo back to his hotel. There was no point in dragging him to chase down Amanda Larson. Kate felt like they had enough information to at least see where the young woman lived and possibly interview her if it felt like the right time.

She found Declan still at the hotel, sitting in the hospitality suite on the penthouse floor. His head was bent over his phone, and he barely looked up when she entered.

"How did the rest of the day go?" Kate asked, grabbing a bottle of water the hotel staff had left for them. She eased down on the couch, not wanting to sit for too long or she'd never get back up again. Her lower back started to ache.

Declan held his finger up for her to wait. He finished whatever he was typing, then tossed his phone on the coffee table between them. "We got a lot done. The hotel staff member who was on yesterday finally arrived. She confirmed that she didn't remember any of the women from the video surveillance in the bar. There is a separate entrance from the street where they could have come in. Because the surveillance was cut, we don't know the door they came in or left out of that night. We don't know where they went after leaving the bar. All we know is that the younger woman followed the security team into the hallway and possibly up in the elevator, getting off at a different floor."

"Amanda Larson," Kate said, surprising him. "Ditch was able to get her name. He matched the photo with one from her college. That's why I came back. I wanted to see if you wanted to go to the address we have on file for her."

Declan cocked an eyebrow. "Interview her tonight?"

"I'm not sure. I want to get a sense of where she lives. See who is around her. Maybe we will catch someone coming or going. She goes to Barnard. That's the same school where Ali Brewer is an assistant professor. They know each other. Amanda is in her class this semester."

"Are you kidding me?"

"It might be a coincidence. Ditch was able to see some of her grades. She's a good student. No problems on campus. She has been involved in some protests." Kate also explained the witness report for the assault on her friend. "I'd say that gives her a motive."

"A weak one in my opinion," Declan said, rubbing his brow. He glanced over at Kate and read her expression correctly. "Katie, I'm not dismissing the girl's anger over the injustice of the criminal justice system. I can't think of any good motive for murdering three men in the way they have. That's all I'm saying. Don't go looking for a fight where there isn't one."

That's exactly what she had been doing. She had to admit to herself that she had been watching Declan carefully, seeing how he responded to things on this case. "Sorry," she said lightly. "All I'm saying is that it's probably not the only assault Amanda has heard about or maybe witnessed. She could even be a victim herself. Sexual harassment and assault are a real problem, not just in the country but around the globe, and barely anything is done about it. I'm not saying murdering these men isn't wrong. Of course, it's wrong. I'm saying that I understand the frustration that can bubble up for women who don't have an appropriate outlet to express it."

Declan stared over at her, knowing she had more to say.

She continued, "As you know, with most terrorism, some people can be more easily radicalized than others. Once they are in that pipeline, it's hard to walk it back. I don't see this case any different than what's happening with the young men being radicalized by these podcasts. For a long time, we have had an issue in this country with young men engaging in school shootings and shootings in stores and movie theaters. It's a pattern of young, white men who have been radicalized in some way. Now, these women, their motive is different, but the acts of violence are the same. These are targeted rather than walking into a school or grocery store and shooting up the place; these women are targeting the direct source."

Kate grew quiet as she considered what else she wanted to say. Declan was still giving her the same dispassionate look. "I believe the woman who is heading this up was possibly a victim herself. I believe she didn't get justice and that anger grew and grew. She no doubt met other women over the years who had experienced similar. She's fed up. One of those women she met, or maybe it was inside of her, had the urge to kill – that turned injustice into a weapon."

"Is that your working theory of who we are looking for?" Declan asked, finally breaking his silence.

"I think so. I think we are going to find that there are two or three women at the top of this who are feeding off each other and radicalizing the rest. If it were just one, she might work alone or she'd work out her issues in therapy. At least two of them came together – one focused on injustice and the other with murderous intent. It created the perfect storm."

Declan still didn't say anything. He got up from the couch and moved to stand in front of Kate. He reached a hand down to pull her up. She tentatively took it, still not sure what he was thinking. He pulled her up into a hug, wrapping his arms around her. She leaned into his hard chest, allowing herself to be held. When he pulled back, Declan leaned down, dropping a sweet kiss on her lips.

The resolve that Kate had been holding like armor cracked. "I thought you were ready to argue with me."

"No," he said, shaking his head. "I know you're conflicted about this case. Honestly, so am I. These are horrible men who have done and said truly disgusting things. They didn't deserve to die the way they did. I have to separate those two things. I'm struggling with it, as is everyone involved in this case. Sharon asked me if we had to solve this one."

Kate's eyes got wide. "Did she really?"

"She did earlier today. I think even Jay Sterling is struggling to care. He called his wife to explain what happened. He told me she said that Nubeck got what he deserved. I think you're going to see public sentiment on this case is a bit mixed. But we still have a job to do." Declan stepped back from her and leaned down to grab his phone. "The podcasters aren't afraid. They are doubling down and taunting these women."

Kate took a deep breath, knowing that more victims would come. She hadn't seen Declan's press conference earlier, but he had texted her to let her know it had happened. "Have you heard from Spade at all?"

"He called me about an hour ago. He knows we are doing all that we can do. There's some political pressure on him now that Nubeck was targeted. There's a collective breath being held in D.C. right now, wondering who might be next."

Kate hoped that these killers stayed within the confines of Manhattan. "I wonder how many of these women have families?"

"Why do you ask that?"

"I was thinking about them killing in other areas of the country. If they have families, it might be another reason why they are staying local to Manhattan and drawing the men here. Many of the other killers we deal with are single men who have transient jobs. The ones who did stay local tended to have greater ties to their communities."

"Are you suggesting we are dealing with professional women?"

"Women with means, for sure. They are women who'd be missed if they were gone too long, whether that means with their jobs or their families." Kate was getting a clearer image of the kinds of women who might join. The scary part was that they would blend easily into Manhattan. They were the kind of women who could, for instance, easily get a hotel key to the penthouse floor. White, privileged women who'd fly far under the radar. "Did you figure out how they got the hotel key?"

Declan shook his head. "It's not the other woman on the penthouse floor. I spoke with her, and she's been involved in meetings and in and out of the hotel at odd hours because of work. She gave me a rundown of her meeting schedule and offered me everyone and their brother to check her alibi. I made a few calls. She's legit. I'm confident she's not connected."

The only other option was someone working at the hotel who had access or could have given the women access. The place had more than one hundred employees. It wasn't just the key, though. It was getting in the tools for torture and the rope that killed Nubeck, not to mention the flowers. Kate assumed they had been staying in the hotel or had access to staff to stash their things. Someone also knew enough to cut the surveillance. There were too many questions and not enough answers.

Declan checked his watch. It was close to ten. "I don't think we should interview Amanda tonight. But let's go check out where she lives and do a little surveillance."

Kate agreed with that. In truth, she was far too tired to go head-to-head with their only lead. "Let's go then. Surveillance, it is."

Luck was on their side that night. An all-night diner sat opposite the aging brownstone in the West Village where Amanda Larson lived. Kate and Declan entered and asked for a booth that looked directly across the street. They ordered coffee and Kate got toast to settle her stomach.

The neighborhood was a mix of older brownstones. The faded red brick with stoops worn and uneven from years of feet that had come and gone lined the streets. A few people strolled by, but the sidewalks felt emptier than Kate had assumed.

They sat in a red vinyl booth with their eyes trained out the window. The glass was foggy with the condensation of the cool air inside meeting the heat of the kitchen, and she wiped a section of it clean with her sleeve.

The diner itself was a relic, a greasy spoon that by the sight of the door had been a staple of the neighborhood since 1941. The floors creaked underfoot, and the smell of bacon and coffee hung heavy in the air, mingling with the distant clang of a skillet from the back. The lights above flickered intermittently, giving the room a half-lit, almost dreamlike quality.

Kate's fingers tapped rhythmically against the chipped Formica table, the sound a sharp contrast to the soft music on the old jukebox in the corner. Across from her, Declan stirred his coffee, his gaze equally focused on the brownstone across the street.

They had been sitting there for an hour watching the second floor. A front light had remained on the entire time they were there, but no one came or left from the building. Kate was starting to think it was a lost cause and they should head back to the hotel for a decent night's sleep when a group of women started to gather on the steps. They came from opposite directions, two of them walking north together, one crossing the street and the other two coming south at different times. Kate didn't notice them until they all convened on the steps.

She shifted in her seat as Declan's eyes flicked to her, then back to the brownstone. "Could be nothing," he said, the words hanging in the air with a casualness that didn't match the tension in his eyes. "They are just standing there. We don't even know that they are going in. It could be friends from college."

Kate shook her head as her lips pressed into a thin line. "No, two of those women are in their forties." She focused Declan's attention on the woman wearing jeans with a red top and another in a long flowing skirt. "I don't recognize any of them from the surveillance video. Can you get any photos or video?"

Declan raised his phone up to the window and focused on the images across the street. "I can't," he said, playing with the light and the zoom. "It's too dark over there. If they were directly under a streetlight, it might work. All I'm getting is shadows. Do you want to go over there?"

Kate gave him a sidelong glance, her voice soft but firm. "Not yet. I don't want them to know we are watching them. We need something solid before we make a move." She watched as the group of women ascended the steps of the brownstone, opened one of the tall glass front doors and went inside. She had no idea after the door closed behind them which floor they were going to. For all Kate knew, it wasn't to meet with Amanda Larson.

"We need to interview her first thing in the morning," Kate said finally.

A few minutes passed as they both sat in silence, watching the building for more activity. The door to the brownstone remained closed, and they were left with the quiet ebb and flow of the West Village.

"All right," Declan said after a long pause. "We'll interview her in the morning and hopefully get enough information for a warrant to search her place."

Kate nodded, her gaze never wavering from the brownstone.

CHAPTER 24

By noon, three days later, Kate and Declan had been denied a warrant to search Amanda Larson's apartment. The judge said there was no probable cause. The fact that Amanda was seen in the bar, even watching Marty Nubeck's security and following them out of the bar, told the FBI nothing. It didn't matter that a group of women had convened in front of Amanda's steps and had gone into the brownstone. Kate and Declan couldn't prove that they were there for Amanda. They hadn't even been able to interview her yet. The woman was elusive.

They had spent days working to find out everything they could about Amanda. They still didn't have eyes on her. They stopped by her brownstone again and again but still didn't see her. They went to the college with the current class schedule that Ditch had pulled up for them, but that didn't bear fruit. Amanda was a no-show for class. They had debated speaking to one of her professors, but the last thing they wanted to do was tip off Amanda that she was being watched. They didn't want to tip off Ali either.

They chose instead to table the search on her until they had more information. So far, it was a lead that was going nowhere quickly. They still didn't know the identities of the two other women who had been with Amanda in the bar that night.

It was frustrating - days spent in Manhattan running down leads that were a dead-end at every turn.

The Midnight Lilies were planned, organized, methodical, and determined. They evaded Kate and Declan in a way no other killer had. In other cases, there were at least some leads to follow. This time, nothing. Even the few leads they had went nowhere.

Kate had tossed and turned most nights, angry and frustrated that they were being made to look like fools in the media. One reporter even asked if she had lost her touch. Maybe she'd lost her edge and these killers were a bit too smart for the FBI.

Kate wanted to bite back, but the truth was they were being outmaneuvered. She had said once long ago that it was a good thing that women weren't prone to serial murder because they'd be far superior to men in organization and planning. They might not have the physical strength to overpower their victims the way men could. But they'd be stellar with planning and covering up the crimes. And that's exactly what they continued to do.

Kate's failure was showcased by two more murders overnight. Two more podcasters. Chad Riker, thirty-two and single, was found in his bed, strangled with signs of torture, his tongue cut out post-mortem, and black lilies all over his body and his apartment. There was a black lily fastened around the door handle that first alerted the woman who lived above him. As she came down the stairs, she noticed it and called the police. She had been watching the news reports and knew right away that whatever had happened was bad.

His podcast partner, Mason Steele, thirty-five and single, was found three blocks over with a gunshot wound to the head, small stabs all over his body, and his tongue cut out. The black lilies led a trail from the foyer entrance to the body, where they were arranged around him like a funeral scene. Black lilies were placed over each closed eye.

Their podcast, *The Iron Creed*, was a mix of bodybuilding, dating, and life advice for men in their thirties and beyond. Their focus was on how men should always lead and women were designed only to be submissive. Anything else was against nature. They touched on that theme with each podcast disparaging working women, single mothers, women in the gym, single and childfree women, any woman who wasn't married with children and working only in the home.

Kate found it ironic that neither of them had ever been married and had no girlfriends to speak of. She wasn't sure what qualified either of them to dole out the advice. The podcast was a lot of them bantering with each other back and forth and occasionally they'd bring on guests. Their podcast didn't rank as highly as Trevor Fontaine's or even Corey Weber's.

What they had done was challenge the Midnight Lilies the day prior. They taunted the women, saying that they had gone after the weakest of the herd. That they weren't brave enough to go after *real men*.

By the next morning, not even twenty-four hours after that podcast aired, they were dead.

The Midnight Lilies were also getting more and more theatrical with each kill.

They were sending a message.

They were deadly serious in their mission that they could get to anyone at any time.

Kate had to wonder about the timing and the precision with which they were killed. Like the others, there were no witnesses. They left no evidence of their identities behind. It was as if a ghost had appeared, created the murderous chaos, and disappeared.

The timing of their murders meant that there had been little planning. The podcast went live at eight that morning. By nighttime, they were dead.

Both men appeared on Ali Brewer's list, but further down in the ranking. Kate had to assume that they might have been targets eventually, but with the threat issued, the group decided to strike right then. Even with that, no mistakes had been made as far as Kate knew. Sharon and her forensics team were still going over the apartments for any traces left behind. As Sharon had told them, the scenes were clean of evidence. She believed the killers were wearing gloves and possibly other clothing to make sure they left no skin cells or hair behind. The Midnight Lilies' meticulousness infuriated Kate. Sharon and her team were having trouble keeping up.

The medical examiner's office was also getting spread thin as the murders were coming in doubles now. It was enough that Kate and Declan were having trouble catching their breath.

Kate was finding something else to be true. She couldn't walk down a street in Manhattan without looking at each woman who passed and wondering if she could be a cold-blooded killer or, at the very least, in some way helping the group.

Ditch had told her that he was sure one of them was skilled with tech. After examining the glitch in the hotel's surveillance, he found a virus that cut out all of the hotel's video surveillance at that time. Not only that. Once Ditch started to work with the city's street surveillance system, he found the same virus had been uploaded, giving a hacker, one he'd yet to identify, remote access. They were able to shut off street cameras at will. And that's exactly what they did the nights of the murders around Manhattan.

Ditch had called it sophisticated.

Sophisticated.

It was a word that had come up a few times during the investigation. It's what Kate had considered the killers. They were leaving nothing to chance.

As the current day wore on and still no leads materialized, Kate found her energy slumping. She checked her phone and it was already nearing two in the afternoon.

"I need lunch," she said to Declan and Leo, who both had headphones on, listening through recent podcasts of potential victims. Kate had asked them to listen to recent episodes in the hopes of identifying the next potential victims.

When neither Declan nor Leo raised their heads, she got up and crossed the room, tapping Declan on his shoulder. He raised his eyes to her, slipping off his headphones. "Did you find something?"

"No," she said. "I need some fresh air and some lunch. Do you want to take a break?"

"Sure," he tapped Leo's arm and asked him the same.

"I'm going to keep at it," he explained, but asked if they could pick him up a sandwich.

"Are you going to be okay here alone?" Declan asked. They had been given space in the lower Manhattan FBI office at the corner of Broadway and Worth Streets. Given Leo's past, Kate had wondered how comfortable he'd be in the building filled with FBI agents who'd love nothing more than to know his real identity.

"I'm fine," Leo assured them and smiled up at Kate for good measure. "Really. I've been working with your art team for long enough that if there was going to be suspicion, it would have happened by now." If he didn't feel comfortable, Declan and Kate would press the issue.

They left the hustle and bustle of the FBI building to find more of the same on the street in lower Manhattan. Even though she grew up in the heart of Boston, Kate didn't like New York City. Boston afforded some quieter spaces where it didn't feel like city life. Other than deep in the woods of Central Park, Kate hadn't found any such peace in Manhattan. It had a static current that ran through the city like a live wire at all hours of the day. The hustle and bustle of the city was mocking her in a way. All those people and zero leads.

"I hate it here," Kate said after they had walked a few blocks. She wasn't sure where they were going. She assumed she'd stumble on an eatery. When Declan didn't say anything, Kate persisted. "It's too noisy and dirty and…" She trailed off, not sure what else to say. She wasn't legitimately complaining; she was saying words to cover what she should have been saying, which was simple – they were failing at their jobs.

Declan had no problem addressing it head-on. "We'll get a lead, Kate. Something will crack open. It always does."

"What if it doesn't?" Kate watched as women dressed for work in designer fashion powerwalked by with their faces lowered to their phones. Two women in leggings with bagged yoga mats slung over their shoulders stopped at a corner to speak to a similarly clad third woman. A young mother tried to wrangle a toddler while pushing a younger child in a stroller. Any of these women could be killers, lookouts, involved in the planning, researchers, or the tech genius. Kate could be staring right at them and she'd never know.

"It could be any one of them, Declan. Any of these millions of women out here could be involved. Did you see the comments on social media after the news articles?"

"I've gone through a few of them. I was trying to see if there were any repeats from post to post, thinking maybe some of the women involved were posting online." Declan glanced down at her. "I know you think they are too organized to slip up like that."

Kate had done the same. "No one cares that these men have been killed. There's a handful of men talking about how the police should be doing more, that the FBI is intentionally not investigating and some wild conspiracy theories. On the whole, people think these men have reaped what they have sown."

Declan sighed. "I've seen the same. It's disheartening, Katie, how completely screwed up society is right now. Murder certainly isn't the way to go."

"No, it's not," Kate said, spotting a deli up ahead. She pointed it out. "Let's take a break and use this as a reset. When we come out of here,

I want a new perspective and my head clear."

Declan reached down, taking her hand as if they were simply a couple on a date. "I think that's the best plan you've had yet."

CHAPTER 25

The door to the deli slammed behind them, ushering in the familiar chaos of New York's lunch rush. The bell above continued to ring a shrill welcome. Kate could feel the heat and the buzz of a thousand conversations rushing over her. She inhaled deeply, the air thick with the smell of roast beef, pickles, mustard, and something else she couldn't quite place.

The crowd was typical – city workers, businessmen, tourists – and the noise was deafening. But in the middle of it all, there was something comforting about the hum of the deli. It allowed her to shut off her thoughts and focus on the immediate sensations rushing through her.

While Kate remained at the doorway, Declan was already weaving his way through the small maze of tables, his broad shoulders bumping against patrons who barely looked up from their sandwiches. There were no open seats. The tables were all filled with people huddled over pastrami on rye, sipping iced tea, or hunched over their phones.

"Over here," Declan called from the back, where a booth tucked in a corner had just been vacated.

Kate nodded and made her way toward him, dodging a waiter balancing a tray of soup and an elderly couple at the nearby table arguing about the price of pickles. She'd barely taken a step before someone brushed past her from behind. Someone nudged Kate out of the way with enough force that she stumbled on her feet.

Kate turned her head to see a figure dressed in a dark hoodie with the hood pulled up and jeans, a stark contrast to the office workers in their suits. Kate couldn't see the person's face. No *excuse me* or *I'm sorry* for bumping Kate. She shook it off and navigated around another waiter to reach Declan.

She slid into the booth, happy to be out of the way. The warmth of the deli pressed in on all sides. She slipped off her coat and draped it over the back of her chair, ready to sink into the familiar comfort of a warm meal. She asked about menus but Declan pointed down toward the table. The menu was already laminated onto the tabletop. She scanned the offerings, typical fare for a Manhattan deli. The server appeared at the table moments later, and they ordered with the quickness and efficiency required for good service.

Kate sat back and let the hum of the surroundings drown out the noise in her brain. She knew Declan was watching her. "How's Sharon liking working with us?"

"The pace is different, and she has to piecemeal the lab sometimes because when she borrows facilities, it doesn't always have what her Boston digs have, but she has some plans for that. I think she's made a nice addition to the team."

Kate was relieved about that. First it was Ditch, then Sharon and now Leo. They were a long way from it being just the two of them, which had been the way for years. "We should ask if she wants some lunch."

Kate reached into the pocket of her coat. It wasn't the cellphone her fingers brushed up against but what felt like a receipt or piece of paper she knew hadn't been in there earlier.

Kate pulled out a small, folded note. Her breath caught, and for a moment, the noise of the deli faded into the background as her mind began to race. She unfolded the crumpled piece of yellow sticky note paper, the edges frayed, the handwriting scrawled in black ink.

White Art Gallery. The meeting tonight will be bombed.

Kate's pulse kicked into overdrive as she whipped her head around. Her sharp gaze darted across the room, suddenly hyper-aware of every person within a ten-foot radius. Kate had cleaned out her coat pockets that morning, looking for a business card she had shoved in there the day before.

Kate's mind traced back to the events of the day, then focused on entering the deli. The figure who had brushed past her. But the deli was packed – too many faces, too many bodies, too many people moving around in a blur. She tried to steady her breath, but the adrenaline shot through her veins like fire.

"Kate?" Declan's voice broke through her thoughts. "You okay?"

She blinked, barely noticing that Declan was looking at her with a furrowed brow. Her eyes flicked to the front of the deli, where the person in the hoodie, who she suspected was a young woman, walked back out the front door and disappeared into the crowd on the street.

"I need to go," Kate said, standing up so abruptly that the table rattled. Her heart hammered in her chest as she scanned the room again, this time with laser focus. She was moving now before Declan could even ask what was going on. Kate wasn't even sure the figure had been a woman. It was an assumption, a feeling, on her part.

"Wait, what? Kate, what—" Declan called from behind her.

Kate was already heading toward the door, her eyes darting across the room. She pushed through the crowd, apologizing as she went. Kate burst through the door back out into the sunlight, but the young woman was gone. Vanished into the streets of Manhattan.

Kate stepped farther out onto the sidewalk, the cool fall air hitting her skin like a slap. The street was as noisy as the deli, filled with honking cars and people bustling in every direction. She scanned the sidewalk, but there was no sign of the young woman.

Kate walked to the corner and stopped, staring down each street looking for any sign of her.

Nothing.

As Kate cursed and turned back to the deli, she spotted a familiar face across the street.

Ali Brewer, standing near a newsstand.

Kate's stomach lurched.

Ali stood perfectly still, her gaze fixed on the street looking north. It appeared as if she was waiting for someone. Kate moved quickly to the corner, waited impatiently for the walk signal to turn green, and booked it across the street toward Ali. She didn't know what she was going to say or do. The adrenaline pumped through her veins had her moving faster, ignoring the crowd pressing in on all sides.

Kate was three-quarters of the way across the street when a familiar face materialized next to Ali, slicing through the crowd with chilling familiarity. It took Kate a heartbeat to register the young woman's features—short dark hair, lips a vivid shade of red, and eyes that were round and dark. Her posture was confident.

The two women stepped back, retreating under the narrow awning of a corner store, and bent their heads together in a low conversation. Kate hesitated, her shoes barely an inch from the curb. She let the rhythm of the crowd sweep past her, the hum of the city muffling her thoughts, but her eyes never left them. They hadn't noticed her. Not yet. It wasn't surprising, given the bustling chaos around them, but Kate's instincts screamed at her to watch and wait.

Ali's face was unreadable, but the woman standing beside her—Amanda Larson—looked troubled. Her brow was furrowed, her lips drawn tight as she spoke. Ali's gaze darted up from their conversation. Her eyes swept over the street, a flash of recognition passing too quickly for Kate to catch. Then, just as quickly, she dropped her gaze back to Amanda, but not before something shifted in her expression, a subtle but unmistakable shift. Concern, maybe.

Kate stopped breathing for a moment, lost in watching the two. She didn't know what was happening with them, but her gut told her that this was more than just a casual encounter between student and teacher.

"What happened?" Declan asked, suddenly at her side, breaking the trance.

Kate hesitated for only a moment before grabbing him by the hand and pulling him up on the sidewalk in the other direction, out of sight from Ali and Amanda. She quickly explained about the note in her pocket, then the chance encounter seeing Ali on the street. "She was waiting for someone, then all of a sudden, Amanda is standing there. Their exchange was intense, more than a discussion about a paper or a grade. The way they leaned into one another when they were speaking, there was familiarity there. We need to follow Amanda and see where she's going."

Kate stepped back out from around the corner in enough time to see Ali and Amanda start down the street. Kate moved into a crowd of people going in the same direction. They made it about two blocks when Ali left off to the right and Amanda kept going.

Kate's shoes slapped the cold pavement with a steady rhythm as she and Declan moved in tandem, their eyes locked on the young woman ahead. Her breath came in short bursts, misting in the chill of the late autumn afternoon. The city felt alive around them, but to Kate, it was as though everything had narrowed to Amanda's every move, every twist and turn. Kate fixed on the quick gait of her walk, the way she kept one hand on her phone and the other swung freely at her side. She didn't look around her, seemed to have no idea she was being followed.

Declan kept pace beside Kate, his face set in that grim determination that matched her own. The last few days had been a blur of dead ends, false leads, and frustrations, but now – now, they had a chance. "She's moving fast," he muttered, his voice low.

Kate's heart was thudding in her chest, every beat urging her forward. She could feel the adrenaline creeping into her bloodstream, heightening her senses, sharpening every detail. Amanda hadn't spotted them yet, and Kate wasn't about to let that happen.

They crossed the street without a second thought, dodging a yellow cab and the rush of pedestrians. Amanda's pace didn't slow. Kate's muscles were coiled, every step purposeful as she closed the gap between them.

All at once Amanda stopped dead on the sidewalk, forcing other pedestrians to step around her. She looked at her phone then ducked into an alley. Kate moved quickly, hoping that Amanda didn't realize she was being tailed. She peeked around the corner and watched as Amanda's shoulders brushed the narrow walls. Kate hesitated for only a split second before following. Declan mirrored her, but the alley was tight, forcing them to slow their pace and move in single file. If Amanda turned, she'd see them. Kate's eyes stayed locked on Amanda's back, a bead of sweat slipping down her neck despite the cold.

Amanda burst from the alley onto 5th Avenue, weaving through a crowd. Kate rushed to close the distance, her eyes never left her target, watching the subtle shift of Amanda's body as she began to pick up speed again. There was something frantic in the way she moved now, something different – she was either about to make a break for it, or she was going to slip into a hiding spot.

"She's heading to the subway," Declan said, his eyes scanning the street ahead.

The streets of Manhattan had started to close in around her, the crowds parting to let Amanda pass, and Kate could feel her pulse hammering in her temples. She was too close now to let this slip through her fingers. The subway entrance loomed ahead. For the first time, Amanda glanced over her shoulder, possibly catching sight of them.

Kate held her breath for the young woman's next move.

Amanda only quickened her pace.

"I think she saw us," Kate said through gritted teeth.

As Amanda reached the entrance, she darted down the steps, the sound of her footsteps ringing in the hollow stairwell. Kate's stomach churned with the cold dread of losing her.

Declan cursed, his voice carrying down the staircase as they followed. The sound of a train rumbling in the distance grew louder.

They reached the bottom of the stairs in time to see Amanda slip through the turnstiles. Kate's heart hammered in her chest. "We can't let her disappear down there."

"Split up," Declan said quickly, eyes scanning the platform. "I'll take the far side. You cover the near."

Kate nodded. She could hear the distant screech of the train, its metal-on-metal cry sending a spike of panic through her. As Kate stepped forward swiping her card and moving through the turnstile, she froze. Amanda was nowhere to be seen. She glanced to her left, but the platform stretched in both directions, dark and empty save for a few people waiting for trains. Her breath caught in her throat.

The hum of a train grew louder, the wind from its approach ruffling her hair. As the train screeched into the station, the faintest shadow moved in the dim corner of her eye. Amanda moved out from behind one of the large pillars into view.

As the train screeched to a stop, the doors opened and Amanda rushed toward the train car. Kate rushed for it too watching down the platform where Declan did the same.

As the doors to the subway car closed, it was only then that Amanda saw Kate right in front of her, a flick of recognition in her eyes. For one heart-stopping moment, neither of them moved. Then, Amanda turned, eyes wild, as if she had been cornered – her body coiled with the tension of a trapped animal.

"There's nowhere to go, Amanda," Declan said, approaching from her back. "We only want to speak to you."

Kate took a tentative step toward her, the other passengers watching them. "We've been trying to find you. You haven't been to class. You haven't been back to where you live."

Amanda's lips curled into a bitter smile, but there was fear behind her eyes.

"You've got nowhere to run," Kate said, her voice tight with resolve.

"I don't have anything to say to you."

"I think you do," Kate said calmly, noticing how the young woman trembled the closer Kate got.

"I can't talk to you." Amanda swallowed hard. "You don't understand."

"I want to understand. I think I can help you." Kate caught Declan's eyes and she communicated with just a look. They weren't letting Amanda off this train without them, even if it meant formally detaining her. "We saw you at the hotel the night Marty Nubeck was murdered. You were there with two women and we saw you following his security to the elevators. We have more than enough information on you, Amanda. You're only hope is talking to us."

For a moment, Amanda just stood there, her chest rising and falling in rapid succession. Then she deflated. "Fine, I'm headed to my aunt's house in Brooklyn. I'll speak to you there."

"You're making a good decision," Kate assured her.

CHAPTER 26

Amanda sat at a small round table in her aunt's second-floor brownstone flat in Brooklyn's Park Slope neighborhood. She lived on Garfield Place in a well-kept brownstone on a tree-lined street. Kate and Declan would have never found Amanda here. The aunt was by marriage, and even though she had divorced Amanda's uncle thirteen years ago, the two women had remained close.

"My aunt isn't going to be home for another hour, so while I have some time, I don't have a lot," Amanda said, crossing her arms. "What is it you want to know? I admit I was at that hotel with some women I know. We were at the bar. As far as I know, there is no crime in that."

Off the street in an environment where she was comfortable, Kate noticed an edge about the young woman she hadn't seen before. The fear that was in her eyes in the subway was replaced with defiance. "Why aren't you staying at your brownstone?" Kate wanted information first and she wasn't going to go straight for the kill. She wanted Amanda loose-lipped and talking.

Amanda's eyes darted to the side in a sure sign of lying. "There's some work being done. I didn't want to breathe in all that dust."

"Interesting. Because we were by there the other night and there was a group of women there to meet with you. I guess maybe the work just started."

Amanda cast her eyes back to Kate. "This morning."

"I see," Kate said, sensing already that truth wasn't going to be something on the menu. "What about your classes? You've been missing those, too. Construction in your classrooms?"

Amanda raked her tongue across her teeth. "I'm taking a few days off. Life has been a bit hectic."

"Sure, serial homicide will do that. It's a lot to keep up with, I imagine."

Declan rubbed his nose to hide his smile behind his hand. He knew Kate didn't like liars, especially ones that did it so poorly. "Amanda," he said her name slowly, drawing her attention to him. "Agent Walsh isn't going to play games with you. She interrogates serial killers and terrorists for a living and she's quite good at it. She knows you're lying. I only have half of her skill and I know you're lying. Stop wasting our time."

Amanda sucked in a sharp breath. "I've been avoiding school."

"Why?" Kate asked, her tone no-nonsense.

"There are some people there I don't want to see. I had some issues with some girls. I needed a break."

"What was the issue?" Kate knew she was now only getting some half-truths. It was better than nothing. When Amanda didn't respond, she asked, "Does it have anything to do with Ali Brewer?"

Amanda's head snapped to attention. "Did you see us speaking on the street?"

"I did and it appeared tense. I know she's one of your professors this semester. This is your second class with her. Do you have a relationship outside of class?"

Amanda lowered her head, staring straight down at the table. "She's been trying to recruit me for a while."

"Recruit you for what?"

"Protests and stuff. She knows I have an interest in women's rights."

Amanda raised her head and looked right at Kate. "She's been trying to get me to go to meetings she has with other like-minded women."

"What happens at these meetings?"

"I don't know," Amanda said with a shake of her head. "I only went to one and it was an introduction of sorts. There were probably fifty women there, all from the college. Ali, that's what she asked us to call her, talked about protesting for reproductive rights and other issues. She said there were things we could be more involved in on and off campus to help the cause."

Kate studied her carefully to see if there were any of the hallmarks of her lying. She didn't see any. "What kinds of things could you be involved in on and off campus?"

Amanda raised her shoulders in a shrug. "There were things like lecture series and being involved politically with student elections and administrative changes. Most of the things on campus were pretty routine on any college campus. It was the things off campus that turned me off."

"What were those activities?" Kate asked, her patience growing thin. She wanted to get to the meat of it but didn't want to jump the gun.

"Protests. Targeting local government for political change. That's not my thing." Amanda stared off past Kate, the disinterest evident in her eyes.

"You've been involved in protests before," Kate reminded her.

"Not anymore."

Kate didn't mince words. "What do you know about the Midnight Lilies?"

Amanda shifted her head ever-so-slightly to the side, her hair covering part of her face. "I've never heard of them."

"You're lying." Kate leaned her arms on the table. "You've heard of them and you might even be among them. They have killed several men, Amanda. Several podcast hosts and a congressman. Marty

Nubeck was murdered at the hotel on the same night you were there."

Amanda's expression didn't shift. If anything, it became colder, her eyes narrowing slightly. "I don't see how that's relevant."

"I'll tell you how it's relevant. You were seen at the hotel the night of the murder. You were in that bar alone when the other women left, coincidentally, when his security settled in. Then you watched them and remained there until you followed Nubeck's security to the elevator. You're also connected to Ali Brewer."

Amanda's lips twitched, like she was suppressing a smile, but it didn't reach her eyes. "Ali Brewer has never been involved in anything illegal."

Kate kept her gaze locked on Amanda. "You expect me to believe that? A group of women killing men for their so-called sins, and Ali Brewer is just a bystander in all of it? You're connected to her, Amanda. And you're connected to this whole mess."

Amanda's breath hitched for a second, just barely. "That night wasn't anything special. We were just at the bar. Having drinks. Nothing else. I don't know anything about Marty Nubeck's death. I wasn't watching his security. If I followed them out, it was a coincidence. Nothing more. The whole thing is nothing special."

"It wasn't nothing," Declan said, his tone sharp. "A man's murder, even for as horrific as he was said to behave with women, isn't nothing. Why were you at the hotel?"

Amanda didn't answer right away. Kate could see her calculating the next move. But there was hesitation in her eyes. "Look, my friend Emily, her husband has been cheating on her. We were there at the hotel to see if we could catch them. When Emily and a friend of hers, Jessica something or other, who I don't know that well, walked off, they asked me to stay. They said there could be a confrontation and didn't want me to be a part of it. They asked me to wait in the bar, both to avoid the confrontation and to see if I spotted him in case he wasn't in the room. That's what we had been doing, waiting at the bar to see if they were coming down. Emily didn't want to wait anymore."

"We're going to need to confirm this with Emily." Kate wasn't sure if she believed her or not. It was exactly what Ditch had said earlier. There could be truth to it, but Kate wasn't so sure.

"No," Amanda responded emphatically. "I'm not giving you Emily's information. She's been through enough."

"Did she catch her husband that night?" Declan asked, causing Amanda to glance over at him.

Amanda shook her head. "They weren't in the room. That's why they called me. I met them upstairs to strategize. Maybe he was at dinner, or maybe the texts she had read were wrong. We ended up leaving the hotel shortly after. I'm not giving you her information. Not if you think we murdered someone. I heard about the murder on television. I don't know Marty Nubeck, didn't see him at the hotel that night, and have never met him."

"You were texting someone right before following them out. Who did you text?"

Amanda shrugged it off. "I don't remember. A friend probably."

Kate tried asking a few more questions about that night. Amanda had a steely resolve and said nothing more, not even the husband's name. They'd have no way to corroborate the story. Kate told Amanda that and she didn't seem to care.

Amanda's breath came out in a sharp exhale. "I can't believe you think I'm involved with this. Do I look like someone who could kill a man?"

Kate leaned back, studying her face. "I think you're definitely involved. I think you know exactly what's been happening, and I think you've been playing a role in it. You and your professor, Ali Brewer. You're all part of the Midnight Lilies, aren't you?"

Amanda's lips parted, her jaw tightening as though the words were trapped behind her teeth. "I'm not involved in any murders. I'm not involved with any of the violence."

Kate believed she was telling the truth about that. She wasn't involved in any of the violence. "We know there are multiple people involved in various roles to make these murders happen. Maybe you're a lookout or involved in the planning. I don't know your role. All I know for certain is that you're involved."

Amanda's face grew red and she balled her fists on the table. She stared down at Kate, her voice growing low. "You have it all wrong. Everything you think you know about the Midnight Lilies is wrong."

Kate didn't immediately respond. She wanted Amanda to catch her own mistake. Kate sat back and appraised her. "If you're not connected to them, then how do you know about them?"

"I…" she stumbled over her words.

"You've already implicated yourself." Kate still didn't think they had enough for a warrant, but they had enough to bring her into FBI headquarters for formal questioning. "You're either going to tell us here or we are going to the FBI office for an official interview."

"I'm not involved," Amanda said, trying to dig herself out of the hole. "I just know things from what people have told me. I can't verify any of it. I don't even know if it's true."

"What do you know?" Kate asked.

Amanda looked between Kate and Declan. "Should I ask for immunity or something? Maybe I need to speak with a lawyer."

"That's certainly your right," Declan assured her, pushing his chair back as if to stand. "If you know something and there's another murder while you're delaying, the charges against you are going to go up."

The silence stretched out longer than it should have. Amanda's eyes flicked to the side, her fingers tapping rhythmically on the table. But when her gaze met Kate's again, there was something hard in them, something that wasn't there before.

"You're wasting your time," Amanda finally said, her voice calm, almost too calm. "You can't arrest me based on assumptions. You don't have anything. Just theories and those aren't even correct." She tipped her head back and held her chin out. "I'm not involved with any of this, but at least someone is finally fighting back. Men need to stop."

"Stop what?" Declan asked.

Amanda snorted as she turned her vitriol on him. Her nostrils flared and her words came out in a sharp staccato. "Stop what? Are you kidding me? Stop attacking us. Raping us. Beating their wives and their children. Do you know most women can't even walk down the streets in the dark without fear of being attacked and it's not an irrational fear. In college, we have to go to parties in packs and watch our drinks so someone doesn't slip something in. We are always on guard and we are exhausted. It's time the men who are not only committing such acts but encouraging this kind of toxic behavior be afraid too, more afraid than we are."

She turned and pointed at Kate. "I'd think of all people to understand this, it would be you. You're a woman. You're one of us. You can't sit there and tell me you were never sexually harassed at the FBI. You were never assaulted on campus or off. Let them continue until every one of them is dead."

Kate swallowed down a mix of emotions she couldn't recognize. "We will not let them continue, Amanda. These murders are horrific. The torture, murder, and the aftermath. I understand that women have been victims. I even understand the exhaustion and the need to fight back. This is something on a whole other level, and we will not let it continue. Do you understand me? We will hunt down every single one of these women and bring them to justice. Now, you have two options – keep quiet and we will come for you too or tell us what you know and we will consider you an asset in this case."

Amanda remained silent.

Kate leaned into the table and stared coldly at Amanda, not breaking eye contact. "I suggest that you cooperate with the FBI. The one thing I never do is give up on a case. I don't fold or capitulate to fear or intimidation. Let me warn you about something else. Agent James was threatened. If any harm comes to him, you will have to deal with me. And I will kill you without thinking twice. Forget the justice system. I don't need this job. I have more money than I will ever use. I'll spend the rest of my life seeking my justice against every single one of you."

Kate shoved her chair back so forcefully, it scraped along the floor and rocked the table in front of her. She didn't wait for Declan. A fire that had been out in her lit up again. It roared to life.

"You understand the feeling they are trying to instill," Amanda said to her back.

Kate didn't turn, but she stopped in the doorway. She didn't acknowledge that Amanda was probably right.

Amanda continued. "I was being honest that I've only heard things. I don't know anything with certainty. What you saw on the street today was Ali's fifth attempt at recruiting me. She runs the Midnight Lilies and most of the women involved were once victims. She has a knack for spotting that in us and seeking us out. I don't know who is involved other than Ali. It's like a cult. She has total control over her followers and they are willing to kill for her. That's all I know, I swear to you."

Kate didn't turn to acknowledge anything Amanda said. She wasn't sure if Amanda was telling her the truth. As she headed for the door, Kate heard Declan thank her for the information and tell her they'd be in touch.

CHAPTER 27

Kate yanked open the door and let it slam behind her. She sucked in fresh air like she hadn't tasted that kind of freedom in decades. She allowed the sun to warm her face while she marched down the street back toward the subway entrance. She was hot, a mix of anger and frustration, and she knew she wasn't being rational. Something about Amanda's dismissiveness had galled her. The way the young woman justified the actions of the Midnight Lilies, daring to ask Kate to let them continue as a bonding of sisterhood.

Kate had never heard something so ridiculous – yet, down deep in a place she didn't want to acknowledge, she understood Amanda's argument for the Midnight Lilies. She knew of cases where a woman killed her abusive husband and she was sent to prison. Another woman who had fought back while she was being raped and killed her attacker only to have manslaughter charges pressed against her. Sometimes, liberty and justice didn't apply to all.

Kate understood the Midnight Lilies in a way she wished she didn't.

"What was that, Kate?" Declan called after her, jogging up to meet her. When she didn't turn, he grabbed her arm, stopping her and turning her toward him. "What was that back there? You threatened to kill people aloud and forcefully. Are you trying to lose your job?"

Kate shook free from his grasp. "She deserved it. She lied so much that I don't even know if what she said at the end was true. I wanted to bring her in right now. We don't have enough. She didn't name anyone but Ali and she's already on our radar. We know she was in the hotel that night and that's all we know. We can't arrest based on that."

Kate realized she was out of breath. She controlled her breathing, tucking her hair behind her ears. "They need to know we are serious. They threatened you. They threatened to kill an FBI agent. I was deadly serious about what I said. They can't go after you without getting through me."

Declan's features softened and he handed her coat to her that she had left in the deli. He helped her put it on as he said, "Katie, we get threatened on nearly every case. It's like any other Tuesday. I know you love me. This is personal and professional, but you never lose your cool like that. Come on, what's going on?"

Kate turned away from him, wrapping her arms around herself as she walked toward the subway station. When he caught up to her, he put his hand on her back. Kate turned her head to look up at him. "I don't know how I feel about this case. I've been saying that all along. I get why they are doing what they are doing. I think what Amanda was trying to tell us is that it's personal for these women. I have to assume many of them, if not all, are victims of crime in some way. That makes it different for me."

"How?" Declan asked. When Kate didn't respond, he pressed her. "Nearly every serial killer we have been up against had a crappy childhood. There was trauma from adults around them. That's not every serial killer, but it's a lot of them. It's never been a factor before now. As far as Amanda goes, I don't know if we should believe her or not."

Kate gestured back toward the house. "The way she tells it, Ali has been trying to recruit her and that was the anger on the street. Why would Ali need her that badly? If Ali is behind this, she has the women she needs. There'd be no reason to work that hard to recruit someone who doesn't want in. That's more of a liability than a help. She's hiding something – she knows more."

Declan shook his head. "I don't think you're going to get it out of her."

Kate didn't think they would either. "We have bigger things to worry about. The meeting tonight at the White Art Gallery is under threat." Kate handed him the note. "Someone bumped into me on the way into the deli. I think they put that into my coat. That place was so crammed with people, I didn't think much of her bumping into me. No one else had access to my jacket and no one else was that close to me all day. I cleaned out the pockets this morning."

Declan took the crumpled piece of square paper. He lowered his head to read, cursing at the words. "We are going to need to get the bomb techs over there to sweep the place." He raised his head to look at Kate. "I assume you believe this is real."

"I think we have to believe it's real. This is going to be a gathering of many potential targets of the Midnight Lilies in a space that supports men like that. Patrice White was having an affair with Marty Nubeck. It's the perfect target for them to take out many at once. Plus, it would make a big enough splash in the press. We've dealt with a bombing in Manhattan before. It might not just be the people in the gallery hurt, but who knows what else around them."

"You don't have to convince me." Declan glanced over at the subway entrance. "Do you think we should connect with Ditch to see if he can get surveillance video inside that deli or out on the street? He might be able to pick up the person on surveillance."

Kate didn't remember the person's face. She had a sense they were a woman or a small man. "Jeans and a black hoodie with the hood pulled up. I couldn't pick them out of a lineup if I had to, Declan. It was a blur of people and it happened fast. We can call Ditch, but I don't want to take him off other work that might yield better results."

"Fair enough." Declan pulled out his phone and placed a call to the FBI office in Manhattan. He got an agent on the phone who could help them and explained about the gallery and the threat. By the time the call was over, Declan had secured a bomb squad team to meet him at the gallery within an hour.

"I don't think Patrice is going to be happy we are heading there." Before she could say anything else, her cellphone vibrated in her pocket. "It's Ditch," she told Declan as she answered.

"I have an address for you," Ditch said in a rush of breath. He started going into the techie part of his work and how he found the address.

"Skip all that and get to the point."

"Where are you?" he asked.

"Street in Brooklyn. I know it's noisy. Just tell me what you found. You said you were able to trace the hack on the street cameras using backdoor something or other. What did you find?"

"As I said before, it was going to be sophisticated and it was." Ditch continued to explain how the hack happened even as Kate grew more and more frustrated. "I have an address for you in Brooklyn. It's at the Brooklyn Navy Yard at one of the warehouses. Given the nature of the hack, she probably has a whole operation over there. I looked up information and those warehouses are for rent. Who knows, Kate, they could be running their entire operation from there."

"Is there any name on the rental agreement?" Kate knew Ditch had done more research than just finding the address.

"Yeah," he said slowly with a chuckle. "It's a little telling. It's ML Corp. I assume they weren't even trying to hide the Midnight Lilies' name. But that's all that's there and it's a dummy corp. There's no website or actual name that I can find attached to anything. I can keep digging."

"Keep digging." Kate went to hang up but stopped herself. "I have something else for you, too. Don't spend much time on this," she cautioned him, then explained what happened to her in the deli. "Black hoodie and jeans."

"I can see if there are any cameras in the area and if they are working. If this woman is trying to help you, then the Midnight Lilies might not have known to turn the cameras off at that time."

Kate hadn't considered that with everything else on her mind. "If you can access it, great. If not, don't waste time on it. Even if we get this person on video, I can't prove they are the one who dropped me the note and we'd still have to identify them. It's low priority."

Ditch promised her he'd be in touch soon.

Kate shoved her phone back in her pocket. "Let's go visit Patrice."

Kate and Declan stood in the center of the gallery, waiting for Patrice. They had walked through the propped-open door, which was letting the cool breeze into the sleek interior of the gallery. The center table that had been there just days ago had been moved and replaced with a chair-like sculpture of a half-human, half-goat type figure poised just about the base. It wasn't sitting but rather looked like it was captured mid-sit. Its right half of the body was the human side with the left the goat. The face of the animal-human beast was disturbing.

"That's terrifying looking," Declan commented, wrinkling up his nose at the bronze piece of art. "It almost looks like…" He didn't finish his thought, mostly because he seemed to have no words for it. He pointed to the ceiling. "Is the space where the meeting is tonight on the second floor?"

Kate assumed so. The high ceilings that stretched endlessly upward didn't seem to give way to accommodate a second floor, but she knew that's what Patrice had told her. "There is also a third floor where she keeps some living space."

"I knocked out the second floor, if that's what you're questioning," Patrice said, walking into the space from around the corner. "The beams you see around the gallery floor are the new support structures." She extended her hand to Declan and the two introduced themselves. "I'm sure you're not here to discuss the construction or the art, for that matter. How can I help the FBI now?" Her tone had a slight exasperation that Kate ignored.

Kate didn't bother explaining. She simply handed over the note that was now in an evidence bag, thanks to Declan always being prepared. "I was given this earlier today by an anonymous person. I believe the person who slipped this into my pocket bumped into me at a deli. I assume they had been watching us and waiting for the right time."

Patrice lowered her head to read the note through the plastic. "This can't be real." She lifted her eyes to Kate. "You can't seriously think that someone is going to bomb the meeting tonight. That's preposterous."

"Is it though?" Kate asked, feeling sympathy for the woman for the first time. She might have been a pretentious art gallery owner, but she had lost someone she loved and now her life was in danger. "You've seen what they are doing. There have been five murders so far. They got to Nubeck in a hotel with top-notch security while his security team was nearby. We have a tech expert, a hacker, who was one of the best in the world. He calls what this group is doing with tech sophisticated. We are doing everything we can to find out who is responsible. But, yes, we believe this is a credible threat. Our bomb experts are on their way to sweep the place."

Patrice seemed to relax into that idea. "You're not asking me to cancel the meeting?"

"I think you should cancel," Declan said. "Of course, we can't tell you to do that. It's our recommendation. At least with the bomb squad going through it affords you some safety. You're making yourself a target by holding the meeting here and by aligning yourself with these men."

"There's still free speech in this country."

Kate didn't want a battle on her hands. "There is and you're entitled to your opinion and your right to host any meeting you want in your gallery. I think what Agent James is saying is that the threat is significant and these women won't hesitate to come after you if they think you're aligning yourself with these men. This evening's salon is gathering many of the Midnight Lilies' potential targets all in one place. If the meeting happens, you are risking their lives, your own, and this entire building. The choice is yours."

Patrice licked her lips nervously and shifted her eyes back and forth as if thinking about where a bomb could be hidden. "Do you think the bomb is already here? Am I in danger now?"

"We don't know," Kate said, trying to make sure Patrice remained calm. "What I suggest is that we get out of the building, send your staff home for the day, and close up. This way, the bomb squad can have access to everything. You can then decide from there if the meeting should go on here tonight. You might want to consider another venue, something that hasn't been publicized, if you want the meeting to happen."

Patrice held her hand up to stop Kate. "I will do all of that. The jury is still out on tonight's meeting. Let's see what, if anything, the bomb squad finds. I don't think it's possible to move the meeting at this time. There are only a few hours until people start arriving."

Kate understood the challenge. "Let me just issue you one warning. If you don't tell the people coming about the threat after the bomb squad clears the place and something happens, the liability is on you." She gestured around the space. "Not to mention the collection of art that you're housing here. I don't think the artist whose work this is would like that you're risking their livelihood for the sake of this meeting."

"Understood," Patrice responded in a clipped tone. "Let me clear my staff and we can go from there. The apartment on the top floor is mine. I don't think anyone could access it to leave a bomb, but I'll certainly give you access to it. I have nothing to hide."

With that she turned on her heels and walked away, leaving Kate and Declan to wait for the bomb squad.

CHAPTER 28

Late that evening, Kate sat with the team in the conference room her hotel provided them. She needed a better base of operations from the outside world and other law enforcement. Things had been leaked to the press and Kate didn't trust anyone other than those sitting in front of her – Declan, Sharon, and Leo. Ditch wasn't meeting with them but he was on the list of who Kate had put her faith in.

The bomb squad had searched the White Art Gallery from top to bottom and found nothing. No trace of any bomb or bomb making materials. They had the dogs in there and still found nothing. Kate didn't know what to make of the note she had been slipped. Neither did her team.

"Do you think it was a fake?" Leo asked after Kate explained the events of the day.

"I have no idea why someone would risk bumping into me and dropping a note if it was fake. It's possible they hadn't planted the bomb yet and have been watching the gallery. Maybe they knew we'd call in the bomb squad and were waiting until they left to plant it. It's one of the reasons I didn't question Amanda about it. I didn't want her to tip them off. I warned Patrice about not going forward with the meeting. She insists they will be fine, especially since she shut the gallery down for the day."

Declan shook his head in disgust. "We tried hard to get her to change her mind. We suggested an alternative meeting place. I said send an email to all those coming and let them know of the change. If they were quiet enough about it, then they'd be safe to still meet. Meeting at the gallery under an active bomb threat, even though we swept it, is insane."

Kate couldn't agree more.

"What's the plan now?" Leo asked, sitting at the far end of the table, watching them.

Declan turned toward him. "We have a raid on the warehouse that Ditch found. We have the FBI SWAT team joining us tonight."

"What do you hope is going to be there?" Leo asked, not having been briefed about what Ditch had told them earlier. "I can't see a bunch of women sitting around a warehouse by the docks."

Kate confirmed that he was right. "Ditch believes the person pulling the tech strings is going to have their base of operations there. He found that they were able to hack the hotel surveillance system to control it remotely as well as tap into the city surveillance system. Ditch found that where there was surveillance, at the time of the murders, surveillance on the surrounding streets was cut. He told us that it had to be someone who had some sophisticated knowledge."

Leo nodded. "I had a person like that on my team. He was critical for many reasons."

"Hackers are the worst," Sharon said with a laugh. "Always stealing data and messing up electrical grids. We have to worry about having power and water because they could take down entire systems."

"It's exactly why we have Ditch on our team," Kate reminded her. "He's the best in the world and it's better we keep him busy on more productive tasks."

Leo hitched his jaw toward Declan. "What can I do to help tonight?"

Kate and Declan had talked about that before. While Kate had been planning to meet with the group gathered at the gallery, she had called it off, given the raid of the warehouse and the active bomb threat. They certainly weren't going to ask Leo to cover for that, but they had something else in mind.

Declan responded. "I want to know if you'd be willing to meet with the people going into the meeting and warn them about the Midnight Lilies, the bomb threat, and the murders. These people need to know what they are walking into. While I believe Patrice when she said she'd tell them, I can't believe anyone in their right mind would still show up. This meeting can't be that important, even if people traveled here for it."

Leo agreed. "Do you want me to go in or just on the street?"

"Don't go in under any circumstances," Kate said, a bit of worry creeping into her voice. "We don't want to put you at risk. The farther you can stand back from the building the better. I just want an FBI presence there on the street. I'm hoping it might deter the Midnight Lilies while at the same time ensuring we are covering ourselves. We asked Patrice for a list of the attendees and she refused to give it to us. We are a little stuck here, but at the same time, I don't want to put you in any unnecessary risk."

Leo readily agreed. "Is there anything you want to know from them? I'm not the trained interrogator, but I know how to question people."

Before Kate could respond, Declan did. "If you're able to find out if they have been threatened like the others, that's important to know. We will know which of them have been targeted already. Find out the nature of the threat, if they still have the evidence and what they are doing about it."

Leo cast his eyes at Kate. He was smart enough not to ask if what Declan said was okay. He simply asked, "Is there anything else you want to know?"

Kate shook her head, not sure how she was feeling about Leo going that far. "Declan covered it all. But again, stay as far away from that building as you can. We have eyes on the place, but who knows what these women will do."

Leo assured her that he wouldn't go inside or stand too close. "I'll be as far away as I can to get the job done." With that Leo left and Sharon said she was headed back to the lab. There were so many samples to still go through from all the crime scenes. It was like looking for a needle in a haystack.

When they were finally alone, Declan turned to Kate. "Are you ready for tonight?"

"As ready as I think we are going to get. I think with this group, we have to prepare for anything."

Even though the night air was cool, sweat pooled at Kate's back. She adjusted her black tactical vest, fingers tightening on the straps, as she crouched behind the large shipping container near the entrance to the warehouse. Her breath was steady, the rhythmic pulse of adrenaline thrumming through her veins as she and Declan surveyed the scene.

The faint hum of distant city lights seemed muffled by the pounding of her heart in her ears. The wind rustled through the metal of the container she hid behind, and the water slapped against the concrete pylons of the dock.

The warehouse loomed at the end of the pier, a hulking structure of rusted steel and faded brick. Its sagging roof seemed barely held together. The walls were scarred with streaks of grime, a testament to their years of exposure to the harsh winds and constant battering of the East River. Weather-beaten windows, their glass long gone, stood as empty eye sockets – silent witnesses to the decay inside. A few lights glowed on the second floor. She saw no movement inside.

A dull gray mist clung to the air, swirling off the river and wrapping around the building like an omen. The pier beneath it creaked with the rhythm of the water's ebb and flow, its wooden planks splintered and rotting. Long-forgotten cargo containers sat in disarray nearby, their rusted exteriors as beaten as the warehouse itself.

A faint smell of diesel and brine lingered in the air, mingling with the scent of wet wood and decay. The hum of distant traffic from the Brooklyn-Queens Expressway was a dull background noise, almost swallowed by the oppressive silence that hung over the pier.

Declan's voice was low, calm, and steady as he finished speaking to the SWAT team. She could feel the years of experience in his tone. "SWAT's already in position," he said to her with the look he always gave her before a mission like this. It was one of great admiration and a promise that he would always have her back.

Declan said, "They're set. We move in on your mark."

Kate nodded, eyes narrowing as she glanced across the darkened waterfront. The warehouse was still. Too still. Her instincts prickled, a low hum at the back of her mind telling her something wasn't right. But they couldn't waste time second-guessing themselves.

She signaled to Declan to stay low, and they moved forward, slipping through the shadows like ghosts, silent as they approached the warehouse's back entrance. She could feel the weight of the gun on her hip, the cool metal of the flashlight in her hand. Every step was calculated. Every movement deliberate.

The team was already in place, crouched at the edge of the building, ready for her signal. Kate held up three fingers and then pointed to the door. Declan gave her a brief nod, acknowledging the plan. She didn't need to speak. They'd been through this hundreds of times before. They knew each other like the backs of their hands.

Her heart steadily beat. She was running on planning and practice. She reached into her pocket and pulled out the small device that would cut the power. A simple flick of the switch, and the building would go dark.

She checked her watch – midnight on the dot.

"On my go," Kate said in a breath. Her hand hovered over the switch.

The seconds dragged by, each one a ticking clock in her mind. Declan was already moving into position, crouching by the side of the door, his weapon drawn.

"Ready?" he asked, his voice low, barely above a whisper.

"Go."

With the flick of her wrist, the building plunged into darkness. The floodlights on the pier flickered for a moment before they, too, went black. The world outside the warehouse dissolved into inky blackness, leaving only the pale glow of Kate's flashlight to guide them.

They were in.

The SWAT team's heavy footsteps echoed behind them as they moved deliberately. Kate led the way, crouching low, the beam of her flashlight sweeping across the walls, illuminating the steel skeleton of the warehouse.

The floor creaked beneath their boots as they advanced deeper into the building, weaving around stacks of metal crates and abandoned shipping containers. The familiar scent of rust and mildew mixed with the underlying tang of oil and steel. There were no sounds of scurrying feet or hissing air vents – just the distant hum of machinery somewhere deep in the belly of the building.

Kate stopped at the corner of a long corridor, scanning the area ahead. She raised her hand in a fist, signaling the team to halt. Declan moved up beside her, his eyes darting back and forth.

"Nothing here," he muttered, his breath clouding in the damp air. "No signs of life. Could be we're too late."

Kate nodded toward the far end of the corridor, where a large metal door stood half-open. "There next."

They moved again, slowly, cautiously. The door creaked open as they approached. Kate swept her flashlight inside, her gaze quickly scanning the room.

It was empty.

Declan advanced farther into the room and then called back. "Nothing here."

Kate moved toward the far corner, where a small office was tucked away. The smell of old coffee and cigarette smoke clung to the air. There was a chair knocked over on the floor. She pulled the drawers out and saw nothing then slammed them closed in frustration.

"We've got nothing," Kate muttered. But something in the back of her mind told her to keep going, to keep looking. There had to be something – something they were missing.

Then she heard it.

A faint ticking sound.

It was so quiet at first, so subtle, that she almost missed it. But there it was again.

Tick. Tick. Tick.

Her blood ran cold. Her eyes locked on the floor beneath the desk. There, tucked against the far wall, was something metallic, something that didn't belong. A small, cylindrical object, covered in wires and blinking lights.

A bomb.

Around it were scattered black lilies.

Kate's heart slammed in her chest.

"Declan…" she whispered, voice tight with panic.

Declan was at her side in an instant, his expression hardening as he took in the sight. He immediately dropped to one knee, his hand reaching for the small device.

He whispered a curse. "It's rigged. We don't have time to disarm this thing."

Kate's mind was racing. They had no time to waste. The team had already cleared the outer rooms. They had to get out now, or they wouldn't make it out at all.

"Back out, now!" she barked. "Move, move, move!"

She turned, her heart pounding in her chest as the seconds ticked away. The sound of the ticking bomb echoed in her ears, a cold reminder that time was slipping through her fingers.

The team bolted into motion, retreating down the hall with all the speed and precision they had trained for. Kate's pulse was hammering as she sprinted toward the exit, Declan right behind her. The sound of the ticking grew louder in her head with every step.

They reached the exit, the SWAT team already outside, the dim light from the streetlamps casting long shadows in the distance.

The ground beneath their feet seemed to shake.

A deafening explosion roared behind them, the shockwave sending them sprawling to the pavement as debris rained down.

Kate's vision swam as she pushed herself to her feet, gasping for air. Declan's voice was distant, shouting something she couldn't hear, but she could see the panic in his eyes as he helped her up.

"Kate, we need to go. Now."

She didn't need to be told twice. She stumbled forward, into the darkness, away from the warehouse – and away from the chaos.

CHAPTER 29

The pressure change from the explosion blocked her hearing. A hum deep inside her head drowned almost all sound. Kate couldn't even really hear what the paramedic standing in front of her, tending to a few superficial wounds, was saying to her. She jiggled her ear and shook her head back and forth, hoping that it would fade. He held up his hand to tell her to stop.

"Be patient," he instructed her as he bandaged up her arm.

Declan had walked out unscathed and so had most of the SWAT team, thankfully. A few of them, like Kate, had cuts and scrapes both from crashing to the concrete outside and flying debris. The explosion wasn't enough to take down the building, but it was enough to blow out windows and cause a cloud of dust, metal, and glass.

Declan had called the bomb squad to have them survey the building again and the surrounding area. He told Kate that he assumed the timer was set to some kind of trip wire, and as they either entered the warehouse or moved through it, they triggered the bomb.

What he didn't know was whether it was meant to kill them or scare them.

Kate wanted to call Leo to make sure that he was okay, but she wouldn't have been able to hear him if she did. She settled for a quick text explaining what was happening and inquiring. She nearly held her breath while waiting for a response. He finally wrote back expressing concern and letting her know that all was well there. The meeting had wrapped up about an hour ago and he was sitting outside the building with an FBI agent as they watched the gallery until Patrice closed up for the night. Leo told Kate he'd meet her in the morning to let her know the specifics of what he'd been told. But he confirmed that a few of the men had received threats.

Kate breathed a sigh of relief that at least all went well there.

Declan finished with one of the SWAT officers and walked over to the ambulance, where Kate sat in the back, legs dangling, not quite touching the pavement. He spoke to the paramedic, finding out about Kate's injuries. She could see their lips moving, but the hum overrode any of their words. She shook her head a few more times, trying to pop her ears. She felt a slight shift in her right ear.

Prescription. Doctor. Tetanus.

She heard those words from the paramedic and watched as Declan nodded. Kate assumed she'd need some follow-up medication. She was even wondering if the cut on her arm would need to be stitched. It had seemed deep to her, deeper than a simple bandage would rectify.

Declan helped Kate out of the ambulance. She swayed on her feet slightly, her balance a bit thrown off. Declan raised an eyebrow. "You okay, Kate?"

Kate assured him she was fine, even though she wasn't so sure herself. "You're okay, right?"

"Yeah, I'm okay. I might have pulled my back a little, but nothing that won't be fine by morning. All the guys got out." He gestured toward the group of SWAT officers standing back from the warehouse. "You okay enough to go have a conversation?"

Kate took a few steps on her own, her balance recovering quickly as she settled back into herself. She joined the rest and assured them she was fine. "Was it a trip wire?"

One of the newly arrived bomb experts confirmed. "On the second floor, once you crossed into that outer room, it was set on a timer. We found the wire. Declan said he saw the timer ticking down. It was a small bomb, enough to blow out some windows. Not enough to take down a building like this. You could have been killed had you not gotten out in time. How did you find out about this place?"

Kate explained how Ditch had traced it. "Maybe we should have assumed it would be rigged. Ditch said the address was hard to find. He had to use a considerable amount of skill to find it, so I assumed they'd have no idea we could track it down."

"I don't think you could have known," the bomb expert confirmed. He explained a little more about the bomb and told her his team would sweep the warehouse, collect any evidence, and bring it back to the lab. He pointed down to Kate's arm. "You're bleeding through that bandage. I'd get some stitches if I were you. We have it here. If we find anything, we know how to reach you."

Kate held her arm up to look at the blood that had soaked through. She raised her eyes to Declan. "Hospital?"

He put his arm around her shoulder and guided her to a waiting car. "You don't even have to ask. It's where I planned on taking you next."

More than an hour later, they were in their hotel. Kate had taken a hot shower with her arm wrapped so she wouldn't get her bandages wet. She had needed close to twenty stitches. The doctor warned her that if she didn't take care of it, the gash would leave a terrible scar.

When she was done and wrapped in the hotel's white robe and had towel dried her hair just enough that it no longer dripped on her shoulders, she made her way to the living room where Declan was watching the evening news.

He glanced over at her and patted the couch next to him. "You need to rest. I know it's just a few cuts and bruises, but I'm already feeling some pain from the blast. You're going to be hurting tomorrow, so you better take it easy now."

Kate wasn't going to argue with him. She eased back on the couch and kicked her naked legs up on his lap. She rested her arm on the couch pillow that she propped on her lap. As soon as she allowed herself to feel the safety and comfort and connection with Declan, her eyelids grew heavy.

Kate yawned. "I heard you on the phone while I was getting out of the shower."

Declan lowered the volume on the television. "It was Leo. He called to check on you. He didn't believe you when you said everything was fine. I assured him it was just a bad cut and you'll be okay soon. Sharon was worried too. She and I have been texting back and forth. Ditch apologized but said he had no idea that they'd try to blow us up. He said he's going to dig a little deeper."

"Yeah," Kate said with a non-committal yawn. "I'm sending the bomb squad ahead next time."

"That's probably the best plan." Declan put his hands on Kate's legs, rubbing her gently. "I talked to Leo about his interviews. Patrice had called all the attendees and told them about the bomb threats. Several of the men had received threats in the past couple of months. The biggest challenge is that these men receive so many threats that it's hard for them to tell what's real and what's fake. They are far too cavalier about it."

"They are men who think so little of women that they aren't afraid." Kate yawned and shook off the impending slumber. "They will continue to underestimate them and end up dead. I'm starting to wonder if we can stop them."

Declan stared over at her, his features a mix of concern and something still on his mind. When Kate told him to say whatever it was, he told her that Spade had called them while she was getting stitched up. "He's concerned because we are no closer to solving this than when we started. Because Marty Nubeck is among the victims and these are all high-profile cases, he asked if we were up to the task. Not that the FBI has anyone else to put on it. Spade asked if we needed help. I assured him that we had everything under control. I'm not sure that we have it under control. Spade is right that we aren't any closer. I think we got set up tonight."

Kate had been thinking along the same lines. "Do you think they left the breadcrumbs for Ditch to find or do you think they just happened to rig the place up in case it was found?"

"I think we were set up. We didn't find any computer equipment there. No signs that it would be the hacker's lair. But with the lilies around the bomb, it's clear they were using the location at one point or at least to draw us there and try to kill us. Ditch said it must have been one of the routing addresses, like the ones overseas. Because it ended at the Brooklyn warehouse, he assumed it was the final address where we'd find them. He believes they left him the crumbs to find. I don't want to stress you out any more than you are."

Kate exhaled deeply through her nose. "Just tell me."

"Ditch said their tech expert might even be better than him."

"That's impossible," Kate argued. "There is no one better than him. I can see why he thought it was the end of the path. It was here in Brooklyn, and for all we know, they did use that warehouse."

Kate didn't fault Ditch for what had happened. He found a local address and they were going to check it out no matter what happened. They had been so focused on the bombing at the gallery, they hadn't stopped to consider they might bomb something else.

"No," Kate said after a few moments of contemplation. "They knew what they were doing. I think it was a setup. They wanted us there to hurt us, if not kill us. I'm still struggling to understand who might have given me the warning about the bomb at the gallery and why it was never planted. Even with that, it doesn't lead us to the warehouse."

"You think that's separate? No connection between the two?"

Kate had been trying to figure that out all night. "I need to speak to Ali in the morning. I need to address what Amanda told me. One of them is lying to me. If Ali is the center of all of this, it certainly makes sense. She has access and a wealth of recruitment at her fingertips. She also has a desire to burn down the patriarchy. What better way to do that than to instill terror."

"Would she go after us?"

Kate didn't know the answer to that. She didn't know what kind of chameleon Ali might be. She had seen the woman on the surface, enough Kate hadn't suspected her. It might simply have been a mask. She expressed all of that to Declan, who agreed with her.

Then she added, "I wonder if the person who slipped me the note will try to reach back out. If they are someone who is trying to stop them, they might try again."

"We can only hope. It might have all been a distraction for something bigger."

"What's bigger than blowing up a room full of—" Kate stopped short. She didn't want to jinx them. Declan shot her the same look of caution. It was one of those questions that they just didn't ask in the middle of a case. There was always something bigger that could happen. They talked for a few more minutes and headed off to bed. Kate barely put her head on the pillow before she was out cold.

Kate was dead asleep when the phone started to ring on the bedside table. She rolled over and reached for it only to hear Declan answer his. The clock on the table read 3:28 a.m.

He sat straight up in bed, said, "Yes. Yes. Okay. We will be right there."

Kate was already in an upright position by the time he rolled over. "How bad is it?"

"Five dead at a poker game on the Upper East Side. One of the wealthiest neighborhoods, Kate. Someone walked in there, shot each one of them in the head, and walked back out like nothing had ever happened. The first cop on the scene said he's never seen something like it. There were no signs of struggle. It looks like the men sat there while they were executed. Each of them had black lilies placed over their eyes. Lilies were scattered around the table and the floor, as well as the white limestone steps leading into the home. A neighbor came home from a night out and saw the lilies. He immediately called the police."

"Who lives there?" Kate almost didn't want to ask because she knew it was going to be bad.

"Avery Lancaster. He's the son of—"

Kate held her hand up to stop him. She knew exactly who Avery Lancaster was. He was the son of media mogul Victor Lancaster. The Lancaster family had their hands in everything from oil and real estate to media and banking. Avery was a known playboy in Manhattan. He had graced the covers of magazines for no other reason than his father's wealth and fortune.

"You said there were five murdered," Kate reminded him. "Who else was there with him?"

"The cop wasn't sure. He got to the scene, then immediately backed out. I don't understand why they didn't just call us from the start." Declan went to the closet and started pulling on clothes. He dressed himself, then called Sharon to tell her where to meet them.

Kate tried to hurry as best she could as her arm started to throb. She wanted to take one of the pain pills the doctor had given her, but it would make her fuzzy-headed. That wasn't going to work.

By the time she got ready, Declan was standing at the hotel room door, staring down at his phone with a scowl on his face. Kate knew it wasn't because she was moving slowly.

"What's wrong now?"

Declan held the phone where she could see it. "It's already made the news. CNN is streaming live from outside the Lancaster mansion. Someone called a tip in to the media."

Kate lowered her head to look down at the floor.

These women were beating them in every way possible.

CHAPTER 30

The early morning air in Manhattan's Upper East Side was sharp with the bite of late fall, laced with the faint, metallic tang of cold rain. The streets on the way there were quiet and not yet filled with the rush of morning traffic. They would be soon. Kate checked the time – 4:08 am. They had made good time getting out of the hotel and calling for the car.

As they headed deeper into the Upper East Side, the houses grew more and more monumental. Kate knew that the Lancaster mansion was in a rare row of still standing Gilded Age mansions — the kind that felt too big for the city to be a one family home and made the gleaming glass of nearby skyscrapers look like cheap costume jewelry in comparison.

Kate had grown up with wealth and privilege, but this was something else. This was old money New York. She knew the Lancasters went back generations to the Astors, Rockefellers, and Vanderbilts. The Lancasters had been among them, and they still owned their Gilded Age mansion. It had been passed down through the generations. Instead of having all of their money in the railroads or oil, they had diversified through the years and weathered all the financial downturns. Kate had read online that the Lancasters' wealth was close to eighty billion and that probably hadn't captured all of it.

Kate felt the weight of it all as she stepped out of the black SUV.

The car had barely come to a stop before she was already pushing the door open, her fingers tightening around the doorframe. A blanket of heavy fog from the nighttime rain hung low over the city, wrapping the block in an eerie stillness, but the moment she stepped onto the street, the oppressive quiet was shattered by the flash of camera bulbs and the hum of idling news vans.

A murder in the heart of New York's most exclusive neighborhood was a rarity, but a massacre? That was beyond newsworthy. Kate adjusted the collar of her jacket, and favored her arm, still throbbing in pain, as she walked toward the scene. Declan was beside her as they passed through the throngs of NYPD officers and turned their heads away from the cameras.

They both stopped at the same time to take in the mansion in front of them. It stood like a silent sentinel at the corner of one of Manhattan's most prestigious avenues, its white limestone façade gleaming cold and impervious. It was a towering structure, four stories of opulence and history.

The building's turrets, their stone faces adorned with intricate carvings, jutted out from the corners, rising like watchful spires. They were both ornamental and imposing, a deliberate statement of grandeur. The roofline was crowned with slate tiles, each one placed with meticulous care, and overgrown ivy clung to the brick in a way that seemed to show both age and preservation, untouched by time, yet undeniably steeped in it.

The mansion sat on a double lot, stretching wide across the corner. The grounds were immaculate, with perfectly sculpted hedges, fountains that whispered in the quiet fog of early dawn, and tall wrought-iron gates that gleamed like polished silver under the streetlights. The manicured gardens sprawled outward, their stone walkways neatly arranged and lined with statues of marble, their faces serene and ageless, as if watching over the property for generations.

A wrought-iron fence, designed with delicate filigree and sharp, pointed tips, separated the estate from the street. The gate was left slightly ajar, as if inviting those who passed by to take a glimpse into this world of quiet excess. The house itself seemed to rise above everything around it, its sheer size dwarfing the neighboring mansions, its white stone casting long shadows over the cobblestone street.

On the front steps, a massive wooden door with bronze hinges loomed, intricately carved with designs that hinted at the opulence within. Above it, tall windows gleamed like dark eyes, their curtains drawn but not heavy enough to hide the glimpse of expensive furniture and décor that flickered in the soft light. It was a place designed not just to live, but to be seen – its every corner built to impress, to overwhelm, to remind you of the world it controlled.

There on the steps, quite out of place, begging to be noticed, were the black lilies. Kate understood now why even in the middle of the night, the neighbor had seen them. The grand staircase leading up to the mansion's heavy front doors was flanked on both sides by a thick carpet of black lilies, their deep, velvety petals spreading across each step like a macabre tribute. There were eight steps in total, each one lined with lilies placed with meticulous precision, their dark beauty almost haunting against the pale stone. The rich, obsidian petals seemed to swallow the light, creating a stark contrast against the soft glow of the early morning. It was as if the flowers themselves had been chosen, arranged, and set in place – deliberate, careful, and eerily out of place in such an opulent setting.

Kate muttered a curse under her breath at the horror of what stood in front of them. The scene outside was like something out of a horror movie. She steadied herself for what was to come inside.

A NYPD detective, a tall man with salt-and-pepper hair and a face that had long since forgotten how to smile, was waiting for them on the front steps. He didn't offer a handshake. There was no pleasantry, only a grim nod.

"Agent Walsh. Agent James. I'm Det. Joe Tobias," he said, his voice hoarse. "We've secured the house. I rushed over here as soon as the call came in. I know you've been working these cases. I didn't want my officers to disturb anything. Trust me, no one wants to be in that house any longer than they have to be. I haven't even called the medical examiner yet. I figured I'd let your team assess the scene, do what you have to do, and we can go from there."

"I appreciate that," Declan said as he stared past the man at the door behind him. "Was there any forced entry?"

"None. No signs of a struggle either. Honestly, it looks like it could be a movie set or some sick, twisted museum display." With that, he showed them where to grab booties and gloves.

Once they were ready, they followed him inside, their footsteps muffled on the marble floors. The interior of the mansion was just as extravagant as the exterior – gold-framed paintings, elaborate chandeliers hanging from the ceiling, and polished wood furniture that gleamed like it had never known a fingerprint. But it felt too still. Too quiet. The kind of silence that had no place in a living, breathing house.

A thin, nervous-looking officer stood by the double doors leading into the back parlor. He barely acknowledged them as he stepped aside, letting them pass. Inside, the cold grip of death hung heavy in the air, like the room itself had been trapped in time.

The room had a sprawling, old-world elegance. Massive windows, once lined with curtains that let in the early morning light, now stood open, letting in only a dull gray mist. An ornate fireplace, blackened with soot, loomed against one wall, but there was no fire in the hearth. Just the smell – metallic, faintly sour, but still fresh.

Kate's eyes immediately scanned the scene.

All five bodies were propped in their chairs, positioned around a grand wooden table in the center of the room. Their heads were tipped back at what would have been a painful angle in life, but in death they stared straight up at the ceiling. Their eyes were closed and covered with one black lily over each eye socket. The burned red hole of a bullet in their forehead. The remains of skull, blood, and brain were dripping onto the polished floor below.

The last cards they ever played were fanned in front of them. Chips stacked in neat little rows. Kate knew it was staged. Each had glasses at their place setting, some with liquid still inside. In the center of the table sat a half-empty bottle of whiskey. The golden liquid shimmered beneath the overhead light.

The black lilies were scattered across the table and the floor – hundreds of them. Their dark, eerie beauty contrasted sharply with the pristine opulence of the room.

Kate's eyes moved methodically over the bodies, cataloging the details with precision. She knew that anything she missed, Declan would see.

Kate didn't need Declan's help recognizing Avery Lancaster. She recognized him immediately, even with lilies covering his eyes. His chiseled jaw had graced the cover of magazines and headlines for decades. But now, his face was frozen in a stillness that betrayed the violence of his end. Shot. Like the detective said, there were no signs of struggle. None.

"How did this happen, Kate?" Declan asked from across the table. "None of them are small men. The angle they were shot means someone had to have been sitting on this table facing them. The table doesn't look disturbed. It looks…" He gestured toward it.

"It looks staged," Kate said with disgust. "Every single aspect of this scene looks staged. There are no other signs of trauma like the other bodies, at least not visibly. They took their time here but not enough time to torture each of them individually."

Declan pried down the jaw of one of the men. "He didn't lose his tongue." He hitched his jaw across the table to Kate. "Check Avery while I check the others."

Kate didn't need to do much examining to figure it out. The blood on the lower part of his face told her that when she moved his lower jaw, he'd be missing his tongue. She put a gloved hand to his chin and checked. She winced at the inside of his mouth. "Gone. Cut out like the others."

Declan pointed to the guy he stood near. "This one too. I don't know who he is, but he's the only other one."

"That's significant. It means the others were probably collateral damage."

Kate crouched down beside the body of a man she still hadn't identified. His fingers were stiff, clutching a glass of whiskey, though his grip had long since failed him. She carefully examined the rest. Same story for each of them – no visible wounds except for a single, fatal gunshot wound. Clean. Clinical.

How had they subdued them? It was a question Kate was coming back to. She remained at the table while Declan worked his way around it again, taking in all the bits of evidence.

Declan bent low to look at one of the bodies. He pulled up the cuff of the sleeve and held the arm up for Kate to see. "No restraints on this one." He moved from body to body, checking each of them. "Nothing, Kate. It's like they sat here and allowed themselves to be shot. Some of these guys are big and could have easily overpowered even a group of women."

Kate had been thinking that too. In the other cases, the men had been alone. She had no idea how many women there had been. They had been restrained and tortured. This scene was something different. Even ten women couldn't have restrained these men, possibly not even fifteen. There sure weren't more than a few who had been in and out of this home. Someone would have noticed that.

"Kate," Declan murmured, his voice low, almost reverent.

Kate glanced at him and saw his eyes lowered to the bottle of whiskey perched under his nose.

"It's poisoned," he said flatly. "I can't quite place the smell, but I'm sure this is poisoned. There is a string around the bottle, like it might have been given to them with a note. Maybe it was a gift. We need to search the house."

Kate wasn't sure she had heard him. "How did they not know?"

"They were probably already feeling good when they opened the whiskey and didn't notice."

Kate nodded, her eyes still scanning the room. "They were subdued first. Then executed." It wasn't a question but rather the most plausible explanation.

Kate stepped into the kitchen behind Det. Tobias, her eyes scanning the scene with practiced precision. Declan was right behind her, taking in the same chaos. The room, despite its lavishly updated features, had an unsettling air of disarray. The once-polished marble countertops, streaked with a thin film of grease, reflected the dim light of the overhead chandeliers. Cabinets that had been meticulously restored to preserve their gilded accents now housed half-empty bottles of top-shelf liquor, some tipped over as if hastily discarded. The scent of spilled bourbon and stale beer lingered in the air, mixing with the faint trace of leftover pizza.

Empty plates were scattered across the long, gleaming island, the remnants of fast food and half-eaten meals clinging to the porcelain like memories of a hurried feast. The once-pristine silverware was askew, a fork with remnants of sauce still on its tines, a wine glass tipped over, its base cracked. Pizza boxes, their edges curling from the weight of neglect, piled high on the counter, alongside crushed cans of soda and scattered napkins. The chaos stood in stark contrast to the polished exterior of the mansion, its wealth now marred by this unsettling display of excess and neglect.

The room was eerily silent, save for the soft hum of the fridge, but there was an oppressive energy in the air. As Kate's gaze moved to the far side of the kitchen, Det. Tobias was pointing out a small piece of folded paper. He picked it up and handed it to her. Unfolding it, her eyes scanned the single sentence scrawled across the page.

The price of betrayal.

No signature, no context, just the cold, cryptic message.

Kate's gut tightened.

This one wasn't just part of their mission – this one was personal.

CHAPTER 31

The shouting in the hallway sent Kate and Declan rushing to the door.

"What is happening out there?" Declan asked as he stepped in front of Kate.

Det. Tobias's loud voice shouted, "You don't want to see this. I need you to vacate the area right now."

A moment later, a tall man with wavy gray hair sticking up all over the place, a flushed face from anger and fear, and wild eyes came face to face with Kate. "I heard you're the FBI. This is my home, and no one has permitted you to be in here. I'm being told I can't enter my property. What is going on?"

It took Kate a moment to realize this man was Victor Lancaster. "Sir," she said, putting her hand up to stop him. She didn't touch his chest, but she was inches from him. She could feel the heat radiating off his body. "Please, is there somewhere we can talk? Let me speak to you. If you still want to go into that room, I'll allow it. You don't want to go in there blindly."

Victor moved toward Kate as if to push her back. She held her ground, stopping him.

"Listen," Declan said, drawing his attention. "Agent Walsh is telling you something for your benefit. If I were you, I wouldn't want to see what's in that room. It's one of those things once you see it, you'll never be able to unsee it."

Kate could tell by Declan's tone that even if she was going to allow Victor in that room, Declan wasn't until they spoke to him. Victor wavered for a moment, looking past Kate's shoulder to the open doorway. He stood there for a few beats, then exhaled.

"Fine. Come into my study on the other side of the house."

"Do you want me to go with you?" Declan asked, offering her support.

Kate shook her head. "Sharon should be here soon. Walk her through everything. We can meet when we are done."

Victor stormed ahead of her, a titan in a well-pressed button-down and crisp jeans. He was dressed like he was going shopping on 5th Avenue, not showing up at a crime scene where his son had been murdered, something Kate was sure he knew, given the media coverage. He moved like a man used to commanding boardrooms and countries.

The scent of old money clung to the air like a second skin – oak polish, cigar smoke, aged leather, and something floral that didn't quite hide the rot underneath. Kate kept up with him as they walked through the mansion, zigging and zagging down polished hallways.

"This is my house, Agent Walsh," he growled without looking back. "I suggest you remember that before you try to block another door."

Kate didn't flinch. "And your house is now an active crime scene."

Victor's laugh came sharp, derisive. He didn't stop until he reached the heavy double doors at the end of the corridor. Mahogany, brass handles, and a biometric lock he thought would keep out the world. He reached for it but didn't open the door.

"Mr. Lancaster." Her voice cracked the air like a whip. She stepped forward, hand resting on the holster at her hip, not as a threat, but a reminder.

He turned, slowly. Rage simmered beneath his skin like steam behind a boiler plate. "My son is back there and you had no right to keep me from him."

"Your son is gone, sir. What's in there now is evidence." Kate knew the language this man spoke and it wasn't emotional. That was fine by her. She got him on a level most didn't.

Something shifted in his expression, just for a moment – a fissure in the steel. Then it vanished. "You think I care about your protocols? My son is dead."

Kate matched his gaze. "I'm here to make sure we find out who did it."

He didn't move, but the air thickened between them. Outside, the murmur of uniformed officers and crime scene techs echoed faintly – background noise to the storm building in this hallway.

"You should have called me the second you found out," he said, quieter now. More dangerous. "You had no right to enter without me."

"We had every right. The NYPD was first on the scene. They called us. This is not only an active crime scene but one connected to several other murders." She paused, letting the words land. "Not just Avery. Five people, Mr. Lancaster. Murdered. In this house."

He closed his eyes. Just for a second. Then opened them with the same burning rage. His voice dropped to a whisper, strained and razor-thin. "I still need to see it."

"You need to breathe," she said. "You need to sit down. You need to let us do our job."

Victor's jaw clenched. "He was launching a start-up. Do you have any idea how brilliant he was?"

"I didn't know that. I don't know your son, but that's the kind of information I need. That's how you can best help me in this situation." Kate's voice softened, just a fraction. "Which is why I'm going to say this plainly. Whoever did this wanted to make a statement.

Avery wasn't killed in some alley. This was premeditated. Controlled. Someone wanted to send a message, and they have been sending a message with these murders. You must have seen the news."

Victor's eyes flicked past her to the door. "Midnight Lilies or whatever they call themselves. Is that why there are flowers all over the place?"

"It is," Kate said matter-of-factly. "As we said, this is connected. However, all the other murders were one person. We have identified your son. Our goal is to get to the family before the press, but the news was tipped off. We only just got to the scene. It's a fresh scene. This happened mere hours ago. I have to assume that maybe the killers called the media."

"Killers?" Lancaster said with some confusion.

Kate gestured toward the door. "Can we speak inside?"

Victor turned and opened the double doors, walking in first as Kate trailed behind. The study was cavernous, more like a library one might find in a European manor house. Floor-to-ceiling bookshelves climbed all four walls, filled with first editions and hand-bound journals. A globe bar stood near the tall windows, cracked open, crystal decanter still half full of bourbon. Deep armchairs of burgundy leather sat like sentinels around a marble fireplace. The Persian rug at the center was dark.

Victor moved to a leather chair, worn by years of use. Kate would have expected a man like him to keep something like that in pristine condition. It was the one thing in the room that looked worn.

Kate sat on the couch across from him. "Do you live here? I'm just confused as to why no one else was home. You were close enough that you were able to rush over here."

He blinked. The anger returned, but this time she saw what was beneath it. Grief, unshaped and unwelcome. "His mother is in Germany with friends on holiday. She's been gone for about a month.

I was at my office." Kate was sure he wasn't at his office. Probably in the arms of a mistress, but she wasn't going to press the issue. She knew Victor Lancaster didn't murder his son and his friends. She didn't need to humiliate the man in the process.

"When was the last time you spoke to Avery?"

"We spoke," he said, not quite answering the question.

The response indicated to Kate that there might have been tension there. "How recently?"

He said nothing.

Kate pressed on. "Relationships are hard between parent and child. There's no judgment from me. I'm asking so I understand what you may know. Nothing more or less."

Silence swelled between them. A silence that carried too many things left unsaid.

Victor rubbed his forehead. "Two weeks ago. I wanted Avery to get his life together. As you might have seen in the press, he's known as a playboy about town. That's not the Lancaster brand. We might be wealthy and powerful, but we work hard. We take what we do seriously. My son wasn't a serious man. I was worried his reputation would tarnish what all the Lancasters before us had accomplished. I was at what you'd call a crossroads with him, trying desperately to figure out what to do about his drinking and running around with socialites. He was almost thirty, brilliant but unfocused, except for his start-up. I thought it was promising. I was worried this crowd he was running with would drag him down. Avery has had some issues in the past."

"What kind of issues?"

Victor looked away from Kate and let out a string of curses. "You want me to tarnish my son even in death."

"No," Kate responded sharply. "Most of the men who have been targeted are podcasters who were putting out misogynistic content.

Then there was Congressman Marty Nubeck. He has a long history of sexual harassment and sexual assault. All of these men received threats beforehand. I need to understand how Avery fits into this."

"Could it be that he wasn't the main target? Maybe he was collateral damage."

"No," Kate said, explaining the hard reality that his son had not only been shot but his tongue removed like only one other man in that room. "We don't know the others' identities. Given the extraction of his tongue after death, we are certain your son was one of two targets. The other three men didn't have their tongues removed. They were the collateral damage, at least that's the working theory right now until we can confirm their identities."

He rubbed a hand over his face, suddenly looking older. "This wasn't random."

"No," she agreed. "It wasn't."

Outside, a uniformed officer stepped into view at the hallway's far end, saw Kate with Lancaster, and smartly stepped back out.

"Whoever did this got in without tripping the security system," she continued. "They knew this place. Knew him. It wasn't about robbery or rage. It was about control. Precision. If it's any solace to you, we believe they were drugged before the murders. I suspect your son was either dead or out cold when he was shot."

Victor looked at her. "Do you think this was connected to me? I have made enemies over the years."

"I think this was connected to how your son behaved with women," she responded dryly. "If I know one thing about wealthy families, it's that criminal activities have a way of being swept under the rug and justice being denied for victims. Do you know of any situations like that?"

Victor's expression turned grim. "There were a few," he admitted. "It started in high school, a he said, she said situation. They had all been drinking. It carried over to college. Another woman, who passed out in a dorm room, said my son had assaulted her. There was no evidence, so we paid off the family to make it go away. This was part of the tension between us. I don't know how I raised a man who'd do something like that to a woman. Do you know what they do to sex offenders in prison? What was I supposed to do other than protect him?"

Kate wanted to tell him that she knew. She wanted to say that his son deserved whatever he got, but she wasn't going to throw salt in a fresh wound. "How many situations like this were there?"

"Four that I knew of." Victor tipped his head back and looked up at the ceiling. He expelled a breath. "There could have been others. Women who were too scared to come forward. I don't know."

"I need the names of the victims."

Victor lowered his head, his sharp eyes piercing into hers. "What good will that do?"

"We don't have many leads," Kate admitted. "These women, and we do believe they are women, are one step ahead of us. These murders are planned and executed with a perfection I've never seen in my career, and all I deal with are serial killers of one type or another. These are not just killers, they are political terrorists on a mission to stop misogynistic men from spewing their nonsense and harming women. They have a target list they are working from. The staging around it is meant to terrify. These men aren't taking it seriously either."

Victor took in the information and let it sit for a moment. "How many of them are there?"

"I don't know. I can't answer that because we aren't even close to solving this." Kate held up her bandaged arm. "We thought we had a lead last night. They set off a bomb in the building we were in. I'm starting to believe they left a breadcrumb for us to follow. I know one thing – the women who are doing this were victims of some kind. This is their revenge tour. They are fighting back, and so far, they are winning. If you have names of women your son might have harmed, I need to know. One of them might be involved. They certainly knew how to access this house without alerting anyone. There's no break in and no struggle."

Victor slowly nodded. "I'll give you all the information I can. You said before that you think they were subdued. Drugged?"

"We still need to have forensics in here. Agent James believes he smelled something in the whiskey. The bottle is sitting in the middle of the table and each of them was drinking a glass. The note we found has the same string attached to it as the bottle of whiskey. Why they would see that note and still drink from the bottle is anyone's guess."

Victor stared off past Kate, running a hand down his face. It lingered at his chin as he looked back at her. "It's Avery's drink. If they used whiskey to drug him, then they know him. Knew him." He shook his head at having to speak about his son in the past tense. "If you're telling me there was a note, a threat. That wouldn't stop him. He'd laugh at it. My son's hubris is his downfall."

Kate thanked him for the information. "This is the kind of thing we need to know. It will help us as we investigate. How they were able to get to him is important. It could point us in the right direction. There's still a lot unknown, and every bit of information, even if it seems small to you, is helpful."

They talked for a few moments longer. Then Victor stood. "I need to see in that room, Agent Walsh. You've warned me sufficiently. The risk is my own. I'm willing to live with whatever I see. Besides, I might be able to help you identify the others. I know a handful of Avery's friends."

As Kate had promised, she was going to allow it. "You need gloves and booties and to prepare yourself emotionally for what you're going to see. I'll allow it because we need to identify the others and a promise is a promise."

Kate hoped she wasn't making yet another terrible mistake in the case.

CHAPTER 32

By one that afternoon, the bodies had been cleared from the mansion and all the victims had been identified. Three of the men were Avery's long-time friends. The other man with his tongue cut out was Blake Thornton, yet another podcaster. His name appeared in the middle of Ali's list, attached to a mid-level podcast that didn't garner as much attention as the others. He had not attended the meeting the night before at the gallery, even though he'd been invited. Once he heard about the bomb threat, he chose what he thought would be safer evening activities.

Kate wondered if the Midnight Lilies knew he was here with Avery or if they just got lucky. Either way, she was sure the target was Avery.

Sharon was still working the scene with Declan. The mansion was vast, with many rooms that Avery used, leaving information strewn about carelessly. Victor had promised to call Kate with the list of names of women that Avery had been accused of assaulting. He hadn't provided it to her right away, much to her annoyance. He said he wanted to check with his lawyer first.

Once she got the list from Victor about the women Avery was accused of assaulting, she'd start there. When there was little else Kate could do at the mansion, she waved Declan over. "I'm going to speak to Ali."

Declan's face pinched. "Do you think it's a good idea to go alone?

Maybe you should consider bringing her in for a formal interview."

Kate had considered that. The threat was that Ali was smart enough to lawyer up and then there'd be no interview at all. Kate explained that to Declan. "I can't risk it, not yet. Not when all we have is speculation. Ali and I had a rapport before. I'm planning on using that goodwill again."

Declan didn't look convinced. "If she's the head of this, I don't want you going in alone. She already tried to blow us up once."

Kate shook her head. "She's not going to talk if you or Leo are there. Leo is helping Ditch and you need to stay here with Sharon." She reached out, putting her hand on his arm. "I promise you that I'll be safe. She has a class getting out soon then she has office hours. I'm going to meet her in her office. She won't be prepared for me. It's in public. I'll be fine."

Declan blew out a frustrated breath. "Call me as soon as you leave or if you get in trouble."

Kate leaned up on her tiptoes and kissed him on the lips. They never showed affection in public, let alone at a crime scene. No one was watching them. Declan was surprised by the kiss but not put off. If anyone told Spade about their relationship, they worried that they'd be separated. While relationships at the FBI weren't unheard of, the agency didn't keep those people on the same team.

As Kate stepped back from him, she said, "If you figure out the poison or whatever knocked them out, call me. I can use it in the interview." Any piece of the puzzle would help with figuring this out. This is what Kate needed more than anything – information.

As Kate turned to leave, Sharon called out to her. "I've been calling around to a few florists about the lilies." Sharon had her full attention. "This particular brand of lily is an Asiatic hybrid white lily. There are specific absorption sprays that will dye them black. That's what's been used. These can be grown indoors, Kate. They are the hardiest of the flowers and easily grown indoors. What I was told is that if they are growing them from seeds, it takes about eighteen months. If it's from the bulbs, it can take as little as one hundred days. The thing is they might not bloom the first year but rather the second. I did a deep dive, and no one has ordered the supply of lilies that's being used. Someone among this group is growing them. That means probably upwards of two years in the planning. They are going to need lights and a watering system. It would take considerable space either inside or outside in a greenhouse. Even at that, no one is going to have that kind of land here in Manhattan unless their house is massive."

It confirmed Kate's worst suspicion – they were as good as they were because this had been in the works for a long time. They had time to plan, prepare, and probably even train. "Is there any way to trace the bulbs or seed shipments? Or the dye? The growing equipment?"

Sharon shook her head. "I asked that question. It's probably from a national wholesaler and it's not something that's going to raise any suspicion. If this group is as good as we believe, they also probably bought things at different times so as not to arouse suspicion. They might have also each bought a little part of it, so the full scale couldn't be tied back to one person. That means it could have all gone to different addresses, separate from where it was assembled."

Kate cursed softly, knowing that going the flower route any further was probably a waste of time. "Good work. I appreciate you running down those leads. If you see anything else in the forensics, let me know."

Sharon started to walk away but turned back. "Listen, this is just a guess, so don't hold me to it. If this group is so adept at growing lilies, they could be growing hemlock as well. That could have been added to the whiskey and used as the poison. As I've been going over the scene, there are traces of bleach and other cleaning chemicals. The victims' mouths have also been wiped and cleaned. One of the victims has stains on his shirt. I think a few of them probably puked before their deaths."

"They went to the trouble of cleaning them up and staging this?" Declan asked the question, confusion evident in his tone. "I don't understand. The staging was that important to them?"

It didn't surprise Kate. The ritual of it, the presentation, was important to them. It wouldn't have had the same effect if the FBI had walked in with the victims on the floor with vomit all over the place. They wouldn't have been able to have the bodies look the way they did with lilies on their eyes in that kind of mess. The staging was part of the crime. Kate explained that to Declan and Sharon. "Get the whiskey back to the lab and confirm it. I don't want to run on any speculation right now. We need cold, hard facts and don't let your suspicions slip out to anyone else. Right now, there are only a few of us who know about the poisoning and only three of us who know they cleaned up the crime scene. Let's keep those facts under wraps for right now."

Sharon and Declan agreed to both. She watched them get down to work before making her way out onto 5th Avenue to the waiting SUV. She sank back into the seat and told the driver where she was headed.

The wind hadn't settled any. It cut hard against Kate's back as she crossed the campus to the building where Ali held office hours. The cold slapped at her coat like it wanted her gone. Kate didn't flinch. She had a steely determination.

She moved down the corridor with hard steps, ignoring the reverberations that echoed. Ali Brewer's office sat in a quiet corner of the second floor. Kate knocked once, and the woman called her in, assuming most likely that she was a student.

Kate opened the door and entered the room that smelled faintly of coffee and old paper. Books stacked themselves into precarious towers across every flat surface. On the windowsill, a dying plant drooped. Ali looked up from behind a desk cluttered with notepads, student essays, and a half-eaten apple.

"Agent Walsh," Ali said, sounding slightly rattled. She recovered quickly, her voice smooth, low, and deliberately calm. "I wasn't expecting you. Can I help you with something?"

Kate didn't smile. "I had some follow-up questions from our discussion a few days ago." She didn't wait to be asked to be seated. Kate crossed the room, pulled the chair slightly from the desk, and sat. She gestured for Ali to do the same. It might have been the woman's office, but Kate was in control.

Ali lowered herself to the chair, placing her folded hands on the table. "Is there something wrong?"

"Other than the mass homicide I just came from?" Kate threw it down like a gauntlet and waited for a reaction. Ali's eyes shifted nervously but she remained quiet. It was odd because most people would show shock or ask some questions. Kate relaxed back in the chair. "You're not even curious about who was murdered?"

Ali opened her mouth to speak but nothing more than a breath escaped. She bit her lip. "I assumed if you wanted me to know, you'd tell me. I'm not sure what any of this has to do with me. As we discussed, I'm not involved."

"I'm not so sure about that anymore," Kate responded, not going into the scene at the Lancaster mansion. "Where were you last night?"

"Here until ten. I had a guest lecturer come in and we hosted a seminar with an after-event where she had books that students could get signed. After that, I went home. I spoke briefly to my neighbor and was in for the night. I called my sister around eleven. We video chatted for about an hour. We don't get much chance to speak, so we take the time when we can. I can show you my phone. It logs the chat."

"I'm going to need to see proof of all of it."

Ali picked up her phone from the desk and handed it over to Kate, giving her the code. "There are photos from last night too." She watched as Kate went through it finding all the evidence that Ali said would be there. "I have a list of students and colleagues you can speak to as well. I swear to you, Agent Walsh, I have nothing to do with this."

Kate couldn't argue with the evidence she was seeing in Ali's phone. The call with her sister went until 12:18 am. She had photos from the event that started around seven, and the last one was taken with a group of her students at a little after ten. Kate handed back the phone. "I saw you on the street with Amanda Larson. I need an explanation."

Ali nodded slowly. "Amanda is my student. She is…" Ali trailed off.

"She's what"

"Troubled," Ali finally responded. "She called me and was upset. She told me she had gotten into things that were out of her control. She was afraid and asked me to meet her. I asked her to come here during office hours, but she refused. If you saw us on the street, then you know we only spoke for a few moments. Amanda refused to tell me what was going on. As soon as she saw me, she said she had made a mistake by calling me. I'm sure you saw that she took off. We left going in separate directions. I still don't know what was going on with her."

Kate kept her expression neutral. "Amanda never told you what kind of trouble she was having? She didn't mention anything? Not anything about being at a hotel with two women when Marty Nubeck was murdered?"

Ali's eyes narrowed just slightly. "I had no idea." She paused to collect herself. "I'm sure there were a lot of people at that hotel."

Kate leaned forward. "Amanda was seen with two unidentified women at the hotel bar the night Marty Nubeck was murdered. She was seen watching his security detail, then followed them out to the elevator. The two other women left the bar as soon as the security came in. Mighty suspicious to me."

Ali's eyes got wide. "I swear to you I didn't know."

"About the surveillance camera that didn't get cut or that Amanda was there?"

"Agent Walsh, I don't know what you're talking about. I had no idea that the hotel surveillance was cut." Ali held her hand up to stop herself. "Let me back up. I don't even know what hotel Congressman Nubeck was murdered in. I've only been loosely following the news. What I read said nothing about the surveillance being cut. So, yes, I didn't know about that. I certainly didn't know Amanda was at the hotel that night. She's been missing class this semester. She's had some trouble and has been threatened with dismissal from school. I was simply trying to provide extra emotional support for a student."

Kate stared. "What kind of trouble has Amanda had?"

"I wouldn't feel comfortable disclosing a student's private information like that."

Kate gave her a hard stare. "Not even if that student is the one pointing a finger at you, saying you're the one who is spearheading the Midnight Lilies. That you found her. Groomed her. Brought her in."

Ali inhaled sharply, the first real, audible breath Kate had heard her take. "That never happened. That's not true. The first time I heard of the Midnight Lilies was when you first came to question me. I know what my background looks like to you. I know you've heard my podcast. I know I'm the most obvious suspect to you. I can also understand why you're here after seeing me with Amanda if that's what she told you."

Kate didn't show any response in her features. "If it's not true, why would Amanda say it?"

Ali shook her head. "I have no idea."

"You must have some idea." Kate uncrossed her legs and leaned forward slightly. "You don't even seem all that angry that Amanda would say that about you. I would even venture to argue that you're not surprised. Why is that?"

A knock on the door interrupted them. Kate shouted to go away while Ali got up, crossing the room to open the door. A young woman stood there looking eager. Ali told her office hours were over and she'd speak to her tomorrow. The young woman tried to protest, saying she needed help with the paper. Ali nudged her back into the hall with a promise to email her some information.

Once the door was closed, Ali locked it. "I'm sorry. Where were we?"

If Ali thought Kate would forget where they were, she hadn't been paying attention. "I was asking why you weren't surprised by Amanda pointing the finger at you about the Midnight Lilies."

Ali slowly walked across the office and behind her desk. She locked her gaze on Kate. "I think it's because when this first started, Amanda was someone who came to mind. I didn't want to think the young woman could be involved in something like this – not something so violent and unhinged. When she called me to meet, I was hoping to get information that I swore I was going to turn over to you. Now you're here telling me that she's pointing a finger at me and that she was there at a hotel where a murder took place. I just don't know what to make of it all."

Kate stilled in her chair. "Tell me everything you know right now. Don't leave anything out."

CHAPTER 33

Ali walked to the window, and turned her back to Kate. "Amanda took my class her freshman year and another this semester. She's intense. Smart. Angry in a way that didn't have anywhere to go."

"Angry at who?"

Ali turned. "Everyone. Men. Institutions. Power structures. Herself."

Kate studied her. "What did you do with that anger?"

"I didn't encourage it, if that's what you're suggesting." Ali's chin lifted. "She was my student. I was trying to help. I thought I could get to the root of the anger and help her work through it."

"Did you?"

"Only partially. Amanda told me she had been sexually assaulted in her freshman year. She refused to tell me who did it. She explained that she had gone to the administration because it happened on campus, but that they refused to do anything because she had no proof. They discouraged her from going to the police. She was in my class at the time it happened, and we were discussing sexual assault. I didn't know at the time that she was a victim. We touched on institutional protections. The kind you see with the Catholic Church. The Boy Scouts. All those organizations, once allegations come out, their first instinct is to protect the offender because not protecting them means that the institution itself failed the victim and it opens them up to liability."

"We see that all the time, unfortunately," Kate admitted, knowing several cases off the top of her head like that. Victims rarely got justice. "What was your advice to students?"

"Go past the politics of it. Charge through the administration. If someone is telling you not to report, report anyway. I told them what they could legally do. More than that, what they should do."

Kate knew that reporting didn't always help victims. She encouraged it, but the system wasn't fair. "Do you know if Amanda reported?"

"She did." Ali wrapped her arms around her middle. "It wasn't good, Agent Walsh. She was practically laughed out of the police station. She went in and said she was raped. She had no evidence, no witnesses, and no corroborating evidence. Amanda also changed her story a few times. A detective came to speak with me. Amanda told him that I knew about the assault. She sat in my class, then told me about the assault a few weeks later. Then she went to the cops, who came to me to see what she told me. Amanda told him she had told her women's studies professor. She told me it happened in her dorm. She told the police that it happened in a field near campus. I had to be honest with the detective about what she told me. But as you know, it's not unusual that a victim might change her story."

"It's not unusual if she's still dealing with trauma, no. It makes it difficult to prosecute. I can understand, with no other evidence, that the detective wouldn't have much to go on. Sometimes they can go forward with just a victim statement. If they catch her lying early on, she has no credibility. A defense attorney would be all over that, and the prosecutor wouldn't let her testify. Without her testimony, there is no case. I would assume that the detective wasn't able to get a confession from the suspect. It's one of the reasons why my job is so important – a solid confession is critical for the case. Do you know why she changed her story?"

Ali's mouth downturned in a frown. "Amanda wouldn't talk to me about her changing story. It was shortly after that though her anger increased. It was palpable. I was afraid for her. I honestly don't know what the detective did or didn't do, if the man was even questioned. She was white hot angry and it burned in her for a long time. Even today."

Kate sensed that Ali wanted to talk. She didn't utter another word, just watched Ali for any signs of lying or fabrication in the story.

Ali put her hands on the desk. "I don't know if you're too jaded by the system to see it, but women deserve justice for centuries of abuses. Domestic violence. Sexual assault. Can you imagine that marital rape was still okay until the seventies? That was the first time people started to question the laws on the books. Before that, a husband could rape his wife and it was fine. It wasn't even until 1993 that all fifty states had laws making it illegal for a husband to rape his wife. Then this rise of misogyny and these podcasts. Then we wonder why women are so angry, and there's a so-called male loneliness epidemic. It sounds to me like it's a consequences epidemic. Men who treat women like objects to be used and abused aren't finding partners, nor should they. Women are raging, Agent Walsh. I can't blame them. But I'm certainly not killing those men."

Everything Ali said was true, but still, she was a suspect. "Your podcast. Your classes. All of it could be a ripe breeding ground for this kind of violence. Do you understand that?"

Ali scoffed. "You think I'm radicalizing these young women? Radical feminist collectives spring up all the time. Zines. Podcasts. Blogs. They usually burn out after a semester. But murder? That's not activism. That's madness."

Kate didn't blink. "Amanda told me the group meets in secret. That you preach about power. About striking back. She said you showed them how."

Ali's eyes flashed. "Are you seriously accusing me of creating a death cult?"

"I'm saying your name came up in an active homicide investigation. The young woman who put it there was at the scene of a horrific murder."

Ali looked away.

Kate pressed in. "When was the last time she sought your counsel here other than yesterday in the street?"

Ali walked to a shelf, opened a drawer, and pulled out a small notebook. She flipped through it, her fingers trembling slightly. She provided Kate with a date from a month ago. "Amanda came in late. She said she wasn't sleeping. She asked strange questions about moral philosophy, about whether violence was ever justified if it was in response to trauma."

Kate felt something shift in her gut. "What did you tell her?"

Ali swallowed. "That's not a conversation you have in hypotheticals."

Kate took a step closer. "Did you ever encourage her to act on that anger?"

Ali looked up sharply. "No."

Kate watched her, listening not just to the words, but the weight behind them. "Do you think Amanda could be dangerous?"

"I think she's dangerous," Ali said finally after several beats of silence. "Not because I radicalized her. Because she's been hurt. She carries it like shrapnel. She's looking for somewhere to put it."

Kate exhaled, rage simmering beneath her skin. It didn't excuse murder. But it explained something. "Did you refer her out for counseling? You're not a therapist. It sounds like she needs a good psychologist."

"I tried to get her counseling," Ali confirmed. "She wouldn't go. She said it was all talk and she was tired of talking. That talking without action did no good."

"Did she go anywhere for support other than you?" Kate pressed.

Ali flipped a few pages in the notebook. "I referred her to a local rape crisis program. They have a group for young women who have been assaulted. She said she'd gone to the group a few times. The jury was still out on whether she liked it or not. I don't know how frequently she went or how she engaged while she was there. The center isn't going to tell you anything. Everything is confidential."

Kate would worry about that later. "You said radical feminist collectives usually burn out. This one shows no signs of slowing down. The Midnight Lilies have a manifesto. They have a kill list and years of planning. They are getting away with targeting their victims, murdering them, staging a crime scene, and escaping into the night. There are ten murders, Ali."

Ali didn't respond.

Kate zeroed in on her. "You're educated. Articulate. Charismatic. Amanda described you like a cult leader. She said you have taken in these broken souls and have given them hope of regaining their power." Kate knew she was stretching the truth but sometimes that was necessary to get a reaction in an interrogation – and that's what this was now.

"She was wrong," Ali said calmly, not taking the bait. "I'm just a teacher."

Kate narrowed her eyes. "You're more than that. To her. Maybe to others."

The air thickened. Outside, the wind howled through bare trees.

Kate moved back toward the desk, picking up a paper from the pile. A syllabus. One line caught her eye.

Week 9: Revolutionary Feminism — De Beauvoir, hooks, Solanas.

Valerie Solanas. The woman who shot Andy Warhol.

Kate looked up. "You taught Solanas?" She was a radical feminist who had appeared in a Warhol film and self-published the SCUM Manifesto, a feminist pamphlet calling for the extinction of men. She believed Warhol was conspiring with her publisher, Maurice Girodias, to keep her manuscript from getting published. She shot Warhol in June 1968. Solanas was charged with attempted murder, assault, and illegal possession of a firearm. Later, she was diagnosed with paranoid schizophrenia and sentenced to three years in prison. Kate understood why this was being taught. But she also understood what a young woman like Amanda could hear – violence was sometimes okay.

Ali didn't flinch. "I teach history. Including the parts people would rather forget."

Kate's voice was low. "Did Amanda take this lecture?"

Ali hesitated, then slowly nodded.

Kate didn't let go. "You taught Amanda that revolution comes through destruction."

Ali's jaw clenched. "I taught her that ideology without compassion is just another form of violence."

Another silence. Long. Unblinking.

"Can I see your phone?"

Ali frowned. "Why?"

"I want to see your communications with Amanda."

Ali hesitated.

Kate held out her hand. "I have enough to get a warrant if I need it. I'm trying to go easy on you, Ali. I honestly don't want to believe you are involved in this. I think you're a good professor teaching a valuable subject. Help me help you."

Ali looked at her for a long moment. Then slowly pulled her phone from her bag. Unlocked it. Handed it over again.

Kate scrolled through recent calls. Nothing. The last text from Amanda was dated the night before the hotel incident.

Amanda (2:04 AM): *I can't stop thinking about it. What you said. About fire.*

Kate looked up. "What did you tell her about fire?"

Ali's face was unreadable. "That sometimes burning it down is the only way to see what was there."

Kate's blood ran cold. She handed the phone back. "If Amanda contacts you again, you call me. Immediately. I want a list of everyone else in your classes going back several years. I want to know anyone you think might be radicalized like Amanda. Do you understand me?"

Ali nodded. "It will take me some time to share that with you. I won't tell the administration. If I do, they won't allow me to hand this over. I swear to you, I'm not involved in any of this."

"Then help me stop it." Kate gave her the details on where to send the student list, then started for the door.

"Agent Walsh," Ali called to her back.

Kate turned.

"Amanda is a young woman trying to outrun something she can't name."

Kate stepped into the hallway. The door clicked shut behind her.

Kate had the driver hurry as fast as they could across Manhattan to the rape crisis center that Ali had recommended to Amanda.

The sidewalk outside the Raphael Center for Trauma Recovery buzzed with the usual Manhattan noise – sirens in the distance, horns impatiently stabbing the air, and the low hum of foot traffic. The building itself was a squat, red-brick structure wedged between a dry cleaner and a juice bar, almost deliberately unremarkable. Only a brass plaque by the entrance identified it, the engraved letters catching the dim fall light: Raphael Center for Trauma Recovery. A place that was meant to feel safe. Impenetrable. But Kate Walsh didn't have time for locked doors and quiet rules.

She had her credentials in her hand as she rang the buzzer.

Inside, the center smelled of lavender oil and old coffee. Calming tones. Earthy furniture. Too quiet. The receptionist smiled and made pleasantries as she ushered Kate toward a closed office door.

"Come in," a voice called, firm and clipped as the woman opened and held the door for Kate. She made quick introductions with the woman behind the desk. Linda Morton – mid-forties, polished, with a sharp jawline and a voice that had probably been trained not to tremble. She didn't smile. She didn't stand. She ran the whole agency.

"Agent Walsh, how can I help you?"

"I'm here about one of your clients, Amanda Larson." Kate took a seat, uninvited. "I'm investigating a string of murders. Amanda was at one of the scenes and she's a person of interest."

Linda folded her hands. "I'm sorry. That's confidential. I can't confirm that this Amanda is even receiving services here."

Kate held her stare. "I can come back with a warrant. I don't think it would look too good for your board and donors that you're refusing to help the FBI with a string of murders that have hit Manhattan. I'm sure you've heard about them. The women call themselves the Midnight Lilies."

"Yes," Linda said, her voice stiff. "I've heard of them and they are unfortunate. Still, we cannot share information about a client." She paused. "Or even confirm that this young woman is a client."

"I'm not playing games with you," Kate said, her tone demanding. "I know Amanda is a client here. I need to know if she's violent. If she's exhibited any violent tendencies. Made threats against men. I don't need to know what she has said in the group beyond that."

Linda relented a little. "Amanda is surrounded by professionals. If she's in danger, we'll know." Linda's tone was final, a door slammed shut. "I'm not helping you beyond that. My board and donors will understand. Try to get a warrant if you want to waste your time. This is privileged confidential information."

Kate stood, jaw clenched. The meeting was over. She nodded once, tightly, and stepped back into the hallway, pulse ticking in her throat.

As she passed the front desk, a woman organizing pamphlets glanced up. Late twenties, tired eyes, volunteer badge half-tucked under her sweater. She brushed past Kate, too close for an accident, and slipped something into her palm.

Kate didn't react. Just walked out into the biting wind and told her driver to wait as she took a few steps down the block. She stopped under the awning of a newsstand, shielding herself from view. The note was written in pencil on the back of a group schedule:

I know about Amanda & the others. Meet me at the Perk & Grind. 10 mins.

Kate's pulse jumped. She pulled her phone out, searched the place, and waved off her driver, sending him away.

Kate turned and headed east toward answers that she hoped would finally blow this case open.

CHAPTER 34

The Perk & Grind sat on the corner tucked between an indie bookstore and an upscale women's boutique. The café had a quiet vibe with soft music playing overhead and young people with headphones on while their heads were bent over laptops. Others were reading or talking quietly to their counterparts across a table. A row of leather booths lined the side wall. The scent of espresso soaked deep into the wooden beams of the ceiling.

Kate sat in the farthest booth, facing the door, back against the wall. Her coat lay across the maroon leather beside her, and her Glock lay nestled tightly in the holster at her hip. Her fingers drummed the edge of a ceramic mug. Steam curled like ghostly fingers.

The bell above the door jingled, and a gust of city wind rushed in.

She spotted the girl immediately. She had put on a moss-green hoodie over the sweater she had been wearing. It was the first time Kate noticed that the young woman's jeans hung too loose on her hips. Nervous eyes scanned the café before locking onto Kate's.

She slipped into the booth. "I'm Maya Corbin, a volunteer at the center. I'm getting a master's degree in psychology. I hope that we can keep this conversation a secret. Otherwise, it's going to blow up my life. Not being able to keep things confidential will derail my whole career before it even gets started."

Kate understood. She assured her. "I'll try to keep your name out of this. Let me assure you, given the case I'm working, your bravery and integrity for speaking to me will win out above anything else."

Maya's fingers twisted on the tabletop. "I didn't know who else to tell. It's probably nothing, I just don't know anymore."

Kate softened her voice, professional but warm. "You did the right thing. Just take your time and walk me through it."

Maya bit her lip and glanced around. "Is this safe?"

It was clear to Kate how nervous this young woman was. "Let's get you some coffee and you can take your time." Maya wanted tea and went up to the counter herself, not allowing Kate to get it for her. When she came back to the table, she was visibly calmer. Kate assured her she hadn't been followed and no one, not even her driver, knew they were meeting.

Maya exhaled shakily and nodded. "Amanda Larson has been going to the recovery group for almost a year. Every week, without fail. I've started noticing changes not just with her but a few other girls in the group. I don't lead the group, but I help with it. It's been part of my training."

Kate's brow lifted. "Changes?"

"She was quiet at first. She wouldn't even make eye contact. But a few months ago, she started talking. A lot. She was angry, furious even. Not just at what happened to her, but at everything. Men. The system. Therapy. The women who didn't want to fight."

Kate leaned forward, eyes locked on hers. "Fight how?"

Maya hesitated, lowering her voice. "That's the thing. It started with discussions. Hypotheticals. 'What would happen if someone made their abuser disappear?' or 'What if we turned the tables for once?' I thought it was venting. Sometimes anger is a good breakthrough with trauma – a way to take your power back. It got darker. Calculated."

"What did the group leader do?"

"Nothing at first. The point of the group is to help these women work through their trauma, share experiences with others. There were many women in the group who were angry. That's one of the stages they are working through. For a lot of women, the anger is a sign of healing. Amanda, though, the anger was something else. It was like planning."

Kate's fingers stilled on her cup. "Was it just Amanda who was speaking like that?"

"No. That's what worried me. The more Amanda went on, the more concerned I got. She was kind of egging on the other women." Maya grew quiet, sipped her tea. "I asked the psychologist if maybe we didn't need to address this. I didn't think Amanda's anger was healthy. I didn't know what it was, I'm not that far in my training, but it seemed too much."

"Was it ever addressed?"

Maya cradled her cup. "Finally, after one particularly bad session where Amanda took over the whole group and two women complained that it was starting to scare them," she admitted with a sigh. "That's the thing. It had gone on so far that other women in the group were starting to see what I was seeing. The group leader had no choice but to address it."

Kate knew then it had to have been serious. "What happened then?"

"Amanda backed off for a couple of weeks. She reassured us she was working out a few things in the group that she couldn't work out in her daily life. She told us she wasn't serious. That it was just some revenge fantasies as a way to help her cope."

"Did you believe her?"

Maya shook her head. "The group leader believed her and that's all that mattered. I think she wanted to believe Amanda. She wanted to think Amanda was progressing, and the group was something beneficial for her. No one wants to think the therapy you're providing is having not only no effect but an adverse effect."

"Was it the therapy?" Kate asked, not sure that it was.

Maya shrugged. "I don't know. Amanda seemed to back off, as did the other women she was kind of egging on. That was until another person joined the group. Then it just got weird."

"Weird how?"

"It wasn't directly in the group," Maya started. "There was suddenly this unspoken undercurrent running through the group. A division of people who were thinking like Amanda and those who weren't. It wasn't tangible, so it's hard for me to explain."

"Try," Kate urged her, letting her grip go on the coffee cup that had cooled in her hands. She realized she was sitting on the edge of the booth bench, wanting to pull the words out of Maya's mouth. Kate knew that kind of intensity could scare her off. "Please, just try to explain it so I understand."

"There's a woman – she is called Cassandra Vale. She just started showing up about six months ago and only talks to certain women after the sessions. She's quiet during group. Hard to break out of her shell."

Kate's pulse quickened. The name was new.

"Although she's quiet in the group, there is an intensity about her," Maya continued. "Charismatic. Amanda latched onto her like a lifeline."

"What did Cassandra say?"

"I never heard her say anything inappropriate during group. If anything, she was kind and empathetic towards the other women, but afterward, I overheard some things. Conversations in the hallway. Amanda told another girl that Cassandra was showing them how to take power back. She said they were tired of therapy. Tired of waiting for justice."

"Violence?"

"I don't know for sure but possibly," Maya said in a rush of breath.

"Amanda told this girl that Cassandra said sometimes blood is the only truth they understand. She said men needed to be silenced in the way women have been silenced for centuries. That's a quote."

Kate swallowed hard.

Maya pulled a folded paper from her pocket, her hand trembling. "I wrote down what I remembered. Snippets. Names. I don't know what's real and what's just trauma-fueled talk, but it was enough that it scared me."

Kate took the paper carefully, unfolding it. There were times and dates. Other women's names from the group. First names. Not any that Kate recognized except one – Kristen. "Do you know Kristen? Was she in the group, too?"

"Not while I was there. The group leader said she'd been there in the past. But it was someone Cassandra mentioned to Amanda. Cassandra said she was able to help Kristen get back to normal. She held Kristen up as this shining example of someone who was recovering and more powerful than she'd ever been." Maya stared across the table at Kate, shuddering slightly. "Amanda and a few of the other young women started talking about Cassandra like she was a cult-leader."

"Did you try to address this at all with the psychologist leading the group?"

"I did," Maya said with frustration. "We work hard to maintain a safe group dynamic. It's the only way the group works. I didn't like the after-group chatter. I was told the women had a right to develop friendships in the group – that was part of the purpose. We wanted women to develop a support network from the group."

"It sounds to me like it was toxic."

"In a lot of ways, it was. This was new for me. It was the first time I was in a support role in a support group environment. I didn't know what the norm was. This group was less direct therapy and more support, so the rules were a bit looser. I just kept being told that I needed to have some flexibility."

Kate had to wonder what the psychologist knew and didn't. "Do you think the group leader knew what was going on?"

Maya shook her head. "I think as long as the in-group sessions were productive, she didn't pay attention to much else."

"Are you willing to give me her name?"

"No," Maya said with force. "I don't want to destroy my career before it even gets started. If you think the director of the agency was a tough nut to crack, you really won't get anywhere with the psychologist. There's no point in even attempting the conversation. Even if you get a warrant, I don't think you'll get the information. They preached to me the importance of confidentiality because trust was key for these women. They have fought before in cases going to court and won. I get it to a point."

That begged one question. "Why are you coming to me with this?"

The young woman's eyes filled, a sheen of tears threatening to spill. "I didn't sign up for this. I just wanted to help. These women have been through terrible ordeals. Now it's like some of them are becoming the thing that hurt them."

Kate reached out, her hand gentle on Maya's. "You're brave for coming forward. You may have saved someone's life today."

"Do you think Amanda did it? Do you think she's involved?"

Kate's eyes hardened. "I think she knows more than she's said. Having this list of names from the group helps me tremendously."

Maya leaned forward. "There's one more thing."

Kate nodded. "Go ahead."

"I followed Amanda once. After a session. She didn't see me, I don't think. She met Cassandra at a bar. The Velvet Finch. They went into the back. I waited an hour and left."

Kate's mental map clocked the area in her mind. She didn't know the bar but knew the area. "This helps," she said again. "Is there anything else you think I should know?"

Maya stood slowly. "You'll stop them?"

Kate nodded. "With this information, we have a real chance at it. If Cassandra shows back up at the group, alert me immediately. When was the last time she was there?"

"A few weeks ago." Maya's expression was haunted.

If it was this woman, Kate had seen her handiwork up close. "I need you to be careful. Don't tell anyone you spoke to me, and don't tell Amanda or Cassandra that the FBI is on to them."

"No, of course not. I wasn't even sure I should speak to you." She thanked Kate for making it easy to talk to her, then turned and left.

Kate watched the girl leave, her backpack slung over one shoulder. She sat for a moment, replaying every word. Amanda. Cassandra. The talk of blood and power. The scribbled names.

Kate stood, tucked the note into her inner pocket. As she stepped outside, the wind hit her like a slap – cold and sobering.

That's when Kate saw the familiar dark hooded figure watching her from the end of the block.

Kate made brief eye contact with the young woman, her face half shielded from view by the hood. The other half was covered in a layer of dark hair. The thin slip of her face that Kate could see was eerily familiar.

As soon as their eyes met, the figure turned and ran.

Kate knew then it was the person who had slipped her the note. She took off after her, determined not to lose her this time.

CHAPTER 35

The city pulsed with its usual chaos. Kate ran with all her might, pushed by the sheer determination to catch this unknown figure.

"Hey!" she shouted.

The hooded woman didn't turn around. Didn't hesitate. She slipped between two businessmen like smoke, her movements sharp and practiced.

Kate followed, her coat billowing behind her. The sidewalk turned into an obstacle course. Pedestrians blurred into faceless obstacles. Kate dodged a man wheeling a dolly stacked with boxes, cut between two parked cabs, and sprinted through the intersection against the light.

Cars blared. Brakes screeched. A yellow cab clipped the back of her coat, yanking her sideways for half a heartbeat before she recovered and kept going.

The hooded figure darted across a crowded street. She glanced over her shoulder, then pumped her legs harder, accelerating her forward. The woman cut west down the next block, breaking into a full sprint.

Kate followed, her breath burning her throat, the pounding in her ears louder than the sound of the city. She wove between cars inching through a jam, one hand on the butt of her Glock, the other pushing people aside. "FBI! Move!"

The sidewalk narrowed. The woman vaulted over a stack of construction cones, her feet barely touching the ground before she was moving again. Kate was faster. Stronger. But the woman was slippery, unpredictable. She darted into a side alley between a bodega and a dry cleaner.

Kate followed without hesitation.

The alley swallowed her. The noise of the city fell away. The air turned stale and close, thick with the stench of garbage and urine. The woman was gone.

Kate slowed, drawing her weapon. Her eyes swept the shadows. A dumpster squatted against the wall, rusted and overflowing. Rats skittered underfoot. Her breath came in short bursts, not from exertion, but adrenaline.

"FBI!" she yelled, her voice low and sharp. "Come out now. We need to talk!"

Nothing.

She edged forward, clearing her corners. Every instinct screamed that she was being watched. Her grip tightened on the gun. She forced herself to breathe. To listen.

A rustle. Then the movement.

From behind the dumpster, the hooded figure emerged slowly, hands raised, not in surrender but calculation. Kate took one step forward and the woman bolted again, pivoting left into a narrower passage that looked like it led to nothing.

Kate cursed loudly and broke into a sprint again. Her legs ached. Sweat soaked the back of her neck, trailing down her spine. The chase twisted through a labyrinth of alleys, the buildings pressing in, windows above like hollow eyes watching silently.

The woman hurdled a chain-link fence. Kate didn't think, just launched herself after her, landing hard on the other side and rolling into a crouch. Pain flared in her knee. Her arm screamed in pain. She pushed through it.

Ahead, the woman ran like she knew the path by heart. Kate followed her through a corridor of graffiti-tagged walls and leaking pipes, past a broken fire escape and a door chained shut. There was no sign of hesitation in her movements. No fear. Just a goal.

The woman disappeared around a corner. Kate rounded it a second later and stopped dead.

A brick wall. Dead end.

The woman stood with her back to Kate, breathing hard, her hood still up, face shadowed. Her fists were clenched at her sides.

Kate raised her gun, keeping her arms steady.

"Don't move," she said, her voice edged with steel.

The woman didn't. She didn't run. She didn't speak.

Kate stepped closer, heart hammering against her ribs.

"Turn around. Slowly. Hands where I can see them."

The woman lifted her hands as she slowly turned to face Kate. Then, deliberately, she pulled the hood back, finally revealing her face.

Kate's breath caught. Kristen.

She hadn't recognized her before, not under the shabby clothes. Not under the hood. But now, with her face exposed in the fading light, there was no question.

Kate still didn't lower her weapon. "I don't understand." It wasn't what she meant to say, but it was honest and real and the truth. "The note about the bombing. That was you?"

Kristen took a step back, leaning against the wall for support. "I don't know what you're talking about."

"Don't lie to me," Kate barked, taking a step toward her. "You were following me, and you slipped me a note in that diner. You wanted me to know about the bombing at the gallery. The only problem, there was no bombing at the gallery. There was a bombing at a warehouse that nearly killed me and my team."

Kristen looked over Kate's shoulder. "Please put the gun away. You're scaring me."

Kate knew if she turned to look at whatever Kristen was looking at the girl would rush her, try to break away. Kate wasn't looking and she wasn't lowering her gun. Instead, she stepped to the right, angling her body so she could see Kristen and behind her in her peripheral. There was no one there.

"What is going on, Kristen? You better get talking."

"Not here. Not when they might find me." Kristen stalled for time Kate didn't have.

"Right now. Right here or I'm taking you in." Kate made another move toward her.

Kristen tensed. "Please, Agent Walsh. I'm scared. It's why I warned you. I got into something over my head. I..." her voice trailed off.

"Does this have anything to do with Cassandra Vale?"

Kristen's eyes got wide. "How do you know that name?"

"I've been told she infiltrated a support group for women who have experienced sexual assault. Were you part of that group?"

"Not while she was there. A long time ago." Kristen looked past Kate again. "Cassandra is dangerous, Agent Walsh. I think she's the one who is killing people. I think she's the one who killed Trevor." Tears formed in Kristen's eyes. "I trusted her with information about Trevor. She used that to get access to him."

"How do you have information about the bombing?"

"I overheard her talking on the phone during our yoga class. She stepped out of the room and I followed her. I've been suspicious of her from the moment Trevor died and you came to tell me about the murder."

Kate lowered her gun but didn't holster it. "Why were you suspicious of her?"

Kristen licked her lips nervously. "I'm not sure exactly. She's the kind of woman with strong opinions. She was always telling me what I should or shouldn't be doing in my relationship. She was a casual friend, someone older who I met in yoga. We got friendly after that. Looking back, she pursued the relationship with me after learning I was dating Trevor."

"How long ago was this?"

"A couple of years. Maybe two years ago. It started innocently enough, conversations after yoga. We'd go get smoothies together. She was like hanging out with a big sister. I told her I had been sexually assaulted. She was interested in that, pressed for information and I told her. After a few months, things started to turn."

"What was she saying?"

Kristen's shoulders relaxed as she opened up more. "I had told her about the assault and dating Trevor, and she was horrified about it. She'd ask about the relationship, then trash who he was as a person, telling me that men like that aren't worth anything and that the world would be better off without them. She would joke about what would happen if all the women banded together and started killing off men like that. I honestly laughed. I didn't think she was serious." Kristen wrapped her arms around herself. "Who'd be serious about something like that?"

"Cassandra." Kate knew this was the woman. She didn't need more evidence than that. But she did for court and she'd get that. Right now, she wasn't going to deny the tingling all over her body – her instinct coming alive and guiding her. "Did she ever tell you how she'd do it?"

"She told me stories about how, before, when women couldn't get divorced, they'd poison their husbands. She even said that in some places, there were women who'd help mix the poisons for these women. They were helpers. It was like a whole underground system to protect women from abusive men. She said that we needed to get back to that."

"How did you respond to that?"

Kristen took a deep breath, her chest rising and falling apparent even under the hoodie. "I didn't know what to say. It was hard to know if she was serious. I didn't agree with her, if that's what you were asking. My comment back was something along the lines that it was a good thing we could divorce then." Kristen tugged at the string on the hoodie. "I don't condone violence. I don't want any part of violence, Agent Walsh. Even if men are hurting women in their marriages, sure, the system isn't set up to help them, and I agree self-defense is justified. I don't think it's okay to just go around murdering people."

Kate could agree with that. That was the rub on this case. Self-defense was fine. Premeditated torture and murder were not. Kate wanted to know more about the bomb, but she wanted more than anything to learn more about Cassandra. "Did she tell you why she felt this way?"

Kristen shook her head. "I asked if she had a bad marriage, if that's why she seemed to hate men so much. She denied that."

Kate stopped her. "Denied hating men or denied having a bad marriage?"

"Denied the bad marriage. She never came right out and said she hated men. It was obvious to me, given the things she was saying," Kristen confirmed. "I think someone close to Cassandra was hurt and she had a lot of rage because of it. I even asked if she had experienced an assault or something like that. She denied that, too."

"What else do you know about her?"

"I don't think the last name she gave me is real. One of the days that we were out to lunch, I watched as she pulled her credit card out of her wallet. I couldn't see the last name clearly, but it started with the letter *M* and I believe ended with a *k*. I didn't want to question her about it. Maybe she went back to her maiden name." Kristen shrugged. "Honestly, I just got the sense that it probably wasn't good for me to ask too many questions."

Kate asked a few more questions, including where the woman lived, places she was known to go, others she spoke to, a phone number – anything. But Kristen knew nothing. They met occasionally at yoga and would go out afterwards. That was the extent of their relationship.

"You said at the start that you suspected her because of Trevor. Tell me about that."

Tears welled up in her eyes. "Look, I know he wasn't a good person. I know what everyone says about men like that. It was a bit of fun for me. After I was assaulted, I needed control back in my life. With Trevor, I had control. He was a terrible person, but he afforded me the kind of control I needed."

"I'm not judging you for the relationship," Kate assured her. The last thing she needed was for shame to prevent Kristen from sharing the full truth. "How have you left things with Cassandra?"

Kristen wiped her eyes. "A few months back, I started avoiding her. It was too much. She wasn't my mother or even a good friend. She had no right to tell me what to do like that. Cassandra kept pushing, asking me questions, trying to make it seem like I was a victim in the situation with Trevor. I ended up feeling like Cassandra was trying to dig around in my psyche for something."

"A weakness," Kate said without meaning to interrupt. When Kristen looked at her with confusion on her face, she added, "She was looking for a way in to exploit you. To take your pain and trauma and exploit it for her benefit. If she could do that, she could convince you that killing was justified."

Kristen shuddered. "Is that what she's doing?"

"It's an educated assumption on my part right now." Kate wasn't going to tell her where the information came from, but she would disclose a little. "I believe Cassandra is exploiting women with abuse histories to carry out her manifesto. She's grooming these women to kill for her or at least help her kill. These cases have a lot of moving parts. When was the last time you saw her?"

Kristen wrapped her arms around herself. "It was that day at yoga. She seemed hyped up. Too hyper to be at our yoga class. I asked her if everything was okay and she told me that all her plans were coming together. I asked her what plans. She wouldn't tell me, but she got a call in the middle of class. I don't know why, but I followed her out into the hallway. I heard her mention a bombing at the gallery. I started right then to suspect that maybe she was the woman you were looking for."

"Why not come to me directly?"

"You already suspected me, Agent Walsh. And I'm connected to two of the victims."

Kate recalled what Patrice had told her. "Congressman Nubeck?"

Kristen nodded. "I was afraid if I came to you with information, you'd think I was a part of it. I saw you on the street that day. I wasn't following you. Then I saw you in that diner and knew it was my only chance to get that information to you. When the gallery didn't get blown up, I thought I had done something good by helping."

"You did," Kate admitted, understanding why Kristen didn't come to her directly. "Do you know anyone else who is involved with Cassandra?"

"No," Kristen said with a frown. "I only see her at yoga and smoothies after. I never fell into her crowd, you know. I had my own life. I didn't like most of what she was saying. I even thought about ditching the yoga class so I wouldn't have to see her. I was at that yoga class first."

"Has she contacted you recently?"

"We never exchanged numbers. As far as I know, she doesn't even know where I live."

Kate doubted that. "I'm going to take you back to your place. You're going to pack a bag, then you're coming with me. We are going to put you up at a hotel until this is over. I want to keep you safe."

"You think I'm in danger?"

Kate did. "I think anyone who gets in Cassandra's way is in danger."

CHAPTER 36

Kate stared at the board they had created with all the case information. She had fully taken over one of the hotel's small conference rooms. The whole team, including Ditch, was there to discuss the case so far. She had come back from her day of running around the city gathering leads and needed more than anything to talk it over with everyone. They ordered dinner in, ate while they discussed the day then huddled in for the night to discuss the case, hoping to make some progress.

"First and foremost," Kate started, "I don't have anything on Ali Brewer to tie her into this case. She has an alibi for last night, and I don't get any sense that she's lying to me about anything. She's a good place to point the finger, but there's nothing there."

Ditch poked his head above his laptop. "There's nothing in her background either that tells me she's good for this. I understand she has that feminist podcast and she speaks on topics that might make her suspect number one. I just don't see it in her temperament."

Kate glanced around at Sharon, Declan, and Leo to see if any of them disagreed. When none of them had a counterargument, she moved on. "After today, I think I have a better sense of what's happening. This woman, Cassandra Vale—"

"Not her real name," Ditch said, cutting her off. He apologized. "I thought it was important we state that right away. There is no

Cassandra Vale anywhere in the database. She's a ghost. She doesn't exist."

"Anywhere?" Declan asked. "Driver's license. Maybe it's her maiden name."

"Nope." Ditch moved the laptop to the side. "The name Cassandra Vale, around the age of the woman described and in a ten-year window older or younger, doesn't appear anywhere – not in birth records, driver's license, voter registration, and the list goes on. I don't just mean here in Manhattan. I mean everywhere around the country."

"You have access to all of that?" Sharon asked, skepticism in her tone.

"I'm not going to explain my process." It meant that Ditch wasn't legally gathering the information. It was something that Kate and the team had continued to turn a blind eye to in situations like this.

Declan shot Kate a look and she moved on. "Let's not worry about what Ditch has been doing to get the information. We need to focus on identifying her."

"Video surveillance at the yoga studio?" Leo asked.

"No," Declan responded. "There is no footage of the yoga studio and the smoothie shop where she and Kristen meet, doesn't keep the footage more than forty-eight hours. It runs on a loop, constantly erasing if the footage isn't needed."

That was the only thing Kate had asked of him upon her return. She needed him to get any video feeds from the yoga studio and the smoothie shop where Cassandra had gone with Kristen. He came back empty-handed.

"No one remembered them?" Sharon asked.

"The person at the desk in the yoga studio was new. We are waiting on a return call from the instructor of the class they take. As per the smoothie shop, it was a crush of people in and out of there just in the twenty minutes I was there. The people working there barely looked up. They aren't going to remember two women who looked like every other woman in yoga pants coming and going from the shop. If you asked me who I saw in there today, I couldn't tell you. They were like clones of one another."

Sharon tsked. "That's too bad. We don't even have eyes on this woman?"

Kate turned her attention to Sharon. "We need to show Kristen and Maya the hotel's video surveillance to see if one of the unknown women is Cassandra. Both Kristen and Maya are working with a sketch artist to come up with a composite image of her. The video surveillance isn't great. If we get a good enough image of her, I can start quietly circulating it. I can go back to the rape crisis program and other groups in the city and tell them they need to be on the lookout for this woman."

Leo cocked an eyebrow. "Media?"

"Most likely," Kate said, glancing over at Declan to see if he agreed. He didn't push back. "I think with ten murders, we have to go public. The more public, the better at this point. Maybe we run her underground and she stops. Maybe someone involved grows a conscience or gets afraid we are getting close. I don't know, but we have to do whatever we can to get her to stop."

"What about setting up a sting?" Sharon asked, glancing between Kate and Declan. "You have Kristen sitting in a nice hotel. She's had contact with this woman. What if you get her to text Cassandra to meet up? Then you have her."

Kate had been considering that. "Kristen doesn't have her phone number. I don't think I'd want to do that even if we could get a number or find a way to contact Cassandra. I don't want to put Kristen at risk."

Declan cleared his throat. "Do you think Cassandra would hurt her?"

Kate explained how Kristen had been pulling back from Cassandra. "After she took the call about the bombing at the yoga studio and Kristen overheard, the FBI showed up and wrecked the plan. Cassandra might have already connected that it was Kristen who tipped us off. I don't trust that Cassandra wouldn't hurt her."

"Have you considered that it was a setup?" Leo asked, running a hand down his chin. When Kate didn't immediately respond because, no, she hadn't considered that, he added, "If she was trying to recruit Kristen and she was resisting, Cassandra might have tested her to see if she was suspicious. It might have all just been a test. Cassandra might never have considered bombing the gallery at all. It was just something she said to see what Kristen would do with it. Has Kristen seen Cassandra since that yoga class?"

"No," Kate said, realizing that Leo might have hit on something. "Trevor was also the first victim and connected to Kristen. Marty Nubeck was also connected to Kristen. Cassandra had already been trying to influence her. Leo, your observation of this might be accurate. It might have simply been a test to see if Kristen would come to the FBI, and she did."

Sharon shifted in her chair. "What about Amanda? It sounds to me like Amanda was recruited by Cassandra. It doesn't even sound like it took all that much effort. Do we have any idea who assaulted Amanda?"

"No," Kate said with frustration in her tone. "I checked with the NYPD and they wouldn't disclose the information to me because the case went nowhere. The detective has yet to call me back, but the other detective I spoke to on the phone said they didn't think Amanda was credible. Because the case went nowhere, they didn't feel comfortable disclosing the name of the man since the allegations were never proven."

"He might be in danger," Declan said evenly.

"I tried that." Kate had been frustrated with the lack of collaboration with the NYPD. "I don't think that matters at this point. What we need to focus on is finding out who Cassandra is and stopping her." To Sharon, she asked, "Where are we with evidence?"

Sharon flipped open a file and read off a few of her findings. There were still no fingerprints found or DNA, nothing that could indicate a suspect. The crime scenes were free of anything that could help them catch a killer. Sharon jabbed her finger down on the page. "The most significant was the ground-up hemlock put into the whiskey. We have confirmed that from the bottle. The medical examiner is still doing the post-mortems, and it will take a while before the toxicology gets back. I'm sure, based on what I've already uncovered, that's what will be confirmed. We have quite the gardener on our hands. First, the lilies and now the hemlock."

Kate let out a heavy breath. There were so many working parts to this case, it surprised her that the Midnight Lilies were able to go undetected for as long as they had. A serial killer working alone, she understood. A whole group of women keeping a secret for this long was something else. Usually, even in traditional terrorist activities, a lone wolf was hardest to catch. A cell normally gave itself up in some way or another.

Sharon continued, drawing Kate's attention back to her. "As his father said, someone knew Avery well enough to know that the whiskey would be opened and drunk that night, even with the threat. I assume the threat was used as a challenge to entice Avery to drink it. If there wasn't a threat with it, then he might not have bothered."

"Then it's someone who knows him well," Leo added. "Is there a way to explore Avery's circle of women to understand who might have set him up?"

Kate was still waiting for Victor Lancaster to provide her a list of the women that Avery had allegedly assaulted. It might give her a clue as to who was involved. She turned to Ditch. "Anything on his background catch your eye?"

"Nothing out of the ordinary for an entitled billionaire's son who was involved in a tech start-up. He has an office in Manhattan and investors; the primary investor is his father. He has a handful of staff who run the office. I'm not getting much back on what they are doing. It looks to me like it's some surveillance technology. I can't figure out more than that. There's not a lot out there."

Declan sighed. "What about staff? Does the website list any staff?"

Ditch nodded. He rattled off a few names of men who worked for Avery. "There is one woman, a young woman named Raegan Pike. She's a twenty-five-year-old New York University student who is working on a master's degree, according to her bio. She is listed as Avery's assistant and also does some human resources work for the company."

Declan cast a glance over at Kate, and she read his expression without any words exchanged. An assistant would be the perfect person to know Avery well, where he lives, and the ins and outs of his life. She'd know him better than most. He asked, "How long has she been employed?"

Ditch focused back on the laptop. "A few months, according to this. She seems like one of the newest employees. The few others say founding member. I assume she's not a founding member because it doesn't say so."

They would have to interview her. "It's another lead," Kate said. "Honestly, there are several women who might be involved in this. Cassandra was out there recruiting. According to Maya, she has charisma about her. Who knows how many women are involved. I think our primary focus should be on finding her real identity."

"What about Amanda?" Leo clasped his hands on the tabletop. "Do you think you can get her to tell you more, Kate? Wouldn't you have enough to bring her in after everything Ali said?"

"I do," Kate agreed. "Declan and I are going over to her first thing in the morning. I don't think we have enough for an arrest. We certainly have enough now to bring her in for a formal interview. If she lawyers up, she lawyers up. I'm tired of playing games with her. She's the one person I know for certain is involved in this. If I have to make a deal with her, that's what we will do."

"You don't know that she killed anyone," Sharon reminded her. "What can you get her on?"

Declan gestured with his hand as he spoke. "Conspiracy to commit murder. In a case like this, being involved in the conspiracy to murder these men will hold the same kind of criminal sentence as someone who did the killing. All of them are on the hook."

Kate agreed with that. "The goal would be to get her to give us names. I don't want anyone walking from a case like this. We can work with the prosecutors to reduce sentences. I don't want to give anyone full immunity, not with this many deaths and the egregious nature of them." Kate knew that Amanda was a victim, and she might be faced with several other victims. She hated that she had to take such a stand. The heinous nature of the crimes made it impossible for her to bend. The prosecutor might, but it would not be the FBI's recommendation.

Leo's face drew a pained expression. "Have you given any consideration to what they are doing with the tongues? You have seven bodies whose tongues have been cut out. Is that correct? Three of the victims from the other night still had them."

That was correct. Kate explained, "We don't believe the three were the main targets, which is why they didn't have their tongues cut out. They were collateral damage. Serial killers will often keep trophies. I don't know if that's what Cassandra is doing. I don't have any way of knowing." Kate hadn't wanted to give too much thought to that gruesome detail.

"Where do we go from here, Kate? I've put feelers out to everyone I know to see if I can identify the hacker they are using. This is someone good, better than most." Ditch had a smug smile on his face. "I wouldn't say better than me but close. She's had to have done something before this. Someone has to know something in the underground channels I run in."

"You haven't heard anything?" Kate asked.

"No. She's a ghost, too. This whole case…" Ditch shook his head in disgust. "I've never seen anything like it."

"Neither have I," Declan agreed, checking his watch. "Is there anything else before we break for the night?"

When no one had anything else to add, Kate told them, "I'll reach out in the morning with a list of what each of us can tackle. Go get some rest. We need to be fresh in the morning. I want an arrest tomorrow, or at least a solid lead that leads to an arrest. If not, the whole country is going to have our heads."

Kate had the sinking feeling that even if they solved the case and brought all the women to justice, a shift had occurred in the community consciousness – a bell that couldn't be unrung.

CHAPTER 37

Kate woke the next morning actually feeling refreshed from a good night of sleep. Declan had felt the same and started something that morning that they had little time for given the day of work ahead. Kate couldn't resist so she had to hurry her shower, twist up her hair barely blow drying it, and was out the door managing to still be on time.

"You need to stop smiling like that," Kate said as Declan handed her a coffee in the lobby of the hotel. He had left her to finish her morning routine and promised her a cup of hot coffee before they headed out into the mean streets of Manhattan. "We are investigating ten homicides and you're smiling like a fool. If the press sees you…"

Declan laughed and pulled her into his side for a hug. "No one is seeing me standing in this hotel lobby. It was a good morning. I'm allowed to be happy about it. We need more mornings like that and nights and maybe even afternoons."

Sometimes in their line of work, they had to compartmentalize or they'd make themselves insane. Kate said, "Let's go see Raegan first then we can head over to Amanda. She's going to be the tougher interview."

The morning light fractured against the polished glass of the midtown skyscraper, its angular architecture jutting into the sky like a blade. Kate stepped out of the black SUV, her eyes scanning the reflective façade of the tower above. The building was sleek, sterile, and new – like most things in this part of Manhattan.

Declan followed close behind. "What's the suite number?" he asked, glancing at her.

Kate didn't answer immediately. She stared up at the thirty-second floor, where Raegan was waiting. Declan asked her again, and she responded absently. Her mind was focused on the approach to the interview. "I want her rattled," Kate said at last. "But not too rattled."

Declan nodded. "I wonder if there will be others in the office. If there are, do you want me to interview them while you get Raegan alone?"

Kate looked over at him. "That's a good idea. She's the only woman who works here. She's not going to give me a straight answer in front of them. And they might offer her a lawyer."

Inside, the lobby was a cathedral of chrome and glass. Cold air wrapped around them. The security desk waved them through after they flashed their badges and mentioned the address. The man behind the desk gave a solemn nod. The news had already broken about Avery's murder. Kate assumed security in the building had been expecting them. They took the elevator in silence as Kate watched the numbers climb, her heart ticking faster as they rose. She took deep breaths through her nose to slow her heart rate. There was no reason to be this worked up this early in the morning.

They stepped into a different world on the thirty-second floor. The open-concept office was all Scandinavian minimalism and design. There were matte-black workstations, hanging succulents, standing desks. Natural wood walls softened the light, and pendant bulbs glowed like tiny suns above unused desks.

And there she was. Raegan. Mid-twenties. Coppery red hair pulled into a messy knot. Thin, dressed in black jeans and a wrinkled silk blouse. She stood near the windows, pacing with erratic energy, chewing the edge of her thumbnail like she meant to draw blood. It was not the image of the young woman on the website who had a neat, coiffed appearance, like she never had a hair out of place.

She turned sharply when they entered. Her icy blue eyes went wide. "What are you doing here?"

Declan flashed his badge and introduced them. "Is there anyone else here in the office with you?"

Raegan shook her head. "The office is closed indefinitely. I'm sure you're here about Avery, our boss. He was murdered. The others aren't here. They are out scrambling to find other work. I'm not even sure why I'm here. Sense of responsibility, I guess. There are still invoices to be paid and there's work to be done." She looked past them. "I'm sorry there's no one here for you to speak to today. I don't think anyone is coming back."

Kate heard the way she stressed the word *responsibility*. "We are here to speak to you."

Raegan focused her eyes on Kate. "I'm a nobody here, just an assistant. Why would you be here to speak to me?"

"You knew Avery," Kate said evenly. "We are trying to speak to everyone in his life. I'm sure you knew him well, you were his assistant for a few months, correct?"

Raegan started to shake her head, then stopped. "I was the office assistant. Avery used me for more than that. I'd handle his schedule and other personal things. I've only known him for a few months. I'm not sure what I can tell you."

"Let's sit down," Kate said, gesturing to a conference table ringed with ergonomic chairs. Declan moved to the far wall, giving them space but remaining in her peripheral vision. A quiet presence, but a reminder that she wasn't alone. He always had her back.

Raegan sat stiffly, fingers knotting in her lap. Her gaze flicked to the door, the windows, and back to Kate.

"What did your personal work for Avery entail?"

Raegan shrugged off the question. "It wasn't supposed to be anything. That's not why I took the job. I'm the only woman who works here. I have a background in human resources. I was supposed to start that department for him. The company is small now, but we were growing. Instead of allowing me to do my job, he treated me like a personal assistant."

The edge in her tone didn't escape Kate. "You don't sound too happy about that."

Raegan licked her lips. "I probably shouldn't speak ill of him since he's gone. The company is gone now too, so I'm not sure that it matters. I was thinking about quitting. It wasn't working out for me here."

Kate nodded. "Tell me about that."

"I'm not sure what more I can say." Raegan knotted her fingers. "Have you ever had a job that it was one thing when you were hired but turned into something else completely?"

The only job Kate ever had was with the FBI. Still, she could empathize. "Sometimes the FBI isn't all that it's cracked up to be. I'm not home much. Cases take me all over the globe. Yeah, I do things I didn't sign up to do. It doesn't sound quite like that for you."

"No." Raegan zeroed in on Kate. "You work with a lot of men."

"I do. Sometimes that's not easy."

"Any of them ever sexually harass you?"

Kate dodged the question. "Is that what was happening here?"

"Not at first. And by at first, I mean the first week. They gave me enough time to settle in. Then it started. It wasn't just Avery. It was all of them. I stopped wearing skirts. I wore higher collars. I stopped spending time on makeup and my nails. I was doing everything possible to make myself as unappealing as possible."

Kate had heard this from women before. "What was the outcome of that?"

"It didn't stop. I got teased more for not making an effort. But the harassment didn't stop. I've been actively looking for another job." Raegan bit her bottom lip. "I thought this was going to be my chance at the ground floor of an up-and-coming company. The Lancasters have power and prestige. I thought this might be my big break out of college. I'm still paying for grad school."

"How did you find out about the job?"

Raegan started to speak but seemed stumped by the question. It took her seconds to recover, her eyes drifting to the side. "Through school, I think. I heard about it a few places. I applied and got the job right away."

Kate knew she was lying. "What other kinds of activities did you do while you were here?"

Raegan narrowed her eyes at Kate. "I told you about the sexual harassment. Don't you care about that?"

"File a complaint," Kate said, not sure how much she believed her now. "As you said, Avery is dead. The rest of the staff have gone. I'm sorry you had that experience. It's terrible what women put up with in the workplace. Unfortunately, that's not why I'm here."

"Why are you here?"

"To find out who murdered Avery and the other men like him." Kate waited to see if Raegan would respond. When she didn't, Kate pressed. "Did you hear about the murder? Five of them at Avery's house. They were drugged and shot. Avery and another man had their tongues cut out." If Kate was expecting Raegan to wince or show some signs of horror, the way most people would, she was disappointed. Raegan had no emotion. If anything, her pupils dilated slightly with interest. "What personal errands did you run for him?"

"The usual. Dry cleaning. Food shopping."

Kate nodded. "And his whiskey runs?"

Raegan blinked. "Excuse me?"

"Avery liked the Macallan Rare Cask, correct?"

Raegan stared right at Kate now. "How do you know that?"

"Because, Raegan, we know that you told someone. We know that you told them what whiskey to buy so they could drug Avery and his friends before killing them."

"No," she said with a fierce shake of her head. "No." Raegan stood and started to walk toward the window, back where Declan was sitting. He moved his hand to his gun.

"Raegan, you have a rare opportunity to help us here," Kate said, sure now just by the woman's reactions that she had been involved. "You seem afraid. Tell me what you're afraid of."

She turned back to Kate, fear in her eyes. Raegan opened her mouth. Closed it. Her hands trembled now. "I didn't…" she started. "I didn't know about the others. I didn't think they'd kill him."

Kate held up a hand. "Who are they, Raegan? The Midnight Lilies?"

Raegan's eyes welled. She clamped her lips tightly, shaking her head violently.

"They aren't going to protect you. They're using women like you. If you helped them get to Avery, you are complicit in murder. If you help us stop them, you might walk out of this."

Raegan whispered something.

"What was that?" Declan asked.

"I said I didn't know what they were, not at first." Her voice cracked. "It was a forum. A place where women talked about harassment. Abuse. There were hundreds of us. Maybe more. It felt safe. Empowering."

Kate sat back, heart thudding. This wasn't the first radicalized digital community she'd come across, but it was the first built on something that resonated so deeply with half the population.

"And then?"

"Then it got darker. A woman messaged me privately. Told me

about this job with Avery. She said all I had to do was apply and catch him harassing me. She said once I turned the evidence over to them that there would be a lawsuit and I'd make enough to pay for my college loans."

"You have evidence of the harassment?" Declan asked, standing now and walking over to her.

She glanced up at him and nodded. "I had it. I don't have it anymore. I had to drop the recordings off at a P.O. Box. They told me not to keep a copy." Raegan crossed the room to her desk. Kate stood then, and both she and Declan's hands went to their guns. Raegan pulled open a drawer and lifted a key. They relaxed. "This is the key to it. I had to drop the recordings once a week in there. I wanted to just use my phone, but they said they didn't want a trace of where I was emailing the recordings."

"Who's your contact?" Kate asked. "Did you ever meet them in person?"

Raegan shook her head. "I only know her screen name. Violet_8282. We never met. She knew everything about me and Avery. She said that we had to take him down. I thought she meant in court. Next thing I knew, I saw on the news that he was dead." Raegan wrapped her arms around herself. "I swear to you I had nothing to do with his murder. I didn't know they were going to kill him."

Kate believed that. "Let me see if I understand what you're telling me. You joined a group chat with women who had experienced harassment and abuse. Someone with the screen name you mentioned reached out to you privately and asked you to help bring Avery down. You got the job here, taped the harassment, and turned the recordings over. What else did you share about Avery?"

"Everything. They heard everything, not just the harassment. I didn't have to tell them anything. They learned about him through the recordings." Raegan glanced over at Declan, then back at Kate. "I swear I didn't know they were going to kill him. Do you think they will come after me now?" Raegan looked up then, and the raw panic in her eyes was clear.

"I think it's possible," Declan said, his tone tight. He looked at Kate for an answer.

Kate nodded at Declan. To Raegan, she explained, "We'll take you into protective custody. You'll need to surrender your devices and walk us through everything. Every message. Every post."

Raegan gave a shaky nod.

As they led her toward the elevator, Kate glanced back at the sleek office space. On one of the desks, a dried lily in a vase tilted slightly sideways, petals dark as blood.

Kate's mouth tightened. They knew Kate would come for the young woman.

They were watching. Always watching. One step ahead.

CHAPTER 38

Kate finally felt like they were getting somewhere. Given the information Raegan had given about the Midnight Lilies online forum, the first thing Kate did after getting the young woman in her secured hotel room was to send Ditch over so the pair could work together.

If Ditch could identify the forum and get some screen names, he'd be able to track the information to some IP addresses. Ditch wasn't sure, based on what he'd already seen from their tech person, that he'd be able to trace anything. Kate knew he was suddenly doubting his skills and an insecure Ditch helped no one.

It took a little buttering up and heaping some praise to convince him that he was still the best in the world. He seemed to get along well enough with Raegan when Kate brought him over to the hotel, but she had taken Leo with her and left him there to keep an eye on things. Leo was quickly becoming a good babysitter for Ditch and he didn't seem to mind it.

When Kate was preparing for her interview with Amanda, Declan had run down a few leads with the other men who had worked at Avery's start-up. None of them admitted to harassing Raegan, but Kate didn't think they would.

It gave Kate enough time to prepare for her meeting with Amanda. She'd need to go in hard and not waste any time. While Raegan and

Kristen both had contacts within the Midnight Lilies, neither seemed to have a direct enough connection to find any information about Cassandra Vale. Raegan had never even heard the name.

Kate would have to wait for a warrant to get any information from the post office. She had called Spade to ask if he could hurry the process. Once he heard they were making some real progress, he was more than happy to handle the court for her.

Once Declan got back, he and Kate set out first to Amanda's aunt's place and found that she was long gone, according to the neighbor. She had high-tailed it out of there the day before and got into a cab.

They went back to the original address they had for her, the brownstone where they saw the women meeting. They climbed the stairs to the second floor and knocked loudly. When Amanda yanked the door open and she came face to face with Kate and Declan, it was clear she was expecting someone else. There was a scream that held on her lips that wasn't released.

"How did you find me?" she barked when she summoned the ability to finally swallow the scream and speak. Her tone was tight and her posture was rigid. Amanda appeared as if she were in the middle of a fight that Kate and Declan interrupted.

"Are you alone?" Kate asked, peering over her shoulder.

"I'm alone," Amanda said in a huff. "There's no one here but me and now you. I'm going to ask you again. How did you find me?"

Kate didn't understand the question. They had told her they knew where she lived before. "We've had this conversation, Amanda. We've been watching you. I told you that when we met the other day. We need to talk to you."

Amanda's eyes cast to Declan, who stood right over Kate's left shoulder. "What do you want?"

Kate didn't wait to be invited in. She crossed the threshold, stepping around Amanda, into the living room. She left Declan standing in the doorway. "I know what you told me about Ali Brewer was nonsense. You're either going to tell me the truth here or we are bringing you in. It's up to you. We have more than enough information to bring you in."

Amanda let go of the door and stepped back to allow Declan to enter. She turned to Kate, a flash of anger in her eyes. "I don't like being cornered like this."

Kate saw not just the young woman's anger but the fear she was masking behind it. That's what happened with assault. It was the loss of control that many victims found the hardest to process. Kate locked her gaze on Declan and gestured with her head for him to come stand near her. This way, Amanda could focus on the pair of them at the same time and not have one at her front and the other at her back. Kate needed her comfortable enough to talk.

"As I said," Kate started, "I know what you told me about Ali Brewer is false. I also know why you were on the street meeting her. She's worried about you."

Amanda raked her hand through her hair that looked as if it hadn't been brushed in a while. "Ali said she's a feminist and she spouts all this nonsense about taking our power back and living a centered life. She teaches us the history of the movement and even encourages us to protest if that's what we choose. She doesn't do anything. Ali isn't strong enough. I told her that and she didn't even care. She didn't even try to defend herself. She talks a good game, but she's got nothing to back it up."

Amanda's anger was bubbling up. Kate could see that she wasn't even going to try to contain it. "Is that why you tried to blame her? You think she deserves to pay because you think she's weak?"

Amanda stared past Kate without responding.

"They are using you, Amanda. These women in the Midnight Lilies have tapped into your rage and are using you."

"They care about me," she spat the words.

"They don't," Kate said, her tone growing softer, feeling the young woman's hurt under the armor of rage. "There are people who do care about you. I know the system isn't fair and that you deserve justice. This isn't the way to get it. This kind of revenge against these men isn't going to fix the problem in the long run. An eye for an eye leaves everyone blind."

"That's where you're wrong. The man who assaulted me is dead. He can't hurt anyone ever again. That's justice."

"Avery?" Kate asked. Amanda's silence confirmed it.

Amanda took a few calculated steps toward Declan, eyeing him up and down. "I can see why you don't understand me, Agent Walsh. You're blinded by his attractiveness. You think he's one of the good ones. He's got you fooled. That's what happens with the most attractive ones. They get away with more. They think they are a gift to women, and we excuse their behavior time after time."

She advanced on him so quickly that Declan took a step back, holding his hands out in front of himself to stop her. "Back up," he ordered her. She stopped advancing but didn't back up. Declan took another step to provide some distance between them.

"Amanda, attacking us isn't going to do you any good," Kate said, drawing the woman's attention to her. "Agent James isn't the enemy. Most men aren't the enemy."

Amanda turned sharply to her. "You're one of them. You're one of the women supporting the patriarchy. You deserve to die, too."

Kate's hand went to the holster on her hip. There was no point trying to debate an irrational point. "We are here trying to help you. I know about Cassandra Vale and how she came to you, offering you a chance to get your power back. To get some of that control that you felt like you've been missing for a long time. You're hurt, Amanda. That's what's under all of this rage. It's pain. Avery hurt you and you're trying to hurt others."

Amanda faltered a step, rocking from one foot to the other. "You don't know anything about it."

"I know the system didn't protect you. It didn't give you justice. I also know that Cassandra showed up and took advantage of that. She's doing the same thing to you that Avery did, Amanda. I know that you can't see it right now, and it probably doesn't feel that way. You're in a lot of trouble."

Kate watched the young woman turn from her to Declan and back again.

Amanda tugged at her hair again, roughly tucking it behind her ears. "No one controls me!" she shouted suddenly, the tears starting to fill her eyes.

Kate held one hand out in front of her. "Amanda, look at me." She waited until Amanda had turned her body to look at Kate. "You are the one in control here. You're the only one who can help you get yourself out of this. Have you even heard from Cassandra after she made you go to the hotel with her?"

Amanda's eyes were wild, like a caged animal filled with fear. "I don't know."

"You do know," Kate said calmly. "You know what you did, and you know what the Midnight Lilies were doing. You can help us. We can get you the help that you need, Amanda." Kate hoped saying the young woman's name over and over again would ground her in the reality of the situation. "Are you willing to take control back in your life? That's what you can do right here, right now."

Amanda shook her head, not in saying no but in confusion. "They told me…"

"They told you that if you helped them, you'd have the control and the power, right?"

Amanda offered a slight nod.

"You helped them hurt a lot of people. Maybe they weren't the best people, but Cassandra doesn't get to decide that. She doesn't get to decide who lives or dies. That's not going to give you any power back." Kate took a step toward her. "I know you're hurting and you want that pain to stop. You can start doing that by helping us. Right now."

Amanda turned her head to look over at Declan. "I don't want him in here. I won't talk in front of him."

"Okay. He can go."

"I'm not leaving you, Kate," Declan said, standing his ground.

"Amanda and I are going to have a nice talk. You can wait for me outside. We are going to be fine. Aren't we, Amanda?" Kate's gaze never left Amanda, watching the young woman's posture start to relax. The last thing Kate needed was Declan to exert control. If he did, he'd be exactly what Amanda thought him to be – one more bully. "Seriously, Declan, go. We are fine."

Declan stepped toward Kate slowly. "I'll be outside if you need anything." It was as much a threat to Amanda as it was a promise to Kate.

Kate thanked him and assured him once again that they were good. When Declan was gone, she said, "See, Agent James is a good man. He only wants to protect me. That's what we do as partners. I know Cassandra convinced you that all men are bad and that the men who died deserved it. I'm not going to lie to you and say they were good men. By all accounts, they were not good men. I heard some of those podcasts. They were disgusting. They said horrible, vile things no one should say and no one should hear. But they didn't deserve to die in the way they did."

Amanda sniffled, wiping her face on the back of her hand. "No one was stopping them. They were doing damage not just to women but to the guys, even young boys, who listened to them. They have a skewed idea that what these podcasters are saying is what it means to be a man. It's toxic for boys to hear those things. They mimic them. The ones that don't get called out for not being manly. They use words like beta and simp. No one should question someone else's masculinity like that. Young boys have killed themselves over it. Others have committed terrible acts of violence."

There was something about the way Amanda said it. It was almost as if it wasn't her words. "Do you know someone like that? A boy who committed acts of violence after listening to those podcasts?"

"No." Amanda grew quiet, taking a deep breath, seeming to center herself again. When she looked back up at Kate, her eyes were clear and wide. "I heard of one who killed himself from being bullied at school because he wasn't a man. He wasn't masculine enough. He was bullied. He was only sixteen."

"Who was that? Someone you know personally?"

Amanda shook her head. "It was Cassandra's son. It happened a little more than two years ago now. He got bullied at school, and he killed himself. That's why Cassandra is so angry. That's why they all have to pay. They took her son from her, her sweet son. She said he was such a nice kid. I feel bad for her. I wanted to help her. Someone needed to help her."

The pit in Kate's stomach tightened. She was dealing with a mother with intense grief that had turned to revenge. She didn't question if the story Amanda had been told was true – Kate knew in her gut it was true. It was all the motivation that was needed.

Kate offered words of empathy. "That must be awful for her to live with. I don't know that I could. How well do you know Cassandra? Do you know how I can contact her?"

Amanda shook her head. "The phone number she gave me stopped working. I called the other woman that's helping her and that number is disconnected too."

"There are two?" Kate asked, holding up two fingers.

Amanda chuckled in surprise. "There's more than two. There's a revolution coming, Agent Walsh. You're not going to be able to stop them all."

Kate's breath caught in her throat. "Here in Manhattan. Are there two women who are leading this revolution?"

"I don't know how many. I know about three of them," Amanda said calmly. "I only met Cassandra. She was the one who was with me that night at the hotel. She and one of the other women. There's a third woman I've never met, but she's the one who grows the lilies. There is the woman who does the tech, but no one knows her name. I never killed anyone. I just went with them to the hotel and some of the meetings."

"Meetings?"

"We all get together at a bar in the basement. I heard it used to be a speakeasy. That's where they plan everything. There's a meeting tonight."

"You're coming with me," Kate said, waving her over.

"I told you things. I don't want to come with you."

Kate wasn't going to get into a fight with her right there. "It's as much for your safety as it is for anything else. Don't fight me on this, you won't win."

Amanda came willingly, but she refused to speak more, asking for an attorney. It would be on the way back to the police station that Kate would call the prosecutor's office and a local defense attorney to work out a deal for Amanda to be a witness.

Only when the young woman had the right legal protections would Kate interrogate her further.

It was the major crack in the case they had needed.

CHAPTER 39

Kate sat at the conference room table trying to piece together all of the information they had been able to find so far. With her interviews with Amanda, Kristen, Raegan, and Maya, a picture was slowly starting to form of how the Midnight Lilies came to be. A mother's rage had spilled over and inspired others. One woman, Cassandra, had linked up with two other women as bent as her to cause total devastation. They were also recruiting other young women who had also been hurt.

Their collective trauma had given way to extreme rage and deplorable violence.

Amanda was able to give Kate a list of some of the women involved – younger women who took more of a support role. They still didn't know the real identity of Cassandra, the gardener, or the techie.

Ditch was still working with Raegan to identity screen names and trace down IP addresses of the members. This was being passed on to Kate's team. Leo and Declan were diligently working to identify people. So far, they had twenty names in total. A plan was needed for the mass arrests but first, Kate and her team needed to raid the bar where Amanda told them that these women spent their time and their secret meetings were held.

Kate had decided not to go forward with the media with the sketch and video image of Cassandra. The video was grainy, but all of the women were able to identify Cassandra from the video recording at the hotel the night Marty Nubeck was murdered. No one knew the other woman with her. Amanda didn't know the woman's name. She had only met her that night. When asked her name, Cassandra told her that it wasn't necessary that she know. Amanda said the hotel was the only crime scene she had gone to. Otherwise, she was involved in helping to pick the targets and research them thoroughly. She also helped Cassandra find other women who were close to these men to help recruit them, like Raegan.

It was a whole investigative operation with no stone unturned.

After the interview with Amanda concluded, Kate understood why they had been so hard to catch. With the trauma bond, none of the women had been willing to break the code of silence. They were bonded to each other in this toxic web, thinking they were doing what was right and helpful for society by ridding themselves of these men. The hope was that as the murders continued, similar men would take it as a warning and tone down their rhetoric. Those who didn't would be targeted for elimination.

The one thing Amanda said that chilled Kate to the bone was that the women at the top had considerable wealth, privilege, and power. They walked among Manhattan's elite, blending in by day and terrorizing the city by night.

Declan rapped his knuckles at the door as he popped his head into the conference room. "It's a go for the raid tonight at The Velvet Finch. We have the warrant for entry and search. What time did Amanda say the meeting would start?"

Kate raised her head from her laptop. "Ten. I think we get there at ten-fifteen. She said they always start on time and they are sticklers for punctuality. I don't know if they have anything planned tonight, but I don't want this opportunity to slip through our fingers. I want Leo and Ditch to remain working on the tech side of things."

Declan stepped completely into the room and closed the door behind him. He leaned down on the table as he watched her. "We are going to catch them, Kate. We are so close. This is almost over."

Kate knew that it was and she wasn't feeling conflicted about it in the least. Not in the way she thought she might. "This is like any other case. We are taking them down and putting an end to this. Is SWAT ready?"

"SWAT is ready."

"What did you find out about the bar? I know you were going to look into ownership."

"Corporation," he said with a dismissive wave of his hand. "Ditch is still working to find the owners."

It wasn't important now. Their warrant to raid the place was solid.

Later that night, Kate sat rigid in the front seat of the unmarked black SUV, her hands flexing restlessly on her thighs. The Velvet Finch glowed like a jewel box, its mahogany doors framed by gilded sconces and a velvet rope that hinted at exclusivity rather than danger.

Declan leaned forward from the passenger seat behind her, voice low in her earpiece. "SWAT is in place. The rear alley is covered. Thermal's showing movement on the lower level. Deep into the basement. Deeper than anticipated. Did you say this was an old speakeasy?"

Kate confirmed. She stepped out into the rain, her boots splashing in shallow puddles. The bar's brass handles were warm under her grip as she pushed through the door into low jazz and top-shelf bourbon air. The lounge looked like a magazine spread – dark leather booths, polished glassware, and a crystal chandelier that glittered like a thousand tiny knives overhead.

To the left, a hostess looked up. "I'm sorry, we're fully booked—"

Kate flashed her badge. "FBI. Sit down and keep your hands visible."

Gasps rippled through the crowd. A man near the bar started to rise.

Declan was already on him, whispering warnings through clenched teeth. SWAT moved to secure the exits. They called to her that there was a back entrance to the basement.

"Where is it?" Kate asked the bartender, who was standing with his hands raised slightly above the bar.

"What?" he asked, but his voice shook.

"The speakeasy below. I know people are meeting there. That's why we are here," she said, her voice a steady staccato. He gestured to the far end of the bar. Kate scanned the space, noting every detail until her gaze landed on a section of floor near the rear hallway with slightly different tiling, scuffed in a circular pattern. The kind of detail missed by casual eyes. She moved closer, crouched, and ran a hand along the wood-paneled wall nearby and knocked. "Hollow," she murmured.

Declan joined her, his breath hitching slightly. "Got something?"

Kate found the latch – disguised behind a vintage portrait of a Prohibition-era singer – and pulled. A segment of the wall popped outward with a soft hiss, revealing a narrow stairwell descending into darkness. "Let's go."

They descended fast, weapons drawn, the stairwell groaning with age beneath their weight. The smell hit her halfway down – mildew, copper, and something bitter underneath. When they reached the bottom, the hallway opened into a chamber straight out of another era – cobblestone walls, brass railings, low-hung lamps flickering against velvet wallpaper. The speakeasy was alive.

And occupied.

Three women sat at a round table near the back, clustered around a laptop, their heads bent low, focused on the screen amid a tense conversation.

"FBI! Hands where I can see them!"

The women looked up, startled. The one on the left moved fast. She kicked the table toward them and dove behind an old piano as the other two scattered, drawing weapons from beneath their coats.

Gunfire lit the room like strobe lights. Kate ducked, rolled, and returned fire. Splinters exploded from the edge of the piano as her shots tore through its side. Declan charged forward, covering the flanking path.

Kate saw one of the women, eyes sharp with rage, make a break for a side tunnel. There was something familiar about her that Kate couldn't place in the melee.

"Declan! Right corridor!" she barked.

He pivoted, firing a warning shot that sparked off the brick inches from the runner's head. She skidded to a halt, hands raised.

Another woman, the one Kate was sure was the third woman on the hotel footage, lunged toward the map, trying to shove it into a messenger bag. Kate surged forward, catching her in a full tackle. They hit the floor hard, Kate's elbow slamming into the woman's jaw before she could bite or scream.

"Don't even think about it," Kate growled, wrestling her wrists into cuffs.

A SWAT agent had the third suspect down, a bloody scrape across his cheek where her ring had scored him. He held her to the ground with practiced ease, breathing hard.

"Three accounted for," Declan said, escorting the familiar runner back into the main room.

Kate stood, scanning the space. It was larger than she'd expected – half a dozen closed doors lined the walls. She holstered her gun and yanked one door open. The back office off the main room was small and dimly lit. She rushed inside to the desk littered with papers, maps of the city with addresses circled. There in the corner of the room sat another table filled with evidence.

"Declan," she called. "You need to see this."

After handing the woman over to SWAT, he joined Kate inside, eyes going immediately to the centerpiece of the room: a sleek steel table covered in photographs, blueprints, and a single glass box filled with jet-black lilies.

Kate stepped closer. The petals gleamed unnaturally, dyed to a violent shine.

Declan whistled low.

"Yeah," she murmured. "But that's not all."

She picked up one of the documents – typed names, photos, and surveillance notes.

Seven new targets. "Next victims," she said grimly.

Declan tapped one of the names. "This guy was scheduled to speak at Columbia University tonight. I saw a flyer earlier on the street. I wondered if he was a potential."

Kate nodded. "Hopefully, we just stopped his murder."

Kate stared at the lilies again, her thoughts drifting to Cassandra. "Where is she?" she muttered. "She wasn't among those women out there. I thought there'd be more here tonight, too."

Always one step ahead.

Declan turned as more agents flooded in, securing the scene, bagging evidence. EMTs began tending to minor injuries. The three women were being processed.

Kate's gaze lingered on the map again. So many circles. So many names. But this time, they were ahead of the curve. This time, they had something solid. She stepped out of the room and zeroed in on the woman who had tried to run, being treated by the EMT.

Kate stared hard at the woman, trying desperately to place her. Her mind scanned the images of all the people she had met on the case until she landed on the woman she had met at the very start.

Tall. Yoga pants. Understated makeup. The entitlement. Her fingertips were tinged with black.

Evaline Marks. Everyone called her Evie.

She was the next-door neighbor to Trevor Fontaine. Back to where they started.

Kate walked over to the woman, asked the EMT to give them a moment. "You're the gardener. You grew and dyed the lilies. The hemlock too."

Evie glared up at Kate. "I don't know what you're talking about."

"Yes, you do. I wonder if your husband knows what you've been up to. Those kids of yours, too. Where is Cassandra?"

A sick smile spread across Evie's face. "I don't know anyone by that name. I want my lawyer. I demand that you allow me to call my lawyer and my husband."

Kate read Evie her rights and asked SWAT to take her to the police station. "We are going to search your house first, Evie. Then you can make your calls."

As she was led away, she jerked against the SWAT officer, cursing Kate as she was led out of the cold, damp basement. "I'm going to have your job for this. I'm going to get you fired. You don't know who I am! My family." She was still shouting as she was led out of the basement and up the stairs.

"I want to make a deal," one of the other women shouted as she too was being led away. "I can tell you everything."

Kate recognized this woman from the hotel surveillance video. "What's your name?"

"Daniella Bartelle. My husband owns this bar. I swear to you, he had no idea what we were doing. I can tell you everything. I was involved in all the planning."

Kate held her hand to stop the SWAT officer from pulling her away. "I need Cassandra's name and address, now."

"Cassandra Vale. I don't know her address. I met her at a yoga class and then only met her here."

"That's not her last name," Kate insisted.

"It's the only one she gave me!"

"Who is the tech person?"

Daniella shook her head. "We never met her. Cassandra is the only one who contacted her."

Kate waved the SWAT officer off. "She doesn't have anything of value to me."

Daniella shouted to Kate, pleaded with her. "Please, I can tell you everything we did. Everything we planned to do. Please, I'll testify against them. Whatever you need."

Kate stared into the woman's panicked eyes. "You tortured and murdered ten men, cut out their tongues, left creepy crime scenes, and recruited vulnerable young women in some sick twisted game you're playing here. I will not show you any mercy. If the prosecutor's office does, that's up to them."

"Please!" The SWAT officer practically dragged her up the stairs. She turned back. "Wait! I do know something. Cassandra's son was named Adam. He went to The Dalton School!"

Kate thanked her but reaffirmed she wasn't going to be making any deals today.

Once the room was cleared, Kate pulled out her phone and started the search for The Dalton School and a boy named Adam. She added the word obituary to her search. Seconds later the results populated. She stared down at the image of a woman that matched the surveillance video. She finally had the woman's real name. It was as simple as an internet search with the right information. She had been hiding in plain sight all along.

Cassandra Millbrook.

Another quick search gave Kate the woman's address on the Upper East Side, not far from the Lancaster mansion. Kate wondered if the woman had watched them from her window.

"Declan!" she yelled. "Let's go! I found Cassandra!"

CHAPTER 40

The Millbrook mansion loomed before them. Five stories of limestone and arched windows stretched toward the sky, each pane reflecting the harsh glow of streetlights. Ivy crawled up the façade like gnarled fingers, and carved gargoyles perched on the corners, their stone eyes seeming to watch the federal agents below.

Declan moved beside her, his breath visible in the crisp air. Even in the dim light, she could see the tension in his jaw, the way his fingers flexed around his weapon.

The rest of the SWAT team was in position.

The mansion's front door was solid oak, reinforced with iron studs that gleamed like black stars. Kate adjusted her position, her shoulder brushing against the mansion's wall. Through the tall windows, she caught glimpses of the interior – crystal chandeliers casting prismatic light across silk wallpaper, oil paintings in gilded frames, furniture that probably cost more than her annual salary. It was a world removed from the gritty reality of their investigation.

Declan called the countdown. "Three... two... one... Go!"

The world exploded into motion. The front door splintered under the battering ram's impact, wood and metal shrieking in protest. Kate surged forward with the entry team, her boots crushing fallen splinters as she swept through the doorway.

The foyer opened before them like a cathedral. Black and white marble squares stretched across the floor in a chessboard pattern, while a grand staircase curved upward, its mahogany banister carved with intricate roses. Above, a chandelier the size of a small car threw fractured rainbows across the walls.

"Clear left!" one agent shouted.

Another one responded, "Stairwell clear!"

Kate took the stairs two at a time, her weapon trained upward. Each step echoed despite the thick carpet runner, the sound swallowed by the mansion's vast spaces. Portraits lined the walls – stern-faced men in military uniforms, women in Victorian dress, children with eyes that seemed to follow her ascent. Kate wondered why Cassandra hadn't rushed out to see what was going on.

The second-floor hallway stretched in both directions, doors standing like sentinels along its length. Kate moved toward the northeast corner. Behind her, she could hear the systematic clearing of rooms, the sharp calls of "Clear!" punctuating the controlled chaos.

The room at the end of the hallway had a light glowing inside and the door was slightly ajar.

Kate positioned herself to one side. Declan on the other. Through the gap, she could see a slice of the room beyond – mahogany furniture, a fire crackling in an ornate fireplace, the edge of a wingback chair.

"Cassandra Millbrook!" Declan called through the door. "FBI!"

Silence stretched between them, broken only by the distant sounds of the ongoing search below.

"We know you're in there, Cassandra," Kate yelled, hoping she was right. "Let's make this easy."

A woman's voice finally emerged, cultured and steady despite the circumstances. "Come in, Agent Walsh. I've been expecting you."

Kate exchanged a glance with Declan. She'd learned not to trust anything that seemed too simple in this investigation. They breached the room in practiced synchronization. Kate swept right while Declan took left, both weapons raised and ready.

Cassandra Millbrook sat in the wingback chair like a queen holding court. She was, without question, the woman Kate had seen on the surveillance video at the hotel the night Marty Nubeck was murdered. Tonight, unlike that night, she was dressed impeccably. Her tan cashmere sweater, wool slacks, and designer heels were not those of a woman about to run. What struck Kate most were the woman's eyes – grey-blue and completely calm, as if federal agents burst into her private study every evening.

"Please, sit," Cassandra said, gesturing to the sofa across from her. "I imagine you have questions. You've been chasing me all over the city. I'm sure your goal is to get as much information from me as you can. I'll not implicate anyone else," she gestured with her hand, "beyond those who have already implicated themselves."

"I need you to stand and place your hands behind your back," Declan said, his weapon still trained on her.

Cassandra smiled, the expression not reaching her eyes. "First, I think we should talk."

Kate kept her Glock steady while scanning the room. Bookshelves lined two walls, filled with leather-bound volumes and family photographs. A desk sat beneath tall windows, its surface neat except for a single laptop computer. The fireplace cast dancing shadows across everything, creating a surreal atmosphere for an arrest.

"We can talk after I cuff you," Declan said, advancing on the woman.

She did not resist him. She stood and put her hands in front of herself for him. As the metal cuffs clicked around Cassandra's wrists, Kate noticed something shift in the woman's composed façade. Not fear, exactly, but a kind of relief.

Cassandra quietly eased herself back into the chair.

Kate holstered her weapon, studying her face. "Help me to

understand what happened, Cassandra. How could you go from this," Kate gestured around the room, "to committing acts of terror? The brutality of the murders, the skills and precision of the crimes, leaving no traces of evidence. Even the theatrics of it are not something I see too often."

A faint smile formed on her lips. "You want something done right, you send a woman to do it."

Kate could see now the lines of pain and grief starting to form on the woman's face. For the first time, Cassandra's composure cracked. Her carefully controlled features twisted with pain.

"Tell me about your son," Kate urged.

"My son," she said as her voice cracked. "My beautiful boy. Adam was sixteen when he died. He started listening to those podcasts the year before." As Cassandra continued, her voice grew harder. "Those men with their poison about women, about what it means to be a man, how the world owed them something. I thought it was just teenage rebellion."

"It wasn't rebellion, was it?" Kate prompted gently.

"It was indoctrination." The word came out like a curse. "They taught him to hate himself, to blame everyone else for his loneliness. They taught him that women were the enemy, that he'd never be good enough. Any emotion or kindness was a weakness. They told him that the world would be better without weak men like him." Cassandra's voice broke on the last words, her shoulders shaking.

Kate stood and waited while she composed herself.

"He left a note," she whispered after taking a breath. "Quoted their talking points. He said he was tired of being a disappointment to the masculine ideal. Tired of existing in a world that had no place for him."

The room fell silent except for the fire's crackling. Declan looked away from her pain. Kate knew it was too much for him. He'd heard the same words on those podcasts, probably had the same realization that he didn't fit that ideal of masculinity either. The difference was that he was in his late thirties and already knew who he was as a man.

"You decided to make them pay," Kate said.

Cassandra's grief was still there, but now it was armor. "Two days after I buried my son, I researched them. Learned their real names. I discovered I wasn't the only mother who'd lost a son to their influence. I wasn't the only woman harmed. Young women had been brutalized by men like that. I had heard the term rape culture before, but this was different. This was systematic promotion of rape, of degradation of women as if they weren't more than their body parts and how they could service men."

Kate held firm. "You groomed the other members of the Midnight Lilies. They might have never committed such heinous acts without your encouragement and planning."

"No." Cassandra shook her head. "I was a fuse to a bomb ready to explode. Those women understood that the legal system would never hold these men accountable for the damage they caused. They hid behind free speech, behind corporate protections, behind the very system that failed our children. There was no grooming. They wanted vengeance and they got it."

Kate stepped closer, her voice remaining steady despite the horror of what she was hearing. "You formed a terrorist organization."

"I formed a response," Cassandra corrected. "Those men weaponized loneliness and self-hatred. They turned vulnerable boys into walking time bombs. When the bombs went off, they shrugged and counted their advertising revenue. Look at all the mass shootings, Agent Walsh? Young men. They are angry, forgotten, and these men have weaponized them without consequence."

"You murdered ten people. You tortured them. Cut out their tongues."

"I eliminated sources of poison." Cassandra's eyes hardened. "They chose to profit from pain. I chose to end that profit."

"Where are their tongues?" Kate asked, staring at the woman. When she didn't respond, she assured Cassandra, "You might as well tell me. We are going to tear this place apart."

Cassandra locked her gaze on Kate. "They are going to make a nice exhibit one day." She paused. "In court, that is. Think of how that will look in the press."

"Where are they?" Kate demanded.

Cassandra shrugged as a laugh escaped her lips. "They won't be needing them anymore. Send me to prison. I didn't accomplish all I set out to do, but I accomplished a lot. I'll sell my story. The world will know about my son and what I tried to do. More mothers will take up arms against these men. More women will be empowered to right the wrongs. A revolution is coming and there's nothing you can do to stop it."

Kate feared Cassandra was right. "How did you break into their homes?"

Cassandra laughed. "Men don't fear women. We walked right in. Trevor let us in. Corey Weber met us in Central Park of his own free will. They were so easy to manipulate."

"The hotel?" Kate asked. "How did you get to Marty Nubeck's floor?"

Cassandra dared to laugh. "There are so many women willing to help."

Declan moved to secure the laptop from her desk. "What about your husband? Where is he in all this?"

For the first time, genuine surprise crossed Cassandra's features. "Richard? He's at his conference in Chicago. He knows nothing about any of this."

"Nothing?" Kate found that hard to believe.

"My husband is a good man who buries himself in his work to avoid dealing with grief. When Adam died, Richard threw himself into his pharmaceutical research. He's been traveling constantly for two years." Cassandra's voice softened. "He couldn't bear to be in the house where our son grew up. He couldn't bear to be around my pain and my anger. I used his absence to build something he would never understand."

Kate studied the photographs on the mantelpiece – family portraits showing happier times, a couple in love, a young boy with his whole life ahead of him. The contrast with their current reality felt like a physical blow.

Kate listed off the names of the women already arrested. "I know we are missing a few. This is your time. I need the name of the woman running your tech operations and anyone else we missed, like the woman who made the bomb that nearly killed us."

Cassandra hesitated for just a moment – so brief Kate almost missed it. But after years of interrogations, she'd learned to watch for micro-expressions, for the tiny tells that revealed hidden truths. She said, "You have everyone who participated in direct operations. The woman who made the bomb was arrested at the bar. You already told me you have her."

Agents were already searching those women's homes. Bomb making material would be found, Kate was sure of it. The only missing pieces were the tech and the tongues.

Kate walked to the tall windows, looking out at the courtyard below where SWAT teams were conducting their search. "Cassandra," she said, turning back to her. "Help me understand the technical side of your operation. The encrypted communications, the online forum, and how you managed to hack into all the city's surveillance. That requires expertise most people don't possess."

Cassandra's mask slipped back into place. "I'm a very determined woman, Agent Walsh. Grief is an excellent motivator for learning new skills."

Kate could see the lie in the tightness around Cassandra's eyes. She also knew this person they were hunting was better than Ditch, and until now, no one was better than him. Someone else had provided the technical backbone of the Midnight Lilies. Someone with serious skills and access.

One photograph caught her attention. It showed Cassandra at what appeared to be an art gallery opening, champagne glass in hand. The background showed several paintings she recognized – contemporary pieces that had sold for millions at auction.

Kate picked up the frame, studying the image more closely. "Where was this taken?"

Cassandra's carefully controlled expression flickered again. "A gallery. I can't remember where. Boston, maybe. Chicago, possibly. Richard and I were always involved in the arts."

A voice buzzed in Kate's ear. "We found evidence in a study on the first floor. Seems like everything tying Cassandra Millbrook to the men who were murdered – their photos, names, and extensive research on them. No tongues. They're still unaccounted for, Agent Walsh."

Kate told them they'd be down in a moment. She looked at the woman still sitting in the chair, her cuffed hands in her lap. "Cassandra, I need the name of your tech person and I need it now."

Cassandra looked up at her sheepishly. "You have all of us, Agent Walsh. I don't know what more I can tell you."

Kate's phone buzzed in her pocket. She called Declan over to escort Cassandra down to the car to take her into custody. "I'm done with her. She's not going to tell me anything else. I have a call to take and I'll be right down."

As Declan pulled Cassandra up and escorted her from the room, she pulled her phone from her pocket and saw that Ditch had tried to call her twice.

Kate hit the button to call him back. "We have Cassandra Millbrook."

"Good," he said evenly. "I got a hit on an address for the tech person. I finally made it through all the code and firewalls and misdirection." Ditch gave her the address and Kate's stomach turned. She asked if he was sure. "I'm positive, Kate. Leo left to go over there already. He said he thought he might be able to help you."

Kate cursed as her heart slammed into her chest. "I'm on my way."

She had no idea what Leo was thinking. He wasn't prepared for what he was about to face. Kate was sure of that. Cassandra might have been the spark that started all of this, but Kate had a feeling the tech person might be just as dangerous as Cassandra.

CHAPTER 41

Kate stood across the narrow cobblestone street with Declan at her side. Her eyes were fixed on the gallery's glowing interior. She hadn't drawn her gun – not yet.

"You're sure about this?" Declan asked. "Leo is in there alone with her. She met him once, Kate. Ditch said she's the one."

Ditch's voice had been in her ear, convincing her of the truth. "She's the one, Kate. Patrice White is your architect. She wrote the entire communications infrastructure, facilitated that forum, and ran all the surveillance interference for the Midnight Lilies. She's not just part of it – she's the brain. Cassandra might be the heart, but Patrice is the one who has made it possible."

Kate believed him. Ditch didn't get excited unless the data was airtight.

Leo had beaten her there. The woman they were about to arrest was likely three steps ahead of the rest of the world, but Kate hoped tonight, Leo was one step ahead of her. He'd need to be, or they'd find his body like the rest.

Kate moved across the street in silence. The gallery was open, but empty. A "Private Event" sign leaned against the glass, scrawled in silver ink. She slipped inside.

The gallery air was cool. She could hear voices from the main exhibit room, low and flirtatious. Leo's voice, confident, unhurried, and a woman's laugh. She had never heard the woman quite so effusive. Charming, even.

Kate edged forward until she had a clean view of the scene.

Leo stood near the center of the gallery floor, just inches from Patrice. He wore dark jeans, a charcoal blazer, and no tie. He was leaning one shoulder against the wall as if he had all the time in the world, all the trust in the room. Patrice faced him, her hair swept back and her lips painted a red that dared you to look away.

"You've really outdone yourself with this gallery," Leo said. "I've been in the art world a long time and this place is magnificent."

"I thought you had an air about you that didn't scream law enforcement," she said, teasing him. "You're more cultured than the rest of them. Refined. European." She gazed up at him, her eyelashes batting. "I can't quite make out the accent."

Neither could Kate that long ago.

Leo didn't tell her. He simply shrugged. "I consult here and there. It's mostly to pay off my debt to society."

Patrice cocked her head, confusion on her face. "I can't believe you were ever a criminal."

Leo leaned into her, put a hand under her chin, tipped it up toward him as if he were about to kiss her. He didn't, but instead leaned down low to her ear and said something Kate couldn't hear. She roared back in laughter, putting a hand to his chest. "I swear to you. They caught me and brought me in. It was either spend my life in a Russian prison or work with the FBI. What they don't know doesn't hurt me. Can't teach an old dog new tricks. I get off on the thrill of it all. I'm sure you understand that." Leo took her in his arms, this time resting his lips against hers. "You seem like a woman with secrets of her own."

Patrice lingered with him for a moment, then stood back and appraised him. "What do you think of the Midnight Lilies and the murders?"

"Intelligent women get things done." Leo waited for her response as he smiled. "I know that you sided with the men. I think those women were right in what they did. I think justice was served. Some arrests have already happened. It's why I'm here. I needed to let you know they arrested Cassandra Millbrook. They uncovered her identity. It's all over, Patrice. There is finally some justice for what happened to Marty Nubeck."

Patrice offered a tight smile. "Nothing will bring him back. I didn't realize Agent Walsh was so far ahead in the case."

"Agent Walsh is excellent at what she does. I'll tell you that she felt conflicted about it, too. These women were victims in their own right."

Patrice locked her gaze on him. "You mean that, don't you?"

"I do," Leo said with total conviction. "Sometimes, to deliver justice, laws must be broken."

That's exactly what Leo had done for decades before the FBI stopped him. Kate knew he didn't need to lie to Patrice about that.

"Can I show you something? A new exhibit will be on display next month. I have it in the other room. I'd like your take on it." Patrice reached for his hand and Leo allowed her to take it. They walked off to another exhibition room. Kate walked quietly into the gallery with Declan right behind her. She stopped at the wall separating one room from the other and peered around it. So far, neither Leo nor Patrice knew she was there.

Leo nodded toward the display on the far wall. "This installation…" He expelled an audible breath. "It's visceral."

Patrice took a step toward the display. Kate followed her gaze and swallowed hard.

Suspended in individual glass orbs, hung from the ceiling with nearly invisible wire, were tongues preserved in formaldehyde. Each one lit up by a light behind it, glowing, showcasing the brutality.

"This," she said with quiet pride, "is what art is meant to do. Provoke. Challenge. Leave a lasting mark."

Leo's voice broke the silence, low and measured. "I don't know whether I should be impressed or repulsed. You've really outdone yourself."

Patrice's smile was slow, almost predatory. "It's the power of silence. The absence of voice. It makes the act louder, don't you think?"

"Are these?" Leo asked, but there was a slight hitch in his tone. Kate could see the flicker of unease in Leo's posture, though he hid it well. But not well enough.

Patrice wasn't stupid. She was calculating. Her gaze flickered to Leo's face for a fraction of a second too long. Then, just like that, the mask slipped. Her smile faltered, and a cool edge entered her voice. "I thought you said you agreed with what these women did."

"I thought you didn't," Leo countered. "I thought you wanted justice for your boyfriend. I'm just surprised. How did you get these?"

"I come by my art in various ways," she responded dismissively. "Thank you for telling me about the arrests. I think you should go."

Leo reached out, taking her hand. "I thought we might have a drink and discuss art some more."

Patrice eyed him. "What are you trying to do? Seduce a lonely woman?"

Leo dropped her hand and held his up in defense. "I'm only trying to get to know you better. You're a fascinating woman. You can't blame a man for trying."

Patrice walked away from him, out of sight of Kate. Leo stood there watching her for several moments until his face drew tight in surprise.

"Patrice," he said, backing up right into the wall behind him. "Put the gun down. I don't understand what you're doing."

Patrice took a few steps into Kate's view. Her grip tightened on the cold metal of the gun with her eyes locked on Leo. His smile faltered, but his hands were still raised in mock surrender.

"Listen, Patrice, I came in good faith to let you know about the arrests."

She remained eerily quiet as she took a step forward, the barrel of the gun steady against his chest. He took a half step back, his eyes darting toward the gallery doors, calculating.

"You think I'm playing? I'm not," she said, her voice a razor's edge. "You have no idea who you're dealing with."

"The same could be said for you, Patrice."

She jabbed the gun into his chest. "You're like all the rest."

"Patrice, don't—" Leo didn't finish his thought. Before Kate or Declan could react, he grabbed hold of her wrist in a move that forced her to release the gun as it clanged to the floor. She tried to swing at him with the other hand, but he stopped that, too. Leo twisted her around, grabbed her in a hold, and had her down to the ground with her hands behind her back before Kate could advance on them.

"Stay still," he told her, his voice low, nearly a growl. She didn't have much of an option. He had deprived her of her ability to move.

Kate shouted the woman's name and told her to stop. Leo's head snapped up, only a little surprised to see Kate and Declan standing there. Leo kicked the gun far away from Patrice and helped the woman to her feet.

"I want my lawyer," she seethed, not even pretending that nothing had been going on. With one final, defiant look, Patrice White was cuffed and read her rights by Declan and led away. "Good job, man," Declan called over his shoulder to Leo.

Leo wasn't paying attention to them. He was staring at the grotesque exhibit.

Kate glanced over at him. "You good, partner?"

Leo didn't answer right away. His gaze was still locked on the twisted display of tongues. Finally, he lowered his eyes and smiled at her. "Partner."

Kate returned the smile. "You earned it tonight and by babysitting Ditch."

"He's a handful," Leo muttered. He took one last look at the display, then focused on Kate. "I'm good," he lied. "This isn't art. This is an atrocity."

None of them were good. The case would be with them for the rest of their lives.

Now, though, the real work had just begun.

Over the next month, there were raids all over Manhattan, taking in everyone connected to the Midnight Lilies. The files found in Cassandra's mansion gave a good overview of everyone involved and how they were involved. If there was one thing she was good at, it was record keeping. If there was ever a time she was going to go down for the crime, she was bringing everyone with her. Everyone except Patrice. It seemed Cassandra was willing to protect her.

Patrice admitted to nothing. The evidence found on one of her laptops in the gallery though confirmed that Patrice was the one they were seeking.

Some communication found on Cassandra's cellphone between her and Patrice confirmed that they had discussed a bombing for the gallery. In the end, Patrice wasn't willing to blow it up for any cause. She also complained that it would be her in the center of the action, and she wasn't interested in helping that way.

If there was anyone still out there, Kate wouldn't know. They'd have to wait and see if the threat materialized elsewhere.

After the case was fully handed over to the district attorney's office, Kate and Declan finally returned to Boston. The rest of their team had left weeks ago, not needed for the final wrap-up. Leo was back in France helping to catalogue the art on his property. Sharon was working in the lab on other cases for the FBI. Ditch was back doing whatever he did when he wasn't with Kate and Declan.

Kate relaxed into the chair in the living room. The light from the morning sun streamed in through the curtains as she curled up on the couch with a cup of coffee. Declan was out for a run, but she had declined because she wanted to sleep in. The only thing Kate was working hard at was catching up on her sleep.

It's why when her cellphone rang, she was hesitant to answer it. Kate didn't, in fact – she let it go to voicemail. It was only after it started to ring again that she dragged herself from the couch, padded to the kitchen to find it on the counter.

Spade.

"Hello," she said, trying to hide her annoyance that her peace had been disturbed.

"Another case, Kate. This one is a bit wild. Are you ready for it?"

Kate rolled her eyes to the ceiling. She wasn't sure she was ready for anything wild after the last one. But she had a job to do. "Give me the details."

About the Author

Stacy M. Jones was born and raised in Troy, New York, and currently lives in Little Rock, Arkansas. She is a full-time writer and holds masters' degrees in journalism and in forensic psychology. She currently has four series available for readers: the completed cozy paranormal Harper & Hattie Magical Mystery Series, the hard-boiled PI Riley Sullivan Mystery Series, the FBI Agent Kate Walsh Thriller Series and the new Connor Fitzgerald Thriller series. To access Stacy's Mystery Readers Club with free novellas, visit StacyMJones.com.

You can connect with me on:

- http://www.stacymjones.com
- https://www.facebook.com/StacyMJonesWriter
- https://www.bookbub.com/profile/stacy-m-jones
- https://www.goodreads.com/StacyMJonesWriter

Subscribe to my newsletter:

✉ http://www.stacymjones.com

Also by Stacy M. Jones

Watch for the next FBI Agent Kate Walsh Feb 2026

Access the Free Mystery Readers' Club Starter Library
PI Riley Sullivan Mystery Series novella "The 1922 Club Murder"
FBI Agent Kate Walsh Thriller Series novella "The Curators"
Harper & Hattie Mystery Series novella "Harper's Folly"

Sign up for the starter library along with launch-day pricing and special behind-the-scenes access. Hit subscribe at http://www.stacymjones.com/

Please leave a review for Midnight Lilies. Reviews help more readers find my books. Thank you!

Other books by Stacy M. Jones by series and order to date

FBI Agent Kate Walsh Thriller Series
The Curators
The Founders
Miami Ripper
Mad Jack
The Fuse
Dead Senate
Close Killer
Diamond King
The Magician
Helix Syndicate

Connor Fitzgerald Thriller Series

Midnight Judge

Sparrow Down

PI Riley Sullivan Mystery Series

The 1922 Club Murder

Deadly Sins

The Bone Harvest

Missing Time Murders

We Last Saw Jane

Boston Underground

The Night Game

Harbor Cove Murders

The Drowned Boys

What He Saw

Fear City

What Stays Buried

Harper & Hattie Magical Mystery Series

Harper's Folly

Saints & Sinners Ball

Secrets to Tell

Rule of Three

The Forever Curse

The Witches Code

The Sinister Sisters

Scandal Knocks Twice

A Treasure Most Deadly